Once again,
to Veronica

Published by:
Powder River Publishing LLC
1014 Black Mountain Road
Thermopolis, Wyoming 82443

Copyright © 2024
ISBN: 978-1-956881-54-7
Printed in the United States of America

www.powderriverpublishing.com

Contents

'Tired with all these, for restful death I cry' **(Sonnet 66)**

'Speak me fair in death' **(Merchant of Venice)**

'Ay, but to die, and go we know not where' **(Measure for Measure)**

"My necessaries are embark'd: farewell." — Antony and Cleopat-
ra, Act I, scene 3 (William Shakespeare)

And I heard a voice from heaven saying, "Write this: Blessed are
the dead who die in the Lord from now on." "Blessed indeed," says
the Spirit, "that they may rest from their labors, for their deeds
follow them!" **(Revelation 14:13)**

"I was within and without, simultaneously enchanted and repelled
by the inexhaustible variety of life." **(Fitzgerald F. Scott, The
Great Gatsby)**

"Come on up, boys -I'm dead." **(Dylan Thomas, Under Milk Wood)**

"All things on earth point home in old October; sailors to sea, travelers to walls and fences, hunters to field and hollow and the long
voice of the hounds, the lover to the love he has forsaken."
**(Thomas Wolfe, Of Time and the River: A Legend of Man's Hun-
ger in His Youth)**

"What is that feeling when you're driving away from people and
they recede on the plain till you see their specks dispersing? - it's
the too-huge world vaulting us, and it's good-bye. But we lean forward to the next crazy venture beneath the skies." **(Jack Kerouac,
On the Road)**

ONE

In the library on the coffee table by the recliner where her father would always sit and watch old movies and any kind of ballgame that happened to get televised, there remained a pile of books he'd been planning to read if he ever had the time when he was home or if he managed to live long enough to get around to them before the curtain came down on his life, which the curtain did come down before he managed to even finish the first chapter of the first book in the pile. The books had been sitting in this pile untouched for some time now, and there didn't seem to be any date in the future when anyone in the family was going to move them and put them back on the shelves in the family library—which wasn't truly a family library much at all but more a place where her father liked to exile himself when he wanted to watch television those times when he was feeling antisocial with his wife and daughter and two sons, which was a lot of the time and usually meant the library was never uninhabited much because he was generally residing there. There were TVs in everyone's bedroom and another in the den, so nobody in the family ever much went to the library for viewing entertainment, because that area was consistently staked out by her father, and if somebody was to go in there with him around the possibility existed he might decide to begin asking all sorts of questions about your life and mention how it appeared to him sometimes that your life was being wasted or you were going about it the wrong damn way and maybe it was time to do an about face before you screwed everything up completely, so it was better to go to the den or stay in one's bedroom or go off for the night with friends and avoid these occasional conversations. It was a simple solution, and she and her brothers and her mother resorted to it fairly frequently down through the years to keep peace and harmony within the house.

Linda Hayes-Carlton, twenty-seven and married for six years and long out of the house, had found in the past opportune times to retire by herself to her father's library on visits home, social calls, birthdays, Thanksgiving, Christmas Eve if he happened not to be around, and so on this occasion of her father's funeral and the aftermath of post-burial attendees at the reception at her old home she found herself wandering back to this safe retreat to escape her mother and brothers and all the other relations and acquaintances gathered throughout the house and spend some time alone there peering at her father's collection of weird paraphernalia. She skimmed over the groupings of his favorite authors, Faulkner and Wolfe and Fitzgerald and

Joyce, and his sections of non-fiction he'd always deemed important, books on classic cinema and the Titanic and baseball and Universal Monsters. Her father's collections were a curious makeup if a stranger was to look at them without prior knowledge, but Linda could view them all in their familiarity and be once again assured that she had known her father's tastes pretty well during his lifetime, and there were not any surprises waiting to spring out at her now and make her question whether this man she called Daddy had any secret interests still hidden away that she had yet to stumble upon.

But there had always been a few small mysteries that surrounded her father, only making appearances ever so often, hardly to be noticed until someone stumbled upon them like a lost camper might step on a snake that might be poisonous or might not. There were the long days that stretched sometimes into the night when her dad was on his route, stocking vending machines with Twinkies and Snickers and Pepsi Colas, those nights when he was not home for supper at a reasonable time and the family would eat with his plate at the end of the table sitting bare and empty like there had been some kind of death among them because he was not present to liven up the household. He would come in later, sometimes just before bedtime and the evening news, with tales of his truck breaking down in another county or immense traffic jams on the interstates from overturned rigs with spilled product blocking his way back. They would hear all his tales and wonder why he hadn't called and informed them of his plight earlier, but then they would remember how Daddy didn't care much for talking on the phone, had rebelled, as a matter of fact, against the entire concept of cell phones at the first onset and refused to have one on him tying him down and monitoring his movements, and later when his company required he have one in his truck with him for communication purposes he'd allow it to slip down between the seats or get left behind at one of his stops and would thus be free once more to motor down the road to his next stop without being burdened by being told where to go next or have to indulge any of his secret strategies about how he was going to manage to make two days of stops in one and where and what he did when he had free time away from making certain a slew of employees at a trucking company had fresh honeybuns in their machines the next morning or some such like, since his route was full of stops and quirks and every destination had its own story.

One mystery her Daddy thought he kept to himself but everyone else had figured out long before was the fact that he and Mama didn't enjoy each other's company much anymore—hadn't really, in a goodly time—and though they did their best to hide the fact and keep it from the children, David, the oldest, and Linda, herself, the middle daughter, and Franklin, the youngest, it had not exactly been one hundred percent successful. For years the children and the neighbors and family friends had known something was going on between the two, but they couldn't put their finger on it and it was never confessed to by either. The fact was Daddy and Mama had stayed together and never argued or had a harsh word anyone could hear, and they slept in the same bed for quite a while and bought each other presents for Christmas and birthdays, but there was something unspoken that kept them apart on those times even when they were together.

Linda had been suspicious a couple of times and done a little investigating on her own after Daddy died, going through his desk and looking at some papers he had stashed away, but all she'd found were some notes he'd made on another novel he wanted to write (who knew how many more were planned, since there were two already?) and a lot of service manuals on stereo amplifiers and high-tech speakers and cassette players and eight-tracks and CD players and catalogues to order 45 records for his jukebox over in the corner, and that was about it, like everything was this big secret or something. Maybe the plans for writing a third novel was a bit of a surprise. He had never discussed with anyone giving such a notion a thought, but he had written two before, so who knew what had been in his mind?

No one she knew, that was for sure.

***

It had been a busy week since the death of John Clark Hayes, and there had been little time for mourning or reflecting upon his life and passing. John Clark had, to his credit, performed a good bit of pre-planning before his death, and his widow, or ex-wife, Brenda, whichever way she was regarded, was pleasantly surprised at how efficient he had been in making certain all the T's were crossed and I's dotted when it came down to planning what to do with his mortal remains. There had been no need to talk about plots or selecting a casket or planning a service, for John Clark, at some time or another, had gone into Mount Hope's funeral office and set everything down in a notebook, selecting cremation as a means of removal and buying a nice sturdy box for his remains to be stored in and noting in his will how he'd as soon his family and friends decide what to do with what was left of him rather than allow Mount Hope to garner further profits by digging a hole and erecting a monument to denote where his bones and dust were buried in case anyone happened to come around looking for him.

"I'm not going to be available to have a conversation with anybody," he'd told his attorney, "so there isn't going to be any use in anybody needing to know where I am."

John Clark had seen to having the details of walking on all taken care of, which was a good thing he hadn't put it off or waited until the last minute, because it wasn't illness or old age that had sent him along to the Great Hereafter but a couple of slugs from an unregistered handgun, used in an early morning robbery when John Clark had been getting ready to stock the snack machine in the breakroom at the Lancaster Hills Credit Union Financial Center in the Jordan Center Mall two miles east of Saint Simons Square that did the trick. The two men who'd tried to rob the credit union the first thing upon opening hadn't been successful much in their endeavor except to set off the new alarm system that seemed to work pretty well and triggered a whooping siren shriek that no one within three miles could avoid hearing, and so, instead of hanging around to complete the job they'd started and fill their Publix plastic bags with stacks of bills, the two masked hoodie-wearing robbers decided instead to take off for their pickup truck parked a ways down the street and so ran out the credit union door straight into John Clark Hayes, who was wielding his two-wheeler loaded with three cases of Coca Cola and Mountain Dew and a bin of assorted candy bars, packages of crackers, assorted chips, and five boxes of Cracker Jacks, because the cute little dish who operated the drive-thru window was pretty much addicted to them and always gave John Clark a smile and a wink on those Tuesday mornings when he delivered them. Her name was Judy, and although she didn't know John Clark's name she was still saddened to hear what had happened to him while he was out on the sidewalk bringing in her weekly supply of Cracker Jacks.

Out on the screened-in back porch at the old homestead David and Franklin were sharing a joint, which was about the only thing the two of them had done together since the family vacation to Panama City when David was eleven and Franklin was four and they both rode on a miniature train side by side in a seat and traveled through some sort of condensed jungle safari that was set up by a souvenir shop down on the beach. There were plastic elephants and rubber lions and a tiger made of Paper Mache that looked pretty realistic to Franklin, so much that he'd had to hold David's hand and clutch his arm and scream his lungs out until the train completed its circular route and coming to a stop in a lagoon where a cardboard crocodile like the one that plagued Captain Hook stuck its head out of a cove and looked the brothers both over, which prompted Franklin to let go of his brother's appendages and hightail it down the walkway lickety-split to his mother's arms.

The pot had a soothing effect on the two brothers and the events of the day began to fade from the fore of their consciousness, the hour visitation spent in a room at the funeral home, the graveside service conducted here in the backyard of their old house listening to the preacher from their mother's sometime-church talk about what a good father and provider John Clark Hayes had been even if the two of them had never once met, and how sometimes in this life someone is called home early and it is not for anyone to see at that moment in time but to have faith that all answers will be revealed to them in the days to come when all gather before the throne of God, followed by the reception where the twenty or so guests who'd come to pay their respects to their father got to mill through the den and see old pictures and drink punch and nibble on Wheat Thins and cheese. Their father's ashes were not scattered during the service but remained in a box and toted back into the house and set upon the fireplace mantel, the family having decided that in the days to come they would once again gather and take John Clark Hayes someplace they felt he would like to be for eternity, but since his life had been such a mystery up to this point it was perhaps better to wait a spell so everyone could ponder where John Clark's final place might possibly be, since at this time no one had any earthly idea where he might have wished it to be were he around to be asked.

When the police arrived at the Lancaster Hills Federal Credit Union that morning of the would-be heist, the two robbers—now killers—had gotten away somewhere but John Clark was on the sidewalk leaning up against the side of the credit union cornerstone with his hand on his heart like he was fixing to recite the Pledge of Allegiance. His eyes were closed and his jaw relaxed like he was off in a revery somewhere, and maybe that's where he was, but no one knew because John Clark was walking on and couldn't really tell them anything. His load of snacks still lay atop the three cases of soft drinks, and in his pockets was his billfold and a set of vending machine keys for his route, pass keys that fit the cash boxes and truck keys and assorted keys that opened the doors of the various machines on the route that held the products. In his shirt pocket was a fat ink pen like are sold at souvenir shops and gift shops in Gatlinburg or Gulf Shores, split into with a swash of ink along the stitching where a bullet had passed through.

The cab on the truck and the rear sliding door and the two side slide-up latches that could be raised upward to get to the stacks of soft drink cases John Clark had loaded earlier that morning in his meticulous way were locked and loaded with supply. The other drivers at the company sometimes would have to come back by the warehouse and load up more product halfway through the day, but John Clark had never adhered to this practice. He preferred to come in before the rooster had even the first inkling toward rising and crowing and loading his truck in his own particular way, with every inch and foot and area of space taken up and inhabited in a systematical manner where the first items to be delivered on the route were the last to be loaded, thus nothing ever had to be moved or touched a second time until they were next in line to be loaded and carted inside to their destination. Because of his scientific approach and his penchant for early rising, John Clark was always the first route deliveryman to leave for the morning, being fully-loaded and strategically laid-out in sequence for his daily route, and if he wished he could easily beat everyone in for the day and have a goodly portion of the afternoon free for himself, but sometimes he was the last to arrive back at the warehouse, for in a secret manner John Clark enjoyed finishing up his route and then driving to an elementary school playground and shooting baskets at a rim with the Wilson basketball he carried in his truck, an activity that provided him exercise and gave him time for thought, a block of moments away from the world to ponder the days to come and his role within it. When he tired at last from his day's work and his goal of making 200 baskets he sat in a lawn chair stored behind the seat of his truck and watched the cars coming home from work go by and waited for the sun to set behind the trees.

Franklin said to David,

"Did you notice how small the crowd was for the visitation and the ceremony? It kind of snuck up on me how Dad's side of the family is practically non-existent these days. His parents are dead and so is his brother and sister, and I don't think he had much to do with any of his nieces or nephews. I think all his other relatives are either dead and gone or living in another state and he'd written them off long ago. I don't know if any of them would have come even if they knew he'd died, even if we'd known how to get in touch with them."

"I think the feelings were mutual that both sides were either dead already or at least should be, because everybody on his side of the family had outlived their usefulness for each other a long time ago and hadn't seen any need in keeping up appearances."

"To tell the truth," Franklin said, "I think I'm a lot more like Dad than I ever thought I was. I hate to say it, but I'm like him in the way I don't really care if I have anything much to do with people or not. That's terrible to say, I know, but it's pretty much the truth. I'd be lying if I said I miss our grandparents on his side at all. I don't know how you feel about them, but I never liked either one of them much. Granny Hayes was so Church of Christ it wasn't funny, and it's hard to remember her ever cracking a smile or laughing. All she did was prepare food that wasn't fit to eat and purse her lips and tell me not to touch any of her trinkets and statuettes she had out there in that god-awful living room of hers. By the time I was six I'd as soon have been sent to Alcatraz than have to go over to her house on Christmas or any of the holidays or somebody's frigging birthday and have to hang around for any length of time."

"You're not alone, bubba. I couldn't stand her either. For a long time I wondered how Pa Hayes could stand to be around her for very long at all, and when he fell out of his boat fishing and drowned I always wondered if he maybe did it on purpose just so he could get away from her. But he wasn't too much of a prize either. He had about as much personality as a damn bowling ball when it came down to it, and if you weren't going to grab your bag with the ball in it and go bowl a few frames then there wasn't much use for having a damn bowling ball like him around. That's the way Papaw was, only good for one thing, bringing in his paycheck from Public Works. If he hadn't known how to drive a garbage truck there wouldn't have been much need for him to occupy any space on the earth whatsoever, since all he'd ever do was get in the goddamned way."

"You know, David, sometimes the two of us sure don't sound like Wally and the Beaver much."

"I guess we'd better get back inside and mingle a little or we're both going to be on Mama's shitlist."

"I can't think of too many times when I've ever been off it."

The brothers walked back through the door and through the small yellow kitchen where there never had been enough room for the five members of the family to jointly reside at one time. There was the Formica table in the middle of the room with six chairs spread around it, pushed in tight so a normal person could maybe inch past unless they were kin to Jackie Gleason or Mama Cass, and there was the counter where you could fit like one coffee cup upon, and the dish rack loaded down with plates, and an icemaker-less ancient refrigerator that the doors could never open completely outward because they bumped into the oven if you swung them out too wide, and in the corner between the refrigerator and the sink was a bevy of unused appliances that John Clark's divorced widow, Brenda, thought at one time in her life might come in handy someday, an electric carving knife, a waffle iron that had to be dusted regularly, and an automatic chopper bought off of a television infomercial that chewed up whatever vegetables were added to it and only took an hour or so to clean afterward. It was a busy room for a lot of items that were never in use, and strolling through both David and Franklin could understand why their father in his life before his recent departure had preferred eating his breakfasts and meals seated in a chair on the back porch, his coffee cup balanced on the arm and his food items (dry Cheerios, a Spam sandwich, a bowl of Pops Rite—John Clark was an expert at popping popcorn from scratch) in his lap while he thumbed through the morning paper or one of his treasured copies of Famous Monsters of Filmland. Departing the kitchen they crossed into the dining room which was also short of sitting and walking room due to the table and chairs and the piano and the bench, and the RCA stereo console crammed by the opening to the living room, where sometimes Brenda played The Carpenters and Celine Dion and her Soft Rock station on the AM/FM selector, and, if no one was home and he had the house to himself, John Clark blasted out the walls with rock LPs from his wild and wooly youth that had static like bacon sizzling and sometimes skipped.

There weren't too many people left over from the earlier celebration of life service, especially since there had not been that many present to begin with. Representation from John Clark's family and friends was nil because of time and death and feelings of good riddance that had pervaded much of that prior population, and it seemed to David and Franklin, as it had occurred to Linda earlier, that their father had been the last of whatever small society he was a member of while among the living and had graduated early into being a genuine loner. It had been a secret society, not much discussed by John Clark during his moments among his family, and now he was gone and the guidelines and rules of his world seemed to be all vanished with him. What was left was all they and their mother still carried with themselves, which was mostly punctuated by question marks.

The few attendees left looked like they were in the process of leaving, and only Brenda's friends were lingering behind, like if they waited long enough Brenda would consider her duties as a mourner completed for today and ready to go off with them to Red Lobster, where they could talk about the events of the past week and eat shrimp and knock back frozen margaritas. It was, after all, a Friday, and Jessica and Charlotte didn't have to work tomorrow, as did Brenda if things were running true to normal, but as it was, with the death of John Clark, she had benevolence time coming because the city still considered her married to John Clark, so she was off work for at least another week.

"Have you seen your sister?" Brenda asked her sons. "I thought she would stick around to help put some things away and say goodbye to the friends and family, but I haven't seen her the last hour or so."

"She's here somewhere," David said. "Her car's still in the driveway, and it's for sure she's not going to walk five miles home. She's too cheap to call a cab even if she had a broken leg. My guess is she's back in Daddy's library, watching TV and hiding out so she won't get trapped into anything."

"Looking at Daddy's junk, I'd bet," said Franklin, "checking to see if he's got anything back there that might be worth something. Don't you remember how she was always dragging stuff down to the Traders' Post and seeing how much money she could get for the stuff he didn't seem to be using anymore? She was always sneaking contraband out a little at a time so he wouldn't miss anything right away."

"I don't remember her doing anything like that," Brenda said.

"She waited until you left for work or busy doing something and not paying attention."

"Brotherly and sisterly love," Brenda tells her friends. "It's been that way around here forever. Anyway," she said to the boys, "this is the pot calling the kettle black. You all smuggled something of your father's out at one time or another."

Linda has noticed how quiet the house has grown and forced herself to come out of hiding. She has nothing in her hands and so appears innocent of all charges, but there's a satchel tucked away behind her father's desk full of horror periodicals and a couple of Hemingway hardbacks that she'll come back and get later. She's thinking twenty dollars, maybe fifty depending on how rare the books are.

"Well, it looks like the celebration is over and Daddy can be at rest now," she announced. "I was thinking maybe we'd straighten up around here and order a pizza and go through some things."

"I'm not ready to start fighting over the will just yet," said Franklin.

"I didn't say anything about fighting," Linda said. "I just thought it might help Mama out to get rid of some of the clutter around here."

"What your father had that was worth anything wouldn't fill up a Volkswagen Beetle's trunk," Brenda said, "so there's no hurry worrying about any treasure hunt. We should just call a disposal team and be done with it."

It seemed like the right thing for them all to do, to stay around a while after the ceremony and be with their mother, and against their usual instincts David and Linda and Franklin tried to do just that, but Brenda was wanting her friends and her children to vacate the premises and leave her mercifully alone for a few blessed moments. For the past day or so she'd found herself trying to abstain from screaming at anyone around her to get out of her sight and give her some solitude, and now the desire had grown so monumental that she felt like a human volcano getting ready to spew hot molten lava over everyone and everything around her. After all, it wasn't like she was a grieving widow or anything like that, so it was growing tiresome as all get-out attempting to maintain a false face for the sake of her family and friends and anybody who came by to pay their respects.

"Mama, if you're sure you're okay then I'll just run along and pick up the kids and get them home for supper. Daycare closes in an hour, and I've already been late so many times they're liable to kick us out if we violate the tardy rule too many more times."

Linda was like a convict begging for release, and Brenda knew if she didn't hurry her out the door this very instant her daughter's sense of guilt would win out and then she'd be stuck with her the rest of the night. Best to get her on the road now before she takes out her cellphone and starts calling around asking for someone to pick up the children and keep them a while, since it was doubtful that husband of hers was anywhere around where he might be of some help. David and Franklin had both already bolted at the first hint of freedom, and if she could just get Linda out to her car and backing out the driveway she almost believed she might actually make it through dinner without having a conniption fit.

She didn't exactly grab Linda by the arm and push her out the front door, but there was some nudging and herding and finger-guiding as she talked her daughter toward the steps. I'm just fine, she told her. No, I'm not the least bit hungry, and if I get that way just look at all these leftovers—there's enough here for an army to eat for the next week. All I want is a little nap, thank you. Since your father died sleep's been a little hard to come by. So, you just go get the kids and I'll shut my eyes for a minute and you can call me later.

Linda, trying not to show how she was overcome with joy at being allowed to leave and not stay here with her mother to further mourn, climbed into her car and begged for the battery to turn over and allow her to be on her way. She looked back at the porch to wave goodbye, but Brenda was already inside the house, presumably on her way to bed. Linda imagined her mother was probably pretty well-spent, even if it was true she and her father were not on the best of terms anymore and hadn't been for a long while. They'd been divorced six years but might as well still have been married. They continued to sleep under the same roof. Daddy was always around for Christmas and Thanksgiving dinner, and he always gave Mama a gift for her birthday and Christmas, so it wasn't like she and her brothers were orphans and had been forced to grow up in a Charles Dickens novel.

The house was quiet now except for the sounds of John Clark's assorted clocks making their presence known, the grandfather clock chiming on the quarter and half-hours and sounding out sixteen chimes and the hour number at the top of the hour, the cuckoo clock with the milkmaids and accordion players who swiveled out and proclaimed a new time for the listener to dwell on while a bird burst out a closed door and tweeted out whatever number applied, and the collection of beer clocks that were silent but stayed lit and bubbled and illuminated day and night, followed by a Frank Sinatra clock that played a snatch of different selections from Old Blue Eyes on its trip around the dial, "My Way" and "Strangers in the Night" and "New York, New York" and more, and that one novelty clock that really drove Brenda mad, that grated on her last nerve because she knew John Clark had to know how it would irritate her when he'd ordered it off eBay, which was a religious cross with an image of Jesus and Moses and a trio of angels in the clouds above them who were all privy to the voice of James Earl Jones at the top of the hour quoting a verse of scripture, after which the heavenly hosts all sang a brief hosannah and the lights dimmed and the clock grew silent again for sixty more minutes.

Maddening. All those clocks had to go immediately.

Yes, John Clark was gone, she thought. There was no doubt about it and it was all over now, but it was still a strange thing to accept. Not that things were going to be all that different with him not around anymore. Quite the contrary. After all, how many years now had it been that she and John Clark had occupied this house together without seeing each other or being in the same room at the same time unless it was absolutely necessary to maintain the status quo? They'd always come together when they had to, for school plays or conferences or birthdays or major holidays, but all you had to do was blink an eye and that pretense show would be over and the curtain would come down and John Clark would be off in his world again and she would be in hers. It was something that had gone on so long it seemed almost natural in the way they conducted themselves, and now it would go on much the same, other than John Clark would make no more appearances out of obligation and duty anymore. She would be totally alone from here on out, and that would take some getting used to. She had to admit it would take a while for her to stop looking for John Clark and waiting for him to show up.

She decided she would take a nap after all. At this moment she had no desire to go with Jessica and Charlotte to Red Lobster and drink margaritas and reiterate how John Clark was now something to be said good riddance to, to laugh about how things would be different from now on, how she would be free to do what she wanted each day without somehow deferring to this person who wasn't even technically her husband anymore, to wonder if he might approve or not of her next move on the checkerboard of Life. She had the rest of her days and nights to go to Red Lobster or anywhere else. But for now, all she wanted to do was close her eyes. All she wanted was to stop considering the future for the next hour or so, to escape for just a little while to somewhere else.

***

Jimmy Baldwin wasn't planning on going to John Clark's Celebration of Life service. He had meant to drop by for the visitation and let that be it, but Donna had insisted on going to the ceremony and Jimmy couldn't really see a way of getting around it. His initial plan had been to drop by the visitation and say hi and mention what a good person John Clark had been and how Tasty Snacks was really going to miss him and be done with it at that, but then Donna decided they had to go to the service and he knew it would look tacky to everyone if they didn't. Even if he was John Clark's boss for the past eleven years, Jimmy, who other than running across John Clark perhaps twice a week in the afternoons when he had to go by the warehouse for something or another, had never had much contact with him other than that. John Clark would come in from his route all finished for the day because he'd arrived early that particular morning and had, as usual, half his route done by the time the rest of the world was just waking up, and so maybe they would run across each other then, but Jimmy generally made it a point to never have much to do with John Clark Hayes if he could help it, but still the two would invariably cross paths at one time or another and then have to be polite and friendly and ask each other how everything was going. John Clark would go his way after a bit and Jimmy would feel uneasy for a time thinking how John Clark might just make an about-face and come back and inquire of him if the affair between Jimmy and John Clark's wife Brenda was still going along full throttle as it tended to do from time to time, the way it seemed to flare up now and again over the years. Or if, by some chance, John Clark was unaware of such a thing ever going on under his nose by his ex-wife and employer and was truly as stupid as he sometimes acted, which Jimmy was fairly positive was not the least bit likely. Because John Clark Hayes was a pretty smart cookie if you got past the moronic way he sometimes liked act like he was. John Clark Hayes knew a lot of things you didn't think he knew. Jimmy knew he was wise like that.

The reality was John Clark knew damn well that Jimmy Baldwin and Brenda had been sweeties back in college, because John Clark had been right there with them when they were all students together at Coastal Georgia during the time Jimmy and Brenda were going along full throttle, but for thirty years he had never made mention of that past romance, because in the end John Clark had been the one who'd married Brenda two years after Jimmy had met another girl and took up with her and even married her after graduating and moved to Memphis for ten years to work as a P.E. teacher, until the marriage broke up and the divorce happened and Jimmy went to shit with drugs and alcohol and got himself dismissed from his job and had to move back to Saint Simons for a new start. That was when he'd first met

Donna, who was working at the Harris Teeter Jimmy got hired at, and it was a small world, you know, because John Clark Hayes was working there too, and it was funny how it turned out that when Donna left the grocery business to go into teaching she'd ended up on the same high school faculty staff as Brenda, funny like God planned all this out so He could have a good laugh about coincidences and such, because by then Brenda was married to John Clark, who had been a teacher once himself until he'd had to move along to another line of work because there was compelling evidence he'd been seeing his principal's married secretary on the sly, and since such things were not to be done at Abigail Adams High School John Clark had been given the choice to transfer or resign.

John Clark, never a big fan of the education profession to begin with, chose at that time to retire from teaching and go to work in the retail grocery business, and it was during this time at Harris Teeter that Donna Owens came in and applied for a parttime job to help pay off her college debt. Donna remembered John Clark from when he taught at her high school in Brunswick years before, when she had him for Junior English and liked him so much she'd taken an elective class of Creative Writing with him her last semester. She graduated thinking he was one of the best teachers she'd ever had. When she'd asked for an application at the Harris Teeter customer service desk that day John Clark had remembered her name and told her he'd put in a good word for her with the manager who did all the hiring at the store. And she'd been hired, just as he'd promised.

John Clark at last left Harris Teeter after a time under the ever-present cloud that he seemed to stay under and moved on to a job at a Food Lion, and Donna lost track of him until she was offered a teaching position at Carol Garner Transou High School in Saint Simons, and then she ran across him again, only this time it was because he was married to Brenda, who was on the same faculty Donna became a member of.

Donna came to the faculty Christmas party the Friday afternoon and night after school had been dismissed for the three-week holiday. It was only her second year of teaching—she was twenty-three—and she still had not completely settled in to teaching as a profession or being an established member of this particular faculty at Carol Gardner Transou High School. This Yuletide party was the first actual faculty gathering she'd attended in her two years there. She had stayed an hour for the Christmas celebration the year before, but she hadn't been around but a semester by then and knew practically no one and felt totally out of place and had left early and gone home. But this second year she felt more a part of the group, and so had come to the gathering and ate finger food and gossiped and imbibed spiked punch like all the others. She wasn't married to Jimmy yet but he had come with her as her date and typically and very shortly attached himself to Lynn Shipley, a teacher in the Science Department, while she, Donna, stayed among her own friends on the staff, Peggy Lewis and Marilyn White and Sherry Woodley, representatives of the English and Foreign Language and History Departments. Donna was teaching Sophomore Lit at the time, and out of the blue she came across the long-lost John Clark Hayes, who had accompanied his wife Brenda to the party.

This wasn't the first time they had ever met outside the workplace and school. John Clark remembered everything about her from his high school classes and working and eying her at Harris Teeter back in the olden days, and he'd somehow known beforehand she was working with his wife, one of those things Donna took as fairly normal, as she'd decided a long while back there were not many things in this world that John Clark Hayes did not have a good bit of knowledge about.

For this gathering John Clark Hayes was by himself at mid-court in the gym, and Donna could see him standing by the punch bowl studying the inhabitants of the room, interrupting his research only long enough to fill his cup from the bowl and drink long swallows of the spiked contents therein. She observed his behavior for a few moments, and after three further glasses of the concocted punch she figured he had to be intoxicated even if he showed no outward signs of it. This was when she decided it might be safe to venture over to the bowl to get a glass for herself. She thought a movement such as this would at the very least give her something to do beside stand and watch him from afar, since that was all she'd been doing for ten minutes now, having shied away the past few moments from her friends who were busy getting plastered and flirting with men on the faculty they usually didn't have a kind word for.

"I don't know if I like this punch or not," she said. She took the dipper and filled her cup halfway, telling herself that no matter what this would be the last of her alcohol intake for the night. "I can't really taste the flavor because it's totally saturated with whatever booze they've used for the mixer. I didn't even think it was legal to have alcohol on school premises."

"I think they started out with vodka and then switched over to diesel fuel," John Clark offered. "Whatever it is, it's starting to get to me a little. I figure another twenty glasses and I'll be right where I want to be."

"Not me. I'm not used to this. I'm taking a chance even coming back for a refill."

"Well, you don't really want to scrimp when you're in a situation like this. The last thing in the world you want to do is stay sober among all these educational wunderkinds at a holiday gathering, because you can bet your life these folks are going to corner you at one time or another during the festivities and start telling you the story of their lives, how they've risen from lowly beginnings to the exalted positions they have today, and how if you're a good little teacher beginning your educational career around here you can worship at their feet a few minutes and maybe they'll let you in on some of their trade secrets on how to become a roaring success by the time you turn thirty."

"You don't sound like you're overly impressed with my colleagues."

"Au contraire, Ms. Owens, not true at all. The only reason I'm not sashaying around among them this very minute is because I am in a state of awe just observing them going through their entrances and exits on this grand stage of high drama while the holiday spirit is upon us all." He took another reflective swallow from his cup and squinted his eyes and allowed his shoulders to shimmy a slight second.

"This stuff gets worse as you go along," he confided. "Generally when I drown my sorrows the alcohol starts tasting better as I travel along on the road to oblivion."

He looks at his cup and shakes his head at what brain cell destructive liquid he's been sampling, then looks over at Donna and smiles.

"It's good to see you again, Ms. Owens."

He at least still remembers my name, Donna thinks.

"You don't have to be so formal," she says. "You can call me Donna like everybody else does. It's not like we've never met."

"And you can call me whatever you like," he said. "Most people these days like to refer to me as JC, which doesn't stand for Jesus Christ because he and I are not related whatsoever, but for John Clark. As a child I never could decide what I wanted people to call me, but I figured if it was just initials it would be easier and they wouldn't forget who I was so fast."

"JC," Donna smiled. "I'll bet you were a real hit with your first grade teacher."

"I was much beloved in those days. People thought I was destined for great things. But, alas."

It was easier talking to John Clark than standing back observing him, although Donna wasn't sure exactly what the attraction was in this John Clark (JC) so much, because it wasn't like he was dashing or handsome or any of those attributes young women her age seemed to find entrancing; it was more that he was not and never had been like most of the other men she'd come in contact with over the years, all of whom seemed to have an inherit belief that they were dashing and handsome themselves much more than anyone actually realized they were and seemed to hold the assumption that everyone around them—especially young women—would soon arrive at that conclusion too and offer themselves up as a reward to them for their God-given physical appearance and breathtaking demeanor. Her fiancé Jimmy was a lot like that. The good thing about Jimmy was he wasn't quite so bad as the others. He had an inkling that parts of him were full of crap.

John Clark Hayes, though, was of another calling.

The two of them presently felt compelled to take several steps away from the punch bowl at mid-court and locate a more private space over past the corner baseline where they would be somewhat apart and separated from the party going on around them. The goals in the gym had been raised and the basketballs and volleyball nets and tumbling mats removed, and while most of the faculty members gathered in proximity to mid-court where the tables and the illegal booze was or chose to congregate along the free throw circles on both ends, no one much bothered to wander over toward the baselines to where the stairs that led to the second tier of bleachers were, and so Donna and John Clark were able to after a few moments mosey over to the stairs apart from the party and lean there against the stair railing and talk, and in a few minutes decided it would suit them better to climb the stairs to the second set of bleachers and after a moment or two of looking into each other's eyes and seeing what they saw while the spiked punch performed Esther Williams breaststrokes around the pool of their libidos they jointly decided to take further steps beneath the second set of bleachers and there embrace and kiss for an exceedingly long moment with fingers groping and tongues darting down each other's throats while the party and the world took a seat below them far away while they wandered and groped and closed their eyes as they travelled to another world together.

This had been both Donna's introduction and denouement to the physical side of John Clark Hayes, since nothing of this intense sexual caliber ever occurred between them again. Oh sure, there were smiles and waves and how-are-you greetings aplenty whenever their paths crossed, whenever John Clark accompanied his wife Brenda to school functions, but the fact that this intriguing John Clark Hayes had small children and a wife who taught Math at the very school where Donna taught Sophomore English made Donna believe it was probably best to play it safe and let things between her and John Clark Hayes ride. Because, she asked herself, how was she to know that this wife of John Clark's named Brenda who was also a teacher with her had also once been a classmate of her fiancé Jimmy years before at Coastal Georgia? And how was she to know what had gone on between this Brenda and Jimmy before she, Donna, had had the chance to connect all the dots? It was like something out of Days of Our Lives or Falcon Crest. There was so much going on that a person needed a glossary just to see who all the characters were and where they came from and how they were related. There she was on the same faculty staff as Brenda Hayes, and there was Brenda's past history with Jimmy, and it was uncomfortable enough just in that sense without the fact of Brenda being married to John Clark and the mother of his children. And here they all were thrown together by a hysterical God who was undoubtedly laughing his celestial ass off at the monumental soap opera He'd managed to create. Sometimes the four of them found themselves thrown together at school events, Jimmy and Brenda and John Clark and her, and boy did Donna feel creepy being around while those events were transpiring, wondering all the time if Jimmy knew about John Clark or if Brenda knew about John Clark and her or if John Clark knew about Brenda and Jimmy and if any of them felt as freaked-out about it as she did

John Clark Hayes. She couldn't get him off her mind.

A Food Lion was where she had found him those eight years later, after she gave up teaching so that she and Jimmy could form their own business catering snacks and refreshments and coffee to businesses across the city. They needed a driver who knew how to stock and rotate products, and that was just the line of work John Clark seemed destined for when it got described to him on those occasions when Donna would run across him accidentally on purpose at the Food Lion while doing her shopping. After a while it became evident that John Clark had come to believe running a delivery route was what God had placed him on this planet for. John Clark also didn't mind weighing the fact that Donna Owens-Baldwin was going to be his new boss and didn't even mind Jimmy being around in one way or another, since he knew he could tune Jimmy Baldwin out any damn time he wanted, as he'd been doing for years now when things with Brenda and Jimmy started flaring up, and how he always knew where old Jimmy was coming from, which was some behavioral slag heap where sleazebags tended to hang out, so it didn't matter to him whether a jerk like Jimmy was going to be one of his employers or not, since he'd been ignoring Jimmy in his jerkiness since the first time he'd met him back at college and all those times during the off and on affair Jimmy had reignited with Brenda like they were swallows coming back to Capistrano. John Clark had long-ago assigned Jimmy Baldwin the role he always designated for jackasses disguised as men he was forced to rub shoulders with—Jimmy was to be regularly smiled at and nodded at when he drifted by John Clark, like he might regard a discarded hamburger wrapper blowing in a gale. Jimmy Baldwin was like most of the other worthless men of the human race John Clark observed drifting by. He could always see the wrappers (men) floating by and disappearing from sight wherever the wind took them, and wherever that place was John Clark always cared not the least bit about, because the wrappers and the men should in his way of thinking all disappear and be gone with the wind and vanish from the face of the earth as fast as possible. John Clark had long assumed he was himself a sort of god of his own mythology and it was his duty to control the elements around him, to command the wind to whisk away the men and the wrappers so they might never be seen again, the likes of them departed and out of his sight. He didn't much like men or dirty wrappers.

Donna felt like she really should say something about the ceremony on the way home. She couldn't just ignore the fact that John Clark was dead. Something had once more begun churning inside her again these past few days, despite the fact there had been nothing going on between her and John Clark for years now and technically had hardly ever been, and so it shouldn't be tearing her apart like this and causing her to wonder if Jimmy was going to notice how she was spiraling to pieces over losing a route driver and how it seemed she simply couldn't function enough to form any words to express where they'd just been and how it was a shame that something this awful had to happen to John Clark Hayes.

So she decided she should simply make the conversation on the way home about hiring a new driver. Any deeper discussion about John Clark with Jimmy was better suited for another time, or at least that was the way she saw it in her own mind. She didn't know what Jimmy might be thinking, and it was probably best to wait and find out later, maybe a couple of years from now when the subject wasn't so ripe as right this moment. Of course, Jimmy wasn't entirely stupid. She was going to have to talk about this at some point or he would know something was up by her silence.

The thing is she doesn't know why she is feeling so weird about John Clark to begin with. It isn't like she needs to feel guilty over anything that had gone on between them. What had happened with her and John Clark had been a bunch of years ago, and in the grand scheme of world events it had amounted to practically nothing. She'd wager if she was any other woman in the world besides herself she would have forgotten such a thing had even occurred by now. If she was normal then trivial matters like that would have never had the strength to linger very long.

***

John Clark Hayes could have easily lessened all the fears and phobias his family and friends seemed to hold about his personal lifestyle and what he did or didn't know and whether any of his knowledge or lack thereof made any difference in the long run, but he'd had decided from an early age that

18

what was going on inside his head was better left covered up and kept silent to the outside world. He believed that anything he said or any cards he showed would all in some way or another later come back to haunt him and be used against him. The best thing, he decided, was to never give the world the first clue about what he had done in the past, what he was up to at the moment, and what he had planned for the future. He believed he had the right to remain silent.

He had been married to Brenda for seventeen years. It had taken him maybe three of those years to come to the knowledge that the marriage was a mistake, maybe not a big, gigantic, colossal error in judgement that was going to plague him and cause him a plethora of pain and misery for the rest of his life, but rather that it was something he was going to have to acclimate his lifestyle to and know when he should deal with it head-on and when it was best to be avoided, when it was good to just herd it out to pasture and let it graze until it seemed time to bring it back into the barn. It wasn't that he disliked Brenda. Actually, he liked her in a passing sort of manner, the same way he once liked going to the bank and asking a pretty teller—whose name was Melinda, he remembered semi-flirting with her for two years until she got fired for misappropriating funds, or at least this is what happened to her in his mind, because he really didn't know for certain what her fate was since the bank never liked to broadcast internal affairs that had gone wrong with their employees—how she was today and where she was going on vacation this year and anything just to hear her voice and see her smile so he could memorize it in his brain and have the essence of it around to think about later. He did like Brenda that way a good bit. He liked thinking about her when they met and how they couldn't get enough of each other there at the first, and he liked some of the meals she prepared and the way she liked to watch old movies more than something new, which was the way he was and which kept them happy for a while when they watched TV together at night. It was only when Brenda grew silent with him when he didn't want to go places with her, like church every blue moon, or failed to get home at an acceptable time that he knew things were never going to be perfect between them and there was always going to be some friction and tension and irritation when they interacted after being together too much, and that was when it had first come to him that there were times that were not infrequent when it was better for her to be in one place and him to be in another. He didn't want to explain it to her out loud but thought she would come to understand it better if he just allowed their own preferred actions to do the explaining for everything.

So he chose to say nothing about his wife's former and then off and on relationship with Jimmy Baldwin or his own one-night interlude of magic with Donna Owens-Baldwin or to bring up anything that bordered on either ancient history or current events. But because he didn't say anything about The Kiss or acknowledge it in any way didn't mean it had totally escaped his mind. He had a constant and abiding memory of kissing Donna Owens-Baldwin that one particular night and wondering what got into him at the time and, more so, why he never bothered to follow up the event with further attempts at romance. The answer occurred to him in fleeting ways over the years, hinting at answers he never could grasp in their entirety. Most of the answers seemed to latch onto the hypotenuse that on that particular evening while taking a trip to the moon on gossamer wings that he and Donna had reached the zenith of what little time the universe had allotted them together, that it had been culminated in that sixty minute tryst the two had experienced that evening in the continuum of time, and anything that further happened between them would surely be a letdown and a disappointment and mar the magical memory the two of them had shared that one moment in space, and so it was that there was a measure of benevolence in the providence provided them, he and Donna, in this once in a lifetime sense, and so they did not have to suffer the pangs of faded and soured love that may have possibly come along later, as it most invariably does to the majority of lovers in the world.

As it had to Jimmy and Brenda.

Yes, he knew all about their past history back at college and during those first intervals in their marriage when Brenda embarked on an affair with Jimmy once more, probably, John Clark deduced, out of boredom or simply for old time's sake. And although the opportunities for extramarital activities had been there for the taking since that time for him too, John Clark had been resolutely faithful to his own soul all the while, all through his time as a teacher and a retail clerk and a route delivery salesman. He did not think he could have lived with himself otherwise.

The only affair he allowed himself was to spend intimate moments alone, seeing how he was the only one in the world who understood his actions and had a sense of what he longed for deep in his heart, and so by the time he made it to his early thirties and had a wife named Brenda and two children and another on the way he had already learned how to take time away from his occupational requirements and steal off to private lands to share moments and interludes with himself. He would drive to secluded locales, shoot baskets at available goals, frequent distant restaurants, where he could sit in a chair and regard birds flying by outside the plate-glass window or have cheesecake and coffee and stare out at traffic going here and there, perhaps to wander over to a corner and play songs on a jukebox while pondering his own existence. He tried not to be late for dinner. He tried to be around for his wife and children, but after a time he realized that lots of times they seemed to prefer his not being there at all, and so he took that as a sign he needed to give them what they wanted. After all, he didn't really mind. Being absent from them only increased the time he could be with himself.

This solitary lifestyle went along smoothly for twenty years or so, and while at first his family and those who called themselves friends considered him strange and distant and wondered among themselves if there might deep down be something wrong with him, but after some measure of years went by the topic of his sanity or his fitting in with the ways of the world faded from conversations and thoughts and everyone seemed to adapt to his regular state of being John Clark Hayes and accept it without giving it too much thought. The fact was John Clark spent so much time not being in the orb of others that his presence in the physical sense was not missed that much anymore, and people tended to allow him to exist merely in their heads and imaginations and made of him whatever they wanted him to be, and in this way all was fine and everyone grew to a state of satisfaction.

By the time that Tuesday morning arrived when John Clark had just finished filling his order and was on his way into the Lancaster Hills Credit Union at the simultaneous moment the would-be robbers were finishing up making their attempted illegal withdrawal, the Today Show was just coming on and the local morning news had ended, and it would take until a little more up into the morning before the news came out about the robbery and the felony murder and the two escapees who were still on the loose and how they were considered dangerous, and the report said the police were withholding identification of the victim until his next of kin could be notified.

And Judy the Cracker Jack-addicted teller who always smiled at John Clark when he brought in his order thought of him as she watched the police take prints and interview people and the paramedics carry the body away and felt a tug at her heart that she was not ever going to see him anymore and wondered if she'd be able to eat a box of Cracker Jacks ever again.

TWO

Someone new to the proceedings might have wondered why on the occasion of John Clark Hayes' Celebration of Life his brother or none of his close friends showed up to mourn him, but that could be explained by their attendance being non-existent on account the quartet of them had all preceded John Clark to the Hereafter already and unless their ghosts happened to hover in joint presence they were not around to rue the memory of his passing. Charles (Chuck) Hayes had died in Viet Nam long ago, and John Clark's buddies from high school and college had all gone their ways too, from cancer, from a heart attack, and from a hit and run accident along a highway while walking the family dog. All these removals from life came within a twenty-five year span, and it had been over a decade since John Clark had been blessed with having a close friend in the world. There were a lot of people who thought this must have been an extremely sad way for him to go through life, alone with no comradeship whatsoever, but that wasn't truly the case. It wasn't exactly common knowledge, but John Clark and Chuck hardly fit the brotherly bill for a long time before Chuck had his body obliterated by a Viet Cong booby trap in 1969, having already decided they were happier being brotherless some ten years before that, when Chuck was nine and John seven, when after receiving another in a series of daily beatings from his older brother John Clark decided to remedy the situation by picking up Chuck's Louisville Slugger and teeing up his brother's head with it while Chuck bent over to tie the strings on his Spaldings. This action resulted in a three-day hospital stay for Chuck and joint thrashings from John Clark's mother and father, the both of whom, he decided, exhibited the characteristics of loving Chuck more than him, and as he pondered this revelation he soon decided that if this was the case then the best thing for him to do was endure being the family black sheep for however long it took him to get free of his surroundings and then buy a car and go away to college and relegate his family to strictly obstacles he had to endure on Thanksgiving, Christmas, and the occasional birthday.

His three friends from his foggy high school and college career all left the world as if they were dominos and death had lined them up to watch them topple in sequence. John Clark didn't have the dates totally firm in his memory, but it seemed to him that his pals had begun dropping at five-year intervals and it had been much like some form of fateful clockwork until they were all of them worms meat. Somewhere inside him was instilled the old adage that there were no friends like old friends, and since his old friends were all pushing up daisies he found no call to throw himself out into the world and try and come up with substitute comradery to replace them. He also had no need of another brother, since what he'd seen of life thus far pretty much conferred the fact that most members of society he ran across were SOBs and horses' asses in general and would keep those qualities whether they were related to him or not. He early arrived at the belief that he was better off without blood relations hanging around just looking for a way to screw up his life.

Now this did not mean he had no use for mankind whatsoever. He got along fairly well with members of the faculty during his teaching career, and he had no problem with the fellows and girls at the grocery store those years he spent nights working in that environment, and he was friendly enough with the customers on his route who worked in the establishments where he stocked their snacks and soft drinks and made certain they had coffee to drink that didn't raise the hairs on their necks or cause them to lose productive time at their jobs because they were gagging to death. So it wasn't like he was some kind of social outcast out to distance himself from the everyday stream of the human race around him.

As a matter of record, he actually considered himself to be more a member of true humanity than others he crossed paths with each day. Unlike the way he sensed they classified him each time he came into contact with one of their representatives, he actually listened to what words came out of their mouths and had some empathy for the tragedy each person in his path seemed to carry around in their hearts. He didn't despise anyone immediately just because he saw them coming down the street toward him. He didn't tune out what they had to say because he'd already decided that their words were unimportant, nor did he dismiss their lives and problems from his mind because their backgrounds and environments meant little in the grand scheme of things in the workings of the world. No, he cared. He listened. He actually spent some time and effort defining the sorrow of the everyday world and tried to determine what he could do to help his fellow human beings escape the pit they either dug for themselves or unwittingly fell into.

So, no, he was not a bad person. Not by any long shot. He even tried to keep himself from thinking that if all the world around him acted like him and possessed his brand of sensitivity then the planet would spin smoother on its axis and all the petty problems that plagued its inhabitants would dissolve and come to nothing.

Take his own family, for instance.

The romance with Brenda had pretty much run its course before the first anniversary of their marriage. At first, he had taken the blame for this, but as time passed he came to see that while he was certainly not blameless in this dying affection category, it was still not him who seemed to come up with different places to be and nights to be out with friends or meetings at the church or any other social event that seemed to pop up regularly that would keep her from being around to spend time with him. He didn't hate her leaving the house so much, he admitted, because lots of times he was more than happy to see her go so he could be alone to do his own things, to read or write or listen to music or take in an old movie on television, but it wasn't like he encouraged it either. And the truth was he was the homebody of the two during that first year and hardly ever left the house for anything other than to go to work as a teacher. But it was fairly easy to read the writing on the wall and know that nobody is so busy that they go days without having a conversation with their spouse. You could hem-haw about it and make all kind of excuses about why it was the way it was, but in the long run there it was and there was no writing it off as coincidence.

The children came along anyway, because he was a heck of an actor and duty-bound to a fault and so felt it his duty in his role as a husband to fulfill his sexual personage and bring children into the world and allow Brenda to become a mother, even if he couldn't quite decide if that role was what she actually desired or not. She liked children, he could tell that. She wouldn't have gone into education and become a teacher if she didn't, but he was not so certain that fondness transferred over to pregnancy and delivery and having squalling babies in the night or changing diapers and all that motherhood jazz he couldn't see how any woman would ever want for a lifestyle.

Since they didn't particularly like each other and since there were now three children present in the household, most of the sexual sparks that were once present between them soon dematerialized like Dracula used to do when he wanted to vanish into smoke, and though it was never discussed that much it wasn't long before Brenda was going out to additional "meetings" at night and John Clark was watching television in either the den if the kids were at their grandparents' or in the library if they were present and gathered together in the den, and it also didn't take long for John Clark to discover that the recliner in the library and the sofa in the den were both conducive to a better night's rest than the bed in the bedroom that he shared with Brenda, and so he forfeited his sleeping accommodations there and took up nightly residence in either the den or the library depending on when he could be in solitude therein and made it a habit that soon became accepted by all the family and wasn't a cause for great discussion anymore. His children, Linda, David, and Franklin, were all young enough to adjust and adapt to most anything, and so John Clark's self-removal from the master bedroom of the house did not weigh too heavily on any of their minds or freak them out or scar them for life or dismay them in any way much at all, so he continued to get up in the mornings and go to his job as a teacher or a retail clerk or a route delivery salesman and bring in the money to support them in food and clothing and transportation and college tuitions until they were the last of them sufficiently grown and mature and schooled and able to begin screwing up their lives all on their own. He came home at nights and sometimes dined with them or else dined alone, eating sometimes Brenda's cooking or bringing home takeout and then reposing somewhere in his two locations to close the day and get ready for another. After a spell his acts of random parenting and now and then fatherhood and off and on appearances became rather natural to Brenda and Linda and David and Franklin, and after settling in for a few years of erraticism everyone's lifestyle adapted and adjusted and fell in with his patterns of behavior, and if the question could have been asked of them the reply would mostly be theirs was a semi-normal existence once you got past all the weirdness.

It wasn't that his kids had turned out to be total nuts. Linda had managed to make it through high school and college without getting knocked up by any of the legions of jocks she had dalliances with along the way, and finally had married a tennis player from her college and produced two sons so far at the age of twenty-seven, which John Clark at the time of his passing thought was fairly normal fare. David was engaged to be married later in the coming year and already had one son before this coming occurrence, which John Clark realized was not that big of a thing these days and so had never mentioned it or linked it to a scandal. It was and is, he decided, a changing world with new sets of normal, and what had been a major no-no and a lasting taboo to be branded with in his time, these days people were popping out illegitimate kids right and left and nobody thought the first thing about it. The good thing was David had a decent job with a computer repair company doing god knows what but was at least not out on the street selling drugs or carjacking old ladies when they went to the grocery store, so things were all good on that front. Franklin he was not so sure about, as he had always not been so sure about in the past and even right up until the day he got plugged and expired there on the sidewalk, thinking how his youngest son was another of those earthly problems he wasn't going to have to worry about anymore. But he had at least had it on his mind in those final moments when his life was ticking away, wondering what he could do and how there really was no time to do it and being somewhat relieved for it to be that way since what he would do to try and guide his youngest son to a safe place probably would have ended up getting him more screwed up in the long run anyway.

So basically, John Clark was embarking on his new plane of unbeing without much encouragement from his closest friends, who had already gone on to a state of unbeing themselves, but they were not, as he'd assumed, anywhere to be seen or near his proximity to help him out in his life journey whatsoever. He was altogether alone in this way, and he'd come to think that this was par for the course when one becomes unbeing and first begins attempts to adjust to their new surroundings after being fairly comfortable in their old digs while among the living. It wasn't exactly easy or contained any answers he had learned in the school of life he'd just graduated from, but he had to say that he at least had some sort of peace now and didn't feel like someone was fixing to require a miracle on his behalf or demand some sort of deep emotional response from him this time around, which was cool and fine and good as far as he could so far tell. He'd not been very good at such things when he'd been breathing and had something of a beating heart, so it was good now to merely be a watcher and let the people he'd been around for such a limited time compared to eternity learn to live their lives the way they thought best with not a lot of assistance from him.

***

Surprisingly, Mark had already picked the children up from daycare when Linda left her mother's. She hoped Mark would take even more initiative and do something like order pizza for them to eat, considering the fact she had been so busy and stressed out for four days helping her mother put together the celebration of life and plan the visitation and reception, so maybe she'd get lucky and he had done that too. Her dad went so unexpectedly and fast that there was no plan in place if such a thing was to happen, but John Clark had surprised everyone with his prior planning, so there wasn't a lot of worry and stress for her anymore other than wondering if her two children had actually been fed and sufficiently looked after by Mark, who certainly had never before shown a propensity for anything like parenthood for any extended amount of time. But she had to admit he'd done okay the last couple of days. She had asked him to keep the kids at home instead of having them underfoot and running wild at her father's services, and he had actually taken them to restaurants or fed them TV dinners and even bother to wash a few dishes in the sink and load the dishwasher as another added miracle. For the first time in a while, she really didn't have a lot to bitch about.

But it was a short-lived ecstasy. She soon ran across numerous piles of empty clothes. ill-placed dirty dishes decorated the path back to the kitchen, and on the breakfast table open bags of chips and glasses and dirty sippy cups were waiting in formation, a sight which made her wonder if there were any more drinking vessels left in the cabinet clean enough to drink from or if everyone in the family was somewhere in the reaches of the house lying dehydrated and close to expiration. After the first flicker of concern had passed through her, she gave over to her usual feelings of irritation and thoughts of maiming for the members of her household with the exception of Barney the cat, who now inched toward her with a swishing tail. He was obviously hungry, probably a victim of neglect like she expected to find her children soon, and so she reached down to stroke his head, half expecting Barney to rear up and attempt to slash her for leaving him alone these last few days to have to fend for himself. But he was weakened from his fasting and instead fell over on his side and attempted to persuade her that unless he was fed straightaway he would very soon stop breathing, so it was now or never.

Linda poured some Nine Lives into his bowl and watched Barney sniff what was there and then walk away.

"So, you're not starving after all," she told the cat. "You've been lying to me again. Haven't I warned you about the consequences of telling fibs?"

She found everyone in the backyard, Will shooting baskets at his mini-goal and Mark pushing Donnie on the swing set while Donnie howled holy murder because he was scared to death of swaying back and forth and Mark continuing to push him anyway so he'd get over it and not be a baby his entire life, even though Donnie was two and technically still a baby. Linda knew better than to try and explain that to Mark, since she was pretty certain he wouldn't listen anyway.

"I'll take him," she said. She walked directly to the swing and unfastened Donnie before Mark had a chance to speak. "Once he gets hysterical and starts crying there's no getting him through it."

She thought maybe she'd get some sort of rise out of Mark, like he would offer some kind of defense for being an insensitive father, but when she turned around with Donnie in her arms he had already moved away and was getting comfortable in his patio chair. He picked up his beer can which was wrapped in a rubber cooler with an Atlanta Falcons logo on it, and once he'd taken a big long drink he leaned back in the chair and folded his arms and closed his eyes. Obviously, his work was done.

"Did you get your mother all squared away?" he asked from behind his lids. "I was beginning to think you were going to have to spend the night there."

"I don't think she needed me all that much. I think she was glad to see everyone start clearing out from the house, like she was happy to finally get everything over and done with so she could go back to her life of watching television until bedtime."

"Maybe this is all just a form of denial," Mark offered. "Maybe she's just going down different avenues so she won't have to stay in one place and face the facts that your dad is gone and she's a widow now."

"No, I thought I sensed relief from her more than anything else. Anyway, she's not technically a widow, since they'd been divorced for six years."

"Maybe so. You know her better than anyone. Myself, I'm more concerned about how you're feeling. You're the one who's lost a father. Not that you were Daddy's Girl or anything, but I do think your father liked you better than he did David and Franklin."

"There are times when I think maybe Daddy didn't like any of us all that much. I mean, he didn't dote on us and never exactly went to the end of the earth to get us whatever our little hearts desired or anything like that. With him it was all a duty to be accomplished and then scratched off the list. The family was his responsibility to keep from imploding and he paid a lot of attention to keep things from boiling over. He didn't feel like he had to understand any of us or tell us the correct way to live our lives or take a shotgun off the wall and shoot the Big Bad Wolf if he tried to get in the door, but as far as staying awake nights and shortening his life through worry and anxiety as to how we were all going to wind up, that just didn't happen."

She started to continue her analysis, but Mark had already used up his attention span and was ready to move on. She guessed she should at least be thankful he had taken a few days off from the car dealership to take care of the kids during the three days of funeral planning and visitation and the celebration of life ceremony that closed it all out. He did bring the kids by for the visitation for thirty minutes and managed to keep them from running amok around the house or attempting to snatch her father's ashes off the dining room table, so that was good. Will had managed to pick up a photo album and spill out all its contents on the floor when he held it by the binding and shook it to see if anything fell out he could play with, but that had been pretty much it. Donnie only cried after he messed his diaper, and after she had taken him and the foul smell out of the room and changed him Mark had herded them all up and left before any greater disaster could occur.

"We had supper already," Mark said, "in case you were wondering. There's a little pizza left in the refrigerator if you're hungry. I didn't know whether you'd eaten already or not. I thought with all that food sitting around you'd probably find something."

"I think I'm just going to have a peanut butter and jelly sandwich and call it quits."

She sat down with a Diet Coke and a sandwich and watched Wheel of Fortune until some woman from Pensacola who looked like Trisha Yearwood after a four-alarm fire blew the championship round by not being able to decipher "Tutti Frutti Ice Cream" from the category she'd chosen. She had the Ts and Is and Cs but was still dumb enough to miss it. Linda supposed she'd just been lucky earlier in the program and had the good fortune of the spinning wheel going for her.

She looked over at Donnie in his high chair. He was fast asleep already. He was lucky, she thought, being a kid. When you wanted to you could just zone out.

***

After a couple of boilermakers, Franklin Hayes was beginning to feel like he'd just awoken from a pretty stupid dream. In the dream he'd been this grief-stricken young man mourning the death of his father, like he was Eugene Gant and he was hanging out at Altamont waiting for a sculptured angel to come to life to denote something big in his head, which seemed really porous when compared to the way it was in his real existence. Yes, he was a son, and yes, his father was dead just like in Look Homeward, Angel, but it was there that the resemblance ended and the whole shebang spiraled off into subconscious bullshit. Hell, he wasn't grieving. He hadn't lost his father today or anytime in the past he could readily assign a date to. He was as close sitting here at Davey's Sports Bar eating chicken fingers and drinking boilermakers as he had been at any time with his father over the past twenty years. His father's ashes were in a box at his mother's and Franklin had no idea when or where they were going to be scattered, and they might just as well be here on the barstool beside him, because the distance and the emotions would be exactly the same.

Dead or alive, there was no big difference.

Two boilermakers down, three to go. Maybe four. It depends.

All the details of his father's funeral had been basically harmless. Nothing to see here, he'd thought. Nothing to worry over. It's just another anonymous person going in the ground or getting cast to the wind. No big deal. Of course, there was a murder involved in this one, but that's no biggie either. People get blown away around this town every day, so it's not like it's so unusual. In two or three days everyone forgets all about it, generally because there's a new, fresh murder coming along to grab their attention.

Franklin was trying to remember the last time he and his father had talked to each other and how he could be so callous about his death. This was the last day of September, so the closest he could recall was back in the early part of summer when he had spotted the delivery truck parked at the YMCA downtown and on a whim had pulled over and gone inside to find his father. It was a large building and he had to walk around and climb some stairs before he found his dad hunched over the open door of a snack machine. He stifled the urge to scream Boo! And see the old man jump, but just walked up and got within eyesight before he spoke.

"Are you going to do the honorable thing and marry that machine after you've had your way with it?"

John Clark looked up from the recalcitrant bill acceptor and grinned at his son.

"Hey there. I'm just trying to get this thing going again. Some kid thought it would be funny to cram chewed gummy bears into the slot and see if it still worked."

"Another reason why I'm planning to never have children."

"Maybe so, but probably these kids learned every trick they know from their sorry parents, so you've still got to deal with them out in the world. You can't get this mean and destructive without being tutored."

"I saw your truck parked outside and thought I'd come in and say hello."

"I've been meaning to call you, but I'm staying pretty busy."

He was always meaning to call, Franklin thought. He was going to call or come by or maybe see if they could have lunch or dinner together sometime, maybe catch a movie if there was anything worth seeing. But it never happened. It was all pie in the sky and see you real soon. It had been that way for as long as he could calculate, and now it was going to continue for a lot longer, until he, Franklin, turned his toes up and there was never a chance to go anywhere again.

He made himself stop at the fourth boilermaker and walked out to his Camaro. The sun was setting and there was pink and gold over the horizon and if he was a lover of nature's beauty he would be awestruck now, but he was not. Rain or shine, day or night, he didn't give it much thought. All he wanted was to get through classes and work and get nice and buzzed at night and get back to his apartment to crash before doing it again, and that was his great goal in life.

It didn't take much to get moving along in the Camaro. All you had to do was put your foot in it just a little and you'd be where you were going before you were prepared to be there, and that was the way it was this night. It wasn't that he was in a hurry or was trying to set any speed records on his way home, but the twilight cast a serene glow and the world seemed silent to him right then and so before he knew it his toes were pushing the accelerator to the floor and the engine was making appropriate growling noises and the wind came in his window warm and fresh from the Atlantic, and for a few blessed minutes it was him and the Camaro and the road all together for a session of love, and that was when he saw the lights flashing behind him and he knew that he was screwed. Then, to make things worse, when he pulled off the road he managed to uproot a guard rail that had been hiding in the shadows. There was a lot of screeching and groaning from metal being crumpled and bent, and when he came to a stop he had a good idea there wasn't going to be any more fun being had by him this particular evening.

***

David had finished dinner and was settling down in the den to log in a few minutes of The Bachelorette so he could look at some of the women network TV found to act like prostitutes on prime time each week. They were, he'd decided, the same kind of figments of the imagination that were in Playboy and all those other magazines that displayed hot young women and their bodies, but he'd decided long ago that a little stretch of the imagination was good for a growing boy, so he figured it was okay to indulge himself this way now and then. After all, it was stuff like this that allowed a fellow respite from the real world and gave him cause to get up the next morning and go to work.

His cell rang and he looked at the caller identification. It was Franklin and he started for a minute to let it go to message and deal with it tomorrow, but since Franklin rarely called him he decided it might be kosher to answer and make sure everything was okay. As long as his little brother wasn't calling asking for money again he supposed he could talk to him for a minute or so.

"Well," Franklin said with no hesitation, "I fucked up and I need some help."

"What's the matter?"

"I got pulled over for speeding and they busted me for being over the limit on the breathalyzer."

"Shit. How much have you had? Was it close?"

"It was pretty bad. I'd knocked back a few at dinner earlier. I guess I had no business getting behind the wheel. I also scraped a guard rail and moved it down the road a little, which wasn't good either. I was pretty looped when they had me walk the fucking line. I don't think I made it three steps before I went sideways."

"Where are you?"

"Downtown. Demere Road."

"I'm on my way. I'll bail your ass out, but you have to promise to pay me back."

"I promise. Just do me a favor and hurry, okay? I'm not too crazy about the accommodations down here."

"You might have considered that a little earlier."

"Yeah, well who knew?"

***

It wasn't exactly the most honorable thing to do on the evening of your husband's funeral, but Brenda Hayes, after a refreshing nap and being rid of her family and friends for a delicious two hours, arose from her bed and began considering how to spend the first night of her life as a legitimate single woman in almost three decades. The decent side of her told her to open a can of soup and have a few Ritz crackers to go with it for dinner, but somehow the mental picture of her sitting at the kitchenette in her bathrobe slurping down Campbell's Bean with Bacon made her think that anything else she might choose to commiserate such a monumental night of freedom as this one should be spent somewhere with music and bright lights and the sound of human laughter. Perhaps it wasn't the classiest thing for a woman in her position to do, but there was a part of her pricking her brain like an open wound that said she needed to change the course of her life from this moment forward starting right now.

She wasn't sure it would be very kosher to give Jimmy a ring on his cellphone and see what he was doing this night. There had been a few meaningful glances between the two during the visitation and the Celebration of Life and the reception, but most of the time Jimmy had either stayed by Donna's side or drifted off away to other rooms in the house, minding, it appeared, his own business while Donna represented the business and their joint years of knowing both John Clark and Brenda down through the years. To the world, it appeared that the four of them—John Clark, Brenda, Jimmy and Donna—were old college friends and faculty pals for a time and had a lifetime connection with each other after Jimmy and Donna left their jobs to form their own vending company, a successful venture that pretty much dominated the competition around the beach town and bonded them further with John Clark as one of their long-time faithful employees. But it wasn't that way and Brenda knew it, and she knew Jimmy knew it too, and sometimes she wondered exactly what Donna knew and how much, and since he was in his earthly reward now she would never find out what John Clark had himself known, as if she might have discovered this puzzle even if he survived to the ripe old age of one hundred and five.

She had been seeing Jimmy on occasion for a dozen years now, but that wasn't the complete gist of it, because there was also the interlude before that they'd spent being a couple during college, and then they'd parted when Jimmy met a girl at a party and broken off whatever strings of a relationship

33

he and Brenda shared. It was not a tearful goodbye with lasting repercussions or angry words of parting like normal people have, but it was more of the fact that Jimmy simply stopped calling or showing up and Brenda was wise enough to know someone was fixing to get dumped and made damn sure it wasn't going to be her. That's when she'd begun to gravitate over to John Clark Hayes, the solitary, somewhat mystical guy who seemed to hang around on the fringe of everything watching and observing like he was taking notes for some future project. What was it? A novel? An epic poem? Was he in the Stanislavsky school of thinking and immersing himself in certain brands of human behavior so he could bring a true representation of mankind to his role on the stage and screen? Or was he merely shy and a classic introvert and thought it best to leave all the thrusts and ploys and interactions employed by human beings to a group of people that excluded himself. She wondered sometimes if John Clark was dropped on earth at an early time and was an intergalactic spy for some other world beyond the stars, set down here among a certain segment of the human race to collect data and take notes? John Clark Hayes was a strange one, all right; she'd seen that from the start.

But still, there was something about him. There had been something about him all these years, and whether this meant she was once or was still in love with him or was just under the spell of his conduct under the sun moon and stars for a finite amount of time she did not know, but somehow he still held some sort of sway on her and made her think twice about an act of sexual union between her and Jimmy Baldwin on this night after her official farewells to John Clark, or whether this time after his passing might be better spent sitting on the back patio regarding the heavens and wondering exactly where her departed ex-husband was exactly this night in the grand realm of the spheres.

Yes, there was something telling her that the best way to pass this evening was by an act of compromise, so instead of trying to contact Jimmy for companionship or sitting alone to pine a life with an entire array of unanswered questions, she would instead get in her SUV and go order something from the Sonic downtown and take a nice, long, reflective ride somewhere, just cruise along and listen to music and eat french fries out of the bag. Maybe by doing this she could indulge her brain and her stomach and be calm about things for a time. Grease and a soft drink might do the trick when nothing else would.

She got in her Toyota and immediately began searching the dial for something to listen to that would allow her to think but not put her to sleep. She opted for a station that played Classic Rock—whatever that entailed—and backed out the driveway and took a left on Fredrica Rd. and went straight for a while. There was a Sonic around somewhere, she believed, but she just couldn't locate it right now. Oh well, she told herself, that's no big thing. Any old place will do as long as they have a drive-thru. She certainly didn't want to go in someplace. That would require interaction with the human race, and that was not on the agenda this night. She needed solitude at the moment, and the interchange at a drive-thru speaker was about as much as she could tolerate for now.

It wasn't hard to tell that the tourist season was about done for this year. All she had to do was glance at the restaurant parking lots on the way to Sea Island Road and she could see spaces between cars where there were plenty of available spots, not the way the population was normally squeezed in from May to September. There would be a couple of weeks lull until the weather in the north drove the snowbirds to the beaches of the Carolinas and all up and down Florida and the Gulf, and then the cash registers and souvenir shops and restaurants either upscale or dinky would be packed again. That was good, she guessed, otherwise the island and all the other towns dotted down the coastline would dry up and go out of business, the employees and owners soon relegated to lives of crime, burglaries and carjackings and armed robberies every time you turned around. And there was always the chance of a nice hurricane coming along and putting everybody out of business, making sure the town was broken and without power if not dead. It was a year-round notion that festered in whoever was living in these parts. Disaster and tragedy were always only a few days away.

She saw a Zaxby's off to her left and settled on stuffing herself with chicken fingers and fries. She hadn't counted on this venue being everyone else on the island's idea for dinner fare and had to wait longer in the line than she'd wanted, but at last she inched to the window and paid her order to a girl who obviously wanted to be somewhere else. It took forever for the girl to muster the energy to process her card, and she had to stifle the urge to scream at her and tell her to hurry up, but she remained cool and quiet, because she halfway understood where the girl was coming from, and if not coming from, then at least where she was. Brenda had experienced that feeling a few times herself. She knew how it was to be lost on earth.

During her wait she had at least been entertained by a playlist on the car radio that may have been selected exclusively for her—Bread and Jim Croce, Gladys Knight and The Pips and Harold Melvin and The Blue Notes. She was almost carefree and contented when she pulled back out onto Sea Island Road, and it occurred to her that this night of reflection and semi-mourning was not going to be so bad after all. She hated to say it, and she hoped if John

Clark was out there in the Great Beyond watching right now he wouldn't take it personally, how she was having such a good time on the night he was officially no longer part of the world anymore. She tried putting herself in his shoes and seeing how she would take it if it was him driving down the road and her looking on at a recently vacated world, and she sort of had the feeling it might not upset her all that much. And if she, Brenda Chapman Hayes of St. Simons Island, Georgia, wasn't bent out of shape in the afterlife like she'd pretty much always been while among the living then she knew for certain that old laid-back John Clark Hayes wasn't having a gnashing of teeth time about it either, and so it was okay for her to ride along and sing with Bill Withers and get down with Aretha. She could make a big circle of the island and wolf down her chicken fingers and tarry with her fries and be back home in time for The Tonight Show.

She shut off the ringer on her phone and set herself to her journey. She could do without hearing from anyone for the next hour or two.

***

David figured he would have never had a flat tire if he hadn't been driving down Brockinton Drive on the way to the police station on Demere to get Franklin out of the pokey. Whatever it was that had assaulted his tire—a nail, a slab of discarded metal, dry rot—had rendered it useless in only a matter of a minute or so. David stood on the side of the road and examined the tire, wondering if it could be helped by the can of Fix-A-Flat in his trunk. But the way the rubber seemed to seep into the road as if headed for China made him believe the tire was beyond help and would need to be replaced. He thought there was a spare in the trunk but was pretty certain it was one of those temporary pony tires, where you could go about five miles before the whole shebang collapsed. Anyway, he didn't think there was a jack or a lug wrench back there anyway, and even if there was he was too damn stupid and lazy to try and change the tire himself. He knew better. He could see him not being able to remove the lug nuts because he was a weakling and not a real man. He could also see the car falling off the jack and crushing him to death.

Hell no, Franklin was just going to have to wait until AAA got here. He would call in for some smiling bubba wrench monkey to come and get him fixed up and then he'd go see about Franklin.

He thought of Franklin in jail and knew if he was going to get out tonight it was going have to be his brother to arrange bail. How much was that going to be? What was the going rate on springing DUIs out of jail these days? Whatever it was, damn it, he really didn't have it to donate. It wasn't that he wanted to come on like a cheapskate or anything; it was just right this minute he was in the middle of what was commonly known as a losing streak. It seemed like every time he turned around there was somebody with their hand out or some unforeseen bill in the mailbox or his kid or his wife-to-be needing this or that. First, he'd had to spring for a new AC unit for the house. Then the roof started leaking and had to be replaced. Car insurance, now a flat tire on the way to help his worthless brother. No telling how much a new tire was going to cost. It wasn't like he was made of money. It was enough to make you shake your fist at the sky. It was so overwhelming that when his father died the first thought he'd had was to wonder if John Clark was going to leave him any money. It was a terrible way for a guy to be, but there it was. The world was turning him into one sorry son of a bitch.

***

Had he known what was in store for him this wretched night after his father's celebratory trip to the other side, Franklin Hayes would never have stopped in at Davey's for chicken fingers and boilermakers. Instead of looking at the waitresses in their shorts and checking out the town girls who'd come in after work to sit on the patio and look at the sunset, he would have gone back to his dinky apartment and hidden under the bed, something wise and ingenious like that.

It was bad enough being juiced enough not to be able to drive or even fake it, but the worst of it was he wasn't as bad as he'd been in the past and he'd always managed to make it home safe and sound those times, and this night he was a tad below his usual peak and it seemed like a sour deal that he had to suffer the consequences for his acts when they hadn't truly been near the zenith of his real capabilities. After the ordeal began and it was clear to him that this time he was indeed busted, it was depressing at first considering that he was going to sober up long before the shit stopped coming down on his head. He was going to have to suffer through some time being arrested and booked and jailed without being totally out of his tree to buffer the moments to come.

After he'd succeeded in exhibiting his inability to not only walk a straight line but to not even envision in his mind's eye where one might be, he then was encouraged to breathe into a breathalyzer to see where his numbers might rate on the old stinko chart. As he thought, they were well over the limit and were hanging out up there in the double figures area, which told him he was definitely cooked despite the fact he knew he'd been worse off than this and never had to go through this ignominy on those times, which he wanted to offer in protest so that maybe a warning might be issued and all could be forgiven this night save a verbal riposting and a slap on the wrist, but something told him it was probably best to remain silent and see if his good manners helped him through this situation in the slightest way.

It didn't take long to figure out nothing was going to help.

He wasn't really crazy about being informed he was being placed under arrest and having his rights recited to him while his hands got handcuffed behind his back. He didn't bother to offer any thanks when he was led to the car and the friendly patrolman sheltered his head as he was lowered into the back seat. From what he could calculate it wasn't that far a trip down to the St. Simons police station if that was in fact where they were going, but he didn't know whether there were cells at that particular location and thought it just might be he was to be transported to someplace else in Gwinnet County, and that was when he had the horrible inkling that he might wind up someplace where no one could find him to come and get him out of this, that he would be like Steve McQueen on Devil's Island and get his ass locked away for a long period of time and have to eat cockroaches and centipedes just to survive.

God was at least merciful at this time and allowed him to pass out, a state that saved him from staring out from the back seat at the patrolman's neck who was driving and the front windshield that traveled past stores and hotels and restaurants and bars where people who were free were allowed to go, and so he was unconscious for that time and thus didn't have to see and imagine how the world was and would be going on without him for an indeterminate time to be named later.

He had to relinquish his wallet and his keys and change his clothes into an orange uniform that made him feel like a pumpkin walking down the hallway to the cellblock or whatever it was they called it. He had made a phone call to David before being locked up, and the only hope he had was that his brother would come and get him away from this place in hell in what most folks would call a jiffy, and when he walked through a doorway and heard the metal door close behind him followed by the click of a lock he trudged over to what looked like a slab but was probably a bed and sat down. He looked at the lone commode in the corner and thought how he needed to take a piss, but for a while he didn't move but just sat on the bed and felt pitiful and violated, too upset to go empty his bladder because he knew that when he did he would have nothing left in his mind to keep him from considering how absolutely fucked up he truly was right now.

Finally, the call of nature became too great and he had to drain the old radiator, and when he'd finished, prolonging it as long as he could, he sat back down and rolled himself up into a pre-natal ball and faced the wall and waited. First, he tried to figure out exactly what time it was—they'd taken his watch, of course—and since there was nothing he could see from his site as to the moon or stars or the light of dawn's approach he gave that up and started counting the seconds and seeing how many minutes he could stay here without getting up and pounding on the door and begging to be released. Don't flip out, he told himself. Try and be patient. David will be here eventually and this will be over. Nothing lasts forever, no matter how bad it is or how much God hates your guts.

Because in the long run that had to be it. Nobody in the history of the world ever had to go through a frigging DUI and rot in a jail cell on the night of their father's funeral. Providence had to completely despise a guy to go and treat him like that. Might as well they goddamn kill him and go ahead and send him to Hell and get it over with.

He didn't know how long it was he passed out. He only knew that when he came to he was still in a dark place, with only the slightest shard of illumination making it through the bars of the door. At first he didn't know where he was exactly, but then it quickly came back to him, and a wave of sadness came over him and threatened to choke him into giving up the ghost. He was still in a cell. His brother had not come to get him out. He might as well be alone in the world from now on.

That was when the guy who'd shown him in came to the door and stuck a key in the lock. It was a blessed sound, something that connected him to the world again, a lifeline tossed his way to help him escape Hades or wherever it was this dungeon was located.

"Somebody's here to get you," the deputy said. "You're getting bailed out."

Franklin wanted to shout Hallelujah or throw a few choice words this guy's way, but decided since he was this near to emancipation it would be wise to keep his trap shut for now.

"Are you okay?" the deputy asked. "Can you get up and walk?"

"I'm okay," Franklin mumbled. It had been a while since he'd used his voice to speak, so his words came out in a raspy whisper. He guessed once he took a deep breath of air outside the jail his verbal skills might return intact, but for now he busied himself with rising from the cot and hitching up his jump suit and walking toward the open door and taking additional steps toward freedom.

"Follow me," his jailor said.

They walked down a narrow hallway and through another door to a well-lighted lobby. Franklin squinted his eyes at this sudden flash of illumination, like a mole peering out from beneath the ground at the world that has been going on while he has been buried elsewhere. There was an office with plexiglass stretched out at the front of the room with six folding chairs in the space outside it. In one of the chairs sat David, who got up when the deputy and Franklin came in. David had a strange look on his face, which might have been a smile but could be a look of incredulity at such a show of stupidity by his little brother, but Franklin, despite his shame and obligation, was damn glad to see his brother for the first time in years.

He had to sign a release to get his billfold and his keys and his clothes back, then had to listen to the terms of his parole and how he couldn't leave the country and go on a cruise or anything on account he was under criminal investigation, then he was handed his possessions and a sheet of paper that said when he had to be back for his court trial and finally allowed to go back through the door and change from his offender's garb back into his regular clothes. Then he was free to go.

He and David walked out to the parking lot to David's car. Franklin was surprised it was still dark, that dawn had not broken yet. Perhaps he hadn't been incarcerated for as long as he'd believed.

"I had a flat tire," David said. "That's why it took so long for me to get here."

"It's okay. Thanks for getting me out."

"You'll have to wait and get your car back tomorrow. It's been towed in already."

"Great," Franklin said. "This is a day to be treasured with gifts that just keep on giving. Truly a day to remember." He thought for a minute and then added, "I don't think it was running anymore anyway."

***

When they got home from the celebration of life service Donna didn't feel the least bit like cooking, and the idea of eating out and sitting across from Jimmy at a restaurant table seemed about as desirable as riding in an elevator with Saddam Houssein, so she suggested pizza and even offered to go get it, deducing this would get her out of the house for a few minutes and give her time to think and decompress from the day's events. It was a lot safer going to get the pizza anyway, since the last few times they'd ordered delivery it had taken hours to get there and on several occasions had not come at all. Companies and people just couldn't be trusted these days. About the only way she could count on getting anything done was to do it herself.

The Domino's she was driving to was not the closest one to her house. This Domino's was about two miles further away than the one nearest her, but she'd made the mistake of going to the closer one once and was not about to repeat the mistake. The nearest one was in a strip mall next door to a dilapidated Dollar General with a parking lot that hadn't been swept or lined in what looked like decades, and the sidewalks were littered with the homeless and empty liquor bottles and apprentice rapists eyeing her as she walked in the door to retrieve her pizza. She promised God if she could make it out alive with her pizza she would never make the mistake of coming there again, and she had kept her promise. It was worth driving a few extra miles to keep from being violated and possibly sliced up into small parts. Something about divine deliverance made the pizza taste better when she got home.

The extra distance not only gave her time to settle her brain, but also provided her a respite from the stress of being around Jimmy for more hours in the day than either of them were willing to spend in each other's company. It gave her a moment to figure out an original escape route to spend her time removed from him, and also, if she dawdled enough, the chances were good that Jimmy might go out on an errand himself and be gone when she came back.

Some marriage, she thought.

She walked inside to pick up the pizza and was told it was still in the oven. So much for the old thirty minute guarantee, she thought, where if you don't get your pizza in a half hour it's free. She supposed that was another one of those maxims from the past that don't exist anymore. Have it your way. Up, up, and away. Take a puff—it's Springtime. Where's the beef? She remembers all that stuff. Does this mean she's getting old? No, she thinks, thirty-seven is not old, not in the world today. Thirty-seven is just getting started.

Unless you're a woman, a voice told her. Then, as far as men were concerned, thirty-seven meant a woman's life was pretty much over. Heck, Marilyn Monroe was dead at thirty-six, so Donna reckoned her chances weren't looking that good.

She took out her phone and checked her texts and phone messages to see if she's missed anything. Nothing there, as she'd already known. It wasn't that she was lacking in friends or anything these days; it was just there wasn't much to talk about right now.

In another ten minutes her pizza was ready and she paid and started out the door. When she pushed against the glass she glanced toward her car to make sure no mugger was crouching somewhere ready to make off with her purse. There was no one there, but up the hill on the sidewalk was a figure she stopped in her tracks to get a better look at. Did she know him? He looked familiar.

She stared at him a moment until there was a break in traffic and he jogged across the street to the other side. There was something about the way he ran, the strides he took to get to the other side, not exactly a sprint but more a gait better suited for the long run, for endurance and consistency in getting to the place you've set your eyes upon, the area that is within your plan. It was like she was watching a cross country event and distinguishing which runner was the one most likely to finish the race first with all his faculties intact.

She knew this man in motion, this man in the midst of his own important contest.

She unlocked her car and kept watching the man move on down the opposite walk, turn right at a street and move west like the sun in its pattern of finding a place to set.

It couldn't be, she told herself. I said my goodbyes to him already. You can't perform such acts of letting go and then have the departed one come back around again like he was making a circle, completing another lap.

She could not stop herself from pulling off from the Domino's and going to the opposite end of the lot so she could make a straight shot across the street and go down the road the figure had taken only moments before. There was nothing there but mailboxes and parked cars and a man pushing one of those old-timey push mowers across the dying grass of his yard. The man was not who she'd seen. The man was a stranger. She drove on.

There was no sign of the walker and sometimes-jogger, no sighting of his aged New Balances or his black fleece jacket or his hair turned slightly gray. She didn't think he could be this far down the street by now, for she had driven a good ways and was certain she would have overtaken him by now. She slowed and looked on both sides of the road, checked the mirrors to see if she'd missed anything. No one there. She wondered if he had gone into some house before she'd gotten there? Was he inside now looking out the window seeing her looking for him? Had he seen her coming and thought it best to take cover? Did he think it was best to disappear and not be around to answer any questions, to let the world continue its spinning without pausing to solve any problems?

He'd disappeared before. Lots of times, she remembered. It was one of those things he was very good at.

***

He wasn't in any hurry. He was only taking care to be prepared. He did not like starting off a new week not being ready. He had always prided himself on his ability to think ahead and stay on top of things. He didn't like blundering into his challenges with his hands down and his eyes closed and no plan in his mind whatsoever. That was how the rest of the world went about doing things, casting their fate to the wind with no idea where they were going to be at the end of the day. That was not him. He had memorized his steps long before it was time to take them. He knew where he was going. He knew the way it was going to be when he arrived. He made sure he lived in a world of no surprises.

He had seen her all right. He'd made sure to check in on her first. Hell, he had known she was ordering pizza before she did. He wasn't altogether gone when he went missing. He always knew what was going on. If he wanted, he could have written a book. Come to think of it, he had. Several of them.

THREE

Since it was over and done between them for a long time now and had never really lasted that long to begin with, Donna did not think of herself as indulging in an act of betrayal when the idea popped up in her head like popcorn in a microwave, slow at first, a pop here and there, then an increase in activity until it was a flurry of crackles and tiny explosions like someone had fired off a Thompson machine gun or thrown a pack of firecrackers down at her feet and she couldn't help but take notice of them as they were discharging around her ankles. Her brain couldn't for that moment in time concentrate on anything else until the agitation had been dealt with. Once the notion formed in her head and she'd weighed all the pros and cons that came with it, she knew it wouldn't be the worst thing in the world for her to go and do, to have an affair with someone halfway interesting. She figured she owed herself that much.

She was thirty-seven and the way she looked at that was that it was getting down to cases now and becoming close to now or never if she was going to experience the kind of wild love affair she'd read about in books or seen on movies growing up and had always hoped that someone would come along and take her for a ride and a whirl where nothing else mattered for a time and she could one day come back to earth once the journey was done and sit in her chair by the window at home and sip her cup of tea and watch the squirrels and the birds play in her garden and know she hadn't missed out on what life had to offer after all. She didn't even care if it was a long experience or a short one, if the trip to the heavenly stars was enjoyable or heart-wrenching, only that it had happened to her personally and there was no denying that it had occurred and now that it had she would be free for the rest of her life to think about what had transpired and how it had been and know that she was a part of those things that make the world go around and somehow become legends and poetry in one's heart and soul and never go away.

Once it was decided in her mind that she would embark upon a great fulfilling romance before she was too old to experience it fully the quest became an easy task. She knew better than to look for someone within her church at City Methodist, because one thing she'd garnered about Christians through the years was that they were a talkative bunch who loved a good scandal as much as any other faction she could name. If she wanted to keep this private and her own little secret she would carry to her grave then it would be best to cast her romantic nets elsewhere, otherwise she'd be the main topic of conversation in every book club gathering or committee meeting for god knows how long. No, better to change her usual course and take new and different paths in her everyday routine and perhaps by going somewhere different and seeing new lands, she would run across some person she could later identify as her lover.

To tell the truth she didn't much care if this lover was male or female. Either way, it would encompass something totally new, and that was what she was looking for.

Of course, she couldn't deny the fact that she would have preferred that John Clark Hayes was this mysterious secret lover she wanted for this present and foggy future to come. It was true that all they had shared together once was a lengthy stolen kiss in a secluded stairway where no one was bound to venture that particular night. The kiss—and she thought of that interval as one prolonged caress of their lips, like once the first tasting began there had been no breaks in the action—had begun almost before she realized it had started; it was like they were talking to each other and joking about something in the past and laughing and smiling and then suddenly something had skipped a beat or turned a page and they were in each other's arms and she was wondering as she hoped he was why it had taken such a long time for this to happen between them? That surely the two of them must have known there was something going on with them that hadn't been brought up in conversation before but was certainly present for a long time leading up to this moment? And why was it if this great thing was there between them and the magnetic pull and attraction was this strong had they never done anything about it? Why had they not recognized this magical force that brought them together this way, that had the both of them wondering where they had been and what they had been thinking about all their lives up until that single enchanted moment in time?

But it had happened only that one time and then John Clark began to distance himself and turn into smoke and vanish whenever she drew near, and later on she realized that even if she saw him at the warehouse each day and said hello he was still as good as gone and might as well be in another country for the good it would do them both. And now he was indeed in another country and gone from her for eternity and she realized that John Clark being dead wasn't much different than John Clark being alive, that he was nothing but a memory these days either way, and now at the age of thirty-seven she knew memories were not going to do it for her anymore, that she needed something new she could touch and feel and see for a time until that became a memory too, and she figured by the time that came she would be ready for a new memory to go with the old ones, and she could be happy running her business and seeing her children have children of their own and watching more squirrels and birds play among her trees and flowers and not feel the least bit bad about any of it.

Once a month she took a couple of days to drive to each location of the clients of Tasty Snacks and check out the appearance of the vending machines and see if they looked to be well-stocked and in good working order. It had never happened too much, but sometimes she found that her route salesmen were not keeping their products rotated or filled to capacity, and sometimes she'd had to admonish her employees or give them fair warning and a few times even let one or two of them go. This was not her job so much as Jimmy's, who enjoyed being a tyrant and something of a bully and pushing people around to the point of them either cracking and being frightened for their job or else prompted to quit on the spot, usually an occurrence that was planned beforehand by Jimmy because he already had a replacement that he could start immediately and get by with paying that new employee less than he had the departed one. Somehow or another this brand of owner tyranny over lowly employees had become enjoyable to Jimmy more and more over the years, and so he was the one who specialized in it. He liked for the most part that Linda be the good guy and he be the bad guy, the holy terror who needed to be bowed to and agreed with by all means necessary. Of course, she remembered, none of those tactics had ever worked on John Clark Hayes, which she knew irritated Jimmy to no end.

She had made it to only two of her intended visits before she saw a man standing at the top of the concrete incline that led to the second floor of the building. The structure itself housed some of the most profitable vending machines under her supervision. There were five radio stations under the banner of a conglomerate called Coastal Communications, which owned and operated a myriad of stations through Georgia and the Carolinas. On the first floor was a reception desk and two AM stations, one talk, one religious in programming, and on the second floor where she was ascending this moment were three FM stations, a New Country format and a Contemporary Pop and a Classic Rock, of which she recognized the man standing by the rail with his leg up and a cigarette in his hand as the host of the Classic Rock's morning show. She had seen him before. He was tall and lanky and had not a trace of middle-aged fat on his body, despite his graying hair that stayed put by the bright red do-rag that kept it in place. He'd been around town a good while now; Linda remembered listening to him while she was in college at Troy, getting her Education degree. He had been around a long time, but he was not that much older than her. She guessed he had started out in radio as a young man and had never left to do anything else.

She had never been this close to him before. He was a nice-looking guy, no matter how many years he'd been around.

"Hi," she said, making sure she caught his eye. Before he had been staring out at the parking lot and beyond at the vestiges of downtown and the beach traffic in the distance.

"Hey," he told her, taking her in by turning his head and putting out his cigarette in the round urn by the door. He moved over to hold the door for her, a Chesshire-like smile on his face, like he was in the midst of enjoying something only he knew about. "Are you looking for somebody or just taking a private tour?"

"I'm one of the owners of the company that services your snack machines and drink machines and replenishes your coffee supplies," she smiled. "I'm taking a look around to make sure we're taking good care of you with our stock and selections, trying to make sure we're keeping everything full and all the machines are working properly."

"Well, in that case I've got a small complaint to make."

"That's what I'm here for."

"Maybe it's not that big of a deal to anybody else, but I sure wish you guys could keep more chocolate doughnuts in the machines. By the time your guy runs on Mondays we've been out of them up here since Wednesday, then I have to go down the hall and raid the other machine and then go downstairs and hit that one up. By Monday morning when I come in to do the show all three machines are out of doughnuts and I have to settle for a candy bar to go with my coffee, which just doesn't cut it for me. I've asked the route guy to maybe put a couple of extra rows in but he says he's already leaving everything he's got from the warehouse. Maybe you could order more for inventory and do away with some of the other things? Like, I'm not too crazy about Almond Joys. I'll bet the ones that are in the machine have been sitting there since last Christmas or so. I mean, I've never seen anybody buy one or go to pieces if they couldn't get their hands on one on a regular basis."

"I'll see what I can do to get you a better supply of chocolate doughnuts."

"Now they've got to be chocolate, please. I'm not that crazy about those powdered white doughnuts, on account they're sort of dry to begin with and all that white powder tends to bunch up on my lips and chin and nose, and everybody thinks I'm sitting back in the studio doing lines of coke all morning and weirding out to all the tunes only the old dinosaurs want to listen to."

"Chocolate it is, then. I'll make your request number one on today's agenda."

She stopped in the hallway and turned around so he could get a good look at her. It had been a while, but she was pretty certain she still remembered how to send a message. She made sure she brushed against him as she passed by.

"I guess I could treat you to a free cup of coffee to make amends," she smiled. "I suppose you've got an office of some kind where we could sit down and take a little break. I've been one of your faithful listeners for a long time now. I might as well tell you that I probably would have never made it through four years at Troy University without hearing you on the radio in my room or in the car when I was coming home on weekends. You took my mind off the endless drudgery of getting my Education degree. I might have quit altogether if it wasn't for you playing some song I really needed to hear at the appropriate time."

He was getting it now. His hip brushed against hers and there was a twinkle in his eyes that hadn't been there before when she'd first come up the ramp. Then he had been contemplating the world he was viewing from his meditation point and not finding anything out there too inviting or exciting whatsoever, but now his curiosity was activated and he was prepared to put aside whatever it was that had been so blasé and boring and explore this new item that had been sent his way. This was not a bad-looking woman at all, he thought. Not in the least. He wondered why he had never noticed her before. But maybe this was the first time he'd laid eyes on her and she on him, and it was hard to ignore how such a meeting was certainly full of budding appreciation and interest. He was getting to be an old dude these days, and something like this was like a blast from the past. He hadn't noticed the scarcity of such moments as this for a time now. Things like this used to happen all the time back in his younger days, and just as quickly they had stopped and he had believed that portion of his life was over with, that that was it and all that, yet now here it was again.

Maybe here it was. He certainly hoped so.

Donna made sure to walk beside the man, whose name she already knew from her years of listening. She had not been fibbing about that. She and this man had a history, whether each of them knew it before today or not. They had a history and she was certain there was also going to be a future, because she had a way of knowing about such things without being told.

His name was Marty McCool. He was so cool he called himself the Iceman.

The Iceman had been one cool dude around Saint Simons Island for years.

***

It hardly took two weeks before the idea began festering in Brenda Hayes' mind how it might be a good idea, once all the estate issues and will dispersions had been completed, to schedule a trip of some kind before going back to work at the library regularly and re-entering the real world again. She had never really had the time or the finances available to her to embark on such a thing, but now with the life insurance payoff and the contents of John Clark's personal checking and savings account and what was due to him from Social Security and his pension from his years of teaching and retail clerking, there was a tidy sum staring her in the face just begging to be splurged on something, and a cruise on the Mediterranean or a flight to Paris began to take up space in her mind and whisper tempting words into her ear. At first she thought she could never think of doing such daring things, but as the days passed it began to seep into her mind that yes, she certainly could. She was free now. She could do anything she wanted.

Although the idea did pass through her head, she still wasn't fool enough to think she could take off on a trip all by herself. She knew better than that. She didn't really like going places alone, much less out of the country. The idea of leaving Georgia and even going to another state was overwhelming to her imagination. She could see hotel employees taking advantage of her, cab drivers and Uber drivers bilking her out of money, strangers on the street seeing her pass by and knowing she would be an easy target as far as the theft of her credit cards or her purse or anything she might be carrying with her that wasn't attached to her torso like her arms and legs. She was no more going to go on such an endeavor as traveling to distant lands and leaving her safe and secure life behind her unaccompanied and on her lonesome than to try and flap her arms and fly to the moon. She may not be the most experienced person in the world or one who always makes the right decisions but she at least had sense enough to know that she was going to need someone to be with her when times got somewhat disconcerting or outright strange and scary. She certainly was not going to go through whatever trauma might be out there alone.

She wondered if she could convince either Jessica or Charlotte to go along with her on this proposed trip. Jessica was divorced but had two kids at home she probably couldn't leave behind for any extended period of time, while Charlotte's boys were both grown and out of the house but there was still the matter of her husband Chris she probably couldn't trust to not burn the house down while she was gone. She could put the question to them, but who knows if she could get a nibble from either. She certainly wasn't going to ask her sister Louise or Linda to go with her. All she would hear from Louise is a lot of political garbage and Evangelical Christian talk, while Linda would do nothing but turn her nose up at anything her mother might suggest to do. No, in that case it would be better to be by herself and have to fend off evil spirits the entire time. At least they wouldn't keep telling her how in the wrong she was on practically everything she got ready to do.

What she could do is get in touch with a travel agent and get a few ideas that way. She phoned AAA and made an appointment for the next day, and in the meantime sat down at her computer and started looking up exotic locales. There was Hawaii and the beaches, there was Bermuda and the Dominican Republic and Puerto Rico, and there was the expanse of islands scattered all over, St. Croix and the Virgin Islands and Nassau and Barbados. She could fly to Chicago and get on a train and travel to California or take any of the excursion bus trips in any of the tourist towns she chose to visit. There was no limit to the places she could go. All she had to do was screw up enough courage to drop everything in her well-ordered life and simply go. It seemed to her that lots of people other than her did this sort of thing all the time.

And she was right.

Her appointment with her new travel agent had her almost dizzy by the time she left, for there were so many options on the table she hardly was able to consider one without another venue popping into the picture. She saw beaches and sidewalk cafes and blue oceans in her mind, and it had been almost more than she could do not to agree to everything right off the bat and simply resign herself to being on vacation the rest of her life. Even with all her confusion she still was convinced that she had to go somewhere, and now it was only a matter of going by herself or talking somebody into going with her.

Her agent had scheduled her to attend an exploratory meeting the next evening on the possibility of traveling to Hawaii either with a group or as a lone traveler, so she waited all the next day and looked up all the places on the Islands she might visit and tried to make a choice about what she would truly like to see and experience and if she might be happy traveling alone or with a group. By this time she had given up asking Charlotte or Jessica or anyone in her family, because somewhere in the back of her mind she didn't want anyone sharing this moment of her life with her, telling her where to go or what to do next, or even worse, to be present when she made an absolute fool of herself at some function during the trip, as Brenda was certain she would. She didn't miss John Clark's presence at anything much in her regular, ordered life, but he had always come in handy when the time came when too much weirdness and mystery was overcoming her and forcing her into a corner, because John Clark had a way of taking things on by himself and attempting to make things right whether he succeeded or not. He'd try, and maybe he would go down swinging or sometimes make things even worse, but she had to at least give him credit for the fact that he would always step up and face what was coming and handle it the best way he knew how. He was wrong as much as he was right, but he could never be accused of cowardice.

There were maybe twenty-five people who arrived for the presentation, most of them older married couples, but Brenda noticed that she was not the only single person who was interested in going to Hawaii. There were three women who were all together and a couple of men by themselves, one who was younger and who Brenda would bet the ranch was gay, and one who was older than her who seemed to be enjoying the cheesecake and cookies a great deal more than the others, since she saw him edge up to the table and fill his paper dish at least twice. Maybe he was homeless and needed a free meal, but he was dressed too nice for that. He had on a sport coat and a shirt and tie and looked like maybe he had just come from work. Perhaps there had been no time to have dinner before the meeting. Maybe he was starving and attempting to fill up on the free snacks at his disposal. It could be he hadn't eaten all day, and that was why he was being such a pig right now. But one thing was certain—he was certainly putting it away.

She picked up a brochure and began nosing through it. A short introductory film began playing at the front of the room. There were luaus and sandy beaches and volcanos and sunsets galore. Muscled native men performed dances and waved torches while hula girls shook their hips and jiggled leas on their necks and wore flowers in their glistening black hair. Coconuts were halved and palm trees swayed, and in the background she heard Don Ho and ukeleles and someone who wasn't Judy Garland singing "Over the Rainbow." It was pretty impressive, but she wondered if she'd get tired of such a wonderland and paradise setting if she spent three weeks with a group. Suppose she signed up and boarded the plane and by the time they landed in Honolulu or Maui everyone on the tour hated her guts? What would she do then? She'd be trapped, so she thought it might be best to go by herself, but there were plenty of scary connotations to that decision too. What if she disappeared and no one was around to look for her or report her missing? She imagined herself lying on a beach with the tropical sunrise rising from the expanse of the Pacific while she was dead there on the sand with a slit throat and a missing purse. John Clark used to get disgusted when he'd pass through the house and find her watching True Crime television. He knew she was engaging her suspicions and imagining harm coming to herself, and generally would ask her why she didn't watch something without bloodshed and murder for a change. He could never understand why she thought it necessary to always be prepared and be well-schooled in case a killer might venture her way.

She had a brief flash of a thought about calling him now and seeing if maybe he might want to go with her, that it might be fun after all this time like it once was, that maybe a trip to enchanted lands might help out their relationship after so long a time when all had been wrong, but then she remembered where John Clark was, back at the house in a wooden box waiting to be scattered somewhere.

Somewhere over the rainbow, she thought. That's where John Clark is now. Him and all the birds. Too late for me to go there with him, especially by myself. I'd be frightened to try and go there alone.

The two presenters came out and began to talk. The man was dressed in a multi-colored Hawaiian shirt, while the lady wore one of those wrap-around skirts like she was the mistress of some great plantation with a red flower in her hair. Brenda couldn't decide if it was a rose or a hibiscus.

She listened to them talk for a few moments, then found herself tuning them out. It wasn't that what they had to say wasn't interesting and well-thought out, it was just that all at once she knew none of their words were intended for her. Like a great light was being shown on the subject, Brenda could all at once see that the idea of herself spending several weeks with people like these two or the couples gathered in the room was not going to happen. She didn't want to be dropped off at fancy restaurants or have lean and textured Polynesian men and women dance around her or serve her food. She didn't want to hear their music or see whales jump out of the ocean for her sightseeing benefit or look into volcanos or visit Pearl Harbor or anything. Not with these people. Not with a bunch of married people. Not with the lone man in the sport coat who rose now in the middle of scenes taken from a helicopter of mighty cliffs and divers flinging themselves from majestic heights into the sea far below and walked over to the refreshment table for more cookies and cheesecake and fruit on toothpicks. This was not the adventure she had in mind. She was not ready to be surrounded by strangers. She had no idea what she wanted to be surrounded by, but it was not by people speaking words she didn't want to hear, conversations that were never intended her way. She didn't know what she wanted, but this wasn't it.

No, she wasn't interested in what this anonymous group of folks had to say, the same way she was certain they were not interested in her. She didn't want to be the sort of person who reaches a point in their lives where what the world has to offer them is of no importance, but it was beginning to feel that way. She knew deep in her soul that no one wanted to hear what she thought, that no one cared to know her opinion of things. It was a sad state of affairs truly, but it had not always been that way. At least when John Clark was around she was sure she was heard. It was probably true he didn't agree with what she was saying or what she believed, but you could bet your life he was listening. He may have had no comment, but he heard every word she said.

It wasn't that she was in a state of mourning, for anything of that degree had been dealt with long ago, but she could honestly say she was missing old John Clark lately. She'd learned to be without him and not have him around so much, but it was hard to think she couldn't call him on the phone and rant about a few things if the situation warranted. She couldn't go out of her way trying to get a rise out of him. He wasn't around anymore to come through in a pinch, like he always seemed to do just when she'd written him off for good.

From the corner of her eye she made out the figure of someone passing by the front window of the private room beneath the streetlights from the lot. All at once a familiar feeling strolled through her brain and she felt better about where she was and what she was doing. It was like she was at peace with her senses about going on a trip or remaining behind and getting her life in some sort of order, and it was like she was not here in some conference room watching a strange world she had no intention of setting foot on but was instead at home in her breakfast room with her soft rock radio station playing and a cup of coffee in her hands and a romance novel open on the table before her. It was a nice, familiar feeling, a sudden sense of peace.

When she looked back out the window, the figure was gone.

Four

It hadn't been the best week of his life, certainly not something he was going to look back on fondly in the years to come and think what a golden time it had been in those early days of adulthood when he finished up the requirements for his degree and put the finishing touches on his college career. It was only another semester or so and it would all be over with, and he certainly didn't need all this hassle he was having to go through simply because some South Carolina patrolman picked him out as someone to pull over and start taking all the necessary steps to ruin his life. Hadn't it been enough that his Camaro was wrecked from pulling over and wiping out a guardrail and his insurance policy was going to sky-rocket because they might have to tender out a little dough? Wasn't it more than beyond the patrolman's dutiful job requirements to haul him off to jail for the night and have him sit in a cell like he was a Mafia member or something? Especially when he wasn't that intoxicated to begin with. Hell, any fool could have deciphered that. All they had to do was observe him for a couple of minutes, then see he wasn't falling down or slurring his words or trying to pick a fight with anyone he came across. He was okay; he hadn't hurt anybody. He'd even offered to pay for fixing the guardrail. The thought was in his mind that if he'd known what kind of bullshit this cop was going to put him through the rest of the night he would have gone on and cold-cocked the son of a bitch right then. The thing about it was, even if he'd done such a thing, he probably wouldn't have been more shit out of luck than he was right now.

So now his car was screwed up and he was facing a DUI and he was going to have to pay through the nose for insurance and fines and have his license suspended even though he didn't have a car, and he was going to have to go to driving school and possibly spend a couple of days in jail. This is much more than he wants to deal with, and he's driving himself crazy trying to think of ways to get out of a few of these consequences and get everything behind him so he can get back to his life again. Luckily, his dad had paid for his last year at Coastal Georgia and he wasn't going to have to forfeit his sheepskin because of his current legal troubles, but he wondered if the news got to the student affairs office that he, Franklin Hayes, was a budding felon and a menace to society that they might decide they didn't want their name associated with such a lowlife and take it upon themselves to sever all ties with him just so their reputation as a molder of young minds wouldn't be tarnished if the truth was to come out about the form of rubbish they were allowing to obtain a degree from their academic institution?

He wondered if maybe there was a way to get some more money out of his father's estate, just so he might have enough to fix the Camaro and pay off the courts and keep himself out of jail and legal for a while, maybe long enough to graduate and get the hell off this godforsaken island and out of this frigging state. All he wanted was a couple more months of peace and then he would take off for Atlanta or Chicago or Nashville or somewhere he could find a decent job using his B.A., where there was a decent nightlife and enough women around not to get bored. He knew places such as this existed, but they certainly weren't here on St. Simon's Island, where it was nothing but retired islanders living on their pensions and tourists who didn't want the bustle or cost of Charleston or Savannah and came for peace and quiet instead. He'd had enough peace and quiet to last him for at least the next sixty years, and he was convinced by now that the sexual awakening of the next decade was not going to occur here, so if he was waiting around for anything noteworthy to happen he was wasting his time and so might as well be on his way, sooner rather than later. Maybe he could give David a call and run some of his ideas by him. The thing about David was he wasn't prone to be fucked up like his little brother tended to become on the most part, but David could probably use some surplus money too. David might be interested in squeezing the grapes of his dad's leftovers and see if any wine might come out. But he knew it was going to take a joint effort, whether it be him and David or even by getting Linda to join in, because he knew his mother wasn't going to fall in line with any of their plans and schemes without a lot of questions being asked.

His call to David went straight to voice mail, so he supposed David was still working, even though it was after five and he ought to be home by now. Franklin wondered if he should call down at the computer store and talk to David there, but he decided he could get a lot more accomplished in person. Maybe if he just drove down and caught David before he went home he could lay out his plan a little clearer without David's someday wife or the world getting in the way. Whatever the case, he wanted to make certain he discussed his plan with his brother when they were by themselves. He for damn sure didn't want his sister or mother having any advance notice on what the two of them might be up to.

David was walking across the parking lot to his car when Franklin pulled up driving his dad's old Civic. Before Franklin could stop himself he found himself racing the engine and speeding toward his brother as if he was going to run him down. This was something he'd been doing for years, since he first learned to drive, and he'd first done it to David with his mother's immense Buick, bearing down on him in the college's parking lot when David was a senior at Coastal Pines Tech and thought he was hot shit and Franklin was a lowly freshman in high school with a learner's permit. At the time Franklin sensed he'd not only pissed his brother off but scared the shit out of him too, and so it had become something of a time-honored tradition over the years to see if he could cause his brother to wet his pants by aiming his vehicle at him and seeing how close he could come without totally running him down. He guessed he ought not to be so reckless since he was driving his father's Civic, but it was hard to break tradition just like that when his brother was right there and such a handsome target, so he went ahead with his impulse and came right up on David before screeching to a stop, noticing with satisfaction the widening of his brother's eyes and the perceived knowledge that David was wondering at the same time if this time Franklin would stop, or if, actually, this moment was going to be his last.

"One of these days your brakes are going to fail and you're going to run over somebody, and then you'll be in a shitload of trouble," David said. "Then it won't be so goddamned funny to you."

"I don't do this to anybody but you," Franklin tells him. "I've got you trained to know what's coming, so I know if push comes to shove you'll be prepared to jump out of the way. If nothing else, you're an agile son of a bitch. I'll bet if you had to you could jump right over an oncoming car just to stay alive."

"I'd think with your current legal problems you'd be halfway careful when you got back behind the wheel of another automobile, especially when you've borrowed it from your own dead father. But I guess you're just one of those recalcitrants who never learn from their mistakes and just keep doing them over and over again."

Franklin backed into a spot and got out of the car.

"I've got something I want to talk about with you," he said.

"I'm not lending you any damn money," David said, cutting him off at the pass. "I haven't got money enough for myself, much less trying to support your ass."

"That's what I want to talk about, but it's not about you shelling out anything for me. I'm talking about the both of us becoming a little more well-off because of recent circumstances."

David eyed his little brother over suspiciously, taking caution lest Franklin tried drawing him into one of his diabolical traps again, the exact same way Franklin had been attempting to pull him into a hole time and time again since God created the universe.

"Hear me out before you say anything." Franklin could tell already his big brother was sounding the Air Raid alarm in his head, so it was best to get his message through before David disappeared into the recesses of his bomb shelter mind and Franklin would be unable to contact him again until David deemed it safe to come back out. That was the way his dumbass brother was. Always distrustful. Always thinking somebody was out to get him. Maybe that's why Franklin liked messing with him so much. It was because old David was already half-around the bend naturally, so it was easy to push him over the edge. Entertaining too.

"I've been thinking about some things for a couple of days now. For instance, here I am driving Dad's Honda Civic, and how old is this damn thing? Fifteen years? Getting close to twenty? And still, here it is looking good and ready to hit the road and get driven to Bumfuck if that's where you want to go, and with the way things are right now we could get a damn good price on this car if we wanted to sell it. So why shouldn't we sell it? Who needs it anymore? Dad's not going to drive it, so it's just going to sit in the driveway and rot if we let it."

"You forget you need it," David pointed out, "since you destroyed your own car by trying to mate it with a guardrail."

"Insurance will get me a new one. Probably. But it's for damn sure I'll be driving something from this century. This damn car of Dad's is just another example of what a hoarder he was. Everything he owned was old and out of date. It was like he got what he wanted when he turned twenty-one and then didn't bother getting anything new since. He lived in a world of antiques."

"Some of his stuff is probably worth a lot of money, Franklin. You have to hand it to him for hanging on to it so long and picking up things cheap over the years."

"That's exactly the point I'm getting to. How much dough do you think we can get from some of his stuff if we separate it from the estate sale or allow Mother to throw a couple of yard sales and let it go for nothing just to get it out of her way? I say we go over to the house and take a little inventory and make a list of some things we can squirrel away and sell it before Mother or Linda get their hands on it. Hell, that old Wurlitzer jukebox of his alone is probably worth ten grand if we found the right sucker to buy it."

David looked thoughtfully at his little brother for a moment, astounded by the fact that for once Franklin might have a good idea about something. He perused his father's eclectic possessions over in his head, the pristine late model Honda, the jukebox that was twice as old as him, the music collection, the books signed by a bunch of famous authors he would always go and see, the plethora of Famous Monsters of Hollywood and Mad Magazine issues from way back—what such a collection of weirdo belongings might bring in was anyone's guess. The trick would be finding the right buyers, but Franklin was right. Those buyers were out there, and all it took was finding the rock they were under and bringing them into contact with his Dad's collection, and it could be Katy bar the door on what someone might be willing to pay. He thought of all that unsubstantiated money finding its way into his bank account and suddenly it seemed like there were no longer dark clouds in the sky and God was indeed alive.

"I'll have to hand it to you," he told Franklin. "You just might be on to something here."

"I'm not such a dumbass all the time," Franklin said. "Now and then I come up with a good idea."

"Who would have thought?' said David.

***

It didn't matter what time he made it to the Great South Inn on Tuesdays, since the machines were all outdoors and he could drive up and service them any time he wanted. For a long while he'd hit them in the early mornings as he was starting out, since he didn't have to waste time waiting for anybody to arrive so he could get in, but once David got his first parttime job washing cars at the car rental office across the street he adjusted his route so he could stop in and say hello every now and then just to keep up, to make an appearance voluntarily, so to speak, so his eldest son wouldn't be so adamant in his belief that his father was way out there on a regular basis and didn't have much of a desire to spend any time with him or anyone in the immediate family that lived under the same roof with him while they were growing up. Not that the kid would be wrong about it, for it was definitely true that he, John Clark, was much more comfortable away from the family home, in his truck delivering snacks or sitting by himself at some athletic contest or a movie house or even holed up in his study/library/hideout at the backend of the house with his books and records and paraphernalia of all sorts of far-out trinkets. He had to force himself on a regular basis to be a father, which was hard enough, but he also deemed himself to be a provider too. He wondered how other people did it, how they managed to go through life being normal, but in his fifty-plus years he had never discovered the answer. It was everything he could do just to fake it.

When he saw Franklin pull up in the Civic he immediately knew something was up. David and Franklin spent little time together these days, and had never really had much of a close bond going on between them growing up. It wasn't like they fought and argued like regular siblings, but it was more like they took their first look at each other when Franklin was born and David was seven and decided it would be a waste of time trying to be related in anything other than blood and surname. For as long as he could remember the two of them would go the opposite way when they saw each other, so to see them now meeting in the parking lot of David's business meant there was something going on that was probably not proclaimed as above board in anybody's etiquette book. The Corleone brothers would probably be up to a more innocent plan than these two would, whether they were his own sons or not.

He hated wasting time, because there were only so many hours in each day and it was important to get through, to keep up, so he watched his sons out of the corner of his eye as they talked and nodded their heads and reached some sort of unholy agreement. He cringed at the way his Honda jerked when Franklin jammed it into gear and drove off, like he was in a hurry to get somewhere or something, and he watched David unlock his car and look around before getting in, like he was afraid someone was watching, like he had something he needed to hide.

There was a note on the drink machine that said the bill acceptor wasn't working. He took it out and removed the dollar bill that had got crumbled inside and straightened it out. When he tested it again, it worked just fine.

FIVE

The only thing to do was to go ahead and get it over with. It wasn't going to help things one bit to sit around and contemplate it or dread it or imagine all sorts of dire things that might happen because of it, because it's that kind of stuff that will drive you nuts in the end, and one of the few things that Franklin Hayes had learned in his twenty-two years was that it was generally better to go ahead and tackle something head-on and deal with it and then put it behind you rather than letting something fester and evolve and grow into a monster you can never kill that will eventually eat you alive in the end.

It was with this fact sadly entrenched in his head that Franklin went ahead and accepted the date for his 48-hour DUI sentence to be served, entirely so that he wouldn't be driven crazy by having it hang over him until it finally dropped like a guillotine and sliced his head from his body and made it so that never the twain should meet again. At least with the date in his mind he could look at it as a signpost of sorts and tell himself that once he reached that fork in the road and took it to its destination he could begin the process of counting it down and bidding it goodbye and hopefully getting back into some semblance of his normal life once more.

The October Friday afternoon arrived when he was supposed to be downtown at the sheriff's department to check in, so he drove his father's Honda into town and parked in the paid lot across the street, noting that this period of incarceration was going to cost him another fifty dollars just so he could get down here and leave his father's car somewhere where it might be safe. This type of added expense didn't thrill him much. He'd already had to pay a fine for court and a fee for online driving school and had been forced to take out an expensive insurance policy for the next year just so he could drive a vehicle to school and work, a provision that included him not being allowed to drive anywhere for pleasure. No bars or restaurants or movie houses or ball games for the next year. No nights bar-hopping with wild women. That was his fate. He didn't think it was fair whatsoever just for knocking over a frigging guardrail, but it wasn't like he could argue about it. It was a damn racket and they had him dead to rights.

At least it wasn't so bad as he'd previously thought. He didn't have to wear a prison uniform with stripes and a big "P" on his back so the guards would have a good target if he made a break for it. He was allowed to wear his own clothes for the weekend, jeans and a couple of tees and his own Nikes. All he had to do on Saturday and Sunday morning was don an orange vest around him like a lifejacket and wear that around while traipsing around the interstate picking up trash with his own personal grabber and a supply of trash bags. The orange vest, it had been explained to his group, was to keep them safe from speeders and those drivers texting and not paying attention, maybe even those who had been drinking or taking drugs much like they had themselves to put them into this position, so they should be glad the city was protecting them in a way they had never tried to protect others from themselves. The vests then, Franklin surmised, were like he and his group's own personal scarlet letters, and for the weekend until three o'clock Sunday afternoon they would bear them around their torsos announcing to the viewing public that this was their shame and their punishment for acting in a way that was uncivil and unsocial and pretty much a no-no any way you looked at it.

It took an hour Friday afternoon for the roll to get called and for the new group of fifty offenders to get processed and loaded onto the bus, which was an old school vehicle that was orange all over and had big blank spaces along the sides where the lettering had been removed, although the imprint was still visible enough to where Franklin could tell this bus had once been a part of Glenn County Schools and was previously inhabited by elementary and middle school kids getting transported to their respective schools, where they would no doubt learn their reading and writing and arithmetic enough to in the future go out and haul trash or paint yellow lines on highways or prepare burgers for the hungry public. It was all Franklin could do to resist sliding his finger under his seat on the bus just to see if there was some mummified wad of gum still stored there.

The bus rolled along with the beginnings of the Friday rush hour, which was not really so much of a rush hour like most other cities in Georgia, not like Atlanta or Macon or Athens or even Savannah with its bordering Tybee Island where nobody much worked at legitimate businesses or even desired to, but which looked large compared to St. Simons which if you weren't looking for it might slip by without you ever knowing it was there. Franklin sat by himself in the middle by a window and watched a few familiar scenes go by as he was on his way to his incarceration, a sight which saddened him some and made him wonder if Christ Himself might have shared a similar outlook when he was on the road to Gethsemane, wondering if this was the last time he might view the workshop where he learned to be a carpenter or the stable where the mule he rode Palm Sunday reposed in a stall or where the tomb where Lazarus had originally been planted before it was determined he wasn't to stay dead and had to vacate was still sitting there unoc-cupied, and Franklin tried to tell himself that it wasn't as bad as he wanted to make it and how it wasn't likely he was going to wear a crown of thorns or get reviled and spit on and crucified to top it all off, so at least it wasn't going to be as bad as that. It was forty-eight hours was all it was, and here he was on this retired school bus going down the road and it had already been an hour since this whole ordeal had begun, and so if he would just relax and keep repeating all things must pass in his head like George Harrison was in his ear reassuring him, it would be over before he knew it and everything would be just fine.

The bus pulled up to a building that used to be a reform school but which had been closed once the left wingers told the right wingers how juvenile lawbreakers didn't really know better than to break the law and ought to be housed in nicer quarters than this one with its leaking roof and its rotted woodwork and its cracked tile in the hallways where some delinquent not paying attention because he was planning his next curb market robbery might fall into a chasm and sprain a leg and inflict permanent damage upon himself so badly he might not be able to sprint from the scene of a crime or have ample vision enough to aim a gun before saying gimme all you got in that cash register. There was like a wire fence with holes in them on either side of a long hallway, and rooms with bunkbeds were available for four citizens at a time, six on each side for a total of twelve to house forty-eight, and since there were fifty of them and, like Jesus once again, there was no room in the inn presently, Franklin and a Mexican named Carlos got instructed to sleep on cots out in the cafeteria where two trustees who worked on the kitchen crew slept also and who they assured them would watch them like hawks to make certain they didn't try to escape. Franklin didn't say anything but nodded his head, wondering where in god's name he might go if he did venture outside, since it was fifteen miles back to town and mostly all there was were woods and swamp and possibly venomous reptiles lying in wait.

On Saturday morning they all got up at five-thirty and ate oats or Frosted Flakes and made do with a single cup of coffee, then everyone went outside through the chain link gates with the holes in them and loaded back up on the retired Glenn County bus and headed off for Demere Road where Franklin got paired off with a partner and one picked one side of the road while the other stayed on the other and then walked southward and picked up paper and beer cans and empty whiskey bottles and used rubbers and once, when Franklin poked at a shoe box that was lodged by a clump of weeds, the top fell off and he saw a contingent of dead kittens inside. The kittens had been there for a while and were welcoming maggots by this time, so Franklin managed to poke the top back on the box and slide the container further back from a roadside view and not deposit them in his trash bag to leave at the side of the road, and he walked on and tried not to think of the kittens and the maggots and the Frosted Flakes that were now performing gymnastic flips in his stomach.

He wasn't hungry but he got in the bus when it came by to pick them up for lunch, and he sat in the seat with his new roommate Carlos without speaking, since by now he'd figured out Carlos didn't have much of a capacity for English when he had anything to say which was usually not anything at all. He watched the same sights go by and the ex-reform school come into view, and he got in line and went inside and lined up for his bologna sandwich and bag of potato chips and a choice of water with ice or without.

The good thing was they didn't load up back in the former Glynn County school bus and they didn't return to Demere Road to pick up any more garbage or travel to any other thoroughfares around the island to spruce up whatever needed sprucing, but instead were told they had free time which meant that most of the staff was only going to work half the day because of budgetary problems, and so everyone decided to sprawl on their beds and sleep or gather in the cafeteria to watch South Carolina get drubbed by Auburn in the first game of a football doubleheader, to be followed by Alabama mangling Vanderbilt, which hadn't happened yet but everyone knew was soon to be anyway, but they watched the games anyway and some of the other inmates snored and Franklin and Carlos got pulled down to the kitchen to wash the leftover breakfast dishes and throw out the trash from last night and this morning and the paper plates and napkins from lunch in exchange, the trustees said, for them not having to go back out in the morning and pick up trash with the others, which was always a lousy job after the island got trashed by the residents and the tourists on Saturday night. You can wash the breakfast pots and pans, they said, and then take it easy until it's time to take you back to the Justice Center and let you go.

This seemed pretty much a stroke of good luck for Franklin since it assured him of not being out on the highways again Sunday morning with the chance hovering in his head that one of his friends or some female he coveted might drive by in their vehicles and see him in his orange vest and his workhouse-issued ball cap carrying around a heavy-duty trash bag and picking up litter like some scumbag not fit to have breakfast in a nice restaurant on a Sunday morning and knowing in his heart of heart that once recognized he would never be able to set foot on any area of upper crust land again. He might as well join up with Tom Joad and go to California in hopes of picking enough peaches so he might be able to find a place to sleep or eat that was not out by a dumpster with green flies buzzing around his head.

Dinner was served at five-thirty when the sun was setting and the sunset was pink and orange and charming when viewed through the window by the big sink where his hands plunged down into scalding soapy water and he washed the baked beans stain from the skillets and swished out the pot that had boiled the hot dogs—two apiece—for the famished offenders. When he finished up he sat back in his folding chair in the kitchen and listened to the sound of the football game on the television in the cafeteria and watched the night come on and the world turn dark save for one light out back where insects swirled around the orb as if it was still the middle of summer. He wondered how long they would be around now that it was autumn and summertime was now nothing but a memory, but he knew how it was in this island town, how fall was scarcely a season and winter sometimes didn't come at all and spring was well upon you and in full-swing and summer was there jiggling the knob and scratching at the window lattice waiting to come in again.

After the games had ended and the news came on with its reports on how many people had been shot this day and a rerun of Saturday Night Live started, which was new to him because he never saw Saturday Night Live anymore, he was always out drinking and drugging and trying to find a warm body because it seemed to him to be a requirement of sorts, and so he listened to the laughter and some band rocking out while he lay on his cot in the kitchen looking out at the one light with the insects flying around it. He lay there a long time trying to will himself to sleep so the time would go by and his sentence would be over and he could get off the bus and walk to his father's car and drive home and know it was Sunday night and his trials and burdens and troubles were now behind him. He didn't know why this had frightened him so, this term of imprisonment he'd had to face, but he wanted it over now so he could go back to feeling like and acting like he was a hell of a guy again. He'd had some time now feeling like a piece of shit, being treated like one, thinking it was true he actually was one, and now all he wanted was to get away from that scratchy, contagious truth and return to the world where he could tell himself things were not so bad, that he was not so creepy, that in the long run everything was going to be okay.

He had to get back so he could find a way to escape all this, his thoughts, his whereabouts, his life. He didn't know how he was going to do it, if he could talk his way out of it or pull a rabbit from his hat or figure out a way to harvest his father's leftovers and buy himself a ticket to paradise, but there had to be something better than this. There had to be a way to get to where he needed to be, and one way or another he needed to find it.

There were times when all the planning in the world didn't do any good, for there were forces out in the universe and monkey wrenches in the heavens and trials and tribulations supplied by the cruel Fates that conspired at times to try and keep John Clark Hayes from doing his job, that attempted in nefarious ways to stop him from completing his route on dark conspiratorial days. He remembers a morning when he arrived to begin his daily delivery—a Monday that day was—and when he tried his pass card at the gate of the warehouse nothing happened and the message screen read Card Error each time he swiped it. After five minutes John Clark knew this was a software problem that wasn't going to be solved until 7 A.M. or afterward, perhaps on up into the morning, and since it was nearing four in the morning and his alternative was to wait there at the gate or turn around and go home and return later—both options which were unacceptable to him--he decided to pull his car over into a parking slot and determine if there were any openings in the gate where he might crawl through or climb over. The bottom portion of the entrance was a steel column that supported a heavy wire mesh and provided no room for even a garter snake to wriggle through, so he turned his attention to the top of the gate and saw how it extended probably twelve feet in the air. The metal mesh was too narrow for a foot to fit into for leverage climbing upwards, so he decided to take off his shoes and toss them over the gate and use his stocking toes to lift him toward the top of the gate and help him descend to the pavement on the other side. He hadn't decided what he was going to do when that feat was accomplished, how he planned to get his truck back out the gate from the other side, but he decided he would worry about that dilemma when he got to it.

Problems had to be solved cooly and efficiently by deciphering the glitches and taking the necessary sequential steps to solve them.

The solution turned out to be fairly simple. When he walked down and got his truck and drove back up to the gate it came to him very clearly, just as he'd supposed it would. All he had to do was press a button to exit—to leave the grounds didn't require a pass card like it did to get in—so all he had to do was drive through and he was on his way. He looked at the gate in his rearview as he pulled out on Russell Road to begin his route, and he saw how if he had not been determined and ardent to do his job he would still be back there waiting for someone to come along and help him.

Screw that, he had thought. I do not like being dependent on anybody, anytime, anyplace.

There had been the morning when a freezing rain had fallen and coated the city with unaccustomed ice. The streets hadn't been that slick, but he'd had trouble getting into his truck and freeing the wipers from the windshield. He'd had to apply a hot rag from the sink inside the warehouse to the sides of the blades and slowly and softly wiggle them free. The driver's door was frozen shut and he'd had to enter through the passenger door and somehow climb over the gearshift to get to his seat. The sliding side doors were also frozen, and he knew he would have to hand-carry all the cases of soft drinks to the back of the truck and load them that way, which would require more time and effort. After one stop and seeing how slow the process was, it came to him to go deliver to the stops on the route that did not have soda machines, that were candy and snacks only, where he could place the order in a huge plastic bin and carry it in without so much bother. He would save the soft drinks until later, when the sun came up and the temperature rose and the frozen rain melted away and the sliding doors would go up and down again and there would be no climbing and carrying requiring lots of wasted movement and spent time and doubled effort.

He was smart like that.

There had been traffic jams for no reason at times, but he had known how to get around them, what side streets to take to help him get to his destinations. He was no good at written maps but he had a photographic memory of places and structures and how to go about getting to them, and when there was a wreck on the roads he knew how to circumvent the chaos and go around it or back away until the police cars and the blockages were in the distance and he was free to move. When the battery on the truck was going bad he knew it beforehand and reported it, and knowing what he might face he came equipped with a charger to build up the battery overnight, and when the truck still wouldn't turn over he loaded as much as he could into his Honda and delivered his products that way. He'd had to return to the warehouse several times to load, but by the time he came back in the afternoon and the battery was being installed, he was already through with the day's route and did not need it anymore. But he hadn't sat all day waiting for the battery to arrive, and he wasn't just embarking out to his first stop either. He was finished. He had adjusted. Somehow the job was done. There had been problems, but in the end they had not defeated him.

John Clark watched Franklin emerge from the downtown building and walk down the sidewalk and cross the street to the parking lot. He knew what his son had been doing this weekend, and he knew he was now going to get into John Clark's pride and joy pristine Honda Civic and drive back out to the free world again. He would undoubtedly stop somewhere for a drink. It was sad, John Clark thought, how both his sons never learned from their screwups, how, actually, they never seemed to learn anything at all. It wasn't that they were stupid. That wasn't it at all. It was just that they didn't seem to truly give a shit.

***

It would have been better if Jimmy had come right out and yelled at her and cursed her up and down, and it would have been better too if she had come right out and yelled at Jimmy and cursed him up and down for all he was worth too, but neither of them had ever resorted to acting the way real people do and so they simultaneously engaged in veiled acts of sabotage that made each one at some period of time feel like killing themselves to get this over and done with rather than hanging around to kill the other and then have to face the gas chamber or the electric chair or get hung by the neck until dead or spend the rest of their natural days in prison depending on how the state legislature was leaning these days. None of this was in keeping with the rest of the world but was nonetheless the way she and Jimmy had always acted toward each other even when they were dating, back when one would think they were grown up enough by then to act somewhat better. It wasn't that they were uncivilized or anything like that, for they had always been very mannerly while wishing the other would go float in the Atlantic and let a barge coming in from Halifax cruise over them.

"I'm not going to be here for dinner tonight," Jimmy told her as she was going out the door. "A bunch of us are going to the basketball game. I didn't think you would be interested so I'm letting Michael have your seat. I thought that would be okay since you haven't made it to a game in over a year anyway."

"Funny, I don't remember you ever asking me to go during that time. I can't recall anytime recently when you've acted like you had the least bit of interest going anywhere that involved my presence."

"Says she, who's a member of at least seven book clubs at last count—one for each night of the week."

"If you'd only remembered how to read over the last ten years you could have gone with me. We do have men in our group, you know. Of course, if you were to come, we'd have to make allowances and keep all the books monosyllabic so you wouldn't have to spend so much time looking up the meanings to the words."

"I've got better things to do than read about immigrants and the injustices of the world and tragic romance between men and women and women and women and men and men. All that crap is way too complicated for me."

"Life's too complicated for you most of the time."

"I may not be at the warehouse today. I've got a machine that needs some major fixing, so I'm going to go and see if it can be saved or if I need to find another one to take its place."

"Don't dare invest in anything new. It would be a shame to have something out there that works the way it ought to."

"Have you looked at the prices of new vending machines lately? No thanks. I'd have to take out a loan just to replace an old one. And a new one would never pay for itself."

"Suit yourself, but I don't agree."

He was texting with someone when she got ready to go out the door, and she wanted to go over and tear the phone from his hand just to see who it was. She had spent the better part of the morning trying to fix the commode from running constantly and stopping by the drug store to pick up her prescription pills for anxiety and headaches and indigestion, and it had occurred to her sitting in the line at the window with her car idling and a joyous morning radio show going on where the host and the hostess were asking people's favorite places to get ice cream in between playing the mix of yesterday's and today's hits that if Jimmy was to not be around at some point in the future then the possibility existed that she might not need pills for anxiety or headaches or acid in her throat because it could be he was the one who brought these maladies on and if he were somewhere else—say, the dark side of Jupiter—she would have no need to swallow two pills twice a day with meals anymore. She had not thought seriously about divorcing her husband before but mainly of arranging for him to go missing, but on this morning the possibilities reared up in her mind and she thought perhaps she should think on such things more these days, especially since she'd recently had call to converse and take lunch and ride over to a secluded area in a distant park and engage in some heavy necking with Marty McCool before being back at the warehouse in the afternoon. It was working out fine that way. She could get away from the warehouse and the running of the business the hour after lunch, and Marty could leave the station because his shift was over and the two of them could meet beneath the trees by the beach with a view of the Atlantic while the sea birds soared and cawed.

His real name was Gerald but he said he hadn't gone by that name since he was a freshman in college. When he'd started working at a station on the weekend he decided Gerald wasn't hip or with it enough and if he was ever going to go anywhere in the broadcasting business he had better have a name that stood out and wasn't easy to forget. It had taken him a week or so pondering names in a book from the library where expectant parents went to find something to name their children other than Junior or Bubba or Heather or some derivative of a dead relative who was supposed to have been an inspiration to them at one time, so Gerald had looked and pondered and entered possible monikers into a notebook until he had settled on Martin McCool, which could be shortened to Marty McCool, which was in keeping with the kind of persona he had aspirations to be.

So that was how Donna found herself spending her afternoons between work and marriage, making out in the park in Marty McCool's Jeep, which was strange to say the least but was altogether different, which was precisely what she was looking for.

***

In her time Brenda held the inkling she was a fine-looking woman and a lot of men were looking her over and thinking the same thing, and these days she mostly held the same view, even if she was approaching fifty now and had added some weight and her eyes were perhaps not as bright or her hair as rich and lustrous and shiny-black as before and perhaps some wrinkles had been sprinkled in and a few things sagged, that she was still more than presentable to the eye considering her age. All this did not come easy, she liked to say to others; a woman really has to take care of herself or the years will take over and leave her high and dry and take away whatever charms she once held. She liked to think she was a good example to her friends and work colleagues around her, who were not so fortunate in maintaining their feminine qualities. This kind of thought only perpetuated the idea in her mind that the reason she and John Clark's marriage had not remained on a good course was not because her physical appearance had cooled his desires over the years, but that his absence from their bedroom and the household on a regular basis was because of something strange that was within his own id and ego and superego and soul. Sigmund Freud or Carl Jung had not been around to analyze the situation, and Brenda doubted that even if they'd both been present they never would have figured out what in the name of god John Clark Hayes was up to on an everyday routine, which was never routine but often bizarre and never the same one day from the next.

She wasn't sure if it was coping with a loss was what she was doing, or grieving over a death, or giving herself some time to weigh and consider where her life was going now that John Clark was removed from it, but what she did know was this wasn't going to be as easy as she'd initially thought. She wasn't going to be able to go out with her friends and down margaritas and laugh and take cruises or vacations and be the merry ex-wife and somewhat-widow of John Clark Hayes of Saint Simons Island. She was going to have to come up with a game plan to get her through all the nights and days to come. Only over the last couple of days had she come to realize how calm and ordered her life had been while John Clark was alive. Even though

69

he drove her crazy with his ways and actions and entrances and exits and varying disappearances there was still this sense of calm he imparted over her existence, over the household and the world that surrounded it, and it had been a comfort she had not recognized until it was gone. It was as if there had been some supernatural manner he'd possessed to keep an eye on everyone and everything and he had been there all along whether you saw him or not.

Yes, there were strange thoughts swirling around in her head these days, and she didn't know what to make of them. Part of her wanted to say this was all just a case of the usual commonplace taking a new twist, and once adjustments were made all would be well, but there was something else too. Something was gone now and she was having trouble deciding on exactly what it was.

***

The last thing in the world David wanted was for his mother or sister to know exactly what he and Franklin had in mind as far as his father's estate went. He realized there wasn't that much to go around; his father had not exactly been some financial wizard who'd somehow taken small amounts of money and grown them into Rockefeller-like mounds of wealth reaching for the heavens. No, his father had simply been just a working man who had gone to his job each day and not gone overboard too many times spending his money on things that did not matter to him. He provided for his children. He maintained a roof over everyone's heads and made sure no one went hungry. At the same time he was no practitioner of self-denial. He did not make himself do without and tell everyone what a great guy he was in all his sacrifices. No, he had his toys. He had books and records and mementos of things he held dear. He just didn't go overboard. He didn't keep taking and never give. If nothing else, David thought his father had been the most-balanced and fair person who'd ever walked the face of the earth.

This is why he'd waited until Wednesday in the middle of the week when he knew his mother would be at the library and Linda would be at school and Franklin would be either working at the grocery store or in class and the house would be untended with no one around and he'd be able to take his time looking around and formulating a plan on what to do with some of his father's fringe possessions which might bring in some extra cash if he could only spirit them away unnoticed and find the right party. He figured if he could go ahead and separate them from the premises before the actual estate tabulations took place then he wouldn't be saddled with having to share the fruits of his labor by cutting in his mother and sister and even Franklin with the profits he could make.

In other words, he was going to load up a bundle of his dad's things and sneak them away unbeknownst to the others and then keep all the cash for himself. Maybe if he stopped and thought about doing this deed too much he might feel some modicum of guilt, but even that would be better than staying perpetually poor and operating at a deficit for the next thousand years of his life.

Take all his father's Famous Monsters of Filmland magazines for instance. There was a pile of them in cellophane wrap in sturdy cardboard boxes just sitting back in a closet in the library. No telling what a haul they would be worth to the right buyer. His dad had been collecting those things since back in the fifties and early sixties, and out of curiosity one day David had gone into a collectible hobby shop and seen what they were charging for a single issue. One copy's price had knocked his eyes out, and there his dad was with hundreds of them in pristine shape all stored away in plastic wrappers waiting for some classic monster nut to shell out big bucks for. This did not count the numerous shoeboxes of baseball cards, Topps and Fleer, the Mad magazines and you name it, and the vinyl and books strewn practically everywhere throughout the house and the garage. There was no way any member of the family knew what a goldmine his father had squirreled away over the years. It seemed a shame, since David was going to be the one taking the initiative to get all this stuff on the market, for him to have to share the proceeds with anyone else.

He was in the process of making an inventory on a notepad and taking pictures of items on his phone so he could check on the internet and see what the going rate of such currently was when his phone began buzzing and his brother's number appeared on the screen. He didn't really want to answer it this moment while in the early stages of grand theft, but this was at least the third time this week his brother had called and he hadn't gotten back to him yet, and since this idea to procure some of his father's possessions and sell them to the highest bidder clandestinely had been Franklin's initially David decided it was only kosher to see what was going on and learn also if Franklin had survived his weekend in the slammer without too much emotional scarring.

"What's up?" he said, putting a little cheer into his voice like he was innocent of any wrongdoing. Franklin wasn't that smart, he thought. He could be smoke-screened as easily as most of the human race.

"Trying to catch up with you," Franklin said. "I haven't heard back from you in about a week, and I thought it might be a good idea for us to get our acts together concerning all dad's stuff and what we need to do with it."

Perhaps it wasn't a great idea, but David thought it might be best to be halfway honest this once. After all, he could engage in individual covert action later on.

"Actually, I'm over at the house right now," he said. "I thought this would be a good time to take a look around while Mom and Linda weren't in the vicinity. I was going to give you a call when I finished," he lied.

"I was over there yesterday," Franklin said. "I drove by and didn't see Mom's car, so I stopped in and had a quick look-around. There's a lot there, just like I thought. For a little bit we could both get rich."

"I don't know about that," David said coyly. "Maybe if we get lucky we can come up with enough to pay our bills and keep from going to debtors' prison."

***

Linda could have taken the last two workdays off after the funeral and come back again on Monday, but the fact was she was ready to go back to the classroom just to get away from the house and everything else. If it wasn't something going on with the kids that she had to drop everything for and make it happen (because, of course, Mark was just too busy and involved with everything else under the sun than to worry about assuming any parental responsibilities) or her mother calling her up and asking impossible things of her, or, on the other end of the spectrum, not calling her up and going strangely silent when there were so many things going on such as her father's funeral and the will and the execution of the estate. Linda had to say to herself that in all these counts her mother was about as helpful and forthcoming as the members of the realm of the dead that her father had recently become a member of.

The kicker had been when the district attorney's office had left a message on her phone and sent a registered letter to her and her mother and her brothers about what the city and the state planned to do about the persons responsible for her father's death so far as charges to be preferred and bringing them to a trial and would the family be agreeable to a plea deal if one were to be reached, all of which was jumping the gun in her manner of thinking, considering the police and the highway patrol and the murder bureau hadn't taken the suspects into custody yet, hadn't, as it was, even quite identified who they were or if they were still within the city limits or even had not hopped a barge for Argentina and were on their way to pursue a life of crime there in a place where they wouldn't be required to take up residence for life among hardened criminals or perhaps get injected with lethal fluids or breathe in noxious fumes until their bodies decided to cruise away and take up residence in another world.

So it was that naturally she had to curse God for allowing her to be in the forefront of a massive school investigation when one of her students in his fourth grade wisdom decided to bring his mother's handgun to school after slipping it out of her purse as she was chatting on the phone with one of her sorority sisters while drinking coffee and smoking a Benson Hedge Ultra and planning the next sorority auction where they would pawn off floral arrangements to benefit the homeless women out on the street who'd been abused and let down by the men in their lives. Antonio Winters didn't think his mother would mind too much if he took her pistol along to school that day in his backpack, since she'd told him at least a dozen times already this school year how she didn't want him to get picked on by anybody in his class because he wasn't as tall or big and sometimes lagged behind the class in his studies through no fault of his own. That was all on the teacher. It was all on Linda.

It certainly hadn't been nice on this first day back after her father's death by murder and a hasty funeral and all that went with it to come back to school thinking she'd get some peace of mind only to have a pistol fall out of a backpack on the floor in front of her. Not only was it not nice, but it just didn't seem the least bit fair at all. It seemed like God was messing with her.

***

SC Medical had never been one of his favorite stops. It was out of the way from his regular stops, located at the end of a bedraggled, unused road down on the banks of the Altamaha River with not much around other than abandoned cars and a makeshift dumping ground, where some of the Island's less-civilized populace liked to throw bags of trash they had no use for anymore. Mostly the way was strewn with discarded junk that even the unfortunate members of Saint Simons society didn't want around them whatsoever. John Clark basically had to watch the road for debris and hold his nose as he approached SC Medical, since it was the final destination for used hospital supplies and any form of rubbish the medical facilities might accumulate. Thus, SC Medical soon came to be known in his mind as South Carolina Stinky. He always made certain to make it his last stop of the day on Tuesdays, since there was such a coating of stink and slime on him after he finished the only thing he wanted to do was get back home and jump into the shower.

No one at the facility spoke any English that he could see. Actually, none of them spoke much at all, but instead glowered at him and tried to stay out of his vision as much as possible, which he attributed to their perhaps being wanted by the authorities for crimes or illegal entry and afraid of someone identifying them or knowing their whereabouts, or it could be they recognized him as a possible candidate for robbery or theft or maybe murder if the time seemed to warrant it. John Clark made it a practice never to turn his back completely or let his guard down when he saw any of the SC Stinky employees around, and he kept up his guard when he didn't see them, figuring they were dangerous enough to be hiding around a corner or slipping into the back of the truck ready to beat him over the head and take any valuables they could find. But it wasn't so much the crazed and desperate human element he was wary of so much; hell, there were numerous stops on his route where he had to be careful and keep an eye on the clientele and the surroundings all the time, the outdoor machines at the Super 8 where who knows who might be hiding in a darkened doorway, the sleazy rednecks at McCullough Forklift, the winos and druggies who hung around the parking lot at the Knight's Lodge down in the murky section of the island, the desperate characters at the temporary day employment center who sat in folding chairs in a room where the two drink machines and the snack machine were up front and there was no way to service them and collect the money without turning your back to the audience, so you had to be alert and you had to be quick.

The main problem at SC Stinky was that the ancient drink machine—which had to be as old as John Clark—was located in a tiny room where only a few Oz munchkins might be able to cohabit at one time, and when the heavy, immense door swung open there was no way to move forward or to the side or even back up much, all directions John Clark Hayes had attempted to go in when on his first visit he'd opened the door and a rat with a perhaps radioactive-induced growth spurt jumped out from the machine's innards and in its unplanned flight had come uncomfortably close to John Clark's own facial features before landing on the table for dwarfs and scuttling away. In the years since John Clark had not been able to erase that image from his mind when he drove down the trashy avenue toward the scummy portion of the Altamaha and the crumbling structure of SC Stinky, where therein lodged the world's tiniest breakroom occupied by the world's largest rat population, features ably assisted by shady employees and dirt and disease and noxious fumes at every turn.

But it had to be done or there would be no such thing as eternal rest. John Clark Hayes was more than cognizant of this fact. He knew somehow without being told by any keeper of the gate to enter his eternal reward that the route was all there was and who he was and his weekly visits had to be completed before any treasures from the Great Beyond could be deposited on his behalf. There was SC Stinky and the water and sewer department and the teachers' lounges and the factories and showrooms and any place where people worked or congregated. And it wasn't simply the action of scooping up candy bars and bags of chips and chocolate pastries and cans and plastic bottles of soda and throwing them into slots and leaving. No, there were bill acceptors to repair and money to be collected and glass fronts to be wiped off. There were notes taped to the machine—I lost seventy-five cents on Wednesday because the Doritos didn't fall, my honey bun's bag had a hole in it, the Mountain Dews won't come out in the tray, can't you stock more Snickers bars in the machine since they run out every week, can't you get powdered donuts anymore? He had to take care of this at every stop. These were his customers. At every stop he knew who wanted what and who was going to give him trouble when he arrived. It was part of the job. He had to out-think them. He had to have the problem solved before they asked, before they even knew there was a problem in the works to begin with.

This was why he was here at SC Stinky. This was why he could not stop. He didn't find it strange at all. He understood it was what he had to do. He had not expected anything different. He had always known the route was his to complete, dead or alive. It had to be done.

***

After he had been to South Carolina Medical he journeyed to the place of repose where he rested these days and nights and rid himself of the stench and the filth and the odiferous reality of it by taking what amounted to a metaphysical shower, and when he was clean again and fresh and had nothing of the SC stinky fumes about him he transported himself in that way he had now of being where he wanted without actually making the trip. His eyes were open all along but now they saw what he wanted to see and he made out the street and the sidewalk and the store fronts across the street and on either side on the opposite part, and he looked at the double doorway with the sign that said Lancaster Hills Credit Union and the hours of operation posted in an engraved box and a hung sign inside the glass that said that it, the credit union, was closed.

He could make it day or he could make it night and there could be light or there could be dark and it could be anyway he wanted it, and so on this occasion he decided to make it day and light and a morning as it had been those weeks ago when this had been the last place he'd visited before shuffling off to a Buffalo of another realm. It took only what would have been a heartbeat if he'd still had one before the scene began to materialize and become familiar and allow him to perceive that he had seen all this before, that this was a place he knew all too well, and he could watch this instant replay rerun of his life and see once again that sometimes there is no way to control what goes on around you and when your train is coming down the track with the mindset on that it is your time to board and there is no way to miss this stop or have the cars derail that there's truly nothing you can do but climb aboard and rumble on toward what is waiting ahead for your arrival, and when you disembark there will be no other train coming along to take you further, for this is the end of the line and there's nothing more to say or do. You might as well accept it. This is as far as you go on this trip.

That was the way he was seeing it.

There is the truck up there sitting at the traffic light. In a matter of seconds the light will turn green and he will slowly move along behind the Honda Odyssey in front of him, that must have all day to get to where it is going because it is certainly taking its time and poking along, going ever so slow until its turn signal comes on and it pulls into the Dunkin Donuts on the right, and then it is clear to travel another block and turn left into a parking lot and backtrack up the street and park on the curb outside the doorway of the credit union, wait two minutes until it is opening time and someone unlocks the door, and then go in and take inventory of what to bring in this morning to fill the machines. It had only been a couple of weeks since the management had requested a drink machine and a coffee machine to go into the employee breakroom, and he had not been able to establish a pattern as to what the employees liked the most in soft drinks or how much coffee they drank in one week's time, not so much, anyway, as the snack machine with its candy bars and chips and bags of salted nuts and Cracker Jacks and Ro-laids and Lifesavers, which all sold on a regular basis and never required too much in the rotation scheme of things and which he could almost predict what he needed to bring in before he even looked.

He watched himself gather up his numbered cloth bag and his clipboard with his route info there for him to write down the machine number readings and get out of the truck and go inside. He followed himself past the teller windows where the three female tellers—two for the lobby and one for the drive-thru—all see him and smile and wave and ask him how he's doing, and he notices how as usual he chooses to linger on the face of the strawberry blonde Judy and checks to see if she is as pretty and desirable as she always is on his visits, and then he goes down a hallway and enters the breakroom on his right and checks the contents of the machine for supply and money and records the counter numbers. There are no notes of complaint or suggestions, and so he is free to go outside and fill the orders and come back in and stock. It is a thirty minute job, but he can usually do it in twenty. There is a science to it, he knows. If he can cut ten or fifteen minutes off each stop on his route each day he is then free to go and sit and read by the marina or shoot baskets at a school playground before going home to be a non-father and a non-husband and live out his life in a pre-ghostly way that has perhaps prepared him for the here and now of what looks to be eternity.

But he has to finish his route first.

He swings up into the truck—it is not so hard to get up in the back anymore; he is used to it now and it is not such an effort to hoist himself up like before, back when he'd been weak and not toughened up by the route—and goes about filling his bin with snacks and Cracker Jacks for Judy and bags of coffee and unloading however many shells of Cokes and Aquafina and Diet Coke and Mountain Dew needed to fill the soda machine. They are 20 ounce bottles, and they are heavier than the cans by the case, but he hardly can tell the difference anymore, for he is stronger now than ever before. Sometimes he can hardly believe his prowess these days.

When the order is ready he loads the sodas on to his two-wheeler and places the durable plastic bin on top of the bottles and makes his way for the door. This is when he hears the alarm going off and he can't decide exactly where the sound is coming from, this buzzing foghorn sound that pierces the morning air as if to say bomber planes are approaching and everyone take shelter, watch out, watch out, and that is when the two men who are wearing masks as if Covid was still around—and maybe it is, he remembers thinking, maybe I am going out into the world and mingling with people too soon, maybe I should still be holed up in my library at home—and one of the masked men looks him in the eye and it is he who is frightened and not John Clark so much, for John Clark is mostly wondering what it is that is happening around him, affecting the rest of the world but not him the way it has always been with him on the outside of it all looking on, and the masked man raises a pistol and fires before he warns John Clark or before John Clark can tell him to hold on a minute. No, the gun goes off with a flash and a crack and John Clark can see the glass door and the painted white bricks on the side of the building and then the sky and the sidewalk before him and the street like a faraway scene, and for a moment he can see his bin spilled out on the walk with the candy bars and the Cracker Jacks scattered and the shells of sodas turned over and a single bottle of Diet Coke rolling down the street, the cap loosened and the bottle fizzing as it comes to a stop. And he sees it all in its totality again and knows there is nothing he can do about it now or ever, so there's only the matter of letting it be. This is all he can do, he decides. It's like all this that is happening is different from anything that's ever gone on before. This is something brand spanking new and he might as well get used to it.

Six

The talk among the family about having a sale to disperse some of John Clark's possessions that were of no use to any of them in the future offered some small promise, but the thought of having only a slight sum of money coming his way from such a thing didn't exactly set David afire with anticipation. For one thing a sale would only cover those things that had belonged to John Clark and not his mother's, so there would be no huge swashes of fresh income coming in from the sale of antique furniture or automobiles or jewelry or any other big cash items. Any sale involving his father's books and magazines and music collection would end up being basically small change in David's pocket, and small change and petty cash were not going to help him escape the fix he perceived himself to be in, that of being bound to being a perpetual pauper and weighted down with a low-paying job for the rest of his days, already having a child and soon to have a wife. Big burdens, indeed. Without some sort of substantial economic breakthrough David can see himself working with no chance of retirement for the rest of his life, especially if he went ahead and got married and had more children on top of that. His one kid was killing him already, and he wasn't even one year old yet.

He didn't know exactly how he was going to do it or how he was going to keep his actions secret from the rest of his family—that predatory Franklin included—but he was going to have to come up with some way to circumvent the legalities and find an avenue where he would get the lion's share of what might be garnered from the sale of the late John Clark Hayes'—also known as his father—prized possessions. He was sure that some of this paraphernalia his father had found so dear was bound to be of value to somebody somewhere. He just didn't know where to look.

But what he did think he could do was ferret out a few assorted items from the whole of the collection and take it somewhere that bought and sold items like his father had prized, and perhaps if he were to do so then he might be able to determine how much to abscond that no one would miss and what he could get for such merchandise. He thought for a while and decided to take only a few books and four or five LPs and three Famous Monsters of Filmland in to a buy and sell place in Glynn Haven and see what the going price was for them. He could also scour the internet and see if there might

"

be the chance someone on eBay or another site might be looking for just the kind of thing his father had possessed in earnest. Who knows? He might get lucky and strike a gold mine in his research.

On his lunch hour, rather than traveling over to the Sonic and downing a Jalapeno cheeseburger and a portion of onion rings and a large sweet tea, he instead drove to his mother's house and used his key to go in the back door, parking around back in case someone might drive by and see his car there. His mother was at the library and Linda was teaching, but you never know. It was hard to keep a finger on Franklin's whereabouts, since he seemed to have no set schedule in school or his parttime job at the Winn-Dixie. He could be cruising around almost anywhere at any moment, so it was best to be careful. David certainly didn't want Franklin to think his older brother was double-crossing him as far as his dad's stuff was concerned. Of course it was true that he was going behind Franklin's back and what they had earlier agreed on, but that was tough. He had no doubt whatsoever that if he hesitated and kept his promise to Franklin that sooner or later his little brother would break their treaty and be off with the goods himself. It was a matter of first come first served and survival of the fittest.

He found himself tiptoeing through the house for fear someone would hear him, which was stupid, which was the product, he supposed, of a guilty conscience, because no one was around and no one knew he was there. It wasn't like the place was wired for sound or any alarms were going to go off if he mishandled anything, because as far as he knew his parents had never had a burglar alarm or a double-bolt lock or anything to assuage the criminal element from making them victims of misdeeds, but he had the feeling anyway and he couldn't shake it. He kept expecting Inspector Clouseau to jump out from a closet and yell Aha! and chase him room to room throughout the house, but it was perfectly silent and all he could hear was the ticking of his father's mantle clock on its place above the fake fireplace. The clock was pretty old; David wondered how much he could get for it and if anybody would miss it.

He entered the library and peered at all the books lined up on three walls with stacks on each side of the desk, as if his father had placed them there for shelter if illiterate fiction-hating armies might come to destroy him and burn his treasures. David turned his head sideways and read some of the titles, The Great Gatsby, Look Homeward, Angel, The Catcher in the Rye, and thought better of swooping them up and taking them in for evaluation. Somehow he thought his father would know he had done such a thing and would come after him to punish him, not with physical violence as retribution, for John Clark Hayes had never laid a hand on any of his children, but by giving David one of his looks, as if he was observing a snake in his dining room or something, or by icing him over with a continuing blast of frosty silence, a silence that said more than words could illuminate how an oldest son who is supposed to be the apple of his father's eye and has been primed to continue his father's legacy has instead become one of them, one of those ill-bred in the world who will stop at nothing to gain something he will never cherish but only throw away for money or greed or some form of ornament he can decorate himself in and pretend to the rest of the world that he is somebody special after all, even though he knows he isn't and nothing could be farther from the truth.

David knows where the magazines are and he knows where his father has his albums and CDs and cassettes. Everything is in the closet by the desk and in the study connected to the library, only a corridor away as if it was a secret passage. That is where the real loot is, but David stands at the desk with his hand on an immense volume of the Collected William Shakespeare and cannot go to the closet or take three steps through the opening and be in the adjoining room. He can only rest his hand on old William and listen to the silence of the house and wonder how much this volume of Shakespeare weighs and how in the name of god anybody could ever write so many words that a jerk like him would not be able to lift their totality with one hand.

This was but another in a long list of things David could not comprehend. It seemed to him the list was getting longer every day.

***

She'd taken another week before going back to work, something she had mixed feelings about since she'd done nothing but sit in a chair and stare out at the garden and drink coffee all day until her bladder couldn't stand it anymore and she could sit and stare no longer, doing this most of the week except for the times she got in the car and drove over to the park and parked by the lake where people fished when there were no appreciable fish to speak of to catch and sat there looking at the water instead of the garden until her bladder told her it was time to go back home. Then when she went back to work at the library everyone had been kind and caring and asked how she was feeling and if she was okay so much that she wanted to tell them to go away and find someone else to dote on because being alone was what she thought she really needed until she did get off by herself and then found she was driving herself crazy thinking about everything and really needed something to do to divert her attention. It was a vicious circle, this being among friends and being alone, and she thought things would be fine if the being alone and being with friends didn't involve her personally, if she could maybe be in her patio glider somewhere off on a star looking down and watching everybody do their thing while the world went around without her.

The good thing about this period of limbo and grieving was it afforded her children the opportunity, now that they had stood by her during John Clark's death and hung around the funeral home and the house in the pose of a united family, to now simply go back to their separate lives and disappear for a while as if they had grieving and a limbo of their own to go through. Brenda wasn't sure if any of them were really that affected by John Clark's death, since the more she thought of it and regarded it the more it seemed his death nowadays was about on par with his constant periods of disappearance over the years and there was not too much different now from when John Clark was alive and these past few weeks when he was dead. Perhaps this is what people do in real life, she thought, when it is not a novel or a classic film where the deathbed is such a momentous thing and is there to bring the story to a climax, but this is the way people act in real life when the audience has gone away and no one is around to pay attention—folks just get up in the morning and go about doing what they need to do to advance and there is no shedding of tears or throwing oneself upon a grave marker and weeping for what had been and what might have been to come. Maybe it is all an act we play whether we know the role is upon us or not. Maybe it is we know the camera is rolling and this is what we must do, and when some director yells Cut we know we can stop and go back to our real lives where fiction and masquerade are not required any longer.

So Linda and David and Franklin have disappeared back inside their own lives again and the food chains and the phone calls and the invitations to lunch and dinner are over with, and there is no trip to a far-off destination that will do anything to solve this problem of everyday life, so the best thing to do is put one foot in front of the other and move along as best one can without letting the overactive brain play a big part of it. Just relax, she tells herself, and let things happen as they may. After all, since when have you been able to do anything about this business of having the world get in line and behave anyway?

Since she is looking for something mindless to do with herself, she stops on the way to the grocery at a hardware store to take a look at their bedding plants. She's not interested in planting anything for food right now, because she eats too much and too often anyway, so there's no sense in adding additional culinary items to her refrigerator because she's not going to eat what's in there already. She's going to go out. She's going to go to every restaurant in town and have them prepare all her meals. And clean up afterward too, she reminds herself. Let everyone else scrape and load dishwashers and dangle their hands in dishwasher for a while. She's had enough.

Anyway, this is fall now and it's not really growing season, so there's no reason to get carried away on this gardening inclination that's taken over her thoughts.

She wanders among the pinks and yellows and reds and all the colors of the past summer, unable to decide what to buy that won't die and will enhance the yard and keep her busy, so she settles on one of about everything she sees. Before she knows it she has a shopping cart full of perennials and annuals, geraniums and mums and begonias and petunias and poppies and more she cannot name. Poppies, her mind murmurs, she remembers poppies. That's what the Wicked Witch of the West tried to kill Dorothy with. Put her and the Lion and the Scarecrow to sleep. Didn't work on the Tin Man as best she can recall. Everybody else falling into deep sleep which will soon be death. The Wicked Witch scared the panties off me when I was a child. Didn't know then that I was going to grow up and act just like her. Maybe I look like her too, I don't know. Have to check myself out in the mirror when I get home. See if I'm becoming a crone yet.

"You've got one heck of a load there," a man in a green apron says to her. "You must be planting for an entire neighborhood with all this haul."

"Actually, it's just my house," she says. "I guess maybe I'm overdoing it a little."

"No, each to their own. I'd rather have too much than not enough and have to make another trip to get more. At least this way you're not going to come up short. You'll have enough to keep you busy for a while, even if half the stuff you're getting probably won't make it until spring."

He peers into her buggy like he's going to make an inventory of everything she's buying. He looks up at her and smiles.

"If you're done I'll help you get checked out where you won't have to put everything up on the counter and then load it back in the buggy again, then take it out and load it in the car, drive home, then do it all again. You'll be all worn out before you ever get started getting these babies in the ground."

"I don't know if I can get them all planted in one day. I'll probably have to ration it out."

"Well, you don't want to wait too long. You don't want to leave them in these containers without watering them, because they dry out pretty fast just sitting there in that plastic. They need to be in the ground and watered pretty regularly, especially now when it seems like we're in a drought most of the time and before the cooler weather starts moving in."

He rolls the buggy over to a counter and grabs a scanner by the cash register. Soon he is beeping away all over the cart, and Brenda can't tell if he has scanned everything once or twice or skipped over them completely. He is done very quickly and the total is not as bad as she'd thought it would be, but she still doesn't know whether he's overcharged her or missed a few plants or what. It doesn't matter, because she's going to pay him anyway. What's done is done.

"Some of your stuff was on sale," he says, "and some of it was fixing to go on quick markdown so we can make room for the autumn shipments, so I gave you a little discount. Made them buy one, get one free like they were fixing to be tomorrow. I didn't penalize you for coming in a day early."

Brenda thanked him and started to push the buggy toward her car, but the man took hold of the handles and moved it away from her.

"I'll help you load this up. You've got a lot of pretty flowers here and I'd hate for any of them to get crushed on the way home."

He wheeled the cart toward the lot, then waited for her to get in front of him so she could lead him to her car. All the way there Brenda felt he was eying her from behind, but if he was he was keeping a constant conversation going at the same time. Brenda didn't think he could concentrate on being lascivious while exchanging pleasantries on the weather and the coming of fall and how he was always glad to see winter go as fast as possible, since he wasn't as young as he used to be and he couldn't tolerate cold like he once could.

"That's a funny thing too," he told her. "I worked outside for Georgia Electric for fifteen years and the cold weather never bothered me then. Now, once I've been away from that a few years I can't take it anymore. It starts to get below fifty and I'm looking up the long underwear and finding me some earmuffs."

She didn't want to appear unfriendly and untrusting so she agreed with him, said I know what you mean and uh-huh and you're right, and stood there while he loaded the back of her Rav without trying to help, since he acted like he knew exactly what he was doing and she'd only hinder the plan if she got in the way. Soon there were flowers and blooms spaced and scattered across the cargo area, and when he closed the back trunk the blossoms rose up to the glass and poked their petals out for anyone behind her to see. She really had bought a lot of flowers. She hadn't meant to go completely bonkers like this.

"That ought to hold you for a while," he said. "I hope you don't have too far to go."

"I'm just down the road. Maybe a mile or so. It's not far."

"Do you have any help getting all this out? You've got a lot of unloading and digging and watering to do when you get home."

"No, I'm by myself. I was looking for a project to keep me busy. You know what they say—idle hands are the Devil's workshop."

"What were you going to do? Get bored and go rob a bank or something? Pardon me saying so, but you don't look the criminal type to me."

Brenda wondered if she was going to be caught out in this lot all day. It seemed a little odd to her that this man could leave his post in the store and go outside with a customer and just loiter about for as long as he pleased. Wouldn't someone inside the store miss him? Didn't he have a boss who might want him to work on something or wait on other customers or unload a truck? It didn't make a lot of sense, this extra service above and beyond, the friendliness coming from a clerk at a business when everywhere else the hired help was apt to cut your throat if you asked for assistance, the smile on his face and the twinkle in his eye as he spoke—what did it mean? She did have to say he was a fairly handsome man, though. He was pleasant and witty and he certainly appeared to think that she was okay too.

"My name's Billy Joe but my last name isn't McAlister," he grinned. "It's Bradford. I already know you from the library, although I don't know your name. You helped me when I had a book on reserve a couple of months back."

"Oh yes," she said. "I thought I knew you from somewhere." It was a lie but she thought she should at least acknowledge him in some way. She didn't wish to give the impression that she was all wrapped up in her own little world and therefore oblivious of anyone and anything around her.

The next thing she knew she was telling him her address, and when he got off in an hour he would be by to help her get all her multitudes of flowers situated.

***

It wasn't that Franklin didn't trust his brother, but the fact was he knew what kind of sneaky jerk David could be if he wasn't watched like a hawk at all times, so he knew better than to leave him alone with a promise that David would get the ball rolling and then get back to him, because Franklin was nobody's fool when it came to promises like that. Oh, it wasn't that David would overtly lie about things—that wasn't it at all. What he would do is keep the truth out there to be seen and observed like a faraway ship at sea being tracked by a lighthouse miles away back at shore, and from that far distance before the gist of the truth could be perceived a whole tonnage of subterfuge and outright craftiness would go on in the shadows away from the radar and the spotlight, and by the time the truth got around to getting done, (in this case taking an inventory of what sellable peculiar possessions his dad had collected over the years and devising a plan to sell them off unbeknownst to his mother and sister and the profits split between the two brothers equally), some of this collection might go accidentally un-inventoried from being a part of the collection that was not going to be a part of the true inventory for John Clark's sale and was not going to be a part of the collection that was going to be divided up between the two brothers before the time for the opening inventory, but was instead not going to be in the sale or the illegitimate pre-sale to benefit the brothers but was going to simply disappear from either and wind up somehow in David's car trunk and driven to some high bidder who was not going to be considered for the pre-sale or the general sale but who was going to pay David directly before any particular sale ever had the chance to convene.

What Franklin not only suspected but truly knew was likely to happen kept him from allowing David to begin the brotherly agenda with only the older brother moving the plan along while the younger brother waited for a text or a phone call telling him when the festivities were to begin, because Franklin knew David well enough to know that the game would be more than afoot before he ever got told it was ready to start.

Sure enough, on Monday morning when it was time for his mother to be at the library and Linda to be at school and David to be at the computer store pinning on his name badge all it took was taking a cut from his Modern Poetry class and driving over to the old homestead to see he was right in his low opinion of his brother's trustworthiness. There was David's SUV parked in the driveway, or rather, pulled around back of the house so it wouldn't be seen from the street, and Franklin knew his brother was inside and definitely up to no good.

He pondered whether to let himself in and come up on David in the act, or should he merely park and get out of the car—blocking the driveway, of course, where David could not back out with the pilfered loot—and simply climb the porch steps and take a seat on the glider and wait for David to come outside with misappropriated loot and reveal himself to be the untrustworthy lowlife that he was?

He settled for a seat on the porch and set in to play the waiting game. He knew he had outsmarted his brother and had him dead to rights, and since there would be no way for David to talk himself out of this situation, Franklin would have him over a barrel and would be able to strike a much better personal deal for himself through this undertaking because he had caught his sorry-ass brother with his hand in the till and there would be no sugar-coated way of getting around it.

He made himself comfortable and lit a Marlboro for patience, but he couldn't fully relax knowing something was going on inside the house that he didn't know about. He ended up hot-boxing the cigarette instead of having a leisurely smoke, and before he knew it he was up from his mother's glider and using his key to quietly get inside and see what David was up to in all his clandestine sneakiness.

He attempted to be as quiet as possible and do a little sneaking himself, to just come up on his brother from behind and either scare the living shit out of him by suddenly demanding to know what he was doing or to maybe take a flying surprise leap like he was some wild savage attacking an usurper from another land to try and protect his own worldly riches from falling into alien hands, but as he crept through the living room and made his way to the hallway he couldn't decide which way to go. The smart money was the library where all his father's weirdo possessions were housed, but there was also the attic with its rope dangling overhead above him, where he could pull the door and steps would come down and he could go to the attic and see what boxes of records or books or strange otherworldly artifacts his father may have squirreled away up there, but the trapdoor was shut, which meant that David wasn't presently up there, so he decided to wait on the attic until later. There was the basement to check out, but the last time Franklin had been down there it was nothing but old garden equipment and cans of paint and a lawnmower with two wheels missing and a dangling handle. No, David wouldn't be down there, so it was definitely the library where he should go.

He'd only taken a couple of stealthy steps toward his destination when he heard the back door that ran from his father's office—his monastery, he always called it—make a creaking sound like it had always made when someone tried to go through it, one of those things his dad was always going to fix but never did, and he stopped with his stealthiness and his sneaking up and his plotting of a surprise attack and went instead into a kind of sprint, or at least as much of a sprint as Franklin could manufacture these days on account of his smoking and drinking and eating two Big Macs daily along with the fries and the soft drink that came with the meal, and he moved at this somewhat faster clip toward the library and past the books and his father's reading chair where he also watched baseball games and basketball games and college football and the NBA and the NFL and sometimes even hockey if he was bored, despite the fact, he always said, he didn't understand the rules at all, and Franklin attempted to speed into the study before his brother could close the door and load his car and try to make a getaway which he wouldn't be able to make because Franklin had the driveway blocked, but if push came to shove David could always drive through the yard even if he did smash and flatten and destroy all his mother's new flowers.

David had a banana box in his arms as he made his way to his car, but when he heard the footsteps coming up behind him he turned to see if it was the police or his mother or the hounds of hell or maybe his father's dog Wolfie advancing forward to take a chunk out of his posterior or just exactly what was behind him coming up to foil his burglary efforts. When he saw it was only his dumbass brother he stopped and waited and wondered which explanation he offered up would be stupid enough for his brother to actually believe.

He didn't really get to offer up any fabric of fiction worth mentioning, since Franklin was not in a discussive mode and instead seemed hell-bent on getting his brother in a chokehold and a full nelson and applying a forearm smash all simultaneously, none of which were a hundred percent successful but which did manage to pry the banana box from David's hands and have it take flight over onto the driveway concrete, where a score of Aurora Universal Monsters fully-assembled and painted models spilled out from the box and began divesting themselves of their form and postures. There were claws and coffins and capes that broke away from torsos and body features, and the Wolf Man's head rolled away from the preponderance of the wreckage as if The Creature From the Black Lagoon had swiped it off with its prehistoric claw.

"Goddamit, look what you did!" David told his brother.

"Goddamit, look how you were trying to screw me over," Franklin told his brother.

"I was just getting ready to call you and tell you to come over and help me. But with help like this, I wish you'd just stay away and let me do it myself."

"Looks like that was what you were doing already."

"Help me pick this shit up. Maybe we can glue these models back together. Probably not, though. Probably you've cost us a bunch of money just acting like the dipshit you are."

"Maybe I wouldn't act like a dipshit if you didn't always force me into being one."

"That doesn't make a lick of sense, Franklin," David said.

"That's cause you're a bigger dipshit than me."

"Am not," David said angrily, picking up an armless mummy.

"Am too," Franklin said. He was holding the Frankenstein Monster's head in his hand, but he didn't know where the torso had got off to. He kept looking. It had to be somewhere.

***

She wasn't stupid and had known from the very beginning that getting involved in an affair right out of the blue without a lot of prior reflection was not going to be something that went smoothly at every twist and turn.

First and foremost was the simple fact that she had always been a good and decent person since she was a small child. She'd been brought up that way, instructed by her mother and father who were both gone now but seemed to still be around somewhere looking on and charting their daughter's progress along the wicked pathways of the world, seeing if she had indeed listened to them way back when and taken those imparted lessons to heart. Donna had always prided herself on being successful in such ventures during her adolescent and teenage years, being that perfect sort of child who makes excellent grades and rises to the fore and never gets in the slightest bit of trouble. There was never the first sense of trepidation about her going off to school in another state after high school, traveling all the way as she did to Troy University in Alabama to get her Sociology degree, and when she had graduated in four years with good grades and returned home to make her living with her degree she found that the job market for bonafide sociologists with a sheepskin from a state university wasn't exactly brimming over with possibilities, so that was when she'd taken the job at Harris Teeter to help out monetarily and met John Clark again, and was a cashier for a time and a bookkeeper for a spell and finally landed a position as the back door receiving clerk, which meant she got to check all the vendors in with a hand-held computer and log all the company truck deliveries and drive the forklift and stack the empty pallets in a pile and sweep the expanse of the backroom and be available to chat with the head grocery clerk and the head butcher and the head produce clerk and the two co-managers who were just graduated from college themselves, and to mainly hang out Monday through Friday before having weekends off so she could go to movies by herself and stay inside her apartment and watch television and read Harry Potter books and science fiction dystopian novels about worlds where people shot each other with bows and arrows and chopped off their enemies' heads with battle axes. After about a year of this Donna decided to take up with the head grocery clerk and go out to parties and get pregnant and get married and make plans with her husband Jimmy for the both of them to quit their grocery jobs and go into business for themselves. It had taken two and a half years at Harris Teeter and then three more teaching Sophomore English to decide exactly what that enterprise was going to be and how they were going to get it started and how much it was going to cost them to not only get it started but keep it going, and when finally they decided their goal in life was to supply Snickers and Baby Ruths and Almond Joys and Doritos and Fritos and honey buns and candy and Coca Colas and Pepsis and Diet Coke and Diet Pepsi and Dr. Pepper and Mountain Dew and sometimes Yoo Hoos if the machine was adaptable to dispense such to the working public and the businesses and the bosses and the customers who walked through their doors who usually had to take a seat and wait for whatever they needed done to get done. Jimmy fancied himself as a potential successful small business owner who was sort of a hands-on guy who knew some people who'd give him deals on used vending machines that he would be able to work on himself if they were to have mechanical problems, which they did, and so he worked on them and sometimes they got fixed for good or maybe for a month or on occasions a week and every now and then only worked until he left and got into his Dodge Ram and drove away. They bought two delivery trucks at first, and Jimmy and Donna drove the trucks and solicited new routes and gave their new customers better deals than the ones they'd had with their previous vendors, and for a while Jimmy and Donna drove the two trucks and stocked the machines and serviced the equipment themselves, with Donna generally going by to get a machine working properly just after Jimmy had made a service call to fix it earlier.

But it was a hassle for Donna to try and work sixty hours a week and have a couple of babies on the side who needed changing and feeding and get taken to the doctor and taken to daycare and picked up in the evening, and it was a hassle to Jimmy for her sometimes to be a little behind in her end of things and every now and then be late getting his supper on the table, so after another year or so the decision got made to purchase another delivery truck and hire three drivers, with Donna taking up being in charge of the warehouse and ordering all the product and unloading all the deliveries and stacking everything in sections where the drivers could peruse the stock and load their trucks for delivery, while Jimmy placed himself as CEO of Tasty Snacks and took over the role as chief of maintenance and thus freeing himself from the day to day business side of things so he could instead sit at home in his lounge pants and drink Mountain Dew and devise strategies on his gaming computer.

It had only taken thirteen years for the thought to occur in Donna's mind that perhaps there was something different she might be doing, and it came to her that this something different might just be one of those behavior things that people tend to embark upon when they are suddenly being led down the wrong path by the urgings of something not exactly heavenly in their brain. But the thing of it was she was thirty-seven years old now, might as well say thirty-eight since her birthday was looming six weeks away, and she had been a good girl and a good young lady and a good woman all her life, and here she was and what had it really gotten her, what had it brought her way? She had two teenagers and they were both well and fine and pretty much grownup, and she loved them dearly and all that, and she had a house in the suburbs with a two-car garage and a patio and a fenced yard with trees where she could sit and read if she ever found the time. She was a member of the church and attended regularly and liked the minister and the congregation just fine, and the bank account was healthy and she and Jimmy were months ahead in paying off the mortgage. All of that was fine. All of that was what she'd always believed she wanted and she was thankful for it. But it wasn't enough.

She could go along with the flow and the peace and the lack of any controversy, but the truth was she knew in her heart she could do all that even if she was dead and gone and pushing up flowers at the cemetery. She didn't want to come out and blatantly admit such a thing but she knew in her heart and felt in her soul that what needed to happen to her very soon was the chance to dirty her hands a little, the opportunity to walk on the edge by doing something wrong and dangerous for once, if for nothing else to prove that she was indeed truly still alive and kicking and hadn't expired from the real world without ever knowing it.

This was why she had thrown all caution to the wind and gone out looking for something wrong to do. She felt like she had done the right thing for so long now that she didn't even know she was doing it, and it was to her that if she was only acting automatically in her dealings with the world and the way she lived her life then it was not as if she was being a good person in the strictest sense of the description. She was only being good because she didn't know how to be anything else. So it wasn't fair for her to get any credit for her good deeds and acts, because it wasn't like she was making a choice to do so. What she was doing was being a robot. She might as well be a zombie and be dead and only acting on instructions from some voodoo queen as far as it went. It wasn't like she was accomplishing anything much. Anybody with nothing to muster can be a goody-goody. It doesn't take much to be vanilla.

No, the truth was that she had been harboring such thoughts down in her secret place for a long time now, for nine years to be exact. That was how long it had been since that long-ago faculty Christmas party where everyone was laughing and busy getting three sheets to the wind and none of them had noticed that she and John Clark were having an enlightening type of conversation themselves, complete with smiles and shared laughter and the spilling of intimate secrets and the dual and sudden realization dawning between them amid the cookies and the cake and the eggnog and the spiked punch and the music that there was something enveloping them and there was an undercurrent that tugged at them and drew them out away into an alcove where no one could see them and they came together with a kiss that pretty well went on forever and neither of them had any idea what to say or do about it. It was a question and a sensation that hung in the air above them and sidled up to them and made up its mind not to go away after just that one evening but stick around and hang inside their heads for what promised to be forever, or until they acted upon it—which they didn't—or until one of them died and left the other behind—which John Clark did both.

Donna guessed it was this that had happened. There had been that one encounter with John Clark Hayes and it had lingered and never left her, and its solitary happening had been more than any other event that had touched her soul for her entire life, and nothing happened since to change that, and she'd carried it with her until John Clark got himself gunned down on a sidewalk delivering goods for her profit, and now he was gone and what happened between them that was magical and charmed and enchanted was gone with him too, and the truth was she didn't want to be left on this earth alone with only a memory to tide her over until she dropped dead of something sometime in the sweet bye and bye. She wanted whatever that was that had made her come alive then to come her way again.

She wasn't stupid enough to think that having sex a number of times with a local celebrity DJ was going to turn the trick for good, was going to make her contented and carefree and able to forget John Clark Hayes and what might have been, but it was at least a start. At least she wasn't sitting around pining and mooning and thinking about how what had happened had come and gone and now her life, what little of it there was to be savored, was over. At least this way she felt a slight heartbeat and had an inkling of all her senses being in some fair kind of working condition. Maybe she'd be ashamed of herself and change her ways back to normal sooner or later, but for now it was hard to tell. Now all she was looking for was some semblance of a heartbeat, some faint sign that she was truly alive.

She found herself driving to Marty McCool's condominium with the radio playing some song she had never enjoyed in the past but singing along with it too, somehow knowing all the words as if she'd practiced before a mirror. It was hard for her to believe that she was actually lighthearted and carefree like this while she was on her way to commit some awful kind of sin, to act in a creepy manner the same way she had always turned her nose up when the outside world indulged itself the same way. What if her friends could see her now? Her children or the people she went to church with? What about Jimmy himself? It wasn't that she hated him and was wishing to inflict some form of mental pain on him. That wasn't it at all. She didn't hate him. As a matter of fact, she probably still loved him in some offbeat, unexplainable way. She didn't want a divorce or a complete change in the life she was living now. All she wanted was to have some realization that there was something more in her and in her daily walk that was capable of traveling off the beaten path when it chose, that did not require her to keep going in a straight line until her feet grew weary and she could walk no more. All she wanted was a small surprise along the way just every now and then. At this point in her life she didn't think that was asking too much.

But maybe it was. She guessed she would find out sometime and somewhere as this whole scene played out.

Marty was home and waiting for her when she pulled into the parking area. She could see his bright green Jeep parked in its usual slot, the top down soaking up the October sunshine, the gold station pennants in a row across the crossbars placed there to let the other drivers on the road know that they were beside or going past Old School Marty McCool the Iceman and his Green Meanie Machine, and that if they wanted to get in on the scene they needed to tune in Capital City Radio and call into or text the station that they'd spotted Marty and the Green Meanie somewhere on the island and get their name in on the drawing for free giveaways and concerts and such. She looked at her phone sitting in the passenger seat and smiled. No, she wouldn't be calling or texting. It would be about her luck that she'd have to provide the information of where she had seen the Green Meanie and when she had spotted it, and maybe it wasn't such a great idea for her to provide those details while she was pursuing other matters presently. Someone she knew might be listening if they put her on the air live. Jimmy might be listening. It was his favorite station. Because he had it on all the time was how she had discovered it in the first place.

She pulled into a place four or five cars away from the Green Meanie. She didn't want to park too near for some insane fear someone would spot her car beside Marty's and put two and two together, which was ridiculous. She was miles away from home in another part of town, and no one knew her here, and even if they did, no one cared. People were busy with their own lives, their own peccadillos and sins, and they didn't have time to snoop around and see what she was doing. She had to remember that neither her or Marty McCool were the center of the universe, so there was no reason to start freaking out.

Anyway, she thought, as she got out of the car and walked to his door, isn't this what you were looking for when you first got this started? Mystery and intrigue? Some way to add some color to your life? Well, here it is. Consider yourself tainted. Consider yourself another Hester Primm. You're now a full-fledged member of the human race.

Take a bow.

***

92

Jimmy had a feeling.

He wasn't one of those guys who got feelings on a continual basis or had inklings or just sat around and had things revealed to him via telepathy, but every now and then he surprised himself and had something come to him out of the blue and educate him on a fact he previously hadn't known before. It wasn't a daily thing or a weekly thing or monthly or even yearly when it occurred, and he could never predict when it would happen and how it would affect him or if he would even know of its arrival when it came or if he would come to know about it after it had visited and already gone off and left him, like Santa on Christmas Eve while he slept and he awoke to find the presents that had been laid out for him beneath the tree, but eventually his premonitions either came on a non-regular basis or were there when he woke up or stumbled over them later, but the fact of the matter is they did come and he did receive them every now and then whether he knew he was receiving them or not.

It wasn't anything he'd seen and it wasn't anything he'd been told by anyone, but somehow on a Wednesday afternoon when he'd finished messing around on his computer and he'd punched in a few bets on over/under on some college football games and he'd knocked back a plate of leftover spaghetti for lunch and was in the shower cleaning up before going down to the warehouse to make an appearance—well, maybe he would make an appearance at the warehouse, he hadn't decided yet, maybe he would go somewhere else instead and make an appearance there since he wasn't really needed at the warehouse for much of anything these days—the thought occurred to him and the feeling which was unspoken and came out of nowhere brought the subject up in his brain that Donna was acting strange these days, not in a way he could lay a finger on, but not like normal either, not as talkative or ever so often implying that she was doing all the work for Tasty Snacks as the warehouse manager and the personnel director and the payroll master and the inventory specialist and the product receiver and the bookkeeper and janitor of the building on a Monday through Friday basis and he was doing nothing except not very often repair what he went out to repair and search around for refurbished machines to purchase so she could go around to new businesses and attempt to convince them to become clients. Now and again he had to change his routine and go down to the warehouse or out into the field and act like he was actually doing something or else, he feared, Donna might come to the end of her rope and read him the riot act and tell him what she was not going to be doing anymore because it was now becoming his job, so sometimes he had to keep her humored.

But this feeling had nothing to do with anything of the regular variety. This feeling came down to him either from God or some watchful spirit who felt it necessary to inform him that something was in the works and something was in the wind, and that if he was wise and wanted to keep the status quo going, then he'd best be paying attention to the matter at hand.

It came to him that Donna was messing around. It came to him that Donna was seeing someone else. He just knew it. She had never engaged in anything like this during their courtship or their years of marriage, but something told him it was happening now and he had better open his eyes and see what was going down and he had better open his ears and listen to the music and he had better start paying attention to what was going on while he wasn't around, because like it or not, something weird was transpiring and the chances were good he wasn't going to like the end results one tiny bit.

He didn't really know where to start with this. He didn't know if he should simply wait until she got home from work and confront her then with his accusations, but the thing of it was he really didn't have any proof about any of this save for his woman's intuition, which sometimes came through for him but more than often led him down the wrong path and caused him to do foolish shit and reveal himself to be an idiot which was something he didn't like to do, since he had this image of a successful private businessman to uphold and he didn't want anybody knowing that deep down he was pretty much a moron.

He could also drive down to the warehouse and see if she was there and have it out with her right then and there if he detected any guilt coming from her whatsoever, and that was what he did after considering every angle and strategy for a while. He drove up and saw Gilbert's truck there with the warehouse door up. He started to turn around and leave but decided maybe he should talk to Gilbert and perhaps accidentally stumble across some damning piece of information. When he walked in Gilbert gave a startled jump at the sight of him, since most days neither Gilbert or Don or Kenyata or even Donna herself were accustomed to seeing Jimmy show up at the warehouse in the mornings or at lunch or the middle of the afternoon or anytime very often, so the fact that he was here now made Gilbert flinch and caused his heart, which had a stint in it already, to speed up some and skip a little and made him almost drop the shell of soft drinks he was carrying.

"Hey," said Jimmy. "How's it going?"

"Pretty good, Jimmy. Pretty good. I ran out of drinks for my last two stops and had to come back by and load up again." Gilbert shoved the case up into the side of his truck where the doors were up. "You scared me for a second there. I thought I was all alone here. Usually, the only other person I see is Donna, and that's only sometimes. Most of the time she's out doing something else."

"I was looking for her myself. I thought by chance she might be here."

"Just call her if you need her. She's probably out checking on machines and seeing if everybody's satisfied on the route."

"I screwed up and left my phone at home," Jimmy lied. "I was too lazy to go back and get it. Anyway, it's not that important."

"I've been meaning to talk to you. I may have to have a couple of extra days off in the next week or so. I'm overdue meeting up with my heart specialist, and I think he wants to run some tests to see how the ticker's holding up. I don't think it's going to be much. Probably a day, maybe two, but I need to get in and get it done."

"That's fine. Just let Donna know what you need. She can run your route the days you miss. That way you won't be all behind when you get back."

"Thanks."

Jimmy knew Gilbert wasn't all that crazy about Donna running his route while he was out, which was the reason he'd said something to Jimmy to begin with. He knew Jimmy would only do the bare minimum if he ran Gilbert's route, and nothing would be said about it when he came back, but if Donna ran it she would find a lot of things wrong, unrotated stock and bill acceptors that needed to be cleaned and window glass that needed wiping down. She'd wonder why so many of Gilbert's machines were low on stock or empty, and maybe she'd ride with Gilbert a few days afterward and point out a few areas of improvement that needed to happen. This was all well and good, Jimmy thought, but he sure as hell wasn't going to do it. He didn't have time. That was Donna's field of expertise.

He started to call her but decided he'd wait. No sense in jumping the gun about something that may not even exist. Keeping the peace sounded like a better idea. Safer too.

***

This Billy Joe was indeed not a McCallister who'd lept off the Tallahatchie Bridge as he'd announced he wasn't but was instead a Bradford who was originally from Oak Ridge, Tennessee, who had moved away from there after working with bomb parts and uranium waste and an assortment of substances and chemicals the public didn't really know about and furthermore didn't want to either. Billy Joe Bradford said he'd spent twenty-five years working for some branch of the government he said Brenda had never heard of, and during that time he'd had two sons who'd both moved out of the country and a wife who didn't move at all but who after twenty-three years strongly suggested to Billy Joe he see the U.S.A. in his Chevrolet, which Billy Joe Bradford smilingly confessed he'd found to be an excellent idea, so he'd filled out his retirement papers and taken his pension early and moved first to Atlanta and took a job with Georgia Electric for a time and then moved to Savannah to work at a Home Depot and after two years transferred to Saint Simons to work at the Home Depot there. It was a pleasure, he told Brenda, to work among people these days who were not radioactive and to handle goods that were not contaminated and to believe perhaps he might live a few extra years now because of his new lifestyle instead of becoming ashen and glowing inward and being eaten up with cancer and having his teeth and assorted other important body parts fall out and go to seed.

Brenda at first had a little trouble distinguishing fact from fiction from what Billy Joe Bradford spoke to her of, not knowing whether he thought it funny people just dropped dead mysteriously every day while he was at Oak Ridge or whether his laugh was a nervous reaction like that archeologist who died laughing when he witnessed Imhotep the Mummy as played by Boris Karloff take a stroll from the tomb after stealing the Scroll of Thoth but couldn't really decide either way.

Billy Joe Bradford was funny though. He was charming in an incessant sort of way, seeing how he tended to grow on her after she became somewhat accustomed to his humor which was about death and poisoning and people's noses falling off. He did love flowers and knew practically all there was to know about identifying them and planting them and which ones to mess with and which to not take home if they were poisonous to pets who might eat them and then go into Camille mode and drop dead in front of their owners. He had a pickup truck with shovels and hoes and rakes in the back, and when he arrived he brought forth potting soil and peat moss from bags in the cab and spread them around the yard at whichever places she pointed to. Unlike most men she'd known, Brenda found him to be quite helpful. She couldn't help comparing him to John Clark, who despised any form of yard work but was always complimentary of her flowers and any of the gardens she started. When she had the flu one July she remembered him coming in from his route in the late afternoons and watering her plants in the swelter of the sun. She knew he'd despised being out there, but wonder of all wonders, he'd done it without being asked. That was the way he was. He preferred doing things without being required to. He was that way with his family. As long as no one was demanding anything of him he would give ten-fold.

Funny man.

After her car was unloaded and Billy Joe Bradford had spread dirt and potting soil and peat moss and dug and planted and patted the earth, when Brenda looked at him and saw the sweat and circles of dust on his face and his clothes caked with earth and his shovels and rakes and hoes scattered throughout the yard, he looked up at her after smoothing down the last hyacinth and asked would she like to go to dinner with him, perhaps after he'd gone home and showered and put on what he called his courting clothes, and she couldn't help it again, couldn't really keep herself from saying yes.

***

You couldn't come too early because they wouldn't let you in and you couldn't come too late because the one person who was authorized to let you in would sometimes go home early, so you had to make sure it was right around lunchtime when you got there with your order, and you might as well block off an inordinate amount of time because there was always some problem waiting for you that was going to do its best to get you running behind, that and piss you off royally too.

What the problem wholly consisted of was Lena, the woman who ran the check-in desk and coordinated all arrivals and departures like she was air frigging traffic control or something. She had a long desk in the front lobby and all visitors and deliveries had to come through her before they were free to proceed into the innards of the center to visit or deliver fruit baskets, or, like in his case, come in to stock the vending machines in the cafeteria and at the end of the halls on both floors of the building.

The Good Seasons Community Retirement and Rehabilitation Center was located behind a Baptist church on the western side of the island, and John Clark had to park his truck in the church lot by the office and walk down the long sidewalk to the Good Seasons door and get buzzed in by Miss Lena, who sometimes looked up from whatever she was doing behind the desk and let him in the door in a timely manner and sometimes let him push the button and stand there several minutes until she granted him entrance. He knew that Lena knew he was there and had seen him even before he pushed the bell to be let in, but about once a month she chose to let him cool his heels a few minutes outside, possibly so he might realize he was under her power and would have to watch his manners and listen attentively to what she had to say when he finally was granted access to the lobby.

His last Thursday there was no different than the others. Lena made him stand a good three minutes before finally getting up from her chair and peering out at him before releasing the latch. When he first began running the Good Seasons route he had been friendly and polite to her, thinking his personality and efficiency would soon win her over, but that had not been the case. After seven years Miss Lena was still sharp and critical with him, voicing her displeasure about having to take time from her busy duties to let him in and out and having to check his order and make sure the Center was given credit for anything that was out of date, damaged, or had been requested to be removed, which seemed to John Clark to also come under the discretion of Miss Lena, who didn't think elderly people needed candy bars or soft drinks or fresh pastries and stressed at each visit to John Clark the importance of stocking healthy items in the machines, such as unsweetened candy and whole wheat products and diet drinks and water and items that would not get wedged in dentures or cause acid reflux or contain sugar, salt, or other deadly additives, which pretty much eliminated any of the usual stock John Clark carried on his truck. Therefore, it was a constant struggle each week to bring product in that Miss Lena approved of, and so he began stocking the machines with only a small number of choices, which gave way to Miss Lena complaining on her weekly list of crimes and sins he'd committed about the sad variety of choices the residents had to choose from, an ongoing discussion which usually ended with John Clark standing and listening and nodding and smiling, then bringing in two orders, one that Miss Lena would check in and semi-approve of, and the other a hidden supply in his crate under an assortment of cloth money bags which he loaded into the machines so the residents would have something to buy, and after stocking the machines with the hidden order he would spirit the checked-in order out in his clothes or hidden in the delivery tub and store them in his truck until next week, when he would present them to Miss Lena all over again.

Miss Lena was here this day, all right, but he didn't in his current state of unbeing have to wait for her to let him in. He was free nowadays to enter the corridor all on his own time and take the hallway back to the recreation room and the two floors without signing in. Moments like this were what made being dead and gone and a part of the spirit world tolerable and even worthwhile. He would like to know what Miss Lena might think if she knew he was in the building without her knowledge or consent. He imagined her pursing her lips or bordering on a coronary attack just being aware that the one person she enjoyed making life miserable for was now back from the grave doing exactly what he wished and she could do nothing about it. She couldn't call Donna or Jimmy and complain. She couldn't tell anyone her dilemma or she might find herself being carted away to the funny farm, or at least transferred to some other work area where she would not present any level of madness to the public. She might even wonder if she was imagining such an occurrence, that maybe there was no ghost of John Clark Hayes from Tasty Snacks roaming around the building unsupervised and she was going off her rocker in the same way a lot of the residents with dementia had done before getting dropped off here. Maybe if she wasn't careful she might find herself up on the second floor herself, with her room locked during the night and no sharp objects about and a monitor on her actions twenty-four hours a day.

She didn't want to be put away, so she would have to be quiet. Grin if she could and bear it. John Clark liked thinking of her this way.

He loaded the three snack machines with as many sweet and sugary products as he could metaphysically come up with. There were Milky Ways and Three Musketeers and Paydays and Twinkies, chocolate cupcakes and pretzels and potato chips of every flavor, even on the bottom shelf where he would generally stock antacids and cough suppressants he now loaded down with Life Savers and Jolly Ranchers. The way he looked at it was most of the folks living here had been brought to this place to die, so someone should at least make their last days pleasurable. Let their teeth rot out if they still had any, let their dentures stain, their cholesterol go through the roof, their blood pressure and blood sugar take off for the outer limits. Fly me to the moon, he thought happily, and started whistling the tune. Who cared? No one could hear him now.

He forced himself to not do anything ugly to Miss Lena on his way out, even though he had the feeling that without him around to devote her hatred toward she would soon shrivel up and die, and this could be the last time he saw her. Let it ride, he told himself. Take the high road now the same way you tried to when you were one of them. Don't give yourself over and go over to her desk and pull some Claude Rains stunt on her like picking up her stacks of papers and sprinkling them around the room, or taking the phone off the cradle and wrapping the cord around her neck, maybe even taking her bottled water and pouring it over her head—no, he wouldn't do that. He had never given anyone in the world what they truly deserved before and he wasn't going to start now. No sense in stooping this late in the game.

When he got outside he was through for this day. He didn't need his truck anymore so he wished it away. He wondered who was driving his real truck these days? He hadn't bothered yet to go by and see. There was still time to do that later.

Seven

Two months had passed and he still had not come home, but Wolfie and Rebecca had no sense of time going by and the calendar turning, and so it all became like one long day where they slept and ate and waited for his arrival. It was perhaps puzzling for it to be the woman Brenda who fed them now and let them out in the yard, but in the past their John Clark had gone away on trips but he had always returned after a time, and so they waited. The last thing he had said to them on the last morning they saw him was "Be back!" which is what he always told them in the early mornings when he left to go wherever he went during the weekdays, but he'd always returned as he promised, he'd come back the way he said he would, and so they thought if they waited he would be back at some point during this very long day.

Wolfie was a rescue hound and terrier mix who'd come home with John Clark when John Clark had gone by the humane center to service their machines. Wolfie was in the lobby getting ready to go for a walk in the fenced area out back, and John Clark uncharacteristically said to hell with the route for a few minutes and asked if he could walk Wolfie , and so they had gone outside and Wolfie had grinned at him with his teeth showing and howled for a little when a fire truck drove by with its siren on, and so with his teeth and his howl and the fact that he was going home with John Clark and needed a name he became Wolf, after both the animal and the Look Homeward, Angel author minus the e, and so on his second month onto heaven Wolf drove around in the truck for the rest of the route and by the time they got home he had become Wolfie.

It was maybe a month later when Rebecca showed up on the back porch wet and bedraggled and pregnant, and when John Clark opened the door she ran inside and made for the library and took a right and had kittens in his study closet. John Clark managed to find homes for the kittens and took Rebecca (he had named her by then) in to the vet to be neutered, and in the afternoon he picked her up and brought her home to live with Wolfie. Wolfie offered to bite her and chew her up some, but Rebecca said no thanks and laid her claws one good time on Wolfie's nose, and they were friends thereafter.

Rebecca slept in the study and looked out the window at the birds and squirrels, and Wolfie slept in the library and in the breakfast room and in any of the four bedrooms and now and then in the kitchen by the refrigerator and chewed on toys he'd been given and household items that had not been assigned to him and had his dinner and his breakfast alongside Rebecca.

And these years later Wolfie and Rebecca looked and waited and wondered where their John Clark was and when during this long day he might be back.

***

David's pickup had six boxes of goods loaded in it, LPs and magazines and books and a lot of things that John Clark had collected and picked up over the years and kept because they were treasures to him and he couldn't bear the thought of letting them go. David and Franklin had been careful not to go into the library and study and start snatching up things at random, because if they made too big a dent in one portion of their father's stuff then it was almost certain that their mother and sister would spot the absence and know some of the collection had been plundered. They wouldn't have to hire a detective to know who the culprits were. They would know it was Franklin or David or both.

The items were so numerous that it was possible to get a fair representative from each of the genres: two boxes of LP albums from the vinyl collection which still left a dozen boxes behind, a box of old 45s from the fifties and sixties, pristine, shiny, almost new, still in sleeves, periodicals and magazines in plastic wrappers, newspapers saved from the JFK assassination to the first men on the moon, Nixon's resignation, the Twin Towers crumbling to the ground, pristine editions of Hemingway and Fitzgerald and Salinger, baseball cards arranged by teams from the long ago, photographs of movie stars and athletes and notorious criminals brought to justice, the Challenger exploding, Lee Harvey Oswald getting blown away by Jack Ruby. There was so much packed away that a little something absent here and a little something gone there surely wouldn't be missed, since there was no beginning inventory to reference it. As long as they didn't get too greedy David and Franklin figured they could get away with some unauthorized lining of their pockets and no one would be the wiser.

Of course, Franklin didn't desire to be too stealthy in their undercover burglary. Whatever David suggested they take and in what proportion Franklin wanted to at least triple the heist volume. Why take things that might make them a couple of hundred on the side when they could really load up and snatch anything that wasn't bolted down and perhaps rack up a couple of grand when the illicit proceeds got divided up?

"People eat this kind of shit up," he argued. "We could get this crap into the hands of the right people and they'd be throwing money at us right and left. There's probably stuff sitting around here that could make us rich as hell so much we could quit our jobs and go to Europe and play around for the next couple of years."

"There's a lot here, but some of it's junk," David said. "A lot of the people who'd want this stuff can't shell out big bucks for it because they're dead already. We're talking about a limited market here, which is why I say let's skim some of the good stuff off the top before it all gets lumped together and sold as a whole, and that way you and me can at least see a fair amount of cash from it."

Franklin didn't say anything more about it, but David knew his little brother well enough to keep his eyes on him throughout the entire pilfering process. They had to be fairly quick in case anyone happened to come home early or drop by, but that fact, as David suspected, didn't stop Franklin from attempting to hide a couple of boxes of relics behind their father's Wurlitzer, arranging them so the curtains covered them up and they would be there when he came back later by himself to get them. He would have probably gotten away with it too, had not Wolfie, who had watched them steadfastly since they arrived, gone over to the curtains to sniff what was behind them and took his paw and pushed the curtains aside to see for himself.

"What the hell is this?" David asked.

"I was going to load it last," Franklin told him. "I know a place that will give us a great price on it, and it's right on the way. I didn't want to have to dig it out."

"You're a lying sack of shit," David said. "I should have never let you in on this."

"Hell, it was my idea," Franklin said. "I was the one who let you in on it."

For a long moment the two brothers looked at each other, considering whether to return to a time-honored tradition and begin smacking the holy hell out of each other and wrestling down the hallway until one of them was injured and began asking for mercy, which was always the signal to continue the pounding and the vice grips and the smashing because if the one who was winning made the mistake of letting up their attack then the loser would be granted a reprieve and stay of execution and be given the chance to regain lost ground and footing and turn the tables on the aggressor and inflict some damage of their own. But seeing how they were pressed for time and were much more mature these days than in the past, they silently decided within themselves to let this moment pass and return to the job at hand and save the thrashing and the mauling and the beating to a pulp until later.

"If we're going to do this we need to hurry up and get it done," David said. "I have to get back to work sometime, you know. I told my boss I had to go to the doctor, but that doesn't mean I've got all frigging day."

Franklin didn't feel much like brawling this moment either, especially when he considered his lard-ass brother probably had fifty pounds on him and could possibly smush him if he managed to get on top of him during a battle, so he said nothing further and went and picked up the boxes that were behind the curtain. He wanted to give Wolfie a swift kick for revealing his hiding place to David, but he knew better than that. Wolfie was his dad's dog, and Wolfie had never made any bones about how he felt about everyone else in the family. He would tolerate them, but he only loved John Clark. Franklin wondered how many times Wolfie had growled at him when he walked into his dad's study while his dad was reading or writing? At least a million times, he was sure of it. And hadn't Wolfie over his lifetime taken a nip at everyone in the house at least once? Hell, he remembered how it had been a common sight for the damn dog to lay in the doorway of the library and not let anyone get by, just guard the room until John Clark got home, like he was protecting the place from foreign invaders. So, hell's bells, he wasn't going to fool with this crazy dog now, even if his dad was gone and wasn't coming back. The dog didn't know it, and no one was going to be able to convince him otherwise until he dropped dead too.

To be safe, he decided to go back to the walk-in study closet and get another box rather than try removing the two behind the curtain. Wolfie was too zeroed in on them, and he didn't feel like getting bitten in about ten places this afternoon. If David wanted them so badly then he could run the gamut and get them himself.

David was outside moving the boxes around making room for the box of 45s he'd just brought out. He had his hand on one box and as he slid it to one side a top book moved and he saw the cover of the one beneath it. It was a book on giant monsters of the cinema, and there on the cover was King Kong carrying Faye Wray and towering over the New York City skyline. It was an old book and David remembered it from his father's collection. Once, on a Sunday afternoon when he was thirteen and Franklin was six, John Clark had taken them to the mall to the movie theater and treated them to a Sunday afternoon matinee of King Kong, which was getting a special showing on the big screen for movie enthusiasts who were entranced by old flicks. David sat there with his Raisinets and popcorn and watched King Kong stifle dinosaurs and eat natives and derail trains and was in the end totally entranced, unlike his stupid-ass little brother, who cried all the way through the fights and the decimation of Skull Island and the airplanes flying around Kong at the top of the Empire State Building. For months afterward David would sneak into his father's study when Wolfie was not on duty and read the book with King Kong on the cover over and over again.

Without opening the cover he already knew what was inside: King Kong and Godzilla and Gorgo and Rodan and the Beast from 20,000 Fathoms and The Monster That Challenged the World. Hell, he couldn't sell this book. He wanted it for himself. This was like finding an old favorite toy that he had never finished playing with.

He suddenly had this urge to start unloading the truck and take everything back inside.

In the study Franklin all at once experienced an overwhelming curiosity rush through him when he opened the flap of a Washington apple box and saw the fielder's glove resting on top of a lot of sports memorabilia. There were scorebooks and game programs and Sporting News papers and a baseball magazine with Mickey Mantle and Roger Maris crossing bats on the cover and two shoeboxes of baseball cards and an NBA poster with Wilt Chamberlain palming a basketball like it was a Concord grape. What he couldn't keep his hands off was the Wilson glove with its saddle-soaped leather and rawhide strings and the autograph of Minnie Minoso etched across the side. This had been his dad's glove once, and Franklin had been allowed to use it the first year he played Knothole. He was scared of the ball and couldn't catch anything unless it was a miracle of God and the ball somehow landed in the pocket, but he remembered it was the coolest glove of anyone's on the team. When he carried it around he felt like he was really something special. This glove in his hand had once made him somebody.

And now here he was, getting ready to get rid of it forever. It was like closing the door on his childhood, like he was making a statement that it had never existed.

He guessed he could put it aside and come back for it later, but that would mean he was separating it from its friends and family that resided here in the box with it. He didn't have time to begin digging through each box and deciding what stayed and what went, what was important to him and what didn't matter, because there wasn't time for that now. He and David were on a covert mission to exchange these memories and keepsakes for money, and this moment, for maybe the first time in his life, Franklin didn't think having a few loose bills instead of what he held in his hand was worth the trouble. This was a new sensation, and he wondered if he was suffering from too many beers and tokes last night, or if this sudden onslaught of decency was something that needed to be further extinguished tonight? Had he been neglecting his vices and keeping his impulses to a minimum so that he now was considering attempting to begin acting like a normal human being?

This was an eerie and new feeling. He hadn't had upright thoughts like this pass through his brain in years. He wondered what was happening. Was he getting soft and growing maudlin and sentimental in this new stage of adulthood?

He spotted David carrying a box back through the library door and wondered what was going on now.

"Before you say anything, I'm just going to tell you we can't go through with this." David continued on his way back to the study closet and continued with his speech. "It's creepy enough for us to get rid of Dad's things like they were all pieces of worthless shit we need to sell and get out of here, but it's another for you and me to sneak over here and haul off the things he loved without even looking at them. I'm an asshole, Franklin, but I've still got something of a conscience. I can't do it. And it's my truck out there, and I say we're not using it to do this today. Cuss me out if you want, but that's the way it is."

"Whatever. Let's load this stuff back up and get out of here before Mom gets home. I don't feel like spending all night telling her how we've both seen the light and are going to be good boys from now on. I'm feeling dumb enough already right now."

David looked at Franklin like he'd never seen him before, astounded he was getting no argument from him. He didn't know who was freaking him out more—his little brother or himself?

"Let's wrap this up for now," he said.

***

Nothing about this new tryst of hers was working out in any kind of positive way, so Donna was more than ready to call it quits as soon as possible. Marty McCool was a nice enough fellow once you got by his façade of bullshit, his posture as one of the city's biggest swingers and a ladies man of the utmost proportions. The truth was he was none of these things and it was all a show, and he knew it deep down inside himself but had forgotten after spending so many years building up his persona and practicing his web of deceit until now he believed all the fiction he had constructed around himself. It wasn't that he was so bad of a person at all. He wasn't. It was just hard working through the phony exterior he had layered upon himself for years, and even when she did manage to break through just a tiny bit there was nothing spectacular there to see. Marty McCool the Iceman was as tepid and dull as anybody else she knew, maybe more.

Marty certainly didn't measure up to Jimmy sexually, she had to admit it. She hadn't known what to expect when she first got in on this extramarital rigmarole, but she'd gone into it thinking that most anybody would be a better partner for her than her own husband, but now she'd come to the conclusion that Marty certainly was not, and it could be that Jimmy ranked higher

on the scale than she'd ever given him credit for. She almost felt she owed
him an apology for having such low expectations of him, that maybe old
Jimmy wasn't as bad of a husband and a lover as she'd made him out to be.

She was all set to tell Marty see you later and hoped that he would take it
good-naturedly and not cause trouble by trying to make the company drop
them and hire another vending company to come in and keep them stocked
in snacks. She didn't know how much power Marty wielded at the corporate
office, or if he happened to be evil enough to make her pay if she backed out
of an affair with him. She would have to be careful or there would be some
explaining to do on her part.

Like Life had always seemed to do for as long as she'd been around to notice
such things, she didn't have to worry about Marty McCool's reaction or what
low trick he might pull as an act of revenge, because she happened to come
across Jimmy's SUV parked in the business lot as she was pulling in to have
a heart to heart with Marty. It was a Wednesday afternoon, and she knew
the delivery time for the six stations in the group was on Mondays. She also
knew that she had taken no repair calls from the business lately, so she hadn't
forwarded any repair information to Jimmy to where he might come by to
see if he could get a machine working or not, and seeing his vehicle sitting
there made her stomach tense up a little with the thought that maybe he had
found out about her and Marty McCool the Iceman and had come down
here to do something about it. This was not anything she had ever believed
would happen. This could be very bad if it was true.

But she couldn't just put the car in reverse and ignore it, just drive away
and pretend she had never seen Jimmy's car parked here. She had learned
enough in the past that when a problem presented itself to her the best thing
to do was to go ahead and deal with it. Don't tell yourself it's a figment of
your imagination. Don't turn away and attempt to get involved with something else. Don't practice denial to the extent that when the something ugly
that you don't want to deal with does sidle up and take a bite out of you in a
vulnerable place you won't be totally shocked and have your hair turn white
because you didn't think such a horrible thing could ever happen.

She parked and walked up to the entrance and was about to open the glass
door that led to the front lobby when she stopped and peered through the
plate window and saw her husband leaning over the counter at the receptionist's desk talking, she supposed, to whoever was back there behind it.
She thought to herself for a minute and recalled a woman named Dolores,
who was in her thirties and was way ahead of the pack as far as the amount
of makeup she wore and the tightness and scantiness of her wardrobe that
she displayed at work each day of the week. Donna always categorized her as

a floozy, but she'd noticed how a lot of men around the place seemed to like her. Take her husband there. Good old Jimmy. He seemed to like her quite a bit if appearances meant anything.

No, this was not a business visit. She knew Jimmy better than to think anything plausible like that. It didn't take a master's degree for her to see what was happening.

Somebody behind the reception desk was obviously in heat, and Jimmy the Westminster Champion Dog had picked up the scent and was right there johnny on the spot attempting to do something about it. She had seen this kind of behavior before, at Christmas parties and any kind of gathering where alcohol and women were simultaneously present. Once it had been quite a bone of contention in her mind, but for the past few years she had come to believe that Jimmy had mellowed and was content to sit around the house and play on his computer and perhaps, if everything stayed within the lines and on the program, muster up the energy to have sex with her once or twice a month. It wasn't exactly a passionate marriage the two of them were sharing, but it was at least peaceful. She at least hadn't had the desire to maim or kill or divorce him as she did now.

Of course, before she did anything rash and showed her displeasure she had to be honest with herself and call her own name when it came time to play the blame game. At least what she saw of Jimmy this minute he was not engaged in any sort of lascivious behavior. He wasn't leaping over the counter attempting to fling off Dolores' clothing or taking off his pants or busying himself on his phone booking a motel room. No, he was only presently in the I'm-so-cute flirting stage and obviously hadn't quite had time just yet to get down to carnal matters. All of this might be in a state of planning for his future endeavors, but it was a far cry from where she herself was right this minute. She reminded herself how she was not blameless at all, that she was guilty of whatever transgression she was trying to affix to Jimmy, that whereas he might be in the exploratory planning stage she had already embarked on her voyage several times and was at this point in time in a holding stage. It didn't matter that she was going to pull the plug on Marty McCool the Iceman and herself; what mattered was she had already done what she was ready to lay the blame on Jimmy for.

She backed away from the door and walked back down the walk to her car. She thought about waiting there and following him when he came out to see where he might go, but then she thought it made better sense to go home and have a cup of tea and decide what was the best thing to do.

Jimmy had no idea Donna was outside the door observing him. He'd been busy chatting with Dolores for the past twenty minutes, the same way he'd been doing about three times a week for the past month, and he was certain he was making progress in his pursuit of her, but to tell the truth, now that it appeared he was going to wear out her defenses and win her over to giving him a little action he could sense a part of him losing interest in the entire operation. Dolores, after all, wasn't really all that great when it came down to cases. Her face wasn't near as pretty as Sam, his chocolate labrador, and she wasn't nearly as smart either. At first glance she had a body to die for, but on further study he'd determined a lot of this body was packed in or pumped up or enhanced artificially and over-compensated in places so a modicum of attention might be paid elsewhere that on close inspection was sorely lacking. In short, Dolores was okay for a while but had the tendency to wear off pretty damn fast, and he was almost to the point now where he believed today might be the last of his visits to see her and that he might fill his time better playing more games on his computer.

Then he saw Marty McCool come out of the elevator and head through the lobby to his car. Jimmy had only spoken to Marty maybe once since the account for the company had been established, but now he saw Marty almost stop when he saw Jimmy at the desk. He blinked once and continued out the door, and Jimmy wondered what that had been all about. It was like Marty had wondered what Jimmy was doing here, like just because he had an account with the company that was no reason for him to come around. There had to be something else he was here for.

"Don't worry about him," Dolores said. "He gives everyone I talk to a second glance just because he and I used to go out together. I guess he thinks he still owns me or something."

With Marty McCool the Iceman giving him a stare that wondered why he was allowed to be here or anywhere else on the face of the earth, Jimmy didn't much feel like standing at the reception desk shooting the breeze with Dolores anymore. He made up an excuse that he had an appointment on the other side of town in fifteen minutes and left the lobby and climbed in his car and left the parking lot headed for god knows where. He didn't want to stay here with Dolores and he didn't want to linger in the lot in case Marty McCool followed him out and decided to shoot him just out of general principle, and he didn't want to go home either, because by now Donna might be home and if he went there he'd be required to say something, and right this minute he didn't have a word to impart.

Donna didn't hang around the parking lot to follow Jimmy when he came out, because she didn't want him to know that she'd seen him there because he might just wonder why she was there herself. She also was fast to leave because she saw Marty come out the door and head off for the Green Meanie to go somewhere, lunch, she supposed, and she didn't want him to see her either because what she had to say to him still needed rehearsing and it was better to wait a little longer on that. She thought the most productive thing to do was go to the Sonic and order a big grape slush that would make her tongue turn purple and sit on Seesaw Hill at the park and watch the golfers go by playing the iron course. At one time she had played golf some herself, and she hadn't been bad at it, had, surprisingly, been pretty good for a beginner, and she wished she had never stopped playing and had her own clubs and could go out there right now. She wouldn't mind losing herself in something for a while. She might even like whacking the devil out of a ball to see how far it would go. Of course, this was an iron course, no woods or drivers allowed, so she couldn't do all that she wanted here. It seemed there was no place on the face of the earth where she might do exactly what she wanted. Too bad, so sad, she thought. That's the way the cookie crumbles.

It had been some time since she had been here last. She used to grab something to go when she worked at the Harris Teeter a mile away, but back then she couldn't linger too long because her lunch break was only thirty minutes. She couldn't spend any time reflecting or unwinding, just like now. She had to be back to clock in, to do some job, to be responsible for something, the same way it was now, with taking care of Tasty Snacks and getting dinner on the table at a decent hour. Lots of times she had to eat without Jimmy being there, because he was sometimes too busy to get home on time, he'd tell her, there was some machine that needed fixed or some details to work out on a client's contract. It was all a line of bull, and she'd known it all along. What it involved was exactly the kind of thing she'd seen this afternoon, him bent over a counter feasting his eyes on the likes of Dolores the Floozy or some other poor excuse for a romantic entanglement.

Just a few more minutes, please.

There were times when she and John Clark would take their lunch breaks at Harris Teeter together, and sometimes they would come here with just a soda from the machine out on the sidewalk and have a few tokes off one of John Clark's joints he carried around for what he called "emergency situations." If the goings on had been too crazy during the initial portion of their shifts then John Clark would call for a period of adjustment and they'd be allowed two and possibly three sincere inhalations before heading back to take care of business. It was amazing how trivial all the important stuff became in only a matter of minutes and a change of venue and the tiny effort it took to view the business world in a different way. John Clark was a master of survival. He knew what it took to keep the hounds at bay and maybe have them take off somewhere yapping after somebody else.

It was time to go. She didn't know when Jimmy would be home, but she knew she was going to have to talk to him sometime. Serious talk, she thought. The two of them needed to sit down and discuss where their marriage was going. Was it worth saving? Did they need to continue keeping up appearances as they'd been doing for probably longer than she knew, or was it best to not worry about what the rest of the world thought and end the charade and get on with their separate lives? She thought of herself as a single woman, working somewhere (she would not continue on at Tasty Snacks, she knew that already) playing the field as far as men went and waiting for some new exciting suitor to call her on the phone, and the idea did nothing to make her want her situation to go either way. All she could think about as far as men went was John Clark Hayes, who was way out there all right. He was as far away as the universe could take him. It was stupid. John Clark was dead and she was alive and it was always going to be that way. She had to be crazy to keep giving him valuable territory in her mind.

She was going to have to get real one of these days.

***

There wasn't any question that Jimmy believed Donna was seeing someone else and had a big fat affair going on. This was just another example of how stupid he could be sometimes. He could sometimes talk himself into buying in to almost anything, preferring usually to believe what he'd imagined wasn't happening. It simply wasn't in him to think that maybe his wife had been tempted to go astray for a while but had decided it wasn't the best thing to do and stopped. No, what Jimmy didn't want to consider was that Donna and her new lover were jointly playing him for a fool behind his back and having a good time doing it, really enjoying themselves at his expense, and that he was going to have to go into battle mode to keep them from attempting to make him look like an imbecile who couldn't satisfy his wife and had not the first clue what was going on around him.

Of course, Donna could have taken it upon herself to go to Jimmy after leaving Marty McCool behind and tell him how their marriage was at a crisis point, that it was time they either repaired it or went their separate ways, but that solution was not only asking for trouble but way too confrontational to her way of thinking. In the past she would have simply let things smolder and disappear without being acted upon, just, you know, let everything go unsaid and keep on being ignored until something new came along and took its place, but now she knew that wasn't going to work anymore and she was going to have to do something. She was going to finally have to act like a grownup.

She hated that.

She also knew that the more she deliberated on the subject in her mind the more entangled and complicated it would get, so she knew it was time to do one of those adult things she had always avoided and take responsibility for her actions and see what was the best way to rectify it. This started with her having to decide if she wanted her marriage to Jimmy to continue or not. She guessed the biggest question she had to answer to herself was did she love Jimmy or not. Did she love him enough to want to stay where she was right now?

She already knew the answer. Yes, she loved him some. Some, only some, but was only some nearly enough? Could she learn to live through the open gaps and shortcomings and holes in their relationship? She had for a while now, but the fact was it was starting to wear thin, else she would never have ventured off the straight and narrow and started anything illicit up with the likes of The Ice Man. She would have stayed put and continued to continue. But was she prepared to go back to doing that now?

Maybe it was the fact that she was getting older, noticing in the mirror and feeling in her head that she was beginning to get a little long in the tooth. She had never thought much about such a thing happening to her and maybe now it was starting to freak her out.

Maybe that was it, but maybe not.

What she really thought it all boiled down to was she had been riding the euphoria of a long, passionate kiss with John Clark Hayes on a long-ago night at a faraway party that existed now only for her, since John Clark was no more these days. Maybe she had been fine with her memories as long as she knew she was sharing them with him, that he had the same memories smiling in his head, but now that his had been dashed on a sidewalk by a couple of bullets she was having trouble remembering them all by herself.

So, what was this line of thinking going on in her head? Was she ruined for life now? Unable to move on to another relationship because she had once made out with John Clark Hayes? She had been in the vicinity of his company all these years, his aura, sharing the workplace and seeing him walking around the warehouse as a constant reminder that once she and he had been joined in a moment of fire and longing that was much more than stolen kisses in the dark and raging surges of sexual delight. She didn't want to admit to being tied to the past until she finally got to join John Clark in death, as if she was one of those women in cinema or classic literature or even Country Music who carried their feelings for one man through the years and to the graveyard where it would rest until the end of time. This was a whole lot of drama that she simply didn't need anymore. What was past was past. What was done was done.

She decided the sooner she had all this out with Jimmy the better it would be for both of them. She didn't know how much he knew or suspected, but she was determined not to cloak anything in secrecy anymore. Besides, there was the fact that Jimmy was probably not such a choir boy himself, that the possibility was great that he had done a good bit of straying on his own. She couldn't get the image out of her head of him leaning over the reception desk grinning and laughing with the company strumpet. She wondered what he would say if she confronted him with that in her own self defense? She wondered what excuse he might offer for being there, since going out and doing any actual labor seemed to be totally against his philosophy these days.

She saw his truck parked in the drive when she got to the house, so whatever tryst he might have been pursuing down at the radio hub must have been short-lived or scheduled for another time. She told herself not to mention seeing him there as she came in the door. She would just get down to business in a flash and get the show on the road, however it was going to transpire. Still, he hadn't gone off sniffing Dolores' scent after all. Donna told herself not to begin any kind of drama tonight, to let things ride until she knew exactly where she stood and what she wanted to do. She thought it best to wait until she had some vestige of sanity floating around in her being. Certainly, it might be at least a tad better than making a wild decision while the influence and essence of John Clark Hayes was still holding sway in her mind.

Jimmy heard Donna's car drive up and the door close. Down the hallway Judge Judy was on the television. Everybody in the courtroom was worked up about something and trying to out-yell the other. He had been sitting in the recliner off in his head for the last half hour, but now all the arguing brought him back to the real world surrounding him. Had he been asleep? Dreaming? He couldn't say for sure, but he had certainly not been alive and kicking inside this physical house waiting for Donna to get home. No, he had been somewhere else, some land where there was no business or family or loose women in his vicinity, only somewhere beyond his current vision where he had no memory of past transgressions or was sidled with a slate of sins he would someday have to atone for, but was instead in a city where there were no choices to make but the right ones, where he could lie down in bed at night and sleep with only the best of dreams around him, and he'd once again been that person whose life coasted along on magical currents, and there was no such thing as the person he had somehow become messing up the entitled tranquility he possessed. There was nothing foreboding at each corner and turn telling him he was in for it soon, and that the time would come when he would pay for the crimes he had allowed himself to commit.

He heard the door open as the voices from the courtroom grew louder. He raised his head up from the recliner and tried to decide if he should fake being asleep or get up and go see his wife and let the chips fall wherever they wanted. There was strong medicine he was going to have to take some time, and he wondered if he should go ahead and get it over with and swallow it down now. Maybe he should get up and start doing something, then maybe some inspiration might come to him.

Jimmy was not in the living room or the den as she'd thought he'd be. Donna found him back in the kitchen stirring a can of tomato soup on the stove. In the skillet on the other burner was some bread he'd just started grilling, cheese beginning to melt on the top.

"Getting ready to have some grilled cheese and soup," he said. "You want some? Plenty here for you too if you're hungry."

She was hungry. She hadn't known it until she'd seen the sandwiches and the bubbling soup. All of a sudden it was like her hunger had been the only thing in the world that was troubling her, and now that it was here before her everything could be remedied if she would just sit down and begin chewing and swallowing. This is the way people get fat, she told herself. When they have a problem they simply sit down and gorge themselves and hope it goes away. That's me to a tee, she thought, but it still seemed like a pretty good idea. It might be that pigging out was the answer to everything.

***

From somewhere that was not truly anywhere but a place where John Clark could look out at the world and see whatever he wanted, he watched his sons unload the truck and take boxes and tubs back into the house. This was good. This meant that, at least for today, unknown hands wouldn't be handling his possessions and strangers would not be taking them to their homes. Perhaps, he thought, there was hope for his two boys after all.

EIGHT

Brenda had already decided she was going to be a detective when she grew up, so she didn't need to dust for fingerprints or see if anything was missing when she got home, because she could tell from the minute she walked in the door that someone had been there. It wasn't just a lone someone either. She could tell it was more than one person and it didn't come as a complete shock to her that it was two and that the two were David and Franklin, her own darling sons, who had never been able to pick up after themselves or keep from creating a mess wherever they went. They had been sloppy and untidy and created chaos from when they were young boys and they hadn't improved a lot since. You'd almost have to be blinder than Ray Charles and Helen Keller combined not to know when the two of them had been around, so it was no surprise to her to know they had been here while she was gone to work for the day, for they both left a trail of guilt and deceit behind them as a tell-tale sign of their sneakiness and covert foul intentions. She already knew what they were up to and what they had planned, and probably had known what path they were going to take even before they did. She knew them both well enough to know that they were going to resort to some slimy undertaking when it came to dispersing John Clark's things. Lord knows, there probably hadn't been a single moment in the past twenty years when she hadn't noticed David disappearing during the evening to wander into John Clark's rooms to see what might be abiding there, and she was aware of times in the past when David had left with a book or an object of some importance in his hand on the pretense of borrowing it to read or peruse for a time, and how said items absolutely never returned to their rightful place. Whereas David would carry his procured items outwardly as if no misdeed was being committed, Franklin would always try and use his pockets or go so far as sticking something in his pants under his shirt, as if no one could tell he was carting something off beneath his clothing. Most of the time these heists occurred when John Clark was out of the house, in the past or now these last few months when he was really gone, and the belief they shared was these items of their father's were now for sure rightfully theirs and should be used as a profitable way of inheritance. Brenda had known what they were doing all along, how they felt and what depths they would jointly sink to, so it was no surprise they were already in the act of usurping the estate before the actual inventory and sale had the chance to begin.

She walked down to the library and walked in. Other than some occasional vacuuming and dusting, she hadn't frequented John Clark's domain much over the years. She didn't look at his books or the notebooks inside his desk or open the walk-in closet in his study and wonder what treasures might be contained in the boxes and file cabinets there. She had yet to sit down and go over any of his written manuscripts or check out the document folders on his computer. No, she didn't want to totally know what was there, what he had stored or was interested in all this time. She would leave that part to Linda. Linda was John Clark's favorite, the child who was most like him. She could look at his stories and manuscripts and decide if someone might want to publish them in some magazine or another.

All of it, everything that had been John Clark's, could go to her children if they wanted it. She was not in that camp. She had once had access to him but the two of them had mutually decided he was to take his things and his world and go elsewhere, if not physically, then spiritually. They would be married for a while and then amicably divorce but they would not anymore be in the same world together at the same time. It was stupid, but that was the way it had gone. They had somehow made it work.

The thing was, David and Franklin were welcome to the books and music and paraphernalia, but she wished they would not resort to attempting to taking it on the sly. They could perhaps be open about it. They could at least for once in their lives be a trifle honest.

But there wasn't time to worry about the those two right now. She had exactly forty-five minutes to change and get ready before Billy Joe came to pick her up. They were going to another one of his surprise restaurants again tonight. This would be the third one now, and the second this week. She'd halfway believed Billy Joe would have seen the writing on the wall and lost interest by now, but he was still hanging in there coming up on a month now, making phone calls, sending texts, asking her out to dinner and driving her all over town just to show her things he thought she'd find interesting. He'd taken her to the Island Pier and the Lighthouse Museum and driven her over to Jekyll Island to watch the sunset, and on each excursion he'd stopped at some eating place and attempted to fill her up with cuisine. Most of the time it was exotic foods and things she'd never heard of, and sometimes she liked it and sometimes she didn't, but she had to hand it to him for trying to show her a little variety. It had been so long since she'd been anywhere that was un-familiar, so she was at least entertained even if she sometimes found herself wanting to barf. It was a far cry from the days when she and John Clark were an actual couple, however long ago that was, when all they ever seemed to dine on were hot dogs and cheeseburgers and pizzas. And if it was a special occasion, an ice cream cone from any of the tourist shops along the beach.

With all this special attention being lauded on her, Brenda guessed she ought to be more thrilled by it than she actually was. The truth of the matter was she simply hadn't been able to decide about Billy Joe Bradford just yet. He was a nice enough guy and seemed to be decent through and through, but there was something about him she couldn't seem to completely trust, and she couldn't decide what that was. Of course, she had never trusted any man too much, and if the truth was told she'd never really fallen that hard for one either. Sure, it was true she'd been somewhat head-over-heels for Jimmy Baldwin for a time before John Clark endeared himself to her, and she stayed halfway smitten with John Clark for a while all through their courtship and the first couple of years of their marriage before she found herself losing interest. She'd never been able to decide if it was John Clark's fault that she came to be that way, what with his mysterious ways of going off inside himself to that place where no one else was welcome, or if it had been her who turned away and took a step back and left John Clark on his own after he'd done everything in his power to make her fall in love with him. She suspected the latter. A big part of her believed that John Clark had sensed she would never stay in love with him and had released her from the obligation so neither of them would be hurt when the end result came to be. That was the way he was. If he thought he was obstructing the path to happiness for anyone he would do his best to clear the walkway and get out of the way himself. He wanted no part of making anyone unhappy.

She didn't go to any great lengths to spruce herself up for this date with Billy Joe. She had long stopped caking herself with makeup or piling on fake eyelashes and coating her mouth with lipstick. She was not going to look like a girl again and she knew it, so she might as well be comfortable in this transition from middle-age into becoming an old bag. She didn't know how many years she actually had left before this happened, but she'd come to terms with the fact it was inevitable and someday soon she was going to look like Grannie Clampett.

But yes, it was strange to hear the doorbell ring and stranger still to know a man—a gentleman caller as they used to say in the movies—would be standing there awaiting admittance so he could escort her out to a fancy place or an interesting location and make an overt attempt to entertain her and amuse her and make her evening somewhat more memorable than what she'd been accustomed to for at least the past decade and probably more, and that would be escaping with the television or reading another cozy mystery or accompanying her friends out for dinner and awarding herself with a frozen margarita, one and only one, and then coming home to turn on the television again or open a Southern Living magazine before going to bed. Sometimes, maybe, to listen to her messages or check her email or, god forbid, see what was happening on Facebook. Sometimes Linda would call to check on her, but never David or Franklin at night. No, the boys would always wait until everyone was at work before they made contact. That way they wouldn't have to worry over having to come by or making an appearance or fulfilling some sort of appointment. Then suddenly it would be eleven or so and past her bedtime, and she would be free to go to dreamland after she let the dog in and made sure both he and the cat—John Clark's pets—had food and fresh water for the night, and then it was safe to go to bed and sleep seven hours until the alarm rang and it was time to go back to the library for another day, which was a blessing, that going to work, it gave her something to do and filled up the void until the evening came and it was time to do it all again.

But there was a man at her door now breaking up the routine, and in a way she was glad and grateful, but in another way she was sad and resentful, because it meant her old life was a thing of the past and what had once been wonderful, however small and fleeting, was not going to come again.

She did not mention any of this to her friends or her children and certainly not to Billy Joe Bradford, because she did not want anyone feeling sorry for her or worrying she might succumb to a life of sadness and scorn and bitterness, and she didn't want to be known for that. She wanted the world to believe that she was happy, that she had her life in order, and that there was not a thing out there in the world she could not live without. She didn't want anyone looking at her and shaking their head in some expression of pity for the way she had landed during the revolutions of the earth. She wanted to be considered okay. She wanted everyone to turn their benevolence to someone besides her. She didn't want anyone offering a helping hand, because she was on her feet and didn't need one. That was just the way it was.

Yes, the doorbell had rung and Billy Joe Bradford was there on the porch, waiting for her to open the door so he could save her from herself and make her happy again, and she didn't know truthfully if she wanted to be saved or if happiness was a thing she'd decided was overrated, that if you happened to have it you would soon see it go and then sadness would come over you like a wave, and you would be washed out to sea with no island of joy anywhere for you to walk in the sand and watch the tides come in and go out. Maybe it was best not to have it, then you wouldn't feel so bad when it was gone.

Naturally, Billy Joe was ten minutes early. She let him in and explained that she wasn't ready to go yet and he said he was sorry to be early but he just couldn't wait to get here because he liked being with her so much. Brenda didn't know whether this was bullshit or not, but it was at least rather original, since she hadn't had anyone be so entranced to be in her presence in quite a long time. Maybe forever, she amended.

She went off to finish her preparations, however small, and Billy Joe lingered in the dining room. He had not had the opportunity to look around at Brenda's house too much until this moment, so he walked over to the mantle above the gas fireplace and looked at the pictures of her children when they were small. They appeared fairly normal, although the oldest boy did border on looking like a doofus and the younger son looked as if he was looking for something illicit to get into. The daughter looked fairly normal, almost pretty. She wasn't as pretty as her mother, so maybe she took after her father in the looks department.

Speaking of Brenda's dearly departed husband, there were no pictures of him to peruse here with the children, which seemed a little strange. Billy Joe looked first at the small dining room and then off to the kitchen, which both appeared devoid of memorabilia, so he meandered down a short hallway on the opposite side of Brenda's and the other three bedrooms and nosed into a room filled with books on all four sides, each shelf laden with volumes from foot-high all the way to the ceiling. In the center of the room was a desk, which almost looked like one that would appear in an elementary school library. The surface was stacked with books in five piles, and Billy Joe looked at some of the titles and saw such names as James Joyce and Raymond Carver and Virginia Wolff and Ross Lockridge, and he realized these were probably books Brenda's husband had planned to read one day before he'd been killed in his accident, and Billy Joe gazed around the room at the mountains of books and wondered if this was all Brenda's husband's collection.

Off to his right at the corner of the room was another doorway. He started to take a peek inside to see what was there, but at that moment a dog appeared from within the room and stood in the opening peering at him. For a moment the two were frozen regarding each other's presence, each one as if they were afraid to move until they'd given the proposal some thought, and then the dog began to growl.

It was a low growl and one that meant business. The dog was not immense or rugged looking or looked like it would be pleased to tear someone apart at any given moment, but the growl was not one that was composed of yips or yaps or might be emitted from a dog who was singing soprano in a canine choir and was able to hit such high octaves because he or she was not a watchdog or a guard dog or a fighting, vicious type of animal but because it was timid and fearful and wanted nothing to do with combat or survival tests or protecting one's master's possessions from would-be burglars, robbers, and thieves. No, this dog was ready to rumble. Billy Joe could see that. He thought it might be best to leave the room and let the dog have it to itself.

He told himself not to run. He decided it was best to back slowly away while saying such conciliatory words as nice doggie and good boy and take it easy there and inch slowly backwards until he could reach the door and slam it shut and take off for the safety of the living room. He hoped the dog wouldn't bark or howl or throw itself against the door with jaws gnashing and sharp teeth clicking. He didn't really want to explain to Brenda that he'd been prowling around the house checking out the layout. She'd mentioned she had a dog before, but she hadn't told him it was a killer. It sort of made him wonder if she didn't want him around or not, seeing how she'd left him alone to maybe get bitten or mauled by an overprotective pet.

"Two minutes," Brenda called.

Billy Joe started to sit down on the living room sofa, but there was a cat sprawled out at one end, lying on its side with its tail swishing and a glint in its smoky eyes, and Billy Joe knew better. There was something about this cat that spelled trouble. It was just like that demon dog he'd just finished escaping from, something in its aura that suggested malice aforethought. He stayed on his feet and let the cat have the sofa to itself. He backed off without turning his back to it, not giving it the advantage of a surprise attack, which he was sure was imminent, since it had now occurred to him that the animals inside Brenda's house were possessed by some spirit that held sway over them and commanded them to do its bidding, and for the first time he wondered if these animals, the vicious dog and the malevolent cat, were once pets of Brenda's husband before he moved on to another state, and if he was still having them do his will from his place in the Great Beyond. This was a stupid manner of thought passing through his head, he knew that, but there was something in his consciousness that assured him it was true.

The tail swished a little faster and the cat growled low in its throat. Billy Joe decided to go and wait for Brenda by the door.

Brenda was almost ready to go when her phone rang for about the forty-eighth time. It was Linda again, and she wondered what was so important that she would keep calling her every ten minutes. She didn't dare answer it, because then she would have to say she was in a hurry and couldn't talk now, and then Linda would want to know why she was in such a hurry and where was she going, and Brenda didn't feel like concocting a big lie to placate her right this minute. She hadn't yet gathered up the gumption to inform any of her children that she was seeing someone on a fairly regular basis, because she didn't think anyone in the family—herself included—was ready for such a shocking revelation just yet. Not so soon after John Clark's departure. Her children would be slow to grasp the gravity of the situation, and even if they were successful in doing so and more mature than she'd ever given them credit for being, she still doubted her own self and was unsure if she had taken hold of the situation yet or was still living in denial of what was going on in the real world.

She could hear Wolfie barking and raising hell down at the other end of the house, and she wondered what was going on. She had fed him in the kitchen not so much as thirty minutes ago, and as far as she could remember she hadn't been down by the library since she'd gotten home, but that was definitely where all the commotion was coming from. Well, she couldn't go off and leave the silly dog going crazy like this, because, knowing him, he'd decide to eat a shelfful of books as a way of voicing his protest. John Clark had spoiled the dog to no end. If Wolfie didn't get his way he'd make sure there was all hell to pay.

She opened the library door wondering how it got closed and Wolfie bolted out like Jesus had released some demons from somewhere in the house and it was Wolfie's job as head canine to chase them all into the sea, which was at least five miles away but still had to be done. He ran breakneck down the hall and made a hard left at the living room door and stopped on a dime, unsure of whether he should attack Rebecca the cat seated on the sofa with the swishing tail and the menacing growls coming from her throat or the man with his hand on the doorknob opening the front door so as to make a run for safety to his car. Brenda caught up with Wolfie barely in time to grab his collar and keep him from lunging at the figure going out the door to see if he could extract some flesh along with a good portion of the pants the stranger was wearing. It took a good four steps for Brenda to halt Wolfie's forward progress, but she managed to stop him just past the coffee table and three feet from the door and Billy Joe's beckoning rear end that by the way Wolfie was snapping and gnashing definitely needed biting now and certainly in the near future.

"Sorry," she told Billy Joe. "You'd better go out and get in the car. I don't know what's got into him. I've never seen him act like this before."

"It's either rabies or hydrophobia," Billy Joe said, looking back over his shoulder. "This dog's definitely not ready to make nice. Whatever it is, that cat has it too. I was expecting it to go after my throat any minute until the dog showed up. It was like all of a sudden I had my choice of how I wanted to die."

"Go on out. I'll lock up and be right behind you."

The door closed and immediately Wolfie relaxed and went slack. Rebecca curled up in a ball and all was well, and Brenda wondered what had brought this all on and what, if anything, these animals were trying to tell her.

***

Judy Robinette did not make it a practice to go out for lunch very often. There was really nothing much around restaurant-wise that appealed to her, and if she had to get in her car to go anywhere most of her allotted hour would be used up just going back and forth. This was why she generally liked to bring a sandwich from home and sit in the breakroom watching General Hospital and drink water from the soda machine and Cracker Jacks from the snack machine for dessert. She had followed this routine fairly regularly for the past two years since she'd been at this branch of Lancaster Hills Credit Union, and she guessed it would still be the same except for the fact that the new person couldn't seem to keep the snack machine stocked with Cracker Jacks the way the last man had always done, the one who'd been shot that morning during the attempted robbery. The lack of sufficient Cracker Jacks inventory in the machine was only a small indication of how things had changed around her place of employment since that terrible morning. Not only did the nice man who'd stocked their refreshment machines die just like that without any warning that day, but the entire mood of the daily routine changed too. No longer was LHCU a friendly place for its patrons to visit and a nice place for its employees to work, for the prone man dead on the sidewalk had changed all that permanently. Now when someone walked in the door the first thing Judy and her fellow employees did anymore was to see how he or she was dressed and if they appeared to be packing and what their intentions seemed to be and not to smile and greet them first thing and ask what you could do for them. No, overt friendliness was out and preliminary suspicion was in. That was the way it was now.

Hardly a day went by when Judy didn't think of the nice man bearing Cracker Jacks and smiling at her as he passed her slot at the drive-thru window, and how she'd always asked if he remembered her Cracker Jacks today and how he'd pick up a box from his bin and hold it up for her to see. And always when he was leaving he'd go outside and walk by the drive-thru window and place a free box of Cracker Jacks in the tray and say here's something to tide you through until lunch.

His name was John Clark Hayes. She hadn't known it until she read about the robbery in the paper and saw it on the news that night. He'd been employed by Tasty Snacks for eleven years and left behind a wife and three children. She'd known none of this while he was alive bringing in her supply of Cracker Jacks to keep her happy. All she'd ever known to do was smile at him and ask him the same question once a week and tell him thanks when he delivered a free box at her window when he was ready to go. The way she looked at it was he had a crush on her and was too shy to go any further than that. But that had been okay, because he was a lot older than her, and she liked having somebody like that pay attention to her and think she was cute, and sometimes, if she wasn't too busy at the window, she wondered if he thought of her all the time and looked forward to seeing her each week, that maybe he would go to the ends of the earth to find some Cracker Jacks to bring her if his regular supplier happened to be out.

It was mostly in the mid-afternoons that Judy Robinette considered the absence of John Clark Hayes. The mornings were generally busy and closing time meant balancing her till and securing all transactions and getting ready to go home, maybe to have a date with one of the four men who called her up and requested her company these days, or sometimes to watch The Voice or America's Got Talent and go to bed early if she felt like it, but there were those dead times in the afternoons when she would peer out the window at her drive-thru and see the tray where a box of Cracker Jacks had at one time regularly appeared, and that was when she would miss John Clark Hayes and wish that she could ask her question and smile at him and wave goodbye to him with her fingers again, the way she didn't ask or smile or wave at anyone much anymore these days.

***

They had given him a pass card to get in downstairs, which you also had to use to access the elevator to get to the seventh floor, where Southeast Global's offices were. No one had ever figured out that this pass card could be used at any hour of the day and one who possessed such could come inside at all hours, which John Clark Hayes, seeing as how disagreeable and uppity most of Southeastern Global's employees were, was more than happy to do. On Friday mornings he made them his first stop of the day, arriving sometime between four and five to fill the snack machines and load the soda machine with twenty ounce bottles of Pepsi, Coca Cola, Diet Coke, Mountain Dew and three rows of Aquafina water. It was one of his longer jobs, since it required a good distance from the garage to the door to the elevator and up seven floors, then an inventory to see what was needed, then downstairs to fill the order and cover the distance again.

He found if he was diligent and ordered enough he could finish his task in less than an hour, and if he was successful he always rewarded himself with a seat at a table by the big plate glass window overlooking Beachview Drive where he could sit for five minutes or so and watch the sun rise over the horizon before going on to his next stop, enjoying himself for a moment in time before the hateful employees of Southeastern Global began arriving for work.

He made it so and came in the early hours of the morning this time too, as was his custom, and he performed his spiritually remembered work in plenty of time to see the sun come up. While he was waiting he recalled the stormy Friday morning when he had been in this very place, when lightning had struck and the power in the building and all the neighborhood around went out. He had been forced to find his way to the machines in the dark, since he'd left his phone in the truck so as not to weigh him down which left him without any light, and he'd opened the doors of each machine and filled them with product by memory just as an experiment to see how extensive his knowledge of the place was, knowing what went where on which shelf and how many items he had in his supply and in the end feeling certain he had a perfect score, and when he had finished he found the elevators were out of service too, so he had taken his bin and expandable two-wheeler and made it down seven flights of stairs without falling or stumbling even once. When he made it to the truck the power had come back on, and though he was risking running into an early-arriving employee he couldn't keep from going back inside and riding the elevator up to Southeastern Global's office and checking out his handiwork, seeing if the machines looked right, if everything was in the correct slot and working properly. They were, as he'd known they would be. He laughed to himself then and he laughed now, because the old adage people used all the time was entirely true with him. He could do this job in the dark. He could be blindfolded and do it again the same way now. He could do it with his eyes closed. He could do it in his heavenly sleep.

He was gone before the first employee made it into the garage.

NINE

She'd given Marty McCool his walking papers on a Thursday and he'd taken it like a man. He hadn't whined or asked why or coiled himself up like a poisonous snake and struck out at her, but had simply smiled and said I understand and wished her luck in the future. Guess this was one of those things that just didn't work out, he told her, and he was so calm and decent about it Donna felt like picking up the sugar cannister on the table inside the Island Coffeeshop and smashing his face in with it just because it didn't seem like that big a deal to him. She didn't disfigure his features any, but had just gotten up from her chair and wished Marty a happy future too and left the building in as calm a way as possible, not wishing to draw attention by cursing and crying uncontrollably or running out of the place like she had just seen the way the world was going to end and didn't want anything further to do with it.

This hadn't worked out the way she'd wanted. Not only was the choice to have some variety in her sex life something that had backfired and made her feel creepy, but she was certain Jimmy knew what she'd been doing and was biding his time before saying anything about it. She wasn't frightened that he would do anything like try and kick her out of the house or beat her up, but he might attempt something with the business that would benefit him financially. She wasn't sure what that was, because she was pretty certain Jimmy would never try and take Tasty Snacks away from her because that would mean he'd lost his best worker and would have to do things by himself in the future, which would mean he would have to leave the house and go into work and be seen and have an everyday presence, balance the books and acquire new customers and keep the ship running smoothly, all things she took care of now, and she couldn't see Jimmy diving into those areas willingly. No, he'd be much more likely to come up with something subtle and underhanded for his settlement in such an issue, some kind of devious blackmail that had no classification and couldn't be described in words.

She wanted to get it everything out in the open but decided maybe it was okay this way after all. She no longer would be lowering herself and sneaking around with men she had no desire for; she could continue to handle any crisis of the company without worrying about Jimmy being around to get in the way. The more she thought about it the two of them leading separate existences the better it sounded. Maybe being on her own for a while would give her time to decipher what the big problem in her life that was plaguing her constantly exactly happened to be. Once she recognized what was wrong at the core of it all, she'd be more apt to come up with a solution and shrink it down to size, and whether Jimmy fit anywhere in that answer was anybody's guess right now.

***

They started to all go out and eat at a restaurant somewhere, Linda leaving Mark and the kids at home and David and Franklin coming by themselves, and then the three of them and Brenda would go and eat and discuss the coming sale and how they wished to go about it, perhaps making some decisions on who could have what beforehand if it was that important and meaningful to them, but then they decided they all had better sense than to take this show on the road where the public could observe them and listen in on what was probably going to be a series of arguments and fights and a host of raised voices, so instead they decided to go visit the Colonel and eat fried chicken and mashed potatoes at the dining room table and conduct their disagreements within the privacy of the family manor. It seemed to be about the only thing everyone agreed on. They decided on six as a meeting time, so when Franklin was still not there at half past they went ahead and started without him, especially after he didn't or wouldn't answer his phone when David tried calling him. Everyone took a turn ringing his number before they decided to go ahead and dive in. They were about ten minutes into the meal when they heard Franklin pull up outside, but it was another five minutes before he made it through the door to join them.

He'd been listening to Spotify, he told them. Led Zepplin. It wasn't too difficult to tell he was high.

"I think it's time we go ahead and get this done," Brenda said. "We can't settle your father's estate and get down into the stipulations of the will until this sale and what's going to be in it gets agreed on."

"We already know about the will," Franklin said. "Everybody gets one-fourth of the assets and Mom gets the house. Everybody's got a payment from his life insurance and what we sell gets divided up four ways. There, I've solved it. I think I should be awarded the legal fees, since we don't really need a lawyer now."

"You forget about taxes," David said. "Some of this stuff's deductible and some isn't."

"That's the reason we have a lawyer," Linda said. "He's the one who's supposed to figure this stuff out for us."

Franklin issued a snort.

"What if I don't trust the clown we hired?"

"You should have said something about it two months ago," David said. "It's too late now."

"Whatever the case is," Brenda stated, taking over the floor as she felt was her right, "we need to decide on a plan and all get on board with it, because I'm tired of all this bickering and meandering. I don't know if everyone's aware of it or not, but your father's death has taken a toll on me. Since it happened I've hardly been able to think of anything else. We may have been divorced but we were still a part of each other's lives. Even if your father seemed distant sometimes he was always involved in everything that went on around here." She paused a moment for effect and to perhaps make herself appear uniquely pitiful and deserving of some help facing the situation, but she could tell her ungrateful offspring were waiting for her to get through with her sob story so they could get on with the business of padding their pocketbooks. "I'd think you all would be ready to put this to rest too and not keep living in chaos wondering who's getting what and if everything will be fair and square and when this is all going to end."

"I say we sign off on the original will and turn the estate over to the lawyer to get settled," Linda, being the most even-minded of all the Hayes clan, or at least in her mind, said. "I agree this has gone on long enough. It's almost Thanksgiving. Daddy is probably turning over in his grave now watching and knowing what a complicated mess we're making of everything."

"Daddy's not in any grave," Franklin pointed out. "He got cremated, remember? That was another one of those things we haven't agreed on too. He's still in that damn box back in the library waiting on us to decide where to sprinkle him."

"Daddy isn't watching us, no matter where he happens to be," David stated. "He'd tuned us all out when he was living; you can bet your life he's not worrying about us now."

"Well, this is just ridiculous," Brenda said. "All we're doing is spinning our wheels, acting like if we wait your father is going to appear before us like Jesus did with the Disciples and tell us exactly what we need to do and what will happen after we do it. The faster we all agree to agree and let the lawyer get everything rolling the faster things are going to go and get better for all of us. If we spend any more time shuffling our feet on this then I'll be the next one to go and it will be twice as bad for all of you."

"I'm willing to bet the ranch you'll outlive all of us," Franklin said. "You're pretty much taken care of more than the rest of us. Of course, Linda has Mark who's got a good-paying job and David's fixing to acquire another breadwinner for himself if he can ever set a date, so if they get left alone they'll have Social Security or pensions and benefits coming their way, but I don't have anything right now. I'm the one who's out here on his own in the world trying to get through school with nothing to fall back on if anything bad happens. I used to go in and ask Daddy for spending money when I was fourteen or fifteen or so, and he'd look at me like he didn't know my name or anything, like I was some beggar who'd just walked in off the street. I've known since he died I was going to be on the short end of the stick and be left on my own the rest my life."

"How is it then that you're the only one of us he ever bought a new car for?" Linda said. "David and I had to go to work and save up before we even got something used. But not you. Heck, you don't even have any college debt to pay off."

"I gave both of you money for cars," Brenda said. "Your father paid your insurance too. So both of you need to stop acting so pitiful."

"We still had to make payments," David said. "Franklin sure as hell didn't."

"That's because the car Daddy bought me was as cheap as they get. A Vega, for Christ's sake. There wasn't a worse car anywhere on the road, and that's what I got stuck with driving everywhere."

This was an argument that had been going on for years, who had been treated worse than the other, so it wasn't like they were moving on to new business. It was the same old thing all over again.

"Jesus," David said. "Where do I sign? I can't take another five minutes of this family togetherness crap."

***

This family forum was exactly the sort of thing John Clark couldn't be a part of when he'd been a member of the earth, and even now being pretty much far removed from the grime and the dirt and having the knowledge of the ages that these events not only go on but are eternal it was still not the kind of thing he liked to see and was certainly not what he wished to be a witness to since becoming attached to the hereafter. Even while being embroiled in life and its daily patterns as he had for fifty-two years, he still remained proud of the fact that he never willingly joined in on the circus acts human beings seemed to prefer performing.

The thing of it was he'd watched Brenda and his children for two months now since his departure, and it was pretty clear not much had changed. They all still seemed to interact with each other in the same way, like they thought the other was stupid and thus didn't deserve the rewards and status they were pretty sure was soon to undeservedly come their way. Not only were they all embarked on their same separate paths, but they were lost on the trail more than before and were all seemingly glad to be headed in the wrong direction, like the failure of their journey was inevitable and it was important to make plans the coming fiasco could be laid at the feet of someone else, preferably a family member, since next of kin tended to always bear the brunt of villainy when difficulties arose. John Clark had been steadfast in keeping an eye on this former family of his, watching them from his unknown places as they took the next steps in their lives without his presence being in the world with them after such a long time, thirty-one years for Brenda since their courtship, marriage, divorce, and shared life thereafter, and for his children it was a matter of the time consisting of all their lives. They had never lived a day without him being alive in their world, and now in these months since his death they still seemed unable to adapt to living a life the least bit different from the one they'd experienced so far.

A few days after his passing—perhaps it had been on the very same day, he did not know, since that day when he'd stopped living had been a whirl of last breaths and thoughts and regrets going on within the changing over of his soul's regime and he'd not been able to fully concentrate on others—his earthly family, Brenda and Linda and David and Franklin, had wasted no time attempting to snatch some bit of substance contained within their familial borders and make off with it for themselves. Brenda envisioned keeping the house without him being around like before, and his kids instantly began growing claws that would help them physically and spiritually take hold of whatever vestige of a possession there was, be it physical or ethereal, and claim it for their own. Even now, with the contents of the will revealed and drawn up in as fair a way as he, John Clark, had possibly been able to construe, there was still the grabbing and the clutching and the attempts to jump what fair claims there were simply to take them all for the aggressor and leave nothing behind for anyone else.   How, John Clark wondered, could so simple a matter as his meager possessions on the earth divided in quarters become such a battleground? He had believed in his own foolhardy, trusting way that each of his relations would be happy with the fair way he had divided his estate, but now it appeared it might have been better if he'd done nothing and left everything behind to twist in the wind. They could have scuffled and fought over the proceeds with no rules to follow whatsoever and it would have been at least as peaceful as this. So much, he thought, for the high road and common legality and the swashes of courtesy he determined were no longer around. Why bother with them if it was apparent they didn't exist?

Still, he didn't know why he should be the least bit surprised as he watched these goings-on from his new place, which was like a stream-of-consciousness theater seat if you thought about it the right way, like he had himself a front row seat right by God and the good thing was God wasn't filling his ear with judgements or accusations because it was way too late for any of that now. His time was done and his grades posted and he seemed to have passed despite all those voices that had told him during his sojourn on the planet earth how it was Hell he was bound for and he'd soon see it. But he hadn't seen it. He wasn't in Hell whatsoever, and the only bad thing about this version of Paradise he was inhabiting now was his inability to stop looking back and seeing what a mess folks were making of their lives in his wake.

Nobody seemed to be getting any better.

Linda forced herself to go to school every day and worried about a lot of things that couldn't be altered. Her marriage was never going to be a fairy tale and her husband would never be mistaken for a prince. Her two children were amazingly normal and vanilla as far as little kids went, and Linda worried about how their lives were progressing and what she could do to help them be well-centered and not have behavioral problems when her own existence was dissolving a bit more every day and she soon would perhaps not be visible to the living world whatsoever in a while, and yet she continued to do nothing to change it.

It hurt John Clark to think that his daughter would one day leave no trace of her being on the face of the earth behind her. He didn't think she'd learned that from him.

And David and Franklin. God, he didn't know where to start with those two. There was so much lacking in the both of them that John Clark wondered how either had managed to make it this far without someone deciding the world would be better off without them and took an AR-15 to them, or to have the idea occur privately to both boys over a period of years and individually each come to the conclusion that there was nothing before them within their grasp worth grabbing on to, that all their lives consisted of was a steady myriad of days and years and squandered, uneventful time, and that perhaps drowning it with alcohol and driving into a telephone pole or swallowing a bottle of pills or taking a swan dive off the St. Simons Lighthouse would dash away all future disappointments. He wondered how any blood kin of his could have no feelings in their essences about love and magic and joy, but all he needed to do was observe them in their shams and deceits and sadnesses for a time and it was all there for him to see. They did not gain anything from him. Perhaps this was because he had taken a road away from them in search of his own life, but it was not his doing that his sons had no highway of their own. They had chosen to never go to the places that called them. They had chosen to pull over to the side of the road and let the world pass them by.

Brenda was another case. Brenda was the one who had changed. What remained to be seen was if this change had been for the better. He had to be honest and admit that there was a part of him that wished she had never swayed in her abiding love for him, but that had not been the case. She had not understood him at first, his strange compulsion to always pull away from those who loved him most, but she had one day come to an understanding that he would only return to her in brief spurts, momentary interludes, but that these visits were performed by some presence outside himself, an extension of that one who was truly there. It had taken some years to grasp the reality of it, how he was there but not there, present to see in some earthly sense but gone off somewhere that she could never follow. The process was slow and tedious, but she had finally arrived at a point where she was content with seeing him when she saw him, knowing he would be around as a protector and a friend when times got rocky, but knowing in her heart that he was a person who could not stop wandering off or forego his excursions into some strange world where it was him and no one else around but a dream.

So it was true that Brenda had let him go finally and at last, had grown to be content with the fact that she was married but not really, and when she'd finally asked for a divorce after some trial lovers along the way and a continuance of her on again, off again relationship with Jimmy Baldwin, John Clark, not truly knowing what might be in store, had said yes, well of course, and the divorce had gone through in record time, no screeching or threats or expressions of hatred whatsoever, not even of disappointment, for John Clark had told her that no matter what he would never leave her entirely unless she told him to, and they had lived in the house on Morrison Street for fifteen years that way, with him leading his life and she leading hers, and it had been as calm and gentle as an existence could be, and there was never an ill word spoken during all that time. No, he had not been disappointed in the way Brenda chose to live after their breakup. She had her job at the library and her friends and even joined a church where there were luncheons and book clubs and activities for her and the children alike, and over those fifteen years there had been men who'd picked her up for dinner and movies and an occasional concert, and at first he, John Clark, had felt a small pang of jealousy and regret, but very soon he knew this was the way it should be. He couldn't be greedy. He wanted Brenda to go and have the good life she chose.

Yes, he had hung his hat on being gracious and understanding and always making certain Brenda would want for nothing on the material side. He would stay her friend and confidant for good. And when the time came for both of them to move on from each other the path would be clear and the axles greased and their joint departure from each other would be easy and smooth. He would always worry about her somewhat, because he had loved her once and still did in his funny way and probably would for good, but that was the way he was and he knew this was the best for them both. Happiness, he thought. That is what I want for you, Brenda.

He was her watcher still. He trusted her judgement and never had wanted to interfere with anything she had going in her life without him. It was all about her being happy. But there was something about this new man Billy Joe Bradford that gave him pause to worry. Not excessively, not an obsessional sort of thought pattern, but still enough of a question in his post-life mind that he could not quite let settle in, that made him think that perhaps Brenda might be getting in over her head with an unknown commodity. It could be she might require some assistance later on. But it could also be he was still a little jealous in spite of his new circumstances.

And it was moments like this when he knew he was right in not yet moving on. There were too many attachments binding him here, too many tasks left to be fulfilled. It was all about inner peace before transitioning, and he was in the middle of it. He did not know how long it was going to take. It wasn't like he saw the end anywhere in sight. Not yet.

He allowed his mind to go into its random shuffle again, trusting his instincts to tell him where to turn his attention to next. After a deluge of brainstorm categories, he finally centered on a church called the St. Simons Atlantic Chapel. He had not made his stop there since before he left the physical world, and it had been some time now and he had not given the church any attention, and the fact remained that he did not have much faith and trust in how his successor might be keeping it in stock. The Chapel, as they called it, was not truly a chapel in the sense of the term at all, but was instead a long and towering structure that sat beachside southerly of downtown. Many of the local residents had come to call it their church home, and a large contingent of people from the neighboring communities of New Hope and Brunswick and Hickory Bluff drove over for services. There was a large youth gathering and a good proportion of Gen X and New Age-types, and it took some doing to keep the drink and snack machines filled on the three floors and basement of the building.

But what was really compelling John Clark to make the trip to The Chapel was the beckoning of the prayer tower built at the end of the third floor that faced out to sea. Because of the peacefulness and certitude of the place, it was frequented regularly by those members seeking spiritual solace or who just might want to scroll on their phone while sitting and overlooking the ocean for an interlude. John Clark had been instantly attuned to the tower each time his route brought him there, and he'd always made it a point to schedule his visit last on his day's calendars so that when he finished processing the machines and had them all filled to capacity—there were four drink machines and two large snack machines, invariably empty each time he arrived—he would be free to go up to the Chapel and watch the sea turn dark with the setting sun back over his shoulder. He would have come early to see the sunrise, but no one was ever there early enough to grant him access.

It was the way it was with real life and the modern world that he understood but didn't like. Why did a church have to be locked to keep people out? Why did there have to be a time restriction on when one gained spiritual solace? He, of course, had learned to acquire such a thing in his own way, but the rest of the world was not like that. Others were not so lucky as he. Or, he thought pompously, nearly as smart.

He visited the three floors and the basement and made his way up the stairway. There were elevators on both sides of the building he had to use when carting in his big orders, but now he was free to be on his own and rise angelic-like up the steps counting them off, knowing beforehand how many there were on each landing, totaling eighty-four in all from the basement up. The good thing was he did not have to worry if the top floor was inhabited by others or not, for these days he was perpetually and eternally alone whenever he wished, and so even if there were others he could fix it where he did not see or hear or sense them. He was alone here and everywhere, another one of those features and advantages of not being one with the living.

It was night already, way past sunset, but that was no matter to him either. He could make it whatever time he wanted it to be. He controlled the days of the week, the months, the events of each day. He could make it Christmas if he wanted. It was his world now.

He decided to make it a September morning, a golden Indian Summer day with the shadows lengthening and the colors of the world so wonderfully accentuated—yellows and greens and pinks and reds. He looked at the clouds in their shades and shapes as the sun came up. This had always been his favorite time.

TEN

On Monday nights the library stayed open until eight, and Brenda always volunteered for the late shift on those days. There had always been something about Monday mornings that bothered her, even when she was teaching before getting the job at the library those ten years before. On Sunday afternoons the first gnawing feelings began forming in her stomach and festering in her brain. It was like once post-lunchtime came around, after church and eating and perhaps watching television a while or reading or even going out for a movie, the dread feeling began to overtake her and only continued to swell and progress as time passed. By suppertime she would be almost too distraught to eat, and though she couldn't put her feelings into words, couldn't, as it was, explain to anyone why the idea of Monday morning and beginning a new week with the same work dramas and the feeling that she was Sisyphus and the great stone she had struggled with getting up the mountain the week before had slipped from her grasp and rolled away before she could stop it and there it was at the bottom of the mountain, down in the valley far below, and she could swear she heard it laughing at her. It was like Monday morning was some monster bearing a great malice toward her, so it became in her mind a good idea to send others down in the valley and let the beast consume them first, and then when she came down later she would not be attacked with the same level of ferocity. The beast would perhaps be sated by then.

So, she had made it a normal procedure to learn to relax on Sunday afternoons and not have to rush dinner and to stay up a little later than usual and read and not feel the rushes of despair and terror at the thought of another week looming before her right off the bat. These feelings had begun to manifest with the dissolution of her marriage to John Clark, but they had only heightened in the months after his death. She guessed the trepidation had always been with her before. Perhaps it had been held at bay during her time with John Clark, but as he faded from her life the fear returned and bade her take some psychological ploy to keep it at bay. Thus, the postponing of the start of another week chockful of horrors by sleeping in late and allowing the world to go before her. It was probably an exercise of denial, but she didn't care. It seemed to be working.

Monday evenings were generally not as busy as the other times of the week. The library was closed on Wednesdays and Sundays, so most of the weekly action was divided between the Tuesday morning Story Hour for the pre-kindergarteners and the Author Readings on Thursday night and the Saturday onslaught of high-schoolers trying to bone up for reference papers and housewives attempting to get a copy of a book for their book club presentations. Brenda's main job during the week when she wasn't shelving or working the checkout and return desk was to manage the requested books and books on hold and keep the files in some sort of order. When a requested book was returned it was her job to call whoever was next on the list of requests and let them know verbally and by email that their book was waiting for them. She always marveled at how it was generally just a few books which were on demand the most, that of all the books in print it was only a smattering of them that the throngs all wanted at the same time. It was like in some strange fashion women's literature had evolved into a giant popularity contest. If you were Faulkner or Hemingway you need not apply.

She was already beginning to wonder about how serious and how far she wanted this new relationship with Billy Joe Bradford to develop. She tried to remember how many times she had gone out with him over the past month and the answer seemed to be at least every night with plenty of lunches thrown in. It was like he had put the rush on her so that there had been no time to think about it one way or the other, for between Billy Joe and work at the library and getting ready for the sale of John Clark's possessions there was not a moment available to reflect on anything.

The sale was to be held this coming Friday and Saturday at the house. Already the estate company people had been out gathering items up and pricing them, making signs and getting everything ready to go. Brenda couldn't wait for it all to be over, if for nothing else so she could breathe again. She imagined an empty house and how she would have room to do new things with the décor without John Clark's treasures piled up anywhere and everywhere. She could have her book club over without having to shut off half the house, and she could get rid of the old recliner and have something that didn't have dog hair on it or scratches from the cat's claws. And it was not only John Clark's things she could be rid of. While the house was in a state of flux she could have Linda and David and Franklin take along to their own abodes some of their childhood and teenage paraphernalia too, get it out of her sight and to a new home where they could stumble and fall over it for a change instead of her.

But she would miss a lot of it when it was gone. She knew that. Having it disappear from view and memory would be like closing the book on a vast section of her life, and it would take some time to get over it completely. She knew without dwelling on it that it would not be the physical items not being there that she would miss so much. No, it would be the remembrance of who those possessions had belonged to and been assigned to in her memory. The videocassettes were David's, the outdated X-box was Franklin's, the Barbie Doll collection belonged to Linda. It was time for them to go home with their owners. The recliner too, and the bar stool with the gash in its seat, both were John Clark's. No one used them in the past or now, and there was no reason for them to remain rooted in the house forever. They all served no purpose to her but to remind her of the life she once had. It didn't matter if it was good or bad. She could look at them and the memories would flood in.

And on this Monday afternoon as she arrived at the library she envisioned the opportunity to catch up on a little work and be clear of the persistent activity her life now was for just a little while. It would be nice to concentrate on other things for a change. She walked by the return desk and looked out at the floor. It was not busy. It was almost peaceful. It was a nice change of pace.

It was about twenty minutes into her shift when Billy Joe walked in the door. He looked around a moment until he spotted her, then he waved.

***

It was the night before the sale, and Franklin was getting antsy. If he didn't hurry up and act right away, he could kiss whatever covert profits he intended to make from his father's weird-ass inventory goodbye. Maybe David had chickened out or had a surge of moral decency about bilking his mother and sister from their rightful share of the estate, but he hadn't. He was still of the mind that if he could just get into the house for thirty minutes on his own, he could cart off a few things that would make for a nice little windfall.

He had to wait for the estate people to go home for the day and then hope that his mother would go out for the night. He was pretty certain this was going to happen, since with her new boyfriend she was heading out to restaurants or movies or some form of entertainment practically all the time lately, and so he hoped that this night would not be any different. His mother hadn't as of yet informed her children about the new man in her life, so Franklin wasn't sure if it had come down to getting serious between the two of them or not, but he did know they were keeping steady company. He'd been driving by and observing her actions for about a week now, observing her patterns to see if there was a time he could gain entrance to the house for his own aggrandizement, which was how he'd come across this new romance his mother seemed to be involved in. The same pickup truck seemed to always be there. There was a part of him that wanted to go and squeal to Linda and David about what he'd uncovered and they could all go to his mother and confront her on her personal life, but it was better to wait. He had other tasks to take care of first.

He had to go around the block about twenty times before the silver pickup pulled into the driveway and the man got out and went to the front door. The guy looked fairly normal, Franklin thought, but there was something about him. Maybe he just felt weird about him since he wasn't used to the idea of another man going to bed with his mother, if, in fact, that was what was happening.

It was just something he'd never had to consider much before.

The truck drove off and Franklin pulled in around back so no one could see his dad's car. He wasn't supposed to be out driving on his suspended sentence, but he told himself if he was careful he could get away with it.

When he used his key to get in the back door, he was met there by Wolfie, who sat in the entrance to the kitchen like one of the hunchback's gargoyles, his body erect and his eyes following Franklin's every move, and when Franklin spoke to him, said Hey Boy and then attempted to step by him, Wolfie sprung forward with gnashing teeth and wrapped himself around Franklin's jeans and his North Face boots and proceeded to bite and chew and gash at whatever substance his teeth could locate.

"Goddam, Wolfie! Stop! Stop, goddamit!"

Wolfie hung on while Franklin jigged around the kitchen, finally letting go when Franklin made a circle and got back to where he came in. He used the door to scrape Wolfie away from his lower self, and shut the door and stood there listening to the dog throw itself against the wooden frame. He had never seen Wolfie act this way before. Sure, he was his father's dog and had nothing to do with anyone else, but he had never gone to extremes like this. It was like all of a sudden the damn dog had been issued a license to kill, like he was Old Yeller's first cousin and the same wolf had bit him and made him crazy too.

Franklin limped out to his car and rubbed his feet a moment before swinging them into the car. He knew his leg was bleeding, not enough to kill him, but one that would take a while to heal. He told himself he was not going to get into the house this night to appropriate anything for re-sale. He was going to have to go back to his apartment and hope he didn't contact rabies from this visit. Best laid plans, he thought. He was going to have to drop back and punt and let everything run its natural course. He might be losing some extra cash he'd been counting on, but it wasn't worth dying for.

Damn dog. Damn his father for having such a mutt. Damn everything, he thought, once you get down to cases.

The night before the sale, Linda thought it might be a good idea to go over to the house and see how the estate sellers had progressed and make sure they hadn't missed anything in getting ready. She would have let her mother do this and have the final say, but Brenda had been acting strange lately and Linda didn't think she could truly count on her to take care of things properly. It was like her mother was distracted these days and this sale was just another one of those things that needed to be taken care of nice and fast. This kind of haste made Linda uneasy. It was almost like her mother was ready to get rid of any and all traces of her father's existence and was prepared to throw out the family treasures with the accumulated clutter just to have available space in the house again.

It was the strangest thing. When she turned the corner to get to the house she could swear she saw Franklin in her dad's old car speeding up the street, and she wondered if he had merely driven by, or, like her, gone in to see that everything was copacetic for tomorrow. This kind of action, though, seemed uncharacteristic of her little brother, so what she really thought was he had been up to something before she got here. Brenda was out somewhere—she hadn't answered her phone, so she was off in some mystery place too—and it could be that Franklin had come by when he knew she wasn't there. He was sneaky like that. Always had been.

This would require some investigation on her part.

Wolfie was raising all sorts of Cain when she got out of the car, so something was up for sure. It took a lot these days to get her daddy's dog to get off the chair in the library and nose around for anything other than to go outside to relieve himself or chow down for breakfast and dinner and any kind of snack to be had in between. She unlocked the door and came inside and Wolfie sat and thumped his tail at her at the entrance to the hallway that led to her father's side of the house, the bedroom, the library, the study, the small kitchenette he'd made in an abandoned space that led to the backyard, his teapot and coffeemaker still in place, several cups and mugs and glasses and a box of Bugles, still open and shut with a plastic clasp. She toured the areas with Wolfie trailing behind her, either curious or with a willingness to impart some information if she could only speak canine, or hoping perhaps she was going to open the desk drawer and pull out any of the assorted dog treats inside, nestled there beside packages of Bonkers and Meow Mix. It was funny, Linda thought, how her dear old dad always had more provisions for his pets than he did for himself or his family.

But that wasn't really a very fair assessment. Her father loved his pets, that was for sure, but it wasn't like he ever let her or her brothers or her mother go wanting for anything. Maybe for his time and attention sometimes, but that was all. She could never remember being denied much of anything she asked for, herself or anyone else in the household. There was always food and spending money and funds for clothes and new shoes and school functions and you name it. She couldn't fault her father for any crime of omission like that.

What she could lay blame on him for was the fact that all this generosity and benevolence and, yes, tokens of love and affection were always bestowed from some distant, faraway region where her father resided, some invisible all but mythical place where it seemed he looked down from on high to chart the progressions of those for whom he had deemed himself to love and be responsible for, and the feeling had always been within her that such a relationship he showed to his family and those he held dearly was not natural. It was not a love and rendering of affections as others gave and received but different in a strange and undecipherable way. It was a love like no other. It was like being looked after by some phantom from another world.

Satisfied that nothing had been tampered with, she started to turn the lights back off and go, but something made her stop in the dining room and walk over to a section of coffee mugs on the table labeled and marked for tomorrow's sale. In the midst of this assortment was an off-white diner mug with a Krystal logo emblazed on the front. It was a souvenir her father had procured from a restaurant somewhere during all his meanderings in his youth in the South, and she remembered him drinking from it back when she was a little girl sitting in his lap in the rocking chair by the back porch on certain Sundays. This was back before he began to disappear. He would read the paper and sip from his Krystal mug and she would watch from her place in his lap the birds and squirrels dance on the fence and the tree limbs in the garden sway with the wind.

Something gripped her and she suddenly decided she was not alone in the house. It was quiet and there was no one there to see but it didn't matter—she could sense the presence of something, someone. It was not Wolfie here at her heels that made her feel this way. It was something else. She looked down at the dog and saw how his ears were cocked, standing straight up like they'd always done when he was engaged. Dogs see and hear things better than we do, her father used to say. They know things before they even happen. We might be in the dark for quite a time while a dog has been sizing up a situation for minutes before. That was what she thought when she looked at Wolfie with his ears pointed straight up and his head bent to one side as if he was taking in a message. There was something going on, all right.

Within seconds Rebecca peered around the corner of the library door to see who or what it was that had changed the dynamic of the silent house. The woman Brenda was gone and the younger man who had always set such store on tiptoeing around trying to get away with something he shouldn't be doing or something he shouldn't have was gone too—he was someone Rebecca had always had to watch, some person in the house who couldn't be trusted—and now it was the woman who had been kind to her when she was a kitten but who was mostly gone now, but there was something else in the house too, and Rebecca sensed it. It was something the cat was familiar with and hadn't sensed for some time now, and when Rebecca looked over at the dog ahead of her in the short hallway she could see Wolfie was aware of it too. The cat and the dog and Linda all stood semi-frozen for a moment, waiting in unison for this thing that was there in the house with them to reveal itself. After a moment Rebecca's tail swished and Wolfie's entire body began to wag.

They both knew who was there.

Linda waited for a number of heartbeats for the spirit to speak, wondering if this was like Hamlet and this was some form of King Hamlet's ghost come back from the dead and beyond to tell her something, to give her some form of warning about something evil in the world that was lurking and creeping around. But she had no sense of danger in those anticipatory moments. It was not like she was going to be informed of some horrible future event that she needed to fear and avoid. It was not like that. It was more that she was standing here in her parent's house where she had grown up and something was telling her she was not alone, that she had never been altogether alone in all those times before even when she believed she was, and that she was not alone now, not during her twenty-seventh year upon the earth when she was supposed to be a practicing adult but could not for the life of her completely extinguish the raging inadequacies of her youth and how she carried them around with her still, hidden, yes, disguised, of course, but still present so that she would recognize them in the dark of the night on those occasions when she awoke in her bed with her husband asleep beside her and the children in their beds down the hall and lay there alone and frightened in the dark for those few abject seconds and wonder if she would ever get over it completely. Maybe not, the presence seemed to say, but you are not alone in that regard. Everyone in the world awakens from their sleep at one time or another and senses the great fear coming to get them and carry them away. They are demons and monsters and banshees and devils, and they are only there for a second and then they are gone.

She wanted her father to speak. She waited for him to reassure her. Mainly she just wanted him to tell her it would all be okay, the way he used to all those years ago, but now she knew he was somewhere else where words could not be spoken and he could not field the questions she wanted to ask him. But the thing of it was he was here now, somewhere in the corners and confines of this house of her girlhood, somewhere among his ancient possessions that made him so himself and kept him in her consciousness back then and now, whether he was present for a time or gone away somewhere to that place no one else could ever travel to, but that didn't matter so much this instant. What mattered was she knew he was around.

And she wasn't going crazy either. She could see Wolfie sniffing along the baseboards and Rebecca staring up at the ceiling with her tail going back and forth, to and fro, her eyes dancing with the presence of the one who had gone, her body alit with a magical sense once more.

Linda guessed she ought to go home, that she should leave and consider these new sensations in her own time and place, but she didn't want to leave just yet. She wanted to stay in this moment a while longer. So she stood for a time and listened for a sign.

***

Wolfie and Rebecca had not communicated to each other in any sort of fashion, but they did manage to talk by way of animal telepathy. Rebecca already knew what Wolfie was barking at before the dog ever opened his mouth, because the arrival of a hostile intruder had lept into Wolfie's mind and instantly transferred down the hallway and into the library and around a corner to Rebecca, who had raised her head and blinked once before jumping down from the study chair and going to investigate. She heard the voice that Wolfie did and immediately placed it as belonging to the youngest of the human pack that John Clark had cared for and knew the carrier for the unpleasant person he was. This person was not one who stroked fur or provided treats, but was one apt to kick either Wolfie or herself out of the way by manner of impatience. Rebecca did not want this person here, especially by himself, and she growled low in her throat trying to decide if she should go on the attack. She watched Wolfie and could tell he was mulling over the same thing. She would join the fray if Wolfie did. They would oust this bad person for good. But for some reason the man had chosen to leave. Whether he was frightened or had a change of his black heart Rebecca did not know, but she watched him go out the door and heard the car start up outside, and so she went back to her chair in the study to take another nap.

In a few more minutes the younger woman arrived. She nor Wolfie were accustomed to so much traffic going in and out the doors lately, so they both knew something strange was going on. They wondered if the man they loved was coming back home.

***

On the Friday morning of the estate sale, David did everything in his power to keep from going by the house to see who was buying what or viewing his father's possessions. In the end he failed exactly as he had known he would. It was a morbid way to spend a morning and would do nothing to assuage his feelings completely, but he went ahead and called out sick for the day anyway and got ready early and ate a granola bar and downed a cup of coffee and drove over and was in the house before the sale ever got started.

The first thing he noticed was that his presence wasn't exactly appreciated by the members of the selling staff. His mother had already left to go out for breakfast and then go somewhere else for the day since the library was not open, and Linda had already told him she wasn't coming by until Saturday afternoon around when the sale was ending, and who knew what Franklin might do? He could show up at any time or not at all, and whatever he did David was fairly certain a commotion and hard feelings would follow along with his actions either way. David himself didn't know if he should simply find himself a chair a little ways separate from all the action or if he should walk around the rooms and observe what was getting picked up and carted off and what was being left behind for the family to deal with afterward. He wasn't sure that if something went unbought if the estate folks would leave it behind or pay a nominal fee for it and have it carted off to a junk shop or a salvage store and get rid of it that way. All he knew was he wasn't going to allow himself to get all maudlin over something his dad once owned and buy it for himself. He was afraid if he allowed himself that freedom he might go overboard and start loading up on everything.

There were already cars in the drive and parked along both sides of the road when he got there, idling sedans and minivans and pickup trucks with people sitting inside drinking coffee waiting for the magical opening time. David could sense how when the second hand touched the top of the hour the people would swarm out of their vehicles like ravished bees hurrying to fill themselves with the nectar of merchandise for the taking, buzzing through the house feeding off his father's earthly juices. A part of him wanted to stand on the front sidewalk and hold his hand outstretched and tell them all to either stop or come forward in an orderly manner and not go busting the doors down and rampaging through the house. He wanted to let them know how this was a holy shrine they were entering, that it would just not do for them to be grabbing and haggling over prices and snatching items up like they had no history or prior term of importance in the world. The entire situation seemed to him to be bordering on sacrilegious actions, a complete disrespect for what a former member of the planet once held dear.

Somehow the perched birds of prey manner in which these cars' inhabitants sat alarmed him and made him wonder if he ought to take cover to make certain he didn't get pecked to death once the onslaught began.

There were two ladies sitting at a long table that had been set up in the living room. One was busy shuffling papers and paperclipping things together while the other was talking on her phone and held up one finger to David as she finished up her conversation. He looked at the table in front of them and saw two cash boxes and two card readers placed side by side, cash, check, or card, and it looked to him like the two of them were loaded for bear and ready for the big rush that was to come.

"Can I help you with anything, hon?" the silver-headed lady on the right asked him. "The sale doesn't really start for ten minutes or so, but you can look around if you want. We'll bend the rules just for you."

"I'm one of the family members," David explained, even though he wondered if he ought to impart such information or not. Who knows? They might tell him he needed to either stay way the hell out of the way or just altogether leave. "I thought I'd drop by and make sure there weren't any hitches in the operation that maybe had just popped up out of the blue."

"Everything's fine and taken care of," she smiled. "That's what we're paid to do."

"I wasn't sure if my mother had explained everything fully or not. Sometimes she forgets things in the heat of action."

"I can't think of a thing to worry about. It will go so smoothly you'll hardly know anything has gone on at all. By tomorrow afternoon I anticipate there won't be much to do but take down the tables, empty the trash and count how much money's been taken in. I think you'll be surprised."

"Everyone gets cold feet before these things get going," the second lady said. "It's just hard to sit back and allow absolute strangers to handle your loved one's items. It takes getting used to the idea."

"I'll do my best not to get in the way. But I do want to look around a little."

The two women smiled at him even though he knew they considered him a nuisance. Too bad, he thought. In two days they'll never see me again and vice-versa. In the meantime it's best for me to move out of here and make my way to other parts of the house.

He went left. This way he could first veer off from the living room and the table of moneychangers and check out the dining room and the kitchen. There was not much to see on the dining room table that reminded him of his father, only a few of his mother's old plates and drinking glasses. A tea set he could never remember seeing stood by some saucers and a sugar cannister, flanked by a butter dish so fancy David was certain the family had never used it. There was no hint of his father in here. It was a room he had used mostly for passage into the kitchen. It looked to him like his mother was trying to get rid of anything that reminded her of his father, his stuff and hers and everything else.

He saw his father's old coffee mugs and tried to remember a setting from the past that had occurred with each one. There was the fabled Krystal diner cup, white and enameled and thick enough to be used as a lethal weapon if need be. David could remember it well, just as he could quite easily recall the cup from the Smoky Mountains with the bear on all fours on the front, the yellow cup from Silver Springs, Florida, with the alligator and its mouth open wide, pictured with the words "Come on in, the water's fine!" etched on the face of the mug. He remembered sometimes on Sunday mornings being allowed to stay home from church with his father, and sitting across from the breakfast table tracing the image of the alligator with his finger while John Clark read the paper.

Drinking my orange juice and eating my Count Chocula. Daddy laughing and saying, "Listen to this. Jimmy Carter says he has lust in his heart and it makes him crazy sometimes. All I've got to say, buddy, is what man do you know who doesn't feel the same way?"

Past the kitchen and out to the breakfast room where Daddy used to read while he was supposed to be watching us play in the backyard. Had my swimming pool and the driveway was paved where I could go up and down to the fence and back to the garage on my tricycle. Linda only a baby then, Franklin not born yet. Sometimes when daddy was home Mama left me with him while she took care of Linda. Take a nap with her on Saturday and Sunday afternoons and I'd stay with Daddy. Riding by the screen window where he could see me. Look at me, I'd want to say, and sometimes he would. Other times he would open one of his books and read. Daddy was always reading.

Down the steps and into the backyard. Remember the tall wooden fence Daddy had installed so the neighbors couldn't spy on us too much. Had a man come by and climb up a ladder to install a wooden backboard and a rim. You can shoot here when you get older, Daddy told me. Watched him drink beer some weekend nights and shoot baskets himself while the radio played. I'd tell him nice shot whenever the ball went in the basket. Starched white net that made a whooshing sound when the ball went through. Hear that? Daddy would ask me. String music is what that is. One of the best sounds in the world. And sometimes to sit on his back piggyback. Be given the ball and hear him say, drop it in, David. And I got to be pretty good. Not afraid to ride Daddy's shoulders or reach up with the big orange ball and make it go past the rim and nestle through the net.

We pitched ball out here, even though when I got big enough to catch the ball every time it came back Daddy wasn't around as much anymore, so I had to go out behind the house and take a rubber ball and throw it against the foundation and above the basement window and on up above the bedroom windows just below the attic. Ground balls and line drives and long flies to the outfield. Soon had my own rules and my personal playing field all marked off. Games all day from morning to night in the summertime. Waiting for Daddy to get home. And generally it was so dark when he arrived it was too late for playing ball by then. It was too dark to see. And he was tired. He'd worked from before the sun came up until twilight. I wondered what he did for so long out there, where he went for such a long time every day.

Over at the corner of the drive, just outside the garage doors where we stored everything but cars, that's where he pulled his lawn chair out into the air and sat at night with his radio inside the garage tuned to out of town baseball games. He'd twist the knob until he could dial in Joe Nuxhall with the Cincinnati Reds or Jack Buck with St. Louis or Ernie Harwell with Detroit—he'd stay with any of their broadcasts as long as the airwaves brought them in nice and clear. Sometimes I would walk out into the moonlight and see his shadow sitting right here where I'm standing now, a game going on, a cold beer in his Tigers souvenir cup resting on his knee, looking off into the heavens as if searching for his own personal image of God, and sometimes it seemed to me he had indeed found it. I would stand and watch him for a time, knowing better than to interrupt his revery, and then I would go inside again to my mother and sister and crying little brother, because that was where we belonged, with him but away, and that was the way I learned it would always be.

Daddy always had a second car. Mama had the family car, which was new and shiny and had all the bells and whistles available for the time, but it was Daddy's cars I was always fascinated with. They were the ones I would open the doors and look inside, sit behind the steering wheel and pretend I was going down the road, stand outside and run my fingers over the smooth metal of the body. He had a Super Sport convertible and a GTO and a Triumph TR-3 that hardly ever ran but looked classy just sitting in its place in front of the garage. Most times he would cover it with a custom weather guard, and I would lift it up and look at what was there beneath. In time there was a fancy El Camino and a Ford Mustang that looked like Steve McQueen's a little—he told me that—and once he took me to a theater downtown that was showing "Bullitt" on their screen as a retrospect, and I got to see the Mustang fly down the highway the way my daddy wished he could do in his Mustang.

There's his old Zenith table radio sitting in its same place on the shelf inside the garage door. Turn it on now and it's all static. Guess the AM signal doesn't come in except at night. Come out here sometimes if there was no game and he'd be listening to Rhythm and Blues out of Nashville. Clear channel, he would say. One of these days I'll let you hear the Grand Ole Opry. Start to turn the knob to see what I might hear, but then I stop. Seems like sacrilege to change the channel. Anyway, they've got a sticker on this radio. Seven dollars and fifty cents. Pull the plug and stick it under my arm. Nobody else is getting it.

There's his old lawn chair too, over in the corner by itself. Spider eggs and ancient webs coated on the polypropylene seat and back and along and beneath the metal armrests. Overlooked here. Missed the dumpster when they came through removing junk and pricing what they thought would sell. Off in a corner by itself. Wonder how long since it's had someone sit in it?

Pull it out and lower the seat. Probably cost four dollars total back in the day, but Daddy got his money's worth. How many times did he sit in this chair?

Brush it off and sit down myself. Sort of like saying another goodbye to dear old dad. Use his chair one more time for old time's sake. It comes to me he'd probably like that.

Creaking sound and feel the fabric ripping under my weight. Butt falling through. Material so rotten a mouse couldn't sit in it without plunging to its death. Just glad I got up before it completely collapsed. Can just see myself finding my own death out here among my dad's memorabilia.

David becomes aware of people walking about now, inside the house and sticking their nose out the back door to see what else there is for sale. He moves along because he doesn't want to hear or watch them among his father's things, picking up and pawing what was his and making comments about it. Probably he should have known better than to come here today. He should have stayed away.

But if he had he wouldn't have this radio, would he?

He clutches it under his arm and goes back inside the house. The living room is full of people now, so he goes the opposite way down the hallway and enters the library. There are a few people milling around, and here and there are empty spaces on the shelves where books once reposed. Already the room is beginning to look violated, stripped of what has adorned it for so long. He wonders if he has the heart to poke his head around the corner into his father's study, because the sight of it being trespassed upon may be more than he can stand to see.

One thing that is noticeable is the absence of Wolfie and Rebecca on the scene. David guesses they have gone to Linda's for two days until the sale is over, and then they will come back to live with his mother. He can't be totally sure of that, though, for his mother has never been totally bonded with the two animals that much in the past. But she has kept them around these months since his father's death, so maybe that assumption is not altogether true. Possibly she is with the dog and cat like he is with the radio; she needs something around to remind herself of her former husband, even if he was not legally her husband anymore and hadn't been for a while. It could be she at least wants something around to help her recall John Clark as he was when he was alive and not have to continually keep in mind that he is now dead and there is nothing left of him for her.

There is no one in the room at this moment, and by the way it looks it seems no one has made their way back here yet. The boxes that he and Franklin had loaded up several nights ago are still sitting on the desk and in the floor where they had brought them back in from the truck. David takes a copy of Famous Monsters from the top of a box and stares at the cover art. It is a picture of Boris Karloff in his Egyptian garb, a turban on his head and menace in his eyes. Ardath Bey, David remembers. It comes into his head fast and clear, old information he has in his memory that he didn't know was there until now. That was his modern name. But his name in ancient Egypt was Im-ho-tep. That was right. He had learned that from his father. His father had talked about it at one time or another and David had listened. It had lodged in his brain from he didn't know when or where. His dad would be happy to know this now. He would be proud of David for remembering such a fact.

He would take the box of Famous Monsters of Filmland with him too, along with the radio. He didn't know whether he would have to pay for them or not.

They were his father's things, and David was this minute his father's son.

It had been a while.

***

There were other places he felt he needed to be, machines to fill and stock to be rotated and added, but there was no keeping John Clark from stopping by the house on this first day of the sale of his things to see what was being taken away and what was going to remain for a different fate. It was not that he was totally idealistic and assigned godlike qualities to those things that were his while he lived on the earth, but, like the way he saw his own life now, they meant something for what they were, much like his own self played a large part in the world that had sprung up around it. They and he had inhabited the world at the same time and were joined together, and in some unspoken manner they were bound together for eternity, so it was im-

147

portant for him to know where these tokens and totems resided on this plain he was leaving behind, and he had this need to know such things before he departed.

He was altogether pleased to see David present on this day, and more so when he saw his eldest son appropriate some of the things his father had held dear for his own. John Clark looked upon the unfolding scene as a redeeming reminder of what he had always thought of the way the planet spun, that one could never tell what surprises were to come during a moment's flashing, that one could never predict an outcome to be forever categorized as good or bad, but that the unpredictability of the canopy of life would always have to be viewed until it reached its eventual end, and who knew when or where that might possibly be?

He had not been happy when he watched his sons first begin plotting ways to make money on his prized possessions, nor had he cared much for Brenda and her wish for things to merely disappear so she could have space for her new life, or Linda wanting the entire procedure over so her business acumen for order could kick in and everything would be arranged as to her own wishes. What a bunch of simple and selfish creatures I have fostered during my life, he'd surmised. Why was he taking the time to view this spectacle and have the sadness of it drummed into his head to take with him for eternity?

But he had seen something sparkling in these last few days. He had seen hope. Not hope for him, because his quest was close to finished now, but hope for these people he had found himself forced to separate from and leave behind before he actually did go. He saw Brenda recalling the peace he had given to her after their long struggles together, he saw Linda coming to understand that her father loved her even when he was somewhere over some rainbow in his existence, and his sons had somehow begun to have their blind eyes see something of him he had left behind that needed to be salvaged and recalled. Perhaps none of these people would have perfect lives in the years to come, but there was a glimmer there somewhere for them all. There was the possibility he had never felt before that maybe they would be all right after all.

And maybe he would be okay too, if only he could complete his route before it was time for him to go.

ELEVEN

Instead of going with the rest of her faculty friends to Cutthroat's for a few drinks to celebrate Friday afternoon, Linda's curiosity got the best of her, so she decided to drive over to the house and see how the first day of the sale had gone. She was fairly certain her mother would be there by now too, even though she had insisted she was not going to come home until the sale was officially over for the day and the estate team was ready to leave. It was like her mother was attempting to convince the world at large that the sooner she was completely rid of John Clark Hayes and his bevy of quirky possessions the better off she was going to be. Linda had heard her argue this point numerous times even before her father's death, even while he was still alive and living under the same roof, and she had yet to believe it. The lady doth protest too much, she thought.

Her mother was home, but there were still several cars in the drive. Two of them belonged to her mother's friends Jessica and Charlotte, but two or three of the other vehicles she didn't recognize. She guessed the estate team hadn't left just yet. Probably they were going over with her mother what went well and what went badly and how they were going to do things on Saturday to ensure the whole procedure was a success.

The front door was open and when she entered the living room there was one woman at the front desk separating credit slips and checks and cash. She recognized Linda from earlier in the week and told her everyone else was back at the other end of the house, in the library, she thought.

Charlotte and Jessica were in the living room when she entered, the two of them sipping bottled water and trying to act as if they weren't listening in on what her mother and the three women standing by the doorway to the study were talking about. There were big gaps on the library bookshelves in different places, but not so much that the room looked barren or in danger of being empty. Linda had the initial feeling that perhaps sales of her father's collection had not gone as brisk as hoped for. Maybe that's what the discussion was about, everyone trying to decide how to get tomorrow's attending browsers to laden themselves down with her father's books, magazines, and vinyl.

No, the library didn't much appear as if a frantic shopping spree had gone on at any time during the day, and Linda was curious to see if her dad's study had fared any better. She walked by her mother and the estate women and gave a finger wave, then poked her head through the study's doorway to see what it looked like in there. Except for a box of magazines that had been sitting on John Clark's desk, it looked as if nothing had been touched. She wondered if someone had accidentally locked the door and no one could get in, or if the buying market for old scratchy albums and horror movie memorabilia and posters of Casablanca and North By Northwest and a plethora of films dating back to the thirties had dried up these days, that the citizenship of St. Simons Island and its environs were not enamored of those sort of artistic creations anymore, that whatever they needed in such a line of interest could be readily and more easily found and procured on Amazon and eBay. Whatever the case, there was a whole lot of stuff still sitting in there, and it didn't much appear as if it was in a hurry to go anywhere.

She'd had the temptation to take a few things for herself from this room earlier, but hadn't because she thought it might piss her mother and brothers off, her taking things for free that might have sold and brought in a nice profit. But now she knew better. It was at the point of being open season as far as snarfing up items for free. She was damned if she was going to have folks come in at the end of the sale tomorrow and start loading stuff up for re-sale to vendors or to have the remainder end up at the city dump.

She ignored her mother and the estate women and walked in and began looking around. There was a lot here she wouldn't mind having after all. She had never thought so before. Whoever would have thought such a thing possible, her having an affinity for her father's junk?

***

Other than the fact that the estate sale was not making much in the way of money, Brenda was still pleased with the way things were moving along. A decent amount of John Clark's possessions had dwindled in one day's time, although it had mostly been small items like coffee cups and beer steins from the kitchen and some old stereo equipment that had been stored in the garage for a few decades. John Clark was never one to get rid of anything, so Brenda was glad to see the 8-track players and the VCRs find themselves new homes. She'd even been halfway surprised at the way his wardrobe had sold, all his tee shirts of rock bands and sports coats with patches on the sleeves and every pair of athletic shoes he had ever owned—it was like the word got out that there was going to be a run of vintage clothing this afternoon, and every hipster in St. Simons had rushed over to pick up a few items.

Really, all that was left was what was in the library and the study, and though some books had been sold this first day, there was still a vast supply anchoring down the library shelves and a number of boxes of hardcovers and vinyl and old magazines crowding the study. Earlier, she'd seen Linda carting a few boxes out the door to her car and had said nothing about it and done nothing to stop her. In a way it had been refreshing and almost touching to see her taking away some things of her father's. It was like Linda was forgiving John Clark of his past transgressions, letting it slide that he had not exactly been the father she would have liked him to be. But Linda was always particular about everything. She always wanted her way and made no bones about it. This afternoon, maybe just for a little, it looked like she'd backed off of that stance a little.

The estate ladies said David had been by earlier, so Brenda supposed that was nice too. Perhaps there was some sort of post-mortem peace being acted upon here, the children acknowledging that maybe John Clark hadn't been such a bad dad after all, despite his absences and disappearances and prolonged periods of silence which leaked over into his husband status also; maybe the whole family had concentrated so much on what John Clark didn't do that everybody else did and never noticed that he did some things no one else ever considered doing themselves, so maybe in the end it all evened up.

No sign of Franklin, but that was to be expected. You couldn't expect Franklin to be around unless there was something in it for him. He'd show up when the profits started getting divided up.

"Maybe after tomorrow there won't be a trace of John Clark left around here," Jessica offered. She'd helped herself to some orange juice from the refrigerator. "I'll bet that on a Saturday all the bibliophiles and music lovers will be over here in droves stripping John Clark's rooms bare."

"I don't know," Charlotte said. "Usually on an estate sale the real serious buyers show up on the first day. If that stuff didn't disappear today, Brenda, you're liable to be stuck with it from here on out."

"I'm not worried about that. Whatever's left is supposed to be picked up by some private companies, and they pay by the load. So it will all be gone by Saturday night."

Brenda listened to herself write off John Clark's pride and joy collection as if the contents had mattered little to anyone but him. She halfway wished her two friends would disappear and go to dinner without her. That way she could go back to the study and look through John Clark's boxes and see if there was something there she'd like for herself. She'd bet there was. She could remember hearing music coming from the library on lots of nights, when they were married and afterward, and always it seemed that something would play she'd forgotten about or hadn't heard in a while and was surprised to remember how much she loved the tune and the words. The same went for books. Sometimes she would find a book in her bedroom John Clark had found somewhere and thought she'd like, and he had always been right on the money. It was funny the way he was, and she guessed she knew it better than anyone. He could be gone but be right there. He could not say a word but speak volumes. He could go long periods of time not touching her, yet she could feel his presence through it all, like he was a ghost or something. It was a weird courtship and a strange marriage and a mysterious aftermath. She didn't know how to describe any of it and she knew she never would. But most of the time, a preponderance of the minutes and hours and years, it had been a real ride. John Clark Hayes had always been a trip.

She sat in the backseat of Charlotte's Subaru and thought about John Clark and children and life and death all the way to O'Charley's. When her phone rang on the way over she looked down and saw it was Billy Joe, and she clicked it off and dropped it down in her bag. Not now, she thought. I need a little break.

***

Bob Seger had finally finished lamenting about how the night moves had about got the best of him, and Jimmy, sitting at a Sonic finishing off a Jalapeño Cheeseburger for his lunch, was thinking how the goings on in his own life were taking a toll on him too. So far he hadn't been able to come anywhere near the momentous sexual heights old Bob had sung about, nothing concrete to write home about in the adultery department, since most of his efforts at obtaining some outside action had gone unrewarded for some time now. He was beginning to think he was expending a whole lot of effort for nothing.

Take this woman working the receptionist job down at the radio complex. You couldn't tell him that she wasn't giving it out to everybody in his brother that she saw every day, but it sure wasn't coming his way no matter how much he tried. How many times had he stopped by and gone in and talked to her? Ten? Fifteen times? And what had come of it? Nothing. He might as well just pull in the parking lot and drive by the lobby door and toot the horn and it would be the same result. He could try to get her to go out with him until the cows came home and he was never going to so much as give her a ride in his car in the end.

She wasn't the only one either. He couldn't count how many women on the route and in some of the dives he frequented he'd hit on the past couple of months, and so far not the first thing had happened. It was like he was trying to commit this big sin and break one of the big Commandments and God was simply not letting it happen. It wasn't that he wanted to act this way so much, but what's a guy to do when he's convinced his wife has been doing

152

the same thing behind his back for a while now? He's got to get even one way or another.

Of course, he wasn't completely certain Donna had really been cheating on him. It was just a theory he had. It could be she was as pure as the driven snow and he was just imagining things to compensate for his own sorry behavior and there was no way to know for sure. But she was sure acting funny these days, so he had some legitimate reasons for being suspicious.

Donna's car was in the garage with the door open, so Jimmy wondered if she was home for good or planning to go back out later. Whatever her plans, he made up his mind it was high time to go ahead and have this out and get it over with now before he drove himself crazy thinking about it, before the kids got home to maybe witness a knock-down drag-out discussion that might freak them out for the rest of their lives. He might not be the best husband and father beneath the sun, but he at least wasn't an asshole. He didn't ever want to do anything that might hurt somebody intentionally.

Donna was emptying the dryer in the laundry room when he found her. For a minute he didn't really know how or where to begin, but he didn't have to make any kind of decision since she started the conversation for him.

"I think it's time we had a talk," she told him. "I don't think I've been completely honest with you lately and I don't like the feeling. I'm starting to feel really creepy."

"Don't feel like the Lone Ranger. I'm not too thrilled with myself either. I've been wanting to talk to you too."

"Come on," she said. "Sit down. Let's have a cup of coffee."

Jimmy had never seen Donna drink coffee this late in the day before, so he knew something must be up. He watched her add three heaping teaspoons of sugar to her mug and stir in about a quart of cream. This was definitely getting serious.

"We've got some real problems with our marriage, Jimmy," she began, "and I feel like a whole lot of it starts and ends with me. I don't think I'm being a very good wife to you lately."

"That's not true."

"Let me finish. I stay about half-pissed off at you all the time, and it has to be me, because you're not doing anything different than you always have."

"You're probably more than justified in being pissed. Hell, if you look at it I don't do a damn thing to help you out either around here or at work. You do all the housework and cook all the meals Dand run the show at work, and half the time I'm here playing games on my computer."

"Well, you are the one who had the idea of starting the company. You put everything together and brought in the first accounts while I watched you do it, thinking the whole time you were losing your mind. But it was because of you that I was able to quit working at a grocery store and teaching in a squirrely school system and able to get out on my own, and I've never regretted any of it the least little bit."

He started to tell her what a sorry bastard he was, how he'd looked at other women and plotted and spent a lot of energy trying to arrive at some point where he could consider himself the island's top cocksman, but if he really examined the scene and thought about it logically he could see that none of these women he told himself to go after were on the level with Donna, so what was the point? He could confess to all of it now and ask for forgiveness, but he didn't know what she knew and he didn't want to know what she'd been doing. Better, he thought, to leave those stones unturned.

"Before we get into this and start saying a bunch of stuff that's better left unsaid, why don't we make a truce?" He reached out his hand across the table and was close to amazed when she took it in hers. "Let's just say we've both been acting goofy," he said. "Let's just decide we're going to both try to do better. I can live with that if you can."

***

So, Donna takes his hand and supposedly that seals the deal and all this murky rigmarole that's been going on between them and behind each other's backs is all over now and the two of them can go back to normal and be happy and contented without a lot of drama with the two of them constantly being on the verge of nervous breakdowns. Donna supposes this is a good thing once you get to examining it closely and weighing the pros and cons, but she still wonders if even if her life becomes tranquil and she's not beset with worrying about adultery and divorce and who gets what in the settlement, that maybe the whole of it doesn't get down to and solve the big question that's at the bottom of everything and got this entire shebang started to begin with.

She may be here in this house and married with almost-grown children and running a profitable business and not have to worry about being the world's greatest sinner any longer, but there is still something sleeping below down at the bottom of the quiet sea in her soul that is not only bound to but is going to rise to the surface from time to time and that's all there is to it, and she's going to have to learn how to deal with that creature from the depths on those occasions when it decides to come up for air and say hello.

John Clark. She still finds herself thinking about John Clark Hayes, whether it be on the cusp of sleep or deep within a dream or simply the act of driving down a road somewhere on the island and seeing some business that had a snack machine or a soda machine that was on his route, and then out of the blue there he would be again, walking along the portal of her brain, driving his truck through her memory as if there was something in her that was empty and it was his job to come into her soul and fill it up.

John Clark is gone but John Clark is here. What is she going to do about John Clark Hayes?

Well, she could go on like she has for years, remembering one night and a long, eternal, and never-ending kiss, and she could think how her life would be different if that kiss had occurred before it did, before her marriage and the beginning of her journey to be a wife and a mother with another man and children John Clark Hayes had nothing to do with helping to create, or she could do what she'd attempted to do and had come close to being successful trying, and that was to push John Clark and his passionate one-night kiss out of her head and tell it to evaporate and disappear like the memories of other kisses with other boys before, but neither of those two options had lasted or been enduring, and it always came back to that moment when John Clark Hayes would return from a far country or rise from the dead or pass her in an opposite direction as she motored down some highway. It was a problem and a dilemma that had gone on for more than a decade now, and just when she thought she had learned how to circumvent its effects and implications, it would appear to her from out of the smoke and fog of her thoughts and materialize in her sight to take up residence in her soul once more.

John Clark Hayes. What was she going to do?

The only thing she could think of to avail herself of all her personal mind-boggles was to stop herself from thinking so much by getting busy doing something that required her attention to be focused elsewhere. Cooking dinner was a good idea. She deduced if she started preparing some monumental feast here in the middle of the week then there would be no time for her thoughts to trail off chasing a phantom by the name of John Clark Hayes. If she somehow could figure out how to keep herself busy all her waking and sleeping moments of the day she'd be all right. Maybe it might not be so easy, the sleeping part, when dreams were free to amble in and make themselves comfortable painting repressed possibilities on the easel of her mind and whispering suggestions on how to circumvent reality and revert to pleasant memories in the world of unbridled imaginings. Maybe it was she couldn't totally rid herself of John Clark Hayes during her somnambulate states, but at least he wouldn't be in control of her brain one hundred percent of the time. Right now, such a balance would be a big improvement.

The first thing to do in her quest for mental taxation was to go to the store and pick up everything she needed for this evening's feast. She needed to keep busy performing domestic acts, even if it meant walking through Harris Teeter on a busy afternoon with the aisles crammed and people in the way and children running amok up and down the rows of food. She worked in a grocery store for seven years. She knows how it is. Chaos rules.

Naturally, the lot was packed, so she had to circle around looking for a parking slot. She pulled the CRV into a space about a half mile off and got out to go inside. Too late to warn herself, she glanced across the street and saw the credit union building where the two armed robbers had shot John Clark in their haste to escape and found herself stopped in her tracks staring across at the scene of the last moments of John Clark's life, and while there was nothing or no one on the sidewalk this moment she saw him again coming toward the door, pushing his two-wheeler, ready to enter and stock the credit union's breakroom machines with chips and candy and soda.

It was like the world suddenly stopped.

She wheels her cart through the produce department and past the bakery, picking up potatoes and bread, then begins walking each aisle to impulse shop and get more steps in for her daily walking curriculum. She passes the juice section and canned fruits and arrives at the snacks, chocolates and candy bars and bags of hard candy. She sees packages of cookies and individual bags for packing lunches, and her eyes settle upon a label that says Famous Amos, and she reaches out to touch it and hold it in her hand.

These are the cookies I was so addicted to. I had to have a big portion of these chocolate chips every day, else I believed I would die. John Clark would catch me sometimes raiding the inventory, opening a case and removing a bag to take back to my desk. Thief, he would call me. Sugar Addict. There goes this week's profits. Don't you know those things are fattening? And that one day you'll die of diabetes from wolfing so many down all the time? And I would wonder if he was hinting that I was getting fat? Because as much as I tried to ignore the thought I did want him to always find me attractive. To forever look at me and think of me and sigh. Remember what I'd felt like in his arms. And most days when I'd come in to work there'd be a package of Famous Amos cookies on my desk. He'd be long gone on his route but I knew he'd stopped that morning and fished out a package to leave there. And I knew that even so early in the morning he'd taken the time to think of me.

She places the cookies back on the shelf and looks to her right toward the end of the aisle. A figure passes by in a blink, a kind of blur with a handcart, and she stares a few seconds trying to decide if what she'd seen was real or not. She quickly wheels her buggy to the aisle's end and looks around, but all she sees are people.

Real people, she thinks.

She walks past rows and rows of chips and pretzels, Doritos and Fritos and Pringles and Cheetos and Ruffles lined up for the taking. She sees these items loaded up in cases, views them in the machines at the places along the routes of Tasty Snacks, and she sees the shadow of a hand opening doors and pulling out racks and sliding the items onto the prongs of the sections that held them. The rack slides back in place, last week's proceeds are emptied into a bag, a notation made, the jangle of keys as the door gets locked. Then he is on his way. She wants to cry, Stop, but he is gone. He is in his truck and driving away. He was never one to waste time, to linger.

It is ten after five on a Wednesday afternoon, and Donna stands with her cart in the middle of Aisle Six inside Harris Teeter. She has more items to pick up and she needs to get home and start dinner, but for a moment she remains amid the crowd of shoppers and the canned music and wonders if she is really and truly here by herself.

***

He hasn't talked to anyone in his family for at least a week now, but that's not really unusual, since he sometimes goes long times getting in touch with any of them. For a while he didn't take or return calls or texts, as if he was sending the message to his relatives that he was out here in the world going to school and on his own now and didn't need any help from them. There were, though, a couple of times when he'd had to borrow some money from somebody—all of them at one time or another, maybe several times over—but he'd been doing better lately and hadn't had to resort to his old ways. Of course, he'd had to break that streak when he got the DUI and had to call David up for help, but for now he'd like all that past stuff to become ancient history and everyone forget about it and not keep bringing it up at every family get-together for the next forty years.

He wondered how the sale had gone. He had managed to go by the house earlier in the week and grab a couple of boxes of LPs that belonged to his dad and store them in the trunk of the car, but he hadn't got around to pawning them off yet. Something kept telling him to put it off. He was beginning to think he might wind up keeping them, although he didn't know what for. He didn't even own a damn turntable.

***

Yes, he saw her go into Harris Teeter and he'd gone against what he thought he should do and followed her inside and watched her as she shopped. In the past, back in his real life, he would have never allowed himself to indulge in this kind of action, since he'd done his best to be over and done with that one night with Donna that lasted only a small amount of time but had proved

157

to be everlasting as the years went by and had lingered so that he couldn't stop looking back and thinking about it. He'd attempted to train himself that Donna was the wife of another man and the two of them were a couple with two teenagers and a business partnership and he was an employee of both of them. He had no doubt in his mind that Donna had feelings for him that preceded their one night of wishful passion just as he had possessed for her, but he'd lectured himself on the end results of such a night and told himself that their one magical moment, if pursued further, would only dry up and become something regretful and troubling for both of them. John Clark knew how he was with life, especially a life in which there was something similar to love involved. He knew that despite his best intentions he would always find a way to screw it up. He had not wanted his penchant for romantic disaster and sexual tragedy to happen with Donna as it had so many times with others in his past. He had wanted what went on between them to stay fresh and new until at least the week after Forever.

But now that he was in his present condition and was so unsure of what was going to occur in the future, if he was always going to be around or if he'd be called elsewhere and have to give up this place or if suddenly everything would just end and there'd be nothing to see and nothing to remember and it would all be just one big blank of nothingness where what happened once was no more and no one would know and no one would care.

He watched her fill her cart with items and thought how this was the way it was in her world now, this country he was not a citizen of anymore. She had a husband and hungry teenagers to feed, she was a mother and wife, she had duties and responsibilities to perform that were evermore removed from one night long ago when she'd been lost in his arms.

A kiss around a corner in a hallway in the dark. Something telling me I'd found it at last but it was too late now. Remember this, it said. Take this moment with you, because this can't be. This can never happen again.

How I had wanted her then. It was like once my hands were on her and I felt her against me there wasn't any past anymore and all I'd said and done in the moments up until then did not exist as they had until the instant our eyes met and our lips touched. And though I knew this was forever and I knew it was what I'd looked for all the days and nights before I also knew somewhere deep inside that forever doesn't last in this world and when this moment ended I would be lost for good. I told myself not to think of it, not to think about it when it was over, to forget it and tell myself that this was the way it was, the way it goes, that's life and you can't deny it, but I knew I'd go on remembering and looking for it anyway. I knew how I was. I knew I'd be searching for it forever.

He didn't know how long it was—it was probably just ten minutes—but he watched her in the store and followed her and stopped when she did and studied her from afar and remembered how she had felt when she was in his arms those thousands of nights ago. Once, he was almost certain she had glimpsed him, and he wondered if the fleeting sight of him made the memories come alive for her again too.

He couldn't be sure, but he liked to think they did, that her brain started breathing with the mere thought of him. Maybe it wasn't that way, but making believe it was so made him feel a whole lot better. Somehow it made it easier to go.

TWELVE

The sale was over. While it had not been exactly a rousing success and had done nothing in the way of making everyone rich and didn't altogether free up the space in the house for future renovation, it had still helped some in clearing out some of the unnecessary reminders of John Clark Hayes and the life he had afforded to his children and his wife. It seemed that everyone was happy with what they had carried away with them—mementos, books, vinyl records, old collector magazines—and what funds that would be divided in the final settlement of the will. John Clark was never going to be completely erased from anyone's memory, but at least this had helped in making everyone accept the fact that he had moved on. He wasn't around anymore. They could finally come to grips with the understanding that he was not coming back.

Brenda certainly hoped this was the case, if not for her children then at least for herself. Even though the thought that John Clark was gone had been in her head for all these years since the actual divorce, she knew she had never actually accepted it as anything chiseled in stone like Moses and his Commandments, for even though there was that legal document denoting their divorce with all its mumbo jumbo stipulations and letter of the law qualities, there had still never been much of a sense of finality about it, for John Clark didn't actually go anywhere but to another section of the house, and he was home for holidays and birthday meals and in the kitchen drinking a first cup of coffee on the weekends or fixing a lunch or somewhere in the house replacing a light bulb or carrying out the trash to the curb the night before the garbage truck came. He brought in the mail and neatly left hers in a pile on the kitchen bar, paid for her license renewal on her car and applied the sticker to the plate without her having to think of it, so no, it was not like he was gone at all. He was always around like some kind of living ghost taking care of business, and now he was a real ghost, so maybe this time it would be different. Maybe he would do that dead kind of thing that ghosts are supposed to do and go somewhere the living don't frequent.

But with John Clark, who really knew?

There were a lot of questions she had to answer, now rather than later. She had waited and delayed a life without John Clark Hayes being a part of it for some time now, but there was no excuse for such procrastination anymore.

She needed to decide if she was actually going to stay in this house with all its familiarity and memories or sell it and go someplace new. She needed to make a decision about what her feelings actually were for Billy Joe, if she was going to allow their relationship to go forward the way he wanted it to or if she was wary of him being some sort of fortune hunter after a new widow's riches. She had to admit she liked him. She hadn't mentioned it to her children or her friends but she not only liked him but found herself pretty turned on by him sexually too. God, that was new. She hadn't felt like this about anyone except Jimmy and then John Clark back in the olden days, and that had been like comets streaking across the sky, bright and flashy but gone before you knew it. Yes, you'd seen the great light and felt the power of it rush through your body, but it didn't do to have to live with an intense memory like those forever without something else coming along to replace them, and here it was with Billy Joe, finally maybe, and at last possibly, and she didn't know whether to welcome it or not. She was not used to making such profound decisions.

God, she was going to have to grow up. She was going to have to become an adult here in her middle-age. It was scary.

She heard Billy Joe at the door and realized she'd been so busy looking around the house and being lost in her thoughts that she wasn't quite ready to leave with him for whatever restaurant he was taking her to this evening. She hated to have to make him wait on her again, since there was the possibility Wolfie might revert back to his savage state and try and bite him once more, but lately the hostilities between Billy Joe and the dog seemed to have subsided, and Brenda wondered if it was possible the two were getting used to each other. She would have never believed it of Wolfie, since he had always been exclusively John Clark's dog and never taken a shine to anyone else before. Maybe Wolfie was becoming like everyone else in the family. Maybe he was slowly coming around to the realization that John Clark wasn't coming home anymore. Then again, she doubted it. She could maybe see herself and the kids adapting to the idea eventually, but she couldn't see it happening with Wolfie. Dogs have a lot more loyalty than people, she noted. Just because they can't see someone anymore doesn't stop them from loving them just the same. The same probably could be said of Rebecca, which placed both species above human beings as far as faithfulness went.

She opened the door and Billy Joe entered, clad in a sport coat and some trousers that looked freshly-pressed. Maybe he had on a new shirt; she'd never seen it before. He looked nice, all fresh and casual. She thought how John Clark's clothes were always wrinkled and faded, ancient with a button missing here and there.

"I'm running late," she told him. "I'm afraid I started checking out the state of the house and got distracted."

"We're not in any hurry."

He glanced around the room, his eyes traveling around in a circle.

"Where's Wolfie? He's usually out here trying to draw blood from me by now. I don't know how to act."

"I guess he's back in the study asleep. I think he may be getting used to you being around and decided there's no reason for you to die anymore."

"That's different."

"It is, isn't it?"

She started to leave him in the living room while she finished getting ready, but he caught hold of her arm and pulled her close to him.

"We don't really have to go anywhere if you don't want. I'll tell you, I'm not really that hungry. I've been thinking all day and can't come up with a good idea about where to go for dinner. Besides, it's Friday night. Everybody in his brother will be standing in line waiting on a table."

"We could always stay here. I could fix you a grilled cheese sandwich, if that would tide you over."

"That would be great. That would be like a culinary delight for this old boy."

"Are you hungry now, or would you like to do something else?"

"Something else."

He was still holding her hand. He hadn't let go yet.

***

It was a dinky machine that stayed broken most of the time, the lock jammed and scratched from someone trying to break into it with a tire iron and sometimes the glass smashed in out of frustration and the money box pried open and most of the candy gone, and that was the least of it. Where it was located was in the front lobby of a floppy hotel called King's Court, back down the beach away from the square where it was thugs and addicts and petty fugitives from the law, a strip of territory where a guy might not return if he ventured in at the wrong time and happened to meet up with the wrong person. John Clark wondered why Jimmy had ever taken the place on as a client, seeing how the money was generally stolen and the machine was frequently in pieces and there was a good chance the person who went in to stock it might have to depart in an ambulance. John Clark guessed Jimmy had signed the place on when he was first starting the business and needed every client he could find. John Clark was the driver given the honors, and from the beginning he'd adopted his own philosophy in servicing the King's Court Inn. The only time to come was at sunrise, when the night was over and the day not yet begun, when the chances were good all the members of

162

this section of the netherworld had either just collapsed from their night's revels or were yet to come to life to begin their nefarious schemes for the day.

As vampires retreated to their tombs and the sun peeked out through squinty slits of a sleepy eye, John Clark could see that the machine had not been serviced lately, an occurrence he figured was because the new route-man who had been hired in his place had decided not to pay attention to it anymore, since the probability was high that any time he'd come to see about it the doors had been dented and punched and beat upon and the glass cracked or smashed and the six rows of snacks emptied along with the dollar bill receiver and the coin bucket. If John Clark knew anything about Tasty Snacks at all, he knew the replacement routeman had probably informed Jimmy of the problem about a month before and Jimmy hadn't gotten around to taking care of it yet.

Jimmy had always been a diligent kind of guy.

He needed no tools to fix the machine and he didn't worry about who might be sneaking up behind him. This was all in John Clark's mind to take care of the stocking and the repair and getting things operational again. He didn't need his hands or to lift a finger. He could will it through his thoughts and make it so. Three months now and John Clark was still enthralled at the process, how being a spirit beat the pants out of remaining alive. He didn't need clocks or tools or caution; he could service the King's Court whenever he wished.

He had one more place to go before he let it be for a time and allowed the world to spin without him. That was what he had learned, letting it be, disconnecting, allowing whatever was coming down the pike to get there and do what it had been destined for. This was what he had come to see, how he couldn't make an eternity out of controlling every little thing he felt an attachment to or a responsibility for, that at some time or another he had a duty to stop and turn away and simply let it be. Let it play out, and maybe later it could be fixed and maybe not.

He didn't even have to go by the house to know what was happening there this night. He'd seen it coming for a long time now, way before he took two bullets to the chest and entered into another phase, and now without looking he already knew what was coming to be, so he didn't have to go at all.

But he wanted to make sure.

He knew that it had been building between Brenda his once-wife on the earth and the man she had felt an at-last attraction for, and he wanted to know absolutely that she was on this night conjoined with another man and that she was not thinking of John Clark Hayes anymore or longing for him and something that hadn't ever truly existed but that the two of them made up so they would not feel so empty on the face of the earth, that they might actually feel something and care about what was happening between themselves and another person on the planet, and make it so that even if it wasn't totally true they could pretend it was.

He was not inside the house nor was he out, but in a state where some section of his spirit soul hovered between heaven and earth and could see and hear what it desired. This was one of those things he'd always desired and wanted before the time came when he and the world were no more, and he wanted to see it all through to the finish.

When finally he knew for certain Brenda had moved on to a new romance and was not mired in the world with her memory of him he relaxed some, felt some relief mixed with a tinge of sadness for what had never come to be in absoluteness for them, and then he said goodbye to Brenda and farewell to the house they'd lived in, knowing this was one more thing that was behind him now.

***

For the first time in his life David was starting to feel old.

He couldn't put his finger on exactly why he was feeling this way, for nothing he knew of had provided a trigger for these new and deep ramifications. He didn't ache anywhere in his body and he wasn't experiencing any bouts of forgetfulness that might possibly be a warning sign of future dementia, so it wasn't like there was some outside force that was making him feel this way. All he knew was his senses were doing some kind of turning he wasn't accustomed to, and it was giving him pause on a fairly regular basis when he examined what he was now beginning to experience in a new way.

It had to have something to do with the sale of his father's keepsakes. Until that came along he'd considered himself to be proceeding down the highway of life at a somewhat pleasant clip, unaware of any bumps or speed traps or crazy drivers in his lane trying to force him off the road. His relationship with his someday-to-be wife Janice was amiable and devoid of any arguments. She was pretty calm all the time and didn't do a lot to drive him crazy from each end of the spectrum. His mother and his sister had both been more than pleasant in the months since his dad's death, and even Franklin hadn't done anything screwy for a while, or at least not that David knew of, but perhaps that was because his little brother was pretty shifty and always involved in something he tried to keep undercover and below the radar and for a time hadn't been involved in murder for hire or bank robbery or anything major like that. Franklin had been a pretty good boy lately. David figured there was generally a first time for everything.

So it had to be the sale that triggered everything.

Maybe it was that he'd been unusually quiet and lacking in outward emotion since his dad died. Maybe he'd been in shock since it happened. After all, not too many normal middle class sons ever have to deal with their father being gunned down on a city sidewalk in the middle of the morning, so that had to have some kind of effect on his manner of thinking, whether he gave any indication of it or not. It could be he'd sunk into the deep depths of an ocean he'd never swam in before, and because it was so new and foreign he had only been able to concentrate on breathing and coming up with a solution on how to bring himself back to the surface. When something monumental like that is going on in one's personal realm it doesn't seem far-fetched in believing one had to deal with immediate matters first and foremost and put off any modes of reflection or grief until one was safe back in the boat, breathing normally again without pending trauma.

It was his sudden penchant for dreaming that first got his attention. He was unaccustomed to such forays as he'd been experiencing in the middle of the night, being always a hard sleeper who had to bribe himself to open his eyes in the morning. Where before he was accustomed to darkness and white noise within his resting brain, now there were strange sights and ridiculous situations to be dealt with while he was supposedly dead to the world. Men in parachutes landed on the roof of his house. Women smiled at him and then slit his car tires with razor blades. Snakes intertwined around his mailbox and kept him from getting his mail or paying his bills. He opened a jar of peanut butter and it was the color of the rainbow, blue and red and yellow and pink, and he had to debate whether to make a sandwich or not. All this in his sleep, when he was supposed to be resting. It was a menagerie parading by him that made not the first lick of sense.

And so each morning he woke up exhausted. Confused. A distemper in his soul telling him that what this day had to offer was probably going to be bad. Better to go back to sleep. Better to forget how to do anything and possibly have someone take care of it for him. A nurse. A caretaker. Someone with energy who was not decrepit and prematurely old like he was. But then he would remember his dreams, and he dared not fall asleep again for fear of what might be waiting for him and his sub-conscious.

It had to boil down to the fact that his father was dead. There was no way to communicate with him anymore, lest he drive down on the strip by the beach and find some medium who could put them in contact with each other or stand by the mantel in the old house and address his father's ashes. David wondered why he was letting the fact of his father being dead and not alive anymore worry him so much, since in real life his father and he had not had that much to say to each other anyway. Hi. Bye. How's it going? David wondered at times if his dad had any inkling of what his oldest son's life was really like—David could never tell—but if his dad had known what was going on in his son's existence he certainly never expressed it out loud. It was like his father possibly knew all the answers to the life examination David was trying to pass but made it a point not to intrude or intercede to try and steer his son along the right path to some form of success, rather leaving it to his boy exclusively to succeed or screw up on his own.

Maybe it was this lack of interference on his father's part was his way of allowing his son to grow up unencumbered by what John Clark may have considered his own personal mistakes in judgment and a failure to keep solid footing along the straight and narrow in his own past, when he had stumbled and stubbed his toe along the journey and made wrong turns and gone down paths where danger and sadness and sheer foolishness held sway, a place where once one landed there was no coming back.

David wondered if his dad had been aware all along of some of the dumbass things his son did and didn't believe in piling on after David had been tackled by his own inadequacies, and if so, should he be appreciative now of his father's silence and lack of verbal chastisement? Maybe so. David couldn't remember his father ever pontificating about poor behavior or a lack of wisdom on his son's part, and he wondered if he ought to be grateful instead of questioning his dad's parenting skills?

He'd had plenty of people around to tell him when he'd fucked up. Teachers, scoutmasters, preachers, Janice, his mother, who is still right up there at the top of the list. Perhaps he should be happy his father believed in being hands off, not trying to make his son into a carbon copy of himself, but to learn the ropes either the hard or easy way, but learn them in the way it was best for him, pain or gain or loss or to come out of it whistling a happy tune just because he'd somehow managed to survive.

Was he receiving communication from beyond? Now that his father was in another world was he sending David messages to let him know it is always all right in the end, no matter how fucked-up it was presently in the here and now? Tomorrow's another day and everything passes? It would make sense for his dad to do something like that.

It was something to consider. That was for sure.

***

He hadn't seen fit to get in touch with anybody in the family since the mini-estate sale, possibly because one of them might bring up his plan to divert the process and take a lot of the proceeds for himself, but mostly because he wasn't certain he could have a conversation with anyone without bringing up the fact that he'd certainly been feeling strange since the event took place and how it might not be for the betterment of all if he communicated that he had felt his father's presence and might have even heard his voice if he'd allowed himself to listen.

He didn't himself quite know what to think. He'd not up until now felt the need to regard anything his father sent his way since what he called his boyhood, his Missing Years like Jesus had, back when he was fresh and innocent and believed anything that was put in front of him. In those days, when he was seven or eight, he'd thought his dad was the authority on most anything and had accepted everything he'd put before him as gospel. This went on for maybe five years or so, until he hit twelve or thirteen when suddenly everything he was told didn't ring true anymore. All at once he, Franklin Hayes, had all the answers to everything and possessed, he thought, a special gift of insight that gave him the knowledge that he knew more than anybody else and that was the way it would always be.

After flunking out of school once and getting fired a couple of times and spending a night in jail and having a restricted license where he couldn't go anywhere at will anymore everything had combined and congealed and come to him as some sort of message from Yahweh that Franklin Hayes' way wasn't the best and right way anymore, and that it might be wise if he changed his lifestyle like at a obtuse right angle and started doing things different before his present path screwed him over for good. He could get busy and pass his tests. He could graduate. He could try not blowing every penny he had on drugs, alcohol, or girls.

He could, like, grow up.

There was something about the box of his father's books and other possessions that—he would swear to it on a stack of bibles, or in this case, a stack of Famous Monsters of Filmland magazines—were speaking to him and showing him scenes of his past and of things to come he had not seen before. Suddenly, his father didn't seem like such a clown anymore. That smile he remembered that appeared on his father's face came not from being such a fool set loose on the face of the earth but because he had the realization that we were all fools on life's stage doing our own brand of comedy and how all you had to do was back off what was making you act like and be a jerk and watch the show, then you could shake your head and grin and say such words like what fools we mortals be, and now, finally, Franklin thought he was starting to know what his dear old dad was talking about.

It was new, all right, this sudden partiality he'd found for listening to what his father might be trying to tell him. It made him wonder what sort of batshit insanity he might have avoided if he'd engaged in this new practice in the first place. Something to think about. He guessed he'd never know. Too late to go back now.

He thought back to the look on his father's face when he told him he had flunked out of school. He remembered how his father wasn't happy about it but never said out loud what a dumbass his youngest son was and how his life was going to go to hell from that day forward or anything like that, but instead had simply stated that it could be this wasn't either the proper time or the right avenue for Franklin to be undertaking at this juncture in his life, and that maybe he ought to try something else for a while and come back to this question of college at a later time, and maybe by then all the elements would be in place and the process might become smooth the second time around. And he'd been right. Franklin hadn't known what his dad was talking about then, much like he hadn't been able to grasp his father's insights at any time before in his life, but he did appreciate his dad not rubbing his face in the shitpie Franklin had constructed and had not discussed what a failure Franklin was as a son. As a matter of fact, like about a thousand times before, his dad had told him not to worry about it, that he, John Clark Hayes, had screwed up far more catastrophically in his younger life than Franklin had yet to come close to. You don't know, Franklin, his daddy said, what a colossal disaster a life situation can get to be until you get up close and take a gander at some of the deeds I've performed in the past.

That had been about two years ago. Franklin wondered if he had taken enough spins on the planet to go back and rectify some of his past college failures, but the more he considered it the more he knew he had to get himself back in a college setting. Somehow he knew he wouldn't repeat the errors of the past and circumvent the magnitude of his personal flops and not take more dives into the deep end and start digging once he'd hit bottom. Franklin no longer believed he would try to fuck up at a higher clip than before or play the old limbo game where the singer asked how low can you go? Franklin had gone low enough already; perhaps this go-round he would choose some new route in his life where he might actually rise and succeed instead of repeating his past practices of sinking and failing.

He didn't even finish the expensive Rusty Nail he'd ordered, but simply left a tip on the bar and left three-quarters of the drink sitting there. He'd had enough of trying every alcoholic concoction in the bartenders' encyclopedia, and so he walked out through the doors for once without the tiniest bit of a stagger and without a worry over whether he was straight enough to get himself home. Oh, he'd get home all right, but he wasn't going to have to worry about getting pulled over by the cops again, because this time the question of sobriety had no bearing, because he was leaving the car behind this time, he was walking, and so far as he could tell there wasn't a strict law on Saint Simons Island against a young man taking a walk of an evening and breathing in some fresh air and trying to come to some form of plan on what to do with the rest of his life. He wasn't sure of that part of it yet. But he could rightly say that whatever it was it was going to differ from what had gone down before.

Been there, done that, he told himself. Like that old Hollies song he'd heard on his dad's jukebox, it's time for a cool change.

***

Maybe there's hope for Franklin yet. Maybe it's better not to give up on him too fast. It could be he's a late bloomer the same way I was.

Thinking this while I watch Franklin pass my old Civic parked on the curb and continue on down the street, becoming a shadow beneath the street-lights as he gets smaller and smaller. A part of me wants to go walk with him, but I don't, because I'm thinking that maybe he is like his old man this way, maybe the best thing for him to do to learn to figure out things is to get away from the voices and the noise and the lights that make it seem like you're on stage and have to perform for the audience in order to be worthy of a spot on the earth, to just walk away from everything and get out of sight or sound with the world which is a lot of times the enemy in disguise and allow the swirling thoughts in your head to drift downward to some level of serenity and quiet and formulate the future right there.

Maybe that's why I liked running my route so much. In my other vocations there were always people present on a continuing basis, in bunches and groups and herds, great battalions who came to plunder and claim certain portions of my soul, and although I was generally successful in fending them off, sometimes a squad or a single aggressor would break through my defenses and plunge a dagger into some part of me where there was no armor and it would hurt like hell. In those settings it was necessary to stay alert and vigilant all the time, to watch for the next vestige of danger that might be headed my way from the midst of the surrounding throng. It was ongoing and tiring and at times it seemed it would never end. The world would never stop coming.

But on the route it was never that way. Mostly I was left alone to devise my steps and take on the world when I wanted and on what terms. I was not drowned out by wishes and commands, but came and went and left behind what I chose was best for the world I served. After I learned the route and the battle plan was etched in my head there was none of the doubt and feelings of failure ingrained within anymore, for I had learned which highway to take to stop the chaotic faces from blocking my view of the constellations of the day and the light that shines in darkness.

Maybe Franklin is on his way to finding that too. Best not to disturb him.

***

This wasn't the kind of thing that could be discussed via text or through a simple phone call. This required a face to face meeting in order for full comprehension to occur.

Linda had for at least a month now had suspicions about her mother and whether or not there was a man involved with her in some fashion. She could tell by the way her mother was not at home on a lot of nights and didn't pick up immediately or return her phone calls until much later in the evening and generally the next day. Linda was no dummy. She knew her mother was out somewhere doing something, and that something had to be a new male friend, else why would she be so secretive about her private life all of a sudden? Before, when she'd spent time with her friends eating out or going to movies together, her mother had been free and easy talking about where she'd been and with whom, but now the pool of information had dried up, and Linda was convinced Brenda was keeping something back because there was something brewing she simply didn't want to talk about just yet, not with anyone, but especially her children.

Carrie Underwood was asking Jesus to take the wheel. Linda punched the radio knob and landed on the classical station. She didn't recognize what was playing, but it was better than listening to what the other stations were offering. The biggest plus was it had no words, thus she could drive to her mother's house and think without some cookie-cutter celebrity star disturbing her thoughts.

It wasn't that she didn't want her mother to be happy. She wanted her to have a life of her own, and if that involved having a romantic relationship with a strange new man then so be it. For the longest time Linda had to admit she'd worried and wondered about her mother's private life. Was it possible her mother actually enjoyed the intimate company of women? Was this one of the secrets that had caused her mother and father to call it quits on their marriage? Linda had never really known what was behind her parents splitting up. Had it been because her father was a secret Lothario and had clandestine affairs with other women? Did he step aside because he knew his wife desired someone else, male or female, or was it simply a mutual knowledge that the two of them had been good for each other for a while and then that time ended, but that they stayed friends and did their duty as parents to their three children in their own strange and weird ways? It was hard to say. It had never been one of those floating questions out there in the air beyond anyone's reach that could be uniformly and completely answered. All Linda knew was that her parents had married and stayed together long enough to

170

have three children, then divorced but lived together in the same home and remained mother and father the entire time their children were growing up, but in the end no one knew what the other was doing or thinking and yet learned somehow to be comfortable with the entire setup. Perhaps they had continued to love each other from afar, while going on with other facets of their private lives, but no one, not them, nor their children, nor the world, knew exactly what the deal was.

They were weirdos, her parents. Her father was a dead weirdo and her mother a live one. Linda guessed she and her brothers weren't too far behind.

The house was dark. Linda wondered if she should go inside and look around for a minute, maybe to see what might be left over from the sale or to see if there might be some clue lying around that would help solve the mystery of her mother's current behavior patterns. No, she wouldn't do that. She needed to stop somewhere and get something for her supper. Mark and the kids were gone to a movie and probably they would fill up on candy and popcorn while they were there. Mark was supposed to have fed them before they left, but she doubted that had happened. She decided to pick up a pizza, that way she could feed herself and there'd be plenty for everyone when they got home. It was Christmas break and kindergarten and daycare were out and not operating, so it wasn't like there were any set rules right now.

She'd just finished putting in her order and was about to sit down in a booth and wait when she felt a hand on her shoulder. With the way crime was rampant almost everywhere in Saint Simons, she was almost afraid to turn around, but decided it would be better to face her assailant. That way she had a better chance of identifying him later.

"Boo," her mother said. "I got you."

"Hi, Mama. I didn't see you in here."

"I was hiding back in the back." She motioned toward the booths in the corner. "I'm having dinner with a dark, mysterious stranger. Come on back and I'll introduce you. I've been meaning to tell you about him for a while, but I've been sort of a chicken about it. I was afraid of what you or the boys might say."

Linda followed her mother back to the last booth on the left. A man sat with his back to them as they approached, a mug of draft beer in front of him, a pitcher in the middle of the table. It looked like their order hadn't made it out of the kitchen yet.

"This is Billy Joe Bradford," Brenda said, thinking how dreadfully formal her voice sounded right now. "Billy Joe, this is my daughter, Linda. She's my middle child. She teaches English over at Coastal Middle."

Billy Joe was trying to get up and say hello, but Linda reached down and shook his hand before he could.

"You don't have to get up. Hi. It's nice to meet you."

"I met Billy Joe a few months ago," Brenda said. "He works at the hardware store, and he helped me get my bedding plants into the ground so I could get the garden going before the bad weather started. You'll have to come see them in the light, Linda. They're getting prettier by the day. If the weather holds I'll have blossoms all year round."

"I will sometime."

"Why don't you sit down and eat with us?"

"I really can't. I've got to get my pizza home before the kids get there. They've gone to a movie with Mark, and I know they'll be famished when they get there. Nothing worse than hungry children at eight o'clock at night."

"Well, all right then," Brenda said. "Give me a call later on. I'll be home early."

"Okay."

Linda walked to the counter to pick up her pizza after she heard her name called. She was all the way out the door when she remembered she had not spoken another word to Billy Joe Bradford the whole time after their initial introduction. No pleased to meet you, nothing. She had not even bothered to say goodbye. Maybe she was in a state of shock or disbelief. It was hard to tell. She didn't act this way usually. He probably thought she was a jerk.

***

It has been two months and change now since he's been inside this building. He can't really say he was actually inside it then, since he was already dead before they wheeled him in the door of the ER, but he guessed it wasn't official that he was expired for sure until some doctor came along and listened for a heartbeat and checked for a pulse and opened and closed his eyes to see if they were dancing or not and turned his head from side to side to see if he might decide to wake up, and once that was done and he had passed or failed—whatever the purpose of the tests were—and been pronounced dead it would be notated where and when this judgment was determined and that would be taken as he was finally dead when he got here and maybe dead before he arrived. Whatever the case, John Clark had not been back for a visit since that time. In a way, he had been avoiding it.

It was late night and all the visitors were mostly gone. There was not much traffic in the hallways, only orderlies and nurses and the occasional family member who was spending the night or hovering over somebody's death bed. From the open doors of the rooms the voices of Jimmy Fallon and Jimmy Kimmel crept out from where patients lay in bed maybe watching and listening and maybe were not, were perhaps in such a state that the Battle of Bull Run could be going on before and around them and they wouldn't notice. There was a low murmur from the nurses station at the end of the hall, the voices talking about patients and movies and who was going on a cruise and when.

John Clark found it pretty funny that he'd not only bitten the official dust in this hospital but also for five years or so had serviced the snack and soda machines located in the break rooms and the waiting rooms on the four floors that made up the building. There was a commissary on the first floor by the gift shop where he supplied bottled water and coffee, and when he made his deliveries on Mondays and Fridays each week he expected to spend at least two hours getting everything stocked, usually more if the Plague or Covid or Scarlet Fever was in the midst of an outbreak, or if people on the Island were particularly itchy with their trigger fingers or felt the need to insert their knives or pound their blunt instruments into or onto someone nearby, or sometimes if no weapon was available to strangle another until they were somewhat throttled, and if any of those cases or incidents were in abundance then John Clark would stick around longer. Sometimes he'd have to take a number and wait to get to his job, circumstances preventing his progress, the acts of saving lives and the red tape of billing the living and pronouncing the departed dead. But he'd always made certain the job was a hundred percent finished before he got in his truck and drove away to the next stop.

He didn't recognize any of the people on duty as being part of the team that had worked to resuscitate him that morning when he'd been shot, not that it mattered, since even if one of them had been involved in his moment on the ER table they couldn't see him now anyway, because, he'd learned, it was pretty impossible to make him out these days in his current form unless the possible viewer had been somewhat close to him when he was among the living and they both had that in common, and those that had that attribute could only glimpse him in a passing sort of way and not be certain if they actually had seen what they thought they saw or if it was just a figment and not to be mentioned to anyone else in case it might tend to qualify them as perhaps bordering on nuts.

He didn't have to tiptoe or creep or even walk softly when he passed the nurses station, because not only could they not see him but they couldn't hear him either. He could squeak his Nikes as loud as he wanted and there would be no response. He could tap dance with Ginger Rogers or lead the River City Marching Band along the tiles playing Seventy Six Trombones and they would not hear. Their world was different than his and his from theirs. That was what it was like these days.

He had been big news the morning it happened. Every television news station from a hundred miles around covered the event and sent news crews to the scene to tell the story and show the scene to its viewers up close, to let the audience know that this was the kind of world they lived in these days, that no one could take anything for granted, that there were guns and criminals out on the street and it was impossible to know when something like this was going to happen. Interviews were aired with the police chief of Saint Simons shaking his head and vowing justice for the stricken family and soundbites with the victim's wife—he, John Clark, was the victim and Brenda was the wife, although technically she was the ex-wife but no one seemed to grasp that amid all the chaos and tragedy and, besides, it didn't matter that much anyway and it made a better story if he and Brenda's union was ongoing rather than dissolved—and there was further camera time for Jimmy and Donna as his employers and a final word from the pretty teller at the drive-thru who'd been sort of a witness despite not being able to see the actual crime go down because her drive-thru window was on the opposite side of the building around a corner where she couldn't really see the murder and the mayhem as it happened, but since she looked good on camera they interviewed her anyway.

And so he had been on the noon news as a breaking story and the afternoon news as the lead and there'd been some mention on CBS Nightly News of his end as a part of the discussion about gun violence here in America and how communities are beginning to get accustomed to death and maiming as just another everyday occurrence, and then on the local evening news he'd received third billing behind another murder down by the lighthouse where a wife from Augusta shot her husband on the third day of their vacation because she wanted to go somewhere different for lunch than what he'd suggested, which barely beat out the upcoming battle for more school funds between the city schools and the town council and how it looked like compromise was out of the question and one side was going to be unhappy when the outcome got revealed and what the ramifications might be going forward in the near future.

John Clark found himself inside the operating room where he had been pronounced dead that day even though he'd been dead already and to his way of thinking it was sort of a waste of time pronouncing him the same way a second time. He didn't guess much was different around the hospital since the day he entered as a dead person and not as a route delivery salesman. Everything was white and scrubbed and sanitary and all the instruments of surgery were put away and stored in drawers and hanging on hooks waiting to be put to use when the next mangled patient got wheeled in. The lights were turned off where on that morning they'd been on, but other than illumination nothing else about the room seemed different but for the lack of medical personnel present and his own presence as not so much of a gory expired victim anymore but as a spirit making his rounds tidying up and fixing any problem that might have not been rectified before his hasty departure. If there was anyone present and they happened to see him he would simply tell them he was doing a quality check and would be done in a jiffy, but seeing how he didn't really exist anymore there were truly no worries about that.

There were four soda machines, six snack machines, the supply of bottled water and coffee in the commissary to be stocked, and he went about his business quickly and efficiently. As in real life, the visitors and employees biding their time while the business of life and death was being gauged and determined did not notice him as he went about his job. The only way they would note his presence this night was the same as they had noted it during his time among them as a mortal, that being, that when they were hungry or thirsty and felt in their pockets for some sort of currency to frequent the machine and get what they wanted, the machine would work and the product would dispense, and they would be free to go back to what they were doing before and resume the process of living quenched and refreshed without their stomachs growling as much as before.

THIRTEEN

No need to break up the routine, even if in the past three months John Clark has gone from being wholly alive to becoming dead as a frigging doornail just like that. There's something to be said for continuity even if one's status has changed drastically, and that is why he feels on this December night the need to go and visit his best friend Walter, who's dead himself for this past five years but has not made any contact with John Clark while John Clark was among the living, and has yet to do so now after John Clark has joined him in the hereafter, or a hereafter of sorts, that is, because John Clark hasn't quite decided if what he's doing now is going to last or is likely to change any day now, and so is beginning to wonder if Walter is going to make contact during this interlude be it long or brief, and has decided to go and visit Walter at his gravesite and see precisely what is shaking with his friend other than the leaves on the trees, which, as Walter always said, was due to the breeze.

He is disappointed when he arrives at Walter's final resting place. The stone is of course still there, and even though it is December a dilapidated fake wreath from last year's Christmas decorations still adorns the dirt beside it, weather-worn and ragged, and John Clark is not sure who would bring a representation of the happy holidays out here to Walter, his wife or his daughter, both of whom should have known that Walter never had been one to bubble over with the Christmas spirit, much less celebrate it all year long, continually labeling the yuletide period over the years as a time for ghosts to make visitations and to remind one of past failures and beckon weirdos to crawl out from under the rocks where they'd been hiding for the past eleven months and start infringing on one's personal space. Did you ever notice, Walter would say while downing his personal lion's share of Jim Beam, how everywhere you look once it's the week after Thanksgiving there's a vagrant or a cripple or a wino throwing up in the gutter amid all the bustle and the caroling and the anticipation that soon it will be Christmas Day? Nuts and crazies, he said. The season does nothing but attract them.

Walter was not around. It was midnight in the cemetery and if he was a practicing spirit he would surely make his presence known, but all is quiet and there is nothing of him John Clark can detect. It must be that once Walter breathed his last after succumbing to his stroke and his alcoholism there was nothing further he had left to do or say, and so it seems he has foregone hanging around and travelled right away to that place that still has no name or zip code for John Clark to learn. Maybe it is that things are different for everyone who shuffles off, either they stay for a bit or catch the first train out and get gone immediately for good if they have no business to attend to, and that is the way it works.

Some of us are done and ready to go, but some of us aren't through yet and need some time before becoming an official goner. John Clark is coming to understand the way this all works.

***

Brenda listened to Billy Joe snoring beside her, doing her best to become accustomed to having someone so near to her like this in the early hours of the morning. It had been a long time since an occurrence such as this has happened, so it wasn't like it didn't take some getting used to. There had been a partner here and a partner there over the years, but it had been a good while since any man had stayed with her through an entire night.

Not since John Clark.

That had been back in the early days of their marriage, back when it was just Linda and David and Franklin hadn't come along yet. Back then she and John Clark had been more than passionate during their days and nights; it was practically like they couldn't wait to jump in bed together at every opportunity. She wondered what it was that had made them slow down, then finally get to a point where they stopped altogether? She'd considered such a question many times and never had come up with an answer. Most women, wives, mothers, would blame their husbands for this diminishment of outward affection, but it wasn't so simple as that. She had never believed it was John Clark's fault, had never thought she'd become unattractive to him or he was seeing someone else on the side or anything crappy like that. No, in her heart of hearts she had concluded that it had been her that caused whatever rift that had come between them. She was the one who had first begun thinking of how it might be if she'd married Jimmy Baldwin or someone else, if she'd gone to a different college and met another man far removed from John Clark and the world he'd brought her, if she had examined John Clark's strange persona from a close viewing and decided against casting her lot with this kind man who did everything for her but mostly lived somewhere far away in his head.

And she had been the one who had first stepped outside her vows and cheated with another man. Jimmy, to be precise, her old flame from college. And to this day, even now lying in her bed with Billy Joe Bradford sleeping beside her, she wondered if John Clark had become aware of her infidelity and simply took a step back and removed himself from the equation, had done what he always did with everyone, which was allow them to be happy and do what they wanted, while he would keep performing the duties he felt were assigned to him by the stars and go on living dispensing no ill consequences toward anyone, namely her, Brenda, who had initially sinned against him.

Once again the thought popped up in her head, the same way it had been showing its face for years now, and she was no closer to the truth these days than she had been back when the notion first appeared on the magic etch-a-sketch box in her head that was her brain, a question she could never completely dismiss from her mind.

Did she still love John Clark Hayes? Toss aside the fact that their divorce had gone through and their bedrooms had become separate and there was nary even a kiss between them since forevermore—John Clark may have continued living in the house and being a father and paying bills and making certain the roof was repaired and the yard mowed—but despite the fact that sometimes she hated him for his faithfulness and his obsession with doing nothing untoward or low, this man who seemed to be in his actions nothing more than a Thumper figure on the rabbit colony of the world he inhabited, a man who would refuse to say anything unless it was kind, who would make no enemies, who would turn his cheek and walk away but come back to do what benevolent feat he felt was required of him, was it possible that she had failed in what she knew she needed to do and had not moved on to other things and other people and had not begun a new life for herself? Could it be that even though she knew the answers to all the questions of the future and understood what she needed to do to be happy and content, was there still a chance that she had never gotten over the loss of John Clark Hayes and could never forgive herself for it, and deemed her punishment to be to continue loving him whether he was gone in real life or vanished by death?

Was John Clark Hayes still with her? And did she truly want him to go away? She looked at the clock on her bedstand and saw it wasn't three yet. She thought of that old Sinatra song John Clark used to sing whenever anyone asked what time it was. It's quarter to three, he would sing. Make it one for my baby and one more for the road. How many times had she heard those lyrics? But it always made her laugh. The children would groan, but she knew they were smiling at their father and the way he was.

She turned over on her side and regarded Billy Joe's figure. His head was halfway off the pillow and he was smiling in his sleep. She wondered what he dreamed about in the night, what thoughts came to him when his eyes were closed and his defenses down. Did he long for what was gone from his previous life and wish it would return? Or was he looking forward to the coming day, like he was a cliché in himself of it being the first day of the rest of his life?

He was a good man. She was glad he was here beside her on this night. She was glad she wasn't alone.

***

He knew that sooner or later he would have to stop hanging around and hovering like this, that he would have to finally put an end to it, he would have to leave absolutely and allow things to work out their own way, but that time still hadn't come just yet, so here he remained after he'd told himself to go.

He couldn't say it had been disconcerting or terrible when the half-estate sale happened, because he was already accustomed to his standing by then and had come to the awareness that things come to an end and life always has to move on else the universe stopped when one left and nothing else entered to take its place—there would be no balance that way—and so it had not been such a bad thing to watch people he knew and complete strangers come into his house and walk into his rooms and look through the things he loved and take some home with them and know that when they did such a thing his things were not his anymore but theirs, and it was a funny feeling watching it happen but it was not as bad as he'd thought it would be because by this time he understood.

The way it was, and he had learned it very quickly, was that all these items that had belonged to him were now a part of the world of which he was not a member anymore. Call me Emeritus, he thought. I am resigned and retired. All these treasures I garnered up and held in my hand so often are removed from my touch now, far behind me out of my grasp. But they continue breathing in my head. In that way we are all alive together, same fellowship, different realm.

Only a light or two was on in the sleeping house. He was not used to seeing it this way. He remembered leaving for work those dark hours of the night before the first hint of illumination, how even while his family slept there always seemed to be lights on everywhere. Sometimes he would go from room to room all around the house switching lights off to save electricity, but it was like a battle he was waging alone and he could never come out the winner. Brenda kept a light on in her bedroom. Linda fell asleep with the lights in her room blazing, the ceiling light and three or four lamps burning away so she could read and write her poetry until her eyes couldn't stand it anymore. David with his TV on because he couldn't go to sleep unless he was watching something and the low murmur of the television voices lulled him to a land of dreams. And Franklin, who came home so many nights stoned and intoxicated and barely able to get through the doors and wander down the hall to his bedroom without stumbling or bouncing off the walls, would collapse on his bed generally fully clothed and hibernate there until the sun or a hangover finally woke him, his condition so clouded over that he never knew if he was in the dark all night or not.

John Clark discerned that one of the lights on was in the kitchen and the other was from his former study by the library. Possibly someone had been in there looking for something or merely perusing the area and remembering a moment or two when he, John Clark, had inhabited the area and held fort there so many nights and days that no one could imagine it belonging to anyone else but him.

And on this night there was no light glowing in Brenda's bedroom. He knew she was there with her new lover—he didn't need to know his name, it was okay—and the room was dark and maybe it was because Brenda was comfortable and safe with someone at last who wasn't John Clark Hayes. He was glad for her. He was happy she appeared to be moving on from him.

It was about damn time.

It was true that Brenda had begun seeing other men while they were married. She had been the first to cross the line, but John Clark had never blamed her or let it bother him much. She may have been the first to commit this brand of adultery in the physical sense, but he had strayed long before she had, only not physically but in his head, in his mind, deep down in the core of his soul. He had been the newlywed husband who appeared faithful and true and had no trace of fingerprints on any woman out in the real world, but there were faces and voices and visions that led him away from his legal wife before she ever had the first idea he was gone off somewhere else, some place where she or no one else could follow and spy upon him, for he was away from her and the world around him deep within himself where dreams and revelations kept him company, held sway with him and became the women he could not have and did not know back on the grounds of the earth.

And so it was in that realm he was unfaithful. It was there he loved someone else.

He did not bring up what he knew to be true about Brenda, her breech of fidelity those times with Jimmy and then others, though he knew she was aware of his knowledge about her and wondered and waited for him to point an accusing finger her way, but he never did anything like that. All he did was continue. He went to work and fed his pets and listened to his children and tried to solve their problems when they came along and made certain above everything else that Brenda was happy, that she was safe, that she somehow knew she would always be cared for. Even when the divorce came and he moved to the other end of the house to sleep and live it stayed the same. She was loved. She was cared for. She never knew it to be different any of the days and nights and years to come. For that he had never failed his duty.

Another item on the list of Regrets and Wishes that he carried with him like Marley's chains was the fact that he had always taken the blame for whatever shortcomings or failures that came about in his quarter of a century with Brenda, for he had always honestly immediately pled guilty to being at fault for any of the problems that had arisen between them. He spoke very few ill words and bore most of the burdens himself, not because he had some great need to be a martyr or sit on some sanctimonious throne but because he knew this form of servitude was the particular yoke he was destined to bear in his lifetime. He did not resist it. After he discovered his calling on the face of the earth, his apprenticeship growing up and being a young man and seeing what the world was like and what it offered him, he felt the raiment fall across his shoulders and envelop his inner self and fit perfectly in all aspects, and it was then he knew the journey he was on would accompany not only him but the entire kaleidoscope of the world before and around him, and he was placed on the earth to perform the duties assigned to him, to be the man he was deemed to be. Somehow he had known this all along. He did not know how or why, but he knew.

It was good to feel the way he did now, to know that he had run a damn good race and there was little he wished to be different. Even the idea and memory of his passionate embrace and long, far-flung kiss with Donna those years ago at that Christmas party did not linger with him as anything he wished had not happened or desired to go forward. It was strange to imagine, seeing how everyone else in the world had their moments they wanted deleted or given back and never let such feelings get comfortable within them, but it was not the same with him. He was different. He was grateful and thankful all had gone just as it had.

For he was wiser than everyone else he'd come across. He knew how magic was not a permanent thing and how it dissolved and disappeared and how one had to be prepared and learn to experience it for what it was and not constantly continue hoping it was more or less than what it imparted, that it was one thing or another, but that it was magic and it would do as it wanted, which was good, which was why a person had to be glad it made an appearance one way or another and accept what it had given them. Some people never saw this magic, he thought. Lots of people go to their grave and know

nothing of what had passed before them. They had taken their life for granted. They had died wishing they were someone else.

Perhaps this would truly be his last visit to this house of his, bought those
twenty-something years ago, inhabited first by him, then Brenda and the
procession of David and Linda and Franklin, the collection of dogs and cats
that had lounged in the rooms and porches and in the yard, some buried in
the back and some cremated in their containers in the library, their ashes to
be slipped in with his to go with him when his own scattering time came.
The only ones left now are Rebecca and Wolfie, living without him and still
in the house, both constantly waiting for his return. He wondered if animals
knew when someone was gone for good, or if they thought they had just
gone somewhere and would be back soon.

Be back, he remembered. Every time I left the house I'd say to the animals
Be Back so they would know they could take a nap and then I'd be there
when they awoke and all would be as it was supposed to be. Be Back, I told
them. Wonder if they are keeping that thought still?

He made out Rebecca sleeping in the middle of his old bed, in her usual
ball. When she was not outside catching snakes and birds and mice this was
what she did, moving only when it was time for meals or snacks. Once she
had grown older this was the lifestyle she preferred. She required very little
affection anymore. Only to repose on the bed with John Clark while he slept
was enough for her. She'd had a good thing going. It looked to John Clark
that she still did.

Wolfie was another matter. John Clark didn't have to look but knew already
Wolfie was in his bed back in the study. He would not be in the bedroom
with Brenda, whether she was sleeping alone or with a partner like tonight.
It was not that he disliked her; she was fine, he would wag his tail when he
saw her. He would attempt to kill anyone who came in the house to do her
harm. He was her protector in this way. But he was John Clark's dog. Everyone knew it. They had a bond. They were best friends.

There was no way for him to take Rebecca or Wolfie with him. He knew
that. They were just like everything and everyone else. He was where he was
and they would have to stay. But it was not a matter of goodbyes or farewells.
It was not that at all. They were going with him. He couldn't explain such a
concept, but he knew it was true. He was taking them with him whether they
knew it or not.

In his new way he reached and patted Wolfie on his head as he slept. Good
boy, he told him. Wolfie sighed in his usual way and kept on sleeping, and
John Clark moved on.

***

He could feel something while he slept and he knew he was being patted, but when he opened his eyes he saw nothing distinguishable but still knew John Clark was here by the familiarity of the touch on his head and ears and the soft way it lingered there. He had been waiting for the touch for an indeterminate period of time and now that it was here at last he wagged his tail and turned over on his side so the touch could come and rub his belly and the bottom of his chin and neck.

He knew the man's name was John Clark in the same way he knew his own name was Wolfie. He had heard the names spoken so many times over his eleven years that he knew who was who, and he even knew the other people's names who lived in the house or visited there often, but they were not nearly as important as his and the man John Clark. He knew the cat Rebecca too and sometimes the two of them were friends but it was not like it was with John Clark, for he and John Clark belonged to each other. He did not know where the man John Clark had been but he understood that he would have to go there again and that he, Wolfie, would be here in the house until the time came when he could go and find the man again in a place he didn't know where it was yet but knew someday he would, and that was why he wasn't sad or distressed to know they would be apart once more for a while because he knew from the touch upon him this night that it would not be forever. He knew they would be seeing each other again soon. He had no idea how that time period could be equated in dog days and months and years but he knew it would be someday, and so he sighed and felt the touch upon him and in a little while he was asleep.

***

For a couple of weeks now she had gone along and all had been calm and peaceful like she knew it would be. Since her conversation with Jimmy and their mutual decision to try harder at furthering their relationship it seemed as if all the pressure had been removed and there was air in the house to breathe again. Nothing seemed as difficult as before. No distrust occupied the spaces between them. When Jimmy left the house Donna did not turn the idea over in her mind anymore at where he was going and what he was up to. Now she believed him when he said he was going to the store or going to the warehouse or traveling to one of the clients' businesses and seeing what he could do to repair a machine. It had not been that way before.

But where the real difference lay was within herself. She had not realized what a vast amount of space John Clark Hayes had occupied in her mind for such a long period. It was not as if she had confessed his abiding presence to Jimmy during their coming to terms meeting, but somewhere between the lines a button had been pushed or a catch released and the force of John

Clark that was within her and engaging her subconscious musings had been able to escape from the prison she had locked it in and flown from its cage to be free once more and allow her to think of something else. She had not thought it was possible to go through a day without the idea of him in some form or another crossing her mind.

Maybe she had freed herself and John Clark from their constant reflection on what life might have been like if the two of them had met earlier or at a different time or in another land or setting. She had explained it to herself down through the years as an example of cruel fate, of kismet gone wrong, of two people cursed by coincidence to know wild passion and grand romance yet know in the absolute depth of their beings that such a thing as what they had seen and what they had experienced for ever so brief a time was only a glimpse given to them to burn in their minds and punish them for some sin they had committed that the Creator on High could simply not let go without visiting retribution upon them. It might be that by facing the truth and getting down to reality this punishment was now coming to an end, but whatever it was and whichever the way the verdict came in the truth was still that it could be shed of her during the waking hours and during the performance of her duties as a mother and wife and business owner, but there still was the time when she closed her eyes to sleep and had no control of her actions, when perhaps the Creator who was her judge also slept, and that was when John Clark Hayes would come into her life again.

But maybe it was not that simple, for it wasn't like she could hear his voice or see his face in these dreams. She could not taste his lips on hers as they had been that one night in a million, that fleeting moment in time. He was not there like that.

What it was, though, was she knew somehow he was still around. She didn't know where he was or how long he would stay, but she knew in her dreams he was somewhere nearby.

FOURTEEN

It was one thing to decide you were going to turn over a new lease on life; it was another thing to actually do it.

In his twenty-three years Franklin Hayes so far had never really gone to the greatest length of his talents to actually try and succeed in anything, but it had never bothered him that much while he was so busy accomplishing nothing, because the fact that nothing good was coming from his daily actions could all be traced back to the reality that he was not really trying, so it didn't count if his grades were bad or no workplace much appreciated him being around and was generally happy when he decided to move on. If he flunked a test or lucked out and made a D, he was able to justify such a low indication of scholastic progress by knowing in a corner of his mind that the actual grade that was given him didn't truly represent what he actually had learned to that point in his studies, because if he didn't cram for his tests or strive to make good grades it could be explained as being the result that he hadn't attempted any of those endeavors and therefore shouldn't be judged by the result that had come from it. If he had made a mess out of any relationship with a female classmate or person he worked with, he explained it all by the way his mind worked and how he could see from the beginning the faults and shortcomings of others and so believed it was better to dispense with the niceties and move on to the groping and pawing and either find success at that stage or move on to something else. Females, Franklin Hayes had long believed, were not put on this earth to make anyone happy any extended time. Better to treat them like fast food and drive from the premises and not get caught in any of the post-aftermath.

It was this kind of learned behavior and muddled background that was making it difficult for Franklin to move on in his life to blue skies and green pastures. He had begun his new journey by celebrating his birthday in solitude and telling himself he was going to stay straight for a while—maybe not forever, but for a while—and see if by removing pot and recreational drugs and beer chased by a variety of hard stuff that he might rise to a loftier state with a clear vision of the world with no persistent drumming in his head brought on by assorted classes of hangovers, but although he puttered along nicely those first two weeks or so attempting to adapt to a life on the up and up, he was having trouble these last few days and especially the nights keeping himself going forward on the smooth highway and not running off the thoroughfare onto the shoulder and maybe spinning off into the woods or a chasm and denting up the car and himself. He was about at the point where he believed one tiny joint wouldn't hurt a thing, a beer would certainly taste good with the hamburger he ordered, and the sound of some blaring music in one of the clubs down on the beach might settle his head in a way the silence of his room as he attempted to study wasn't cutting the mustard.

Franklin wondered if, at this age of twenty-three, his life was already too far gone for salvaging. When he thought about the long road to respectability and the row he was going to have to hoe to arrive at a point where he might be considered as decent and trustworthy as anyone else his ilk the thought flooded his brain with the specter of failure. There was a good chance that even with the total application of all his energy to be a useful human being and not a piece of slime that in the long run he might not be able to climb such a mountain or clear such high hurdles. There was a good chance he just flat didn't have it in him to be decent twenty-four hours a day.

He did his best to fight it. He turned on the television and watched the news and Wheel of Fortune, engrossed himself in the commercials that ran so frequently to keep his mind from wondering what was going on outside his apartment door and if he should go out and join in on the fun. He studied the female news anchor's hair and lips, he looked at the meteorologist's legs as she pointed out the coastal disturbances, he stared at Vanna White as she turned letters. He knew this was wrong and was only the dark side of his mind telling him these things and leading him into these labyrinths and how he knew better and had known it was going to be like this from the moment he started in on his quest for high-standing, but he had not known it was going to come so often and with such persistence and hounding determination. He wanted to be a good human being instead of remaining a low creature of the earth who would never have a claim to anything wondrous or splendid, but he had not known it was going to be World War Three to get there. He'd been expecting a skirmish but not a full scale war.

He was ready to throw in the towel and call it quits with this being a good guy stuff, but whenever he neared the point of surrender he would stop and back off just the slightest, because it was as if someone had come in the door or peeked in the window and was watching to see what he was going to do, and Franklin had been caught doing the dastardly and shameful too many times in his life already and he did not know if he could take the ignominy of it again, for someone else either known or unknown to him to gaze upon his acts and shake their head at the unprincipled and lowdown code of behavior that propelled it. It had happened too often in the past and he wanted to be done with it. He was damned if he was going to be looked at the same way now and forever as he had for so many times before. Somehow he had to make it end. He had to change.

***

It was still his little secret that he kept to himself and didn't say a word about it and hoped no one would ever notice and ask him about it where he'd be forced to say what he'd done.

He had his daddy's old Zenith set up out in his garage. He'd stored his father's box of *Famous Monsters of Filmland* magazines over in a corner in a plastic tub by all the other junk he had stuck there until some unforeseen day when it might be of use, which was probably never, but David was glad it was there these days and the garage too crowded for anyone to walk in, so it made it easy to stash his magazines with an old quilt over them and plug up his radio in the corner where he could sit during the twilight hours of the day on those occasions when he got home before the sun went down and play the oldies channel on the Zenith while he perused an ancient Famous Monsters copy pertaining beasts and mad scientists and hunchbacks who for reasons all their own made quick work of people who got around them and asked too many questions.

It was not like anything terrible would have come about had anyone known he had visited his father's sale and pilfered items from it. Heck, it would have been fine if he had simply announced he was going to get a few things for himself and taken it away right out in the open, but there was something about admitting his fascination with some of his father's oddities that bothered him, that seemed like an extreme infringement of John Clark's privacy, and he would rather keep it to himself. What business, after all, was it of his mother's or Linda or Franklin to have the idea that he, David, was not the tough oldest son that he was, that he did not feel it necessary for any of them to know that a part of him still missed his father and wished he was still around in his absentee way walking the earth and dropping in on him from time to time. Probably everyone would view such knowledge as an indication of his prior weakness, how David as a boy would pine for his daddy when he was gone for long stretches, would sometimes sit on the porch swing and wait, looking down the road hoping his father's car would appear soon, shooting hoops in the backyard at the goal mounted on the garage or throwing his hard rubber ball against the house playing catch and having imaginary contests between invisible major league teams, straining to hear if a car was coming down the road or entering the driveway and pulling up outside the fence. If there was time his dad would play with him then. He would turn on the Zenith he kept in that old garage at the house the same

187

way David was keeping it in his garage now, and they would listen to his father's rock and roll station while they shot baskets or pitched a ball back and forth until it was time to go in for supper.

David wondered if he should include Janice in his infrequent visits to his own self-procured paradise here at the overladen garage, invite her to share these moments with him. Maybe he would in time, but first he felt it necessary to get whatever brand of mourning this was he was doing for his father who was gone for three months now but probably when it got down to cases for a lot longer than that, for David was aware of John Clark Hayes being in the act of disappearing almost from the start. He was virtually doing a Chesshire Cat-like thing in those days and vanishing but for his smile as long as David remembered. It seemed what David was doing now was trying to reconstruct that smile and restore his father's voice so that somehow in his approaching middle-age he would have something of his father to recall when he thought of him, and maybe he could then appear before the world at large as something real and authentic and not simply a face and a name to fill a slot in the obituary section of the Brunswick News when he bit the dust sometime.

His father wouldn't have cared for a lot of the music that was on the radio these days, just as he didn't like modern horror movies or bestsellers or the designated hitter. David thought of his father's disgust when he had learned that his beloved Major League Baseball was studying a way to speed up its game times for the current impatient fanbase by adding a pitch clock and a limit on throws to first base to keep the runner close, to eliminate this cat and mouse facet, and then to add to its already burgeoning list of sins the placing of a ghost runner at second base to begin extra-inning games so a contest could be over and done with faster and the fans could get home from the park earlier to engage further in their boring and trivial lives. David, therefore, in homage to his father's likes, twisted the station selector knob until he found St. Simon's oldies station so that the Beatles and the Platters and Petula Clark could reign supreme.

Even if it was still a week before Christmas the Sunday morning island sunshine made it feel like Independence Day. David began feeling the sweat on his neck collecting and his underarms beginning to drip. He thought about taking his shirt off and maybe soaking in some Vitamin D so he wouldn't go around looking like Casper, but then he thought about how the preppie number who lived next door, the lady lawyer who wasn't bad-looking at all, might come out in the backyard or look out her kitchen window and see him sitting here in his lawn chair looking all the world like the beaching of Orca. The idea of her viewing his protruding belly made him think of another way of coping with the heat.

He was rather enjoying listening to his dad's music on the oldies station, and it occurred to him that he could still keep listening if he got in the car and turned the air conditioner on high and cruised around town for a while, even if the music wasn't coming from the Zenith. Being it was Sunday morning, there shouldn't be too many drivers about causing traffic jams or trying to run people off the road and maybe kill them while they were at it, so he went back inside to retrieve his wallet and get his keys. He thought he might even stop somewhere and treat himself, have a hot fudge cake or something.

He backed out of the driveway while Creedence Clearwater was telling him about a bad moon being on the rise, thinking about how the song was what his dad called "a classic werewolf tune," and almost instantly he felt his fingers tapping on the steering wheel and his voice singing along for all it was worth. He wondered how long it had been since he had felt this way and actually drove down a street singing unbridled to the heavens and anyone else who might be in the vicinity, and concluded it had been too long a time indeed. He could almost remember when he felt like this all the time, back when he was still unaware of girls or his father's more-frequent absences and his growing realization that the world was not going to be his oyster a whole lot longer.

He'd descended into the slough of despair at far too early an age.

But he was all right this particular day. He didn't know why his spirits were on the rise so but he didn't want to question it too much this moment. It had been so long since he had felt like the world wasn't fixing to swat him like an unwelcome housefly that he wanted to savor it for a while. He figured he had plenty of time to be morose and miserable a little later down the road.

Ray Charles told Jack (whoever Jack was) to hit the road, and David reached into the cup holder and pulled out the vial of mystery pills he'd found in his dad's desk a few weeks back. They were in a prescription bottle with his dad's name on it labeled Benzonatate—take one capsule twice a day for congestion—but these weren't capsules but pills that had a rather ominous look to them, as if they were something foreign and forbidden and might border on the side of illicit. Speed, he wondered? Acid? He didn't know, but he did know his father liked tripping the light fantastic now and again. He had never come right out and discussed it with his children, but David had seen him sitting in his study with a record or a cd on, tripping away in his chair with a smile on his face from viewing something different happening on the other side of a place not visible to anyone else.

David sprinkled a small pill out into the palm of his hand and swallowed it, chased it down with a swig from his water bottle.

Now, he thought, I'll maybe get to see what dear old Dad used to see back when he was around, those happy misunderstood moments he spent before leaving on the jet plane to an airport that doesn't schedule return trips. David had always wondered what the attraction was in getting out of one's mind and losing touch with reality, but he had never tried it much, had, instead, preferred staying in his proper orb and not subjecting himself to strange unknown forces that might whisk him away from his safe existence. He had known of and seen his brother and sister both take their own personal flights before, the two of them venturing out into a realm where the rules were changed and there were no seat belts or tethers to keep them bound to their assigned positions, but he had never done such a thing himself. He had never let himself find out what it was like.

He was a coward. That was the truth of it.

Was one pill enough? Should he take another?

He wasn't that stupid. He didn't know what he was ingesting into his system and didn't need to play the prune game. Is one not enough? Are six too many? He is being daring enough already. No need to overdose or go join his father in the vast expanse this sunny Sunday morning.

Even though he feels he is fixing to start seeing God and the Heavenly Hosts any minute he decides to take a few safety protocols before whatever is in charge of his nervous system right now takes complete control of his faculties. He begins making his way to the town square over by the lighthouse and heads up Dement Road and winds around to Fredrica, then starts making a loop around the main island until he feels journeyed out. Maybe what he has taken is no more than a glorified aspirin and he won't be affected by it at all. But it is best to have a plan just in case.

He listens to Janis Joplin and Smoky Robinson and the Miracles and Otis Redding as he winds along. He has the window down because the sea breeze feels good as long as he is moving and the wind makes him feel more connected with the city as he drives along. This is not a bad place at all, he thinks. He could have grown up in lots of worse places than Saint Simons. At least here it's not urban decay and potential murder everywhere you look.

The volume on the radio seems to go up as the Fifth Dimension head off on a Stoned Soul Picnic, and before David knows it he is dancing off with them, Florence and Ronald and Lamonte and Billy Davis Jr. and Marilyn McCoo. Marilyn was the pretty one he used to study on the cover of his father's old LP. As a little boy he looked her over closely, thrilling in the taboo sin of getting a hard-on for a black woman who was probably old enough by then to be his grandmother. But such things could be ignored. A young boy's fantasies can function quite well without the aid of reality and common sense.

He just decided to keep his feelings a secret and simply drop by his father's study to take a look at Marilyn every day. It wasn't a crime as long as only he knew it. And come to think of it, old Florence hadn't been a slouch either.

"Marilyn and Billy Davis Jr. got married and had their own TV show," a voice says. "I bet you didn't know that. You wouldn't. You were too young. She also hosted "Solid Gold" for a while. She was a big star for a long time."

David looks over to the passenger's seat and there is no one there, which is funny, since he knows he heard a voice. He thinks he recognizes the voice, and then he thinks that maybe he's gone crazy because he's here in the car alone.

"I remember you coming in the study and making moon eyes at Marilyn. Most of the time you'd wait until I wasn't home and come in, but sometimes you couldn't help yourself and you'd come in and look at her on the album cover and act like you weren't doing it, but I was on to you. I knew you had it bad. But guess what? I never said anything because I thought you had pretty good taste."

Now David believes he is freaking out altogether or at least galloping toward it fairly fast. His dead father has spoken to him from beyond the grave and he cannot deny it. He doesn't care if he's on crack or acid or what it is that's taken over, he still knows he's not that far out there. He will go to his own grave believing his father was here in this car this day with him. Hell, he thinks, what do you mean, was? For all I know he's still sitting here in the seat waiting for the next song to play. Invisible, maybe. Dead, for certain. But here.

"By the way, you're not crazy, David," his father's voice tells him. "You've just taken a nice little hit of TLC I'd saved for about ten years to take myself if I decided I needed to vacate the real world for a while. I had three of them to take separately to make the world go away and get the hell off my shoulder or to take all three at the same time and end everything for good. That was back when I had a black viewpoint about life, but I got over it. I almost got to where I enjoyed living for a good long time. Nobody could have told me such a thing before. But everything got better for me just when I thought it never would."

"That's the way it will go for you too, son. Just keep plugging and don't let it get to you is what you do. Don't sweat the small stuff. Everything passes in its due time, sooner or later."

The next song comes on, Grace Slick and Jefferson Airplane. "White Rabbit." Feed your head. David is not sure he's ever heard this one.

"This is another song about drugs," his father says. "Hallucinogenics *and Lewis Carroll, in fact."*

Do tell, David thinks. You learn something new every day.

***

John Clark Hayes had not, up until this time, been the type of attendant spirit who is attached to the ones he'd recently departed from, but had instead been rather removed and apart from the action going on without him and stayed a safe and tolerant distance away so as not to interfere with the lifestyles going on he was no longer a part of, and tried to allow those from whom he was detached the opportunity to live their own lives without being duly influenced in any way by a supernatural whim, and thus be free to screw up their lives sufficiently by themselves without any aid from beyond the veil. John Clark was of the opinion that his children and ex-wife and friends and lovers all had sufficient reasons already to blame him for the pitiful state of their existences, and he did not wish to add any more coal to the fire.

It was, therefore, unusual for him to allow his essence to drift too close to those who had been tied to him previously, but this time he had allowed the notion of him to touch base with his eldest son and give him some form of shoulder to bolster his spirits and a light to shine upon the dark path he seemed to be continuously embarking upon, which John Clark knew from personal experience was a treacherous and harrowing trip and how even a small amount of wise council from an invisible cohort might help to keep David from losing his footing and plunging to the rocks far below.

John Clark was careful not to be too obvious. The image his son saw was not truly his father's, not anymore, at least, for that had changed along with everything else, but what David thought was his father sitting in the passenger seat beside him sharing a tab of TLC was only a conjured wisp of the residue left over in the real world, the dust of what had gone on to the world of the spirit, or Ghost City, as John Clark had dubbed it, but what was there and what his son believed he was seeing were two different things for which there was no explanation and what John Clark believed was better that there wasn't.

His voice, too, was not really present either. The sound David Hayes heard did not come from the almost-real apparition that sat beside him on their tour, but was more like a recording from an audio library that David had remembered and stored in his consciousness over the years, now come forth in sentences and words of advice and knowledge that David had self-programmed in his time with and without his father, resounding now to ease his doubts and fears and tell him which way to go and when to do it and how to go about achieving something good once he had arrived there.

And so, the fact was John Clark was with his son but was not. What could be seen of him was not him in actuality but was a part of him remembered and recalled to be, like Lazarus, once dead but now back among the living, here with his son to guide him for a moment, to keep him from getting lost. None of what David was experiencing of him was real, but it was at least like a game of horseshoes and close enough. It would do.

No, he had never wanted to interfere in anyone's life or be the kind of person who's bossy and insisted on things being either his way or the highway, he had not wanted to be the one who could have a finger pointed at him if and when things went wrong, and he had tried to keep a distance between himself and the goings-on of life and let them handle it the way they wanted while he stayed somewhat out of reach in his land of himself and did what he wanted when he thought the time was right, and sometimes it had worked and sometimes not, but he had made certain he had not been the one to cause the earth to shake or the mountains to come tumbling down as the result of a wrong endeavor. He had worked diligently to assure himself that once the sky fell down on his head it had been no one's fault but his own. He figured he could make enough bonehead mistakes by himself; he didn't need to branch out and infect the others of a realm he was not a member of and make them become victims of his own personal contagion.

Okay, then, the thing of it was he was coming to the realization that this ride with David might be the last thing he could do for his son until his own time ran out and it was his scheduled moment to leave. There at the first it hadn't occurred to him that he was on borrowed time and that this branch of eternity didn't go on forever. There were phases to all this, he began to realize, and once one leg of the journey was through it would be time to move on to the next leg. You couldn't just hang around in one place until the end of time. Even the hereafter has a schedule.

So, accompanying David on this excursion through David's own valley of the shadow was perhaps the last thing John Clark could help him with before the shot clock expired and he either launched a three-pointer or coughed it up to the defense without a chance of scoring. Maybe he could have delayed these formal finalities until another time, but the fact that David had stumbled upon John Clark's emergency supply of THC, which, when he purchased it from a fellow worker some quarter of a century before, was supposedly enhanced by some Dr. Feelgood in a laboratory somewhere to produce massive moments of euphoria and intensified sensory perception and help a fellow see God and all that stuff without overdosing and going off to the Land of Jello like was possible with bad acid. John Clark knew his eldest son fairly well at this point and didn't feel the least bit good about letting the boy go on a trip for the first time all on his lonesome and freak himself out so badly he might never recover. He didn't particularly want to go along as a bodyguard or a keeper or anything like that, but he didn't feel like he could take off for the sky with a clear conscience if he didn't make certain his son didn't do something lastingly dumb, which John Clark was pretty sure David could do, since acts of idiocy tended to run in the family. David had it, Linda had it, and, oh god, did Franklin have it, and John Clark was fairly certain they hadn't inherited it from their mother.

He manned the radio and pointed the way toward turns and new streets and the sighting of familiar landmarks along the way. *Remember when I took you for a walk on the pier, he inferred. You were maybe five and threw your wooden airplane over the rail and out into the ocean. You wanted me to go and get it and cried and had a fit when I told you I couldn't. It was like the first time you realized I couldn't do everything, and I don't know if it made you angry or if it scared you shitless. We watched it float out to sea and you cried for a while and when you stopped you wouldn't stop looking at me. I wondered if you knew already that this was the way it was always going to be. Your father was going to eternally be a great disappointment.*

It's gone now, but over there was the parking lot where I took you to learn to ride a bicycle. You were scared to death and thought I was trying to kill you, but after what was really a short time you were cruising along and going around in circles and laughing and smiling, and the only time you were unhappy was when I got close to try and make sure you didn't fall over. It was like you learned how to do this despite me being around.

I took you to see Old Yeller and you were traumatized for weeks. I should have known better. I tossed you a basketball and it hit you in the nose and you ran to your mother. When we watched The Creature From the Black Lagoon one night in the living room the Gill Man scared you so much you wouldn't go out in the backyard and swim in the plastic pool anymore. You said it was full of monsters.

You said I loved Linda more than you and when Franklin arrived you thought we would keep him and send you off somewhere else to another house and you would have no mother anymore. By that time I already had the feeling you believed you had no father, that I was not your real dad but only a poor substitute. It seemed like every time I came your way something bad happened, and I didn't know if it was bad luck or me or if you were just the strangest kid who ever walked the face of the earth. From the earliest time I didn't know what to do with you, and it got so it carried over to everyone else, you, your brother and sister, your mother, all our family and friends, everyone. And that was when I thought it best to take a step back and give the world some room, that we were getting in each other's way, that we'd do a lot better functioning by ourselves.

Once he was finished reminding David of the way it had been in the past and how terrible it may have seemed then and how it had worked out okay after all, that David was not totally screwed-up like he tended to think he was, John Clark then began to steer his son through the peculiarities and ambiguities his present life seemed to be presenting him these days.

You could have done a whole lot worse than choosing Janice for a wife, he told David's mind. First of all, she's not a bad-looking woman at all. She's maybe no beauty queen, but she's all right when she gets fixed up, if that's what's so important to you. If it is then I'll let you in on a little secret— you may have outkicked your coverage when you got her to say yes to marrying you whenever the day comes. You're not exactly the most hand- some dude who's ever strolled down Broadway, you know. You're cursed by looking something like your father, which is somewhere just above The Monster Who Challenged the World, so it's not like you should be expect- ing the great-granddaughter of Sophia Loren to come knocking at your door desiring your company. And it's not like Janice is stupid or anything either. She doesn't need any help figuring out which leg of her yoga pants to put her foot into, and if you tell her a joke she gets it even if you screw the punchline up. So believe me, buddyroo, you got the door prize in that department.

John Clark went on to say how David's kids-to -be weren't going to be the worst in the world either. It wasn't like his son was going to be Gomez of the Addams Family and there would be Pugsleys and Lurches and Cousin Itts coming after him, running around the yard for the neighbors to see. They would actually be decent and normal children, certainly not as wigged-out and bizarre as David and his sister and brother had been. Not that any of you were all that terrible, John Clark amended. Just space cadets.

Sometimes I got a big kick out of the way you guys acted. I liked how it seemed as if you'd all landed here from Neptune and how each of you could drive your mother completely batshit sometimes in your own different ways. When it got like that I didn't have a hard time knowing you kids were defi- nitely descended from me. Weirdness runs in the family the majority of the time, and I think you got that from me.

John Clark went on.

You have a nice life going, David, believe it or not. You're not going broke anytime soon, no matter how you believe debtors' prison is where you're going to end up. Janice has a good job and so do you. You two could do a whole lot worse. It's not like you're missing any meals and somebody's coming in the middle of the night to repossess your car. Most of what drives you so nuts is all inside your head. I can tell you that's true because I've been through that whole line myself, back in the days when I thought being crazy was a handicap. You just have to learn to do the mental hokey pokey and turn yourself around.

That's what it's all about, son.

John Clark could see David coming off his high and preparing to come back in for a landing. Two hours had passed and the THC had subsided enough that now all David had to worry about was relaxing too much. John Clark knew how it was. David would be okay. He would marvel at what kind of trip he had taken and chuckle some inwardly at how far-out he'd been. It had been pleasant, he would think. It was almost as if he'd made strides toward getting his head together. Maybe a few more times around the block and that would do it.

Maybe he would see David again. John Clark didn't know. But he gave his son a sense of goodbye all the same, not knowing if they would ever meet again.

FIFTEEN

For the longest time she'd believed it would never happen this way with her again, and no one could have convinced her any differently. No one, of course, would have ever been confided in on such a subject by Brenda Hayes herself, because that would mean sharing the secret she had carried in her heart for the longest of time, and that was the fact that deep in her consciousness Brenda was convinced there was no better lover in the world than her ex-husband had been, and as much as she hated admitting it she felt she would go through the rest of her life never experiencing an overwhelmingly intimate moment between herself and another man (she'd even expanded the field to include a woman, though she had yet to cross over into that sort of land) that would please her and satisfy her more than the uncountable times she had been with John Clark Hayes.

Perhaps it was not that John Clark had been the most endowed and physical lover she had ever encountered. She had dated a few burly-types back in college, and yes, it was the sexual revolution and the Summer of Love or maybe a little past but she hadn't been one of those abstaining waiting until holy matrimony girls who circumvented sleeping with anybody no matter how turned on they got. Brenda hadn't been a strumpet or a gutter-slut but she'd flopped around the covers with a few men here and there when the situation seemed to warrant it, but despite a goodly percentage of those trysts being enjoyable experiences she had never traveled so far as the moon and beyond with any of them until John Clark Hayes came along, which was something she couldn't pin a label on, only that John Clark had been different and had always remained that way.

The thing was that none of these previous lovers could keep up with John Clark when it came down to the Effort Department. None of them aimed to please like John Clark Hayes did. They may have gotten hot and bothered and performed like champions while the act was going through its motions, but they were not as prepared in their opening foreplays as John Clark always was, the care and planning he put into what was to come, his staying apart and coming together, his delays and starts, his gentleness interspersed with savagery that rode to a point where Brenda would want it to happen and at the same time never want it to end, and somehow John Clark Hayes was the only man she knew who could accomplish this. It was like he was two or three lovers all at once, and when the lover she had chosen came to her the stars shone and bells rang.

And unlike the rest of her past lovers, who'd already left the scene before the act was done, John Clark always was there with her, whether that part of him was gone or not, the part she loved would never leave her but stayed with her and whispered her name and held her close until it was time for them both to return to the world they'd left behind.

It had been three months since John Clark's death, but it had been much longer a time than that since she and he had first begun to say goodbye to each other. It had been years since they had first begun sleeping in different beds, then divorcing but staying together in the same house for the sake of the children. Those years had gone by and they had been apart for a long time even before the day John Clark died, and when that happened the breach between them became complete.

But she'd not forgotten him or believed the day would come that she ever would, yet now she was beginning to think that too was changing. And she would never have supposed that some man with the moniker of Billy Joe who worked in a hardware store would be the cause of it. On her first glance of him in the garden center, she had not given any credence to the idea that here was a man who would come along and rival John Clark Hayes in those areas that Brenda believed only John Clark was truly accomplished. But she had to admit it. She had to give credit when credit was due. Billy Joe was quite the partner in bed. He was all she had ever dreamed of, even compared to John Clark, even to those long-ago trysts with Jimmy, and she was experiencing delights now she had conceded were gone from her for good, but they were back once more and in full force. They were most certainly back and showing no signs of departing. So yes, it was good with Billy Joe Bradford in bed and out. She was happy again, though she tried telling herself not to be that way too much, to remain faithful somehow to the deceased John Clark and not tarnish what they had once shared together. But this was now, she told herself. What transpired between her and John Clark was a long while ago and getting further down the line with every passing day. She had not had faith she would ever be happy and fresh again, but here she was, and it was hard to feel bad about it.

There was also another thought in the corner of her mind that was growing stronger all the time, and that was it was becoming clearer to her every moment that what was going on was not only making her happy but was doing the same to John Clark, wherever he was, in whatever form he had assumed. After all, this was the way he had always been, watching out for her, making certain she was safe, doing whatever he could to never allow her to be sad.

Somewhere she knew John Clark was glad for her. She did not understand how she knew this to be true, but she did. She was in love with someone besides him, and John Clark was happy.

***

Maybe it was simply the way the process of grieving went, but Linda could tell she was getting over her father's death a little more each day. She couldn't quite put her finger on it, but her thoughts of him were not so constant these past few weeks. She did not spend time wondering why he did the things he did, why he had acted as he had for almost her entire lifetime. She did not know if she was in the process of understanding him or forgiving him or what exactly was in her mind, but it was a welcome relief from the onslaught of mysterious memories she seemed to have collected from her first waking moment as his daughter.

She was not angry with him anymore, which was a new sensation, since anger and bewilderment seemed to have been the common elements of her emotions toward him for the longest while. She was not, in fact, angry or puzzled or disgusted with much of anything that was happening lately, in her thoughts about her father or her curiosity about what her mother might be up to or her two dumb brothers who weren't worth worrying about or her husband or children who ought to be the most important things in the world to her by now but weren't. She was more consumed over what was going on at school and why she lately seemed to want to spend more time with Lynn Peterson the Latin teacher and what that meant in her new line of thinking. In a few years she would turn the ripe age of thirty, and boy oh boy was she beginning to think a mid-life crisis was taking place in her already.

She was afraid to admit it to herself but all indications seemed to point to the fact that her sexual inclinations had taken a sharp turn these days and were traveling in a direction she had never gone in or even considered in her life before. She had never thought of herself with another woman, for it would have been a crime to her way of thinking in the environment she grew up in. It was not really any stifled vibrations from her mother or father—no, whatever faults the two of them had it couldn't be laid at their feet that they were homophobes, or whatever it is you call those folks who think such attractions one might have for the same sex as themselves warranted expulsion or suspension or a good beating with a Louisville Slugger to dissuade them from such proclivities. Linda knew it was her own generation that instilled such negativity in her, and perhaps it was the fact that she was growing older and more apart from her old acquaintances that she was now able to catch the drift of a new idea, a fresh act, some slice of living she had never considered so far in her term on earth.

She was on her way to a basketball doubleheader this December evening, the last school activity before Christmas break. She had done her best to avoid extracurricular volunteer activities at any of the three schools she'd worked at until now, but this night she would be behind the snack counter with Lynn, serving up popcorn and soft drinks for three hours while the girls and boys games were going on, and there would be time, Linda hoped, for the two of them to talk. Linda liked Lynn a lot already as a friend and a co-teacher; she was beginning to want there to be more to it than that. The thing was it was hard to tell whether Lynn felt the same.

She was here thirty minutes early. She wondered if she looked too anxious. She wondered if anyone else on the faculty that was volunteering tonight would figure out why.

This was her first time getting involved in this kind of thing, so she stood in the lobby and waited for someone to get here and tell her what to do. A few people wandered in early for the girls game, looked at the closed window on the concession stand, and went inside to watch the warmups.

Lynn came down the hallway with the American History instructor, a man named Eugene Vick, who as far as Linda knew was married, and Linda felt a sudden rush of jealousy. Could Lynn be running around with him and she hadn't known of such a pairing? Linda immediately wished she'd stayed home. Her own personal life was a downer enough without having to get educated about this.

Eugene broke away to go sit at the admission table and take money with Joel Bosheers, and the way the two greeted each other told Linda the real scandal was going on between the two men, Joel who was a bachelor, and Eugene, the married man who had maybe made a change of course since saying I Do. Linda let this settle in her head for a moment and then felt relieved.

"I'm almost late," Lynn said. She opened the side door of the concession stand and went inside and unlatched the sliding door. Linda took one end and the two of them raised it upward. Lynn switched on the light and took a till she'd been carrying and placed it in the drawer.

"Here's our money till," she said.

"I've never done this before," Linda said. "I don't even know the prices of anything."

"Popcorn is two dollars a bag, a soft drink—Coke and Diet Coke is all we have, a cup of ice and we pour from a two liter bottle—that's a dollar, and peanuts are a dollar a bag. We used to sell hot dogs but don't anymore because the warming oven blew a fuse, which is okay by me since hot dogs were a lot of trouble. If they leave it up to me it will never get fixed."

People started lining up for refreshments, and for twenty minutes there was no time for talk, but just reaching and pouring and scooping and taking money and giving change, and several times they were so busy that they bumped into each other and rubbed against each other. They touched, and Linda enjoyed it. She wondered if Lynn felt the same?

After the girls game started it was fairly deserted in the lobby. There was time for talk. The two women smiled and chatted with each other. It seemed they had a lot in common.

Linda could tell something was happening. She didn't know where it would lead, but it was nice to think of the possibilities. She wondered what Mark would think when the time came to tell him. She wondered how the children would react, what her mother and brothers might say. She wondered if her daddy would stir in his ashes if he found out? Probably not, she thought. He'd never been like that at all. Her daddy had always been pretty much cool with everything.

***

When she thought about it clearly and stopped making excuses for herself and took some responsibility for her own behavior, Donna couldn't lay all the blame on Jimmy for what was lacking in their marriage. She'd always considered herself to be the high and mighty one and Jimmy to be down among the slimy mollusks that inhabited the lower reaches of the earth and had no sense of principle or a desire for wholesome decency, but now that everything in her life had been brought out into the light for examination she could see that it had not been Jimmy working alone who was solely the cause of the negative things that had gone on between the two of them over the years. At best, she thought, they both shouldered an equal share of the blame.

The truth was—and she had to accept it as gospel—was for all her pointing a finger and accusing Jimmy of a litany of foul deeds it had been her who had strayed past the formal line of bond and consent on that one particular night of the long-past Christmas gathering, the evening when she and John Clark had taken the step away from the party and the celebratory people and gone through a doorway into a solitary nook and fell finally in each other's arms and exchanged the long-overdue kiss that had been waiting out in the air for eternity for the two of them to at last take. She remembers the kiss even today and can't seem to let it go, years past, months gone by with John Clark dead and gone and nothing but ashes now, remembers the way it felt to be close to him and touch him and be the one who was in his arms sharing a kiss and how good it felt to know that he was kissing her and she was kissing him and there was no one else in the world keeping them apart for this divine moment, and how she had wished it would never end but had known that it would, and how, like she was certain John Clark was too, she would never forget it and would know in her heart that nothing would ever be so wonderful in her life again.

Perhaps Jimmy had crossed the line before that night, she did not know, but it was one thing for a person like Jimmy to boogie through a mild flirtation and not think anything about it but it was another for her to plunge into a deep canyon of emotion and fall with all her being, her heart and soul and body, into the mystery existence that was John Clark Hayes and all he encompassed, and go there without a thought of broken vows or disregarded promises she was leaving behind as she fell. She could not fault her husband for accepting something temporary while he journeyed alone, for now she knew it had been her who had left him behind so completely and without recall that night, and whether he knew the complete story or not, he was still wise enough to know that his wife was somewhere else and that some part of her wasn't likely to be back. He did not have to have it pointed out to him. Jimmy could always tell which way the wind was blowing, and certainly from that night forward he would have had to have been a fool not to notice the shift in the breeze and how it was nowhere near as warm as it once had been.

No, it was her fault and that was all there was to it. She had been the one to cause the break. She had been the one to fall so deeply and completely for someone else, even if she knew it wasn't going to be, even if she knew this promise of eternal love would only last a moment.

Okay, then, might as well be truthful about it, she thought. No use lying to myself and trying to make myself believe something I know isn't true.

I always had a crush on John Clark, from the first time I had him for a class and from the first day when I came to find work at the grocery store and he was there. There was something about him and I knew it from the start. I was seventeen and getting ready to go off to Troy, trying to decide that last year of high school what I wanted to do. I took Advanced Placement Freshman English and there he was—he was Mr. Hayes back then—and I liked him so much I took Creative Writing with him in the spring, even though I'd hardly written a thing in my life before. It was in this class where I found out he'd published two novels. He used to joke about how nobody ever read them, but I did. I went to the Books-A-Million in Brunswick and ordered both copies and read them. They were pretty good but maybe over my head at the time, since I didn't understand what was going on in the plot half the time. It wasn't that they were bad but more that they were different. I'd never read books where the people in them were all pretty nutty and did weird things to ruin their lives. Some-

times the plots got pretty gruesome but they made me laugh at the same time. I wasn't used to anything like that. I'd been pretty sheltered all my life. I had never done anything wild my entire life.

I was ready to get started, though. Freshman year at Troy I started hanging out with a couple of girls who lived in the dorm, one from Fort Lauderdale and the other from Kingsport, Tennessee, and they were both in to smoking pot and zoning out now and then, so I joined in just to feel like I was out in the world and wasn't such a kid anymore. I can't say I ever got too hard-core like they did, taking speed and dropping acid, because I had a job on the weekends and a night or two during the week, but I crossed the line now and then. Sometimes they'd sneak me into their dorm and I'd spend the night on their couch, and we'd go down to the beach and listen to music and drink beer and pick up boys, or at least they did, Debbie and Sara, and me on occasion but not so much. I had my moments though.

I heard John Clark had given up teaching when I came home for visits and I didn't see him or hear about him for a while. I was looking for a better paying job than the one I had with Kentucky Fried Chicken and went in and applied at a Harris Teeter down the road from school. That was when I saw him again, stocking shelves and running a cash register and working up in the customer service office at the front of the store, cashing payroll checks and sending Western Unions and handing out money to the cashiers when they needed it. He was doing it all and it looked like he knew what he was doing. I wondered how he'd learned all these skills so fast. I asked for an application and he got it for me. I wondered if he'd remember me and he called me by name. Hello, Donna, he said. It's nice to see you again. I said, hello, Mr. Hayes, and he said, no, don't call me that anymore. It makes me feel old. Call me John Clark. Or J.C. if you wish. He took my application when I completed it and brought it back. I'll put in a good word for you, he said. He must have, because I got the job.

I worked there with John Clark for three years during the summers, all the while completing my degree while he rose through the company ranks and became one of the managers. Not only was I around John Clark during that time, but that's where I first met Jimmy, who was working in the Dairy department. Jimmy really put the rush on me for a while, and after a time I finally said yes to going out with him, even if the person I was really interested in was John Clark Hayes. But John Clark was married and had a kid and another one on the way, so I knew that was a hopeless case. I made up my mind to stop dwelling in fantasies and move on. After I graduated, Jimmy and I got married and I took a position *teaching fourth grade at an elementary school in Brunswick and quit Harris Teeter. After a while Jimmy took another job at a Winn Dixie and I didn't hear anything about John Clark anymore.*

Ten years went by, and wouldn't you know it, there I was teaching in a school with John Clark's wife, Brenda. That was why we both ended up at that same Christmas party when I met up with John Clark again. That was the night of the Big Kiss that threatens to live until Eternity. But doesn't everybody have a moment or a memory that lives in their head like that? John Clark and I can't be the only ones. There have to be other people out in the world like this. I suppose in time everybody gets over it or stores it away where it's not on the front burner anymore. I guess I'll get over this eventually, the same way John Clark did. He learned to live without me and life went on.

Yes, she thought, I will do the same. I have a nice life going and I'm not going to let something that happened a long time back color it bad for me. I have my own marriage and two sons and a productive life to go with it. One of these days I'll be a grandmother. I won't have to worry about one kiss with a man who's gone from the world forever spoiling everything else I have going on in my life.

She drove to the warehouse and unlocked the door. It was a Saturday and no one was working, so she wouldn't be disturbed if she took a little inventory and tried to determine what was selling good and what wasn't and if there was any product she didn't need to carry anymore. It was quiet in the warehouse, and she wondered if the mice were listening to her footsteps on the concrete and hiding somewhere.

But it wasn't just the mice who were keeping quiet and watching her. She felt like there was someone else with her, and she didn't have to guess who that someone was. It was like he was always around, and she was accustomed to it.

"Hello, John Clark," she said.

***

This was not going to go on forever. Nothing lasted that long. That was one of the big things he'd found out. That was the major thing he'd had to learn.

From the morning when he'd started in with his two-wheeler at the Lancaster Hills Credit Union at the Jordan Center Mall he'd had no advance warning on how quickly stuff that you thought was always going to be around sometimes just flat went to hell in the blink of an eye. It wasn't that he thought of himself as immortal all the time leading up to that one moment, but it was more that such an abrupt conclusion to all he was accustomed to happened too fast for a whole lot of reflection. He could safely say that he had never been dumb enough to think he was going to be eternal and live forever; it was more like he was just the same way everyone else on the face of the earth was, and that was the unspoken conviction everyone harbored within themselves that even though they knew they were whistling in the graveyard they still carried the idea around that they were never really going to go anywhere, to not die like everyone is supposed to do when the end comes, but that there could never truly be an end to themselves in any way they could think of, because if the end was to come for them then that meant the end of everything else, the world, the universe, everything there was, and how could a thing like that possibly happen? No, it was better to ignore the facts and keep in a corner of your mind the idea that what's always happened to others was not going to happen to you.

It wasn't that he had been wrong so much. After all, he'd believed in all things and him being eternal the same way everyone else had, and it was not like he had feared he might be, that he would come to an end and all things would end with him, or even worse, all things outside himself went on while he did not, but that perhaps everything ended the way he knew it but still went on in another manner, and he had ended in one way but went on for a while in another, and how that would end too but then he would go on to something else. He did not know what that something else was just yet, but he was at least coming to the knowledge that whatever it was was out there and he would come to it soon and understand it then just by being in it, and perhaps when that was done there would be something else but he could not know that now. For that he would have to wait and he would not know for how long that would be. It was all complicated and unclear but he at least understood a lot more of it now than he had on the morning when the bullets entered his body and he was suddenly somewhere he'd not imagined himself to be and had no rules of decorum on how to comport himself there.

This, then, was what he had learned.

He was in a place of departure right now, a sort of waiting room or a learning center where he was being educated on what was coming up for him when he got to his new destination. He wasn't scheduled to go just yet; there were some lessons to be digested before he moved on to his new locale, and there was also a show of benevolence toward him for being in an unexpected circumstance and having to learn a new existence before he was ready for such an event to transpire, which was his being able to stay and linger and not vacate the premises of the earth he had known just yet, not immediately anyway, not until he had been granted the time to get his effects in order and accept what had happened and where he was and who and what was being left behind and how to provide for all of it and tell the whole of it goodbye and feel good about leaving and not think there was something still there that had not been taken care of, that all his earthly tasks had been completed, checklist done, and it was okay to call it a day, a lifetime.

He had even been granted the knowledge that someday in the future the two men responsible for his death would be apprehended in Pensacola, Florida, and that the one who had shot him would be killed by the police during the capture.

But his time here was growing short, he knew that. He had come to accept that this part, like what he had left before it, did not go on forever. There was an end to it soon, and it would be here before he knew it.

He didn't think he had to worry about Brenda anymore. It appeared she was over him. At last, he thought. All this time he had worried about what would become of her after him, even when he was still around and feasible in a sense, and now it looked as if she had been able to finally make the break with him and find someone else to spend the rest of her days with. This is what he has been striving for so long, and while some of it feels good and he is happy he can't help but have a feeling of loss about it. He doesn't want to be so human and such a braggadocio male on the face of the earth that he is sad she has found someone else, a little hurt that she will now bestow her affections and thoughts on someone besides him. He guesses he is not completely finished with the ways of the world just yet; he still has some residue of it within him. Maybe it just takes time, he thinks. Maybe as I transition to some new place and being these feelings for Brenda and what was lost and left behind will subside. Maybe we'll both arrive at a point where when we think of each other it will be in passing and perhaps with a smile.

He guesses he should be shocked or surprised at the abrupt change Linda is going through, but if he is truthful (and this new situation he is in requires such a quality) then he has to admit that he's seen such a thing coming for a good time now. It's just hard these days, he knows, for a fellow brought up in the day and time he was to not have second thoughts about such a new direction his only daughter is taking. He considers how he has spent his entire life attempting to be a kind and understanding person, to not look down on someone because they are different from him, to not consider himself superior or all-knowing or to be residing at the top of the old ethical mountain where all below who didn't act like him or adopt his beliefs or follow the same road he did were not on par with him and were therefore to be avoided—no, he had not done that. He had, in truth, been a chameleon in his behavior toward others. He had let them live and go forward and prosper without an unkind word or gesture from him, and he could not remember ever saying a bad word against anyone for his entire stint on the planet.

There had been people he had not liked much, situations that disgusted him, experiences he would have soon wiped clear off the slate, but he had not taken action against them. He had let them ride. He had hung loose. He had found his place in the world for his body and soul to lurk and never allowed the bad things to enter. He had not been perfect, but he'd been damn close, and as far as he knew living a decent life was like horseshoes and hand grenades, because close did matter.

The way he looked at it was this: if Linda was drawn to a woman, then she was old enough to make that decision, and she was his daughter, and what he had tried to do all his life since she came along was support her and protect her and see that she didn't grow up to be a serial killer. Mission accomplished, he thought. She married. She is a mother and a teacher. She is good at both things. She deserves happiness in her life. If this was what brought that to her, then so be it. Her dad was happy about it. Her dad said good for you, babe. You gave me a couple of grandchildren and made me proud and you loved me all the way even when you didn't understand the first thing I did, when you had to go through life knowing your dear old dad was from another planet. But you came through it. You survived me. You did good.

The more he thinks about it the better it is. He and Linda have had a good run as far as fathers and daughters are concerned. Not a lot of fighting, very little drama. She has been the most level-headed of the crew he sired. He's not going to have to worry about where she goes or what she does in the years to come, because it's going to be like it always has, she's going to do right toward everybody. Maybe she'll have a relationship with Mark like he had with Brenda, where the two of them stay together and find some level between them that works out both ways. Worse things could happen, he thinks. A person just has to do what makes them happy, and Linda has always been among the smartest out there. She will figure out what's best for everybody. She is her daddy's girl. That's a nice thought to have.

The boys, now, they're a whole different ball of wax. There's a lot of tinkering and fine-tuning that still needs doing on both their counts. He could probably hover around here for another fifty years and still not be done with these two yet. Between David wanting to wig out altogether and Franklin seemingly instinctively headed toward a life of crime there's not too many reasons to feel overly confident things will work for the best when leaving them behind. He's not so certain about their ability to fend for themselves just yet, even if they've crossed over from raging male youth to their placid twenties these days. He's not so sure either one of them are going to be adept at handling problems when one comes up and introduces itself to them. He almost thinks David will imagine there is not one problem facing him but twenty, while Franklin will either choose to fight or run and mostly compound the minor into major. Past behavior dictates future acts, so John Clark has some doubts about whether his sons have completed their homework and learned any lasting lessons from them yet.

It would be easy to blame himself for these shortcomings and uneasy predicaments because maybe he hasn't exactly been the role model to his sons that he conceivably should have been. But that would not, he decides, be completely the truth. Wasn't he the one who like a good father bailed out his sons whenever he saw they were in distress, when David got cut from the basketball team and didn't think he'd be able to show his face in the hallways at school anymore because by being cut he was not worthy of any further fun or to date some girl because he was puny and had no athletic ability or anything much going for him other than being able to read a book and tell you what it was all about? Hadn't he gone out with him and helped him buy a used car, an Oldsmobile Cutlass, so he would look cool and have a way of getting around on his own, help him learn to be independent and have other interests besides worrying who was going to steal the ball from him or block his shot? Hadn't he given him money for clothes and taught him how to write a book report? He had.

And when Franklin farted around and didn't have everything ready to write and much less complete the term paper he needed to graduate on time, wasn't it his good old dad who'd spent the weekend helping Franklin construct the text and bone up on the facts and get it all down in a comprehensible style by sitting down and typing and editing it for him. Jack Kerouac and On the Road: The Great American Novel. Boy, did he remember that. He'd had to go out and get Cliff Notes because Franklin hadn't finished the book yet, he'd had to make a list of characters and towns and events and instruct Franklin on how they all came together, Friday night and all day Saturday and Sunday and into the wee hours of Monday, Franklin sleeping sometimes in a chair while he, John Clark, did the work, Franklin peering at him sometimes through a haze where John Clark had to wonder whether his son was high or not with the sad conclusion coming that it was difficult to tell since this was standard Franklin behavior. But it had been done. The paper had been completed and Franklin passed with an A, and so he was able to get into college and muddle his way through a few years until now, and maybe he would finish and maybe he wouldn't, but it was getting to a point where John Clark had done all he could do for both of his sons. His bag of tricks was thinning down and soon they would have to locate their own magic store and purchase those items that would help them navigate the passages and pitfalls and chains and chambers they found themselves imprisoned in and find ways to escape. He wouldn't be around to slip them a key or tell them the way to get out alive.

He thought of how no one had done any such like for him, back when he was young and stupid and needed a line thrown his way to keep from drowning. He had been forced to learn to swim. He'd had to learn how to survive the icy waters by himself. Somehow he had done it. And that was the way it went, he thought. That was how it goes. You sink or swim, and maybe for a while somebody's watching you and ready to jump in and save you if need be, but the day or the night comes when you're out there far from shore and it's all on you to get back. There's no exception for anyone. Sooner or later the time to keep your head above water comes along.

And he knew the time was coming for everyone and everything, just as it had come for him when he lived and when he died, and he would not be allowed to help anymore. Soon he would be past being able to do a damned thing about anything.

SIXTEEN

It was the week after Christmas, which had always been one of his favorite times of the year. John Clark spent the days sightseeing and tooling around, not exactly in any one of his cars he'd owned in the past, but in a sort of traveling manner anyway, like it was a combination of him driving and a chauffeur of some kind driving him to whatever destination came up in his thoughts. Of course, he had learned by now that he could go anywhere he pleased. Presently he was in his old neighborhood playing basketball in one of his friend's driveway with a group of his school pals, trying to get the last letter on each of them in a game of H-O-R-S-E with a variety of running hook shots or long set shots from the edge of the asphalt or his special Reverse Continental Layup, which involved him driving down the right side of the lane at full speed, stopping on a dime and planting his left foot down to do a circular pirouette and then shift directions toward the left underside of the goal and lay the ball up with his left hand. How many letters had he put on his friends with this shot in his boyhood? How had he been smart enough to figure out that most boys were right-handed and were like cripples with their left? It had served him well back then, because only Gary Platt was left-handed among his buddies, and John Clark could always take care of Gary with a simple free throw, since Gary had never been able to master a free fifteen foot shot. He was always either too long or too short, and John Clark was already counting on Gary to miss even before Gary had the ball in his hand. He enjoyed being back in this driveway once more and hung around a while in the December morning, not feeling cold in the Saint Simons air or having to brace himself against any Atlantic wind, because he didn't feel cold or the sea breeze chilling his bones anymore. That was just the way it was these days. Things that had once seemed so important and had to be remedied or else were of no consequence now.

It was nice to now place all the worry he'd known in his lifetime behind him, deleted from his present faculties as if by some magic eraser. He did not have to worry about making a fool out of himself in class or in the hallways of his schools, to not have to concentrate on waiting for something awful to occur and somehow adjust to it, and to simply drop in on places of the past where there had been joy and pleasure and sometimes pain and see them again without a sense of anxiety. He could go sit down at a table in Marty's

RX and Sundries and have a Cherry Coke and listen to the jukebox. Marty's was, of course, gone now, replaced by a salvage store, but in John Clark's world all was as it was, still present for him to peruse. He could go to Neptune Park and climb the steps of the lighthouse, or simply skip the steps and be up on the top balcony immediately. There was the playground where he could sit on a bench and watch the children go around on the carousel or catch the women walking on the sand with their beach hats and sunglasses and long, tanned legs propelling them forth and imagine what their lives were like. One late-summer night when he was here he had shared a bench with Eva Chandler. He was eighteen and getting ready to begin college at Coastal Georgia, and Eva was going off to Savannah State. Eva was black and he was white and it was still probably a good idea for no one to see them like this, but he had kissed her and wanted more, but she was afraid of him then, not so much because he was white but because he was crazy. He could feel her skin now, mingled with the wind from the sea blowing against him. He could look in her eyes by moonlight and stars and drown himself there, knowing it was not to be but knowing also for that moment that it was all right.

He didn't necessarily have to stay on the island. At times he found himself in Atlanta, in long-gone Fulton County Stadium watching the tail-end of a game between the Atlanta Braves—America's team, Ted Turner's people had labeled them—and the Cincinnati Reds, or the Big Red Machine as they were known back then. He saw Phil Niekro on the mound and Pete Rose at bat, Joe Morgan in the batter's box, Tony Perez on deck. Pete Rose was still not in the Hall of Fame, John Clark thought. Isn't it a funny thing the all-time hits leader isn't welcome in Cooperstown? Forgive us our sins, Father, as we forgive practically the whole world who delights in sinning against us each day and for the most part wouldn't have it any other way. He tells himself to let these thoughts slip away. There is no need for them now. For him it has all been resolved. What is left is for the others to decide.

On to Florida, where he passes through Delray Beach, where once he'd driven down in his old Triumph and spent a week when he was twenty, drinking Bacardi on his motel balcony and walking down the sand to a bar called Captain Hook's trying to pick up a new girl each night. He'd struck out five nights in a row but it had still been fun. He listened to the music and watched the girls who did not want him find others, and that was all right. Back then he was already learning how to live in his head, how satisfaction came in different medicinal doses for everyone. And how life ran in cycles. First there's famine, then a feast. When he returned to Saint Simons he slept with three different girls within a week.

In Miami he had an imaginary beer in a tiny dive and thought about how some thirty years before he'd snorted coke for the first and only time in his life in this same bar in the women's restroom where the wife of a guy he knew from college sprinkled powder on her overgrown fingernail and held it on the counter for him to sniff. And he came across a barmaid named Marian whom he'd done this kind of thing with in the long ago, young and pretty still and alluring with frizzed hair and bare shoulders, and she went off with him in a boat with a trolling motor along the canals that stretched to the beach as they'd done in the long-ago, and though they didn't make love this time as they had then, because that was over now, it was dreamlike and magical still.

Sometimes he found himself going back and visiting the same places. It seemed to be that he loved the places so much and had such good memories of what had occurred there that he was reluctant to leave it all behind, but chose instead to re-live certain moments a time or two more. He did not chastise himself for lingering so, for wasting time along his journey, for he was convinced beyond doubt that he would be allowed to complete all that was on his agenda before the time came to walk on. This cheered him to think all would be settled in due time, and he found himself singing along with Hank Snow on the song I'm Movin' On, which was funny and astounding to him, since he had not thought he knew all the lyrics to this one. There were surprises galore these days.

He sat in a restaurant in Memphis, savoring the smell of smoked barbecue and fried potatoes and cornbread, thinking how he had eaten these foods so many times in this spot and practically everywhere he had ever been, in the cities downtown and on the outskirts, up North and down South, each place with their secret sauces and levels of heat, dry and moist. Across the room he heard a table of young men talking. He assumed they were all in their twenties and had been friends for a good while. They were laughing and joking and one stood up to feed quarters into a Seeburg.

"Play some Garth Brooks," a voice from the table called out.

"I ain't wasting my money on Country shit," the man at the jukebox answered.

The men were all on a Wal-Mart night crew. They'd just got off mid-morning and were eating an early lunch and having a few beers before going home to crash. Most of them were from Memphis but there was a boy from Arkansas and a black man from Mississippi. John Clark was glad they all seemed to be good friends. Sometimes he had wished he had been around friends when he was working, but probably he would have grown tired of it after a while. He would have wanted to go back to being alone.

The man dropping coins into the Seeburg was named Henry. He was one of them who was from Memphis and he'd gone to the University of Memphis a couple of years until he got tired of it and dropped out to work a while. He was planning on going back in the fall, but for now he would rather work and be free to do whatever he wanted. Working nights at Wal-Mart let him do that. They paid better than he thought they would, and he got to where he liked going in at eleven at night and mindlessly stocking. He could work his shift and pick up overtime any time he wanted. Pretty soon he could afford a new Dodge Ram truck. He'd already been looking and it wouldn't be long now. But he knew he wasn't going to be doing this forever.

Clifton, who'd moved here from Mississippi, was fixing to start at Memphis in the fall too. Henry and Clifton had a thing going, but both were careful not to let anybody else on the night crew know, because then things wouldn't be so pleasant and easy anymore. Then it would be that one of the boys at the table who didn't really like blacks and didn't like gays and for damn sure didn't like the two of them together might decide that such a pairing might need some shots fired to break it up. John Clark had never been inclined to have a homosexual relationship but didn't much care that others did, and he had never been one to dislike blacks or much of anyone unless they were intending to do him harm mentally or physically, and John Clark had solved that problem long ago simply by making space between such catalysts or removing himself from their proximity completely. He had learned from an early age that disturbances of this sort were going to go on whether he was present for them or not, so he had always chosen the latter path. He sat and watched the men and thought how when he had been in this place before he'd been alone, and he wished it was that way now, since he knew the way it really was with this set of friends.

When Henry and Clifton finished eating they got in separate cars parked in the lot and drove off in different directions. John Clark knew one would circle the block and then follow the other back to his apartment, his house, wherever he lived, and they would spend the afternoon together. John Clark was happy for them and hoped for their own sakes that none of their night crew friends ever found out.

John Clark was surprised how he couldn't seem to stop himself from thinking about Henry and Clifton afterward. He took a final view of the Mississippi River before leaving Memphis and finding his way up I-40 to Nashville. He wondered if Henry and Clifton were still together by then, but he couldn't decide if it had been hours or a week or months since he'd seen them last, and so he couldn't know what had transpired in that time, if they were together or apart or dead or what. People have their own stories, he thought, and sometimes you just never know.

He didn't stay in Nashville long at all, because it looked so much different now, larger and more complicated than he had known it once to be, and so he hurried along through Kentucky past Rupp Arena and through Ohio and Cincinnati and the Ohio River flowing by and Chicago where he and Brenda had come once on St. Patrick's Day to see the river turn green. He drifted up to Detroit to watch Al Kaline play rightfield, and he made a short request to whoever was in charge of such things that the Tigers someday win a World Series again. He hoped he wasn't asking too much.

***

For as long as he could recall, John Clark's biggest interests in life—besides girls, of course, girls were always first and foremost—had been baseball and convertibles. He'd branched out later in his schoolboy days to include basketball in his group of favorites, but it was always way behind his first two loves. Dribbling and shooting and dunking a ball had never compared to the visceral feeling of clutching a tightly stitched baseball and preparing to fire it by a waiting batter or making a strong throw to first from deep in the hole or standing within the chalk lines of a batter's box and timing a swing so as to get the fat part of the bat on the ball and line it to the gap in the outfield, to round first and head for second with thoughts of going to third, to stand up or slide, it was wonderful, it was incomparable, it was God come down to earth was what it was. In his Little League days there had been nothing like it. He had believed back then there was nothing that could ever replace those feelings.

But when he grew older and found there were other attractions in the world—girls, once more, girls were always in the equation—he began to suffer from those pangs that boys all seem to acquire when they reach double figures, in age, early teens. He began to have a sense of a need to leave his house, his neighborhood, to somehow have the freedom to see and be at new places besides the place where he lived or where he went to school or church or arrived at in a car driven by one of his parents, to be out by himself to go wherever he pleased, be it down the street or the other side of town or maybe, just maybe, someday to travel down a highway to be in a new, exciting, golden place, and the only way he could see to accomplish that dream was by being behind the wheel of a car. And as he began to see the cars go by on the road in front of his house he began picking out the ones he wanted for himself, and in time his choices began to dwell on cars without roofs, cars with no top, cars that welcomed the sun and the moon and the air that was waiting out in the world to be inhaled.

His first convertible had come the summer before his senior year of high

214

school, a red used Corvair Monza that had faded with the sun to turn almost a purplish shade of the hue that had lost its battle with the sunlight. The top was rotten and mangled and leaked if it rained steadily, and so John Clark, being without enough money to get the roof repaired or buy a new one, saving as he was for college, went to an Army Surplus store and bought a tarp that fit over the body and covered the seats. It worked just fine for him but the Corvair stayed damp most of the time, and after a few years the dashboard and the steering wheel began to acquire a slimy feel and threaten to soon putrefy. When Ralph Nader declared the Corvair a death risk John Clark thought it best to put it up for sale and look for another car. A convertible, of course. It would have to be a convertible. This was the summer before his senior year at College of Charleston, after he'd gone two years to Coastal Georgia to save money. This was when he got hooked. He looked around the lots in Charleston and found whatever he might want to be beyond his means, and so took to reading the newspaper and viewing bulletin boards around the campus to see what was out there that someone was willing to part with for the price of a song, which was about all he had in his pockets.

When he finally came across a picture of a Fiat Spider that looked like it might be worth having, he walked across campus under the palmettos and magnolias and oaks, watching the girls strolling by as he walked, always the girls, until he came to an apartment building on the edge of campus. In the lot he saw the Fiat he had walked a mile to see and found the picture on the bulletin board had done it more justice than it was actually entitled to, but next to the Fiat was an Austin Healey Sprite, smaller, unassuming, but neat and clean, almost as if it had been in storage for a good time and had just been backed out of its entrapment to taste the Charleston sunshine for the first time in a while. He found the apartment number on the mailbox and knocked on the door. The lock clicked on the other side and the door opened and a man faced him. The man looked like the quintessential sports car owner with his beard and wire-rims and his thinning hair from years of too much wind and rain. When he told the man who he was, it was almost like a look of sadness came to the man's face, and John Clark could tell there from the start that this man who had his Fiat up for sale was not really into going through with such an act and would likely be heartbroken when he did.

The man had his Fiat for sale because the Austin Healey that was outside sitting beside it had belonged to his mother, and his mother had recently died, and since he lived alone and had no need of two sports cars he thought he would let his Fiat go and keep the Sprite, although he liked the Fiat better because the Sprite was a little hard for him to fit into but was in much better mechanical shape. What would you think of selling the Sprite instead of the Fiat, John Clark asked, and the man hemmed and hawed for a minute and went on about what great shape the Sprite was in compared to the Fiat and how he would have to have more money for it than what he had asked for the Fiat because of the good shape and because it had belonged to his mother and there were sentimental attachments that he had not been prepared to deal with this early since her passing. And John Clark said how he had the money in his pocket and he would buy the Sprite right this instant if the man would settle on a price and allow him to do so, and he took the stout wad of bills out of his pants and showed it to him, a thousand dollars in hundred dollar bills and twenties, and the man thought for a moment about birds being in hand and out in the bush and finally told John Clark that yes, a thousand dollars would buy the Sprite.

But what John Clark had not known was how this decision on this clean, well-kept British sports car was going to affect him for the days and years to come, for soon he found himself in a state where he was praising and worshiping this 1967 Austin Healey Sprite one day and cursing it for being a plague from an angry Jehovah the next. He found himself wishing the car was gone from his sight to wanting to drive it forever. He spent exorbitant amounts of money on repairs, money he did not need to donate to a foreign sports car money pit, and yet, on those rare occasions when Irene was running smoothly—Irene was her name, because he liked the old folk song so much and liked to sing it when he was high or inebriated or both—she was the answer to his worries and a song in his heart. How many nights had he driven the streets singing? How many other times had he been stranded along the side of a road, waiting for a wrecker to tow him somewhere so he might donate his money again?

In his mid-twenties, years after leaving college and settling in to life as an adult, the time came when he accepted a job as a teacher in Saint Simons, some ten miles from his apartment. He wisely decided to part with his moody Sprite and invest in a real car that would get him to destinations on a regular basis, and so he sold the Sprite for nine hundred dollars, thinking he had perhaps broken even on the whole experience, and invested in a dependable Pontiac Lemans, which served him well his first years in secondary education despite it being a hardtop. In his second year he met Brenda, who came along to teach Algebra and Trigonometry to juniors and seniors, and who resided across the hall from his Senior English classes, which numbered two that were included in his duties along with Creative Writing and a freshman grammar and composition class three times a week first thing in the morning, which he despised. Grammar and composition were each bordered on facts, which John Clark had no use for, since his entire life had been a continuing flirtation with fiction. During his teaching duties, John Clark had not been able to keep himself while in mid-lecture from glancing across the hall—well, actually staring—at Brenda Dorris, her name then, who had a habit of sitting on her desk at the front of the room and crossing her legs, which were nice legs indeed, so John Clark found himself in the habit of viewing Brenda and her legs across the hall and going further to determine he liked the rest of her just as well, and so he had waited one afternoon for her to lock up her classroom and made sure he was locking his own room simultaneously, and walked her to her car, which was a Nova and not necessarily anywhere near a Corvair, but was close enough anyway for John Clark to discuss with her the merits and hazards of Chevrolets and Pontiacs but how they were at least dependable in a way Austin Healey Sprites never tended to be.

John Clark was not really old but began thinking of himself that way, seeing how most guys his age were married by this time and had children and suburban homes and came across as fairly normal, whereas John Clark still favored playing loud music and going to the movies high on pot and drinking until it was the next day when it suddenly came to him that he had to be at school in a few short hours. Had he not let his mind run away with feelings of dread, he would have been fine. He would have weathered this coming of the onset of middle age without panicking, but he didn't. He fell victim to the voices in his head that told him it was time for him to become a grownup.

On an April night, an Easter Eve it was, he had come to the conclusion that if he didn't act soon he was going to become one of those drunken old alcoholic men who lived in solitude and got sloppier every year, and soon he'd be found out by his employers and let go and his entire existence would soon go right down the old drain, so he concluded the only way to escape this horrid fate was to join the rest of the world as a normal human being, a married man, a someday-father, a homeowner, perhaps not a pillar of the community but at least a brick. Since he and Brenda had begun going out to movies and dinner and necking now and then on her sofa and sleeping together a few times a month, and since Brenda was an attractive woman who wasn't close to being past her prime like he was getting close to being, he asked her to marry him as they walked back through a courtyard after eating at Sal's Neighborhood Pizzeria, laying his to-go box down on the grass so he could kiss her and seal the deal.

For seventeen years they'd stayed married through his careers as a teacher and a retail clerk and a route deliveryman, had three kids and two houses and gone through three family dogs and two cats. John Clark finally decided Brenda needed to be happy, and so he took his supply of mystery and misery away and moved down the hall and dwelled in his end of the house from then on, thinking sometimes to himself how odd it was that just by the act of his own self disappearing he could make the majority of the world happy indeed. Life was still a mystery sometimes.

Once more he found himself standing before his old house, even though he had already made a decree that he would not come back there again, that he would leave Brenda in peace and not make her sense his presence anymore, if in fact that was possible, because he wasn't so sure of that or not. It was hazy and foggy and muddled and hard to tell. He didn't want her to feel like he was feeling this moment, imagining how it had been there at the first between the two of them, where he had liked to feel his hands on her body and hers on his, and how when they kissed for a time his mind did not wander off and look for a higher sensation from some ethereal phantom woman who could not be seen and possibly didn't exist, and how they had kissed so long and passionately until little by little he could tell that it was high time to move on to something else. Perhaps he could have lived with his own inadequacies as a husband, but the time came when he began to sense it coming forth from Brenda too. And for several years the two of them had remained this way and tried to make it work, until at last Brenda couldn't do it anymore and wandered off to her own place of longing, and the night came when John Clark took Donna in his arms and saw what it was like to be in love and experience real passion and how it might have been between them, and he knew then it was best for him to go away, maybe not so far as to be absent in the physical sense, but to go.

***

He is surprised to see the driveway at the house full of cars and that all the company seemed to be his children and grandchildren and Brenda, not counting the pickup truck that was parked out by the garage where he used to sit in his lawn chair and listen to the Reds on summer nights. Once it got dark the frequency came through clearer, and he could hear every word Marty Brennaman and Joe Nuxhall had to say. If he wanted he could make this happen once more, have a game going on and the old Zenith radio fired up and the lawn chair unfolded with a mini-ice chest full of Busch beers there to quench his thirst and aid in imagining the scene going on those hundreds of miles away, but he was too busy for that right now, that scene had run its course, and it was time to begin getting everything in order and stowed away, because the hour, as someone told Hamlet—or was it Benvolio? —is getting late. He hadn't been entirely certain he would be back this way again, but he guesses it is only natural, since this is the house he lived in for almost a quarter of a century and bedded his wife and raised his children and took care of his animals. Here he has mowed lawns and watched classic movies and written stories and novels, several of which have yet to see the light of day, read the great novels and listened to the best music, so it is not too far off the realm of common sense that he would not return this one last time to take a good and final look. It would in reality be a breach of decorum were he not to come here as a parting gesture, for it seems to him the bricks and mortar and walls and floors would be hurt if he did not tell them goodbye before crossing over to his new home, and there was also that sentimental, selfish part of him that wanted to make sure everything was all in its place and lacking for nothing from him before he moseyed off.

And maybe this was not him that was making the effort to come this way again but something else that was meant to be pushing this whole matter toward resolution. It has taken a long moment for the fact to sink in that all who were kin to him that he loved in his own special and mysterious way while he was among them are gathered here now, and could it be that there is some sort of meaning that can be garnered from that? Certainly that has to have something to do with all this. Surely there is an answer contained somewhere in this convention of bodies and souls. Maybe a providential finger moved a piece or pointed toward this place and deemed for all of this to occur, to happen, to be in this place together at one time? It is difficult for John Clark to comprehend such goings-on by some Creator-In-Charge, but he has lived long enough and seen enough strange things transpire to argue against it. He knows better. All he has to do is know that perhaps this is beyond anything he has planned and is out of his control as far as results and answers, so he is to wait here in his place without being an unwelcome spirit barging in on what is happening inside the house, to simply hover here like a good and friendly ghost and wait for a door to open and see who comes out. He will take this as a sign to enter into their world again, whether they are aware of it or not. Sometimes he thinks he is perhaps not so stealthy. Sometimes he gets the feeling that whoever he is visiting has a faint and slight notion that he is around. They can't prove it, of course, but they know there is something. He has seen this happen with Brenda, as if she knows he is in the house and finds herself desiring for him to come to her bed. Linda has sensed him being with her in the library, David in the car on their THC excursion, Franklin in his jail cell the night of his arrest, feeling glad his dear old dad was dead so he wouldn't have to explain this, yet wanting his father to come save him, get him out. And Donna in the grocery store—he knows she saw him that day, caught a glimpse of something she couldn't bring herself to believe—she has a knowledge of his presence too.

He tells himself not to go inside, but to look into the house through the brick walls and see everything that way. This was safer, better. He didn't want to take the chance of scaring anyone if they somehow sensed him being around. He could see David in the dining room sitting at the table eating ice cream. John Clark doesn't have to look any closer. He knows it is butter pecan—David's favorite. He is glad David is having what he likes. The women are all in the kitchen, at the stove stirring pots or frying chicken—tenders it is, John Clark can almost smell them—or sitting at the breakfast table slicing fruit and vegetables for the salad. There is Linda, Janet, and some woman John Clark has only seen recently who's seemed to have taken up with Franklin, the two of them spending a lot of time together lately. John Clark wonders how serious this may become, but he'll have to let that happen without him. He won't be around for the denouement. One can't be everywhere all the time. Life must go on without his attendance.

His grandchildren are playing in the living room, scampering around the coffee tables and chairs as if there is some treasure to be found, and on the sofa John Clark sees Brenda with her new man—Billy Joe is who this is, he remembers, he has heard her speak his name—and the two of them lean forward and laugh at the children playing and take sips of lemonade from the tall, red glasses he brought home for her when he saw them at a yard sale on a Friday when he was winding up his stops and heading back to the warehouse. He remembers paying two dollars for a set of six of them and how they had been plastic but sturdy and kept ice from melting for a goodly period and how sometimes he would squeeze the lemons and make the lemonade himself because Brenda always said he made it better than her but he wondered always if she said that because it was true or because she just didn't like to make it that much and would rather him do it, but that was okay, he didn't mind doing it, he was glad that she liked his lemonade and didn't hate him because he was not the constant love of her life that she had wanted him to be and he was glad that she was trying to get over it and he wasn't even angry when she finally went to bed with Jimmy those times and then someone at the library, because he couldn't really blame her for any of that and in fact had wanted her to do something in that vein so he wouldn't feel so bad himself for wanting to go and being free enough afterward to go and do it even though it was not a complete exit he'd made but was just a departure that took baby steps a little at a time and lasted years for him to fade away until he was gone and she and none of the children had not ever been too distressed seeing him go. Complicated it had been. He sees how this Billy Joe watches Brenda's grandchildren and watches her and how he

leans his shoulder against her without even being aware he is doing it, and
John Clark knows by this action, this touch, this intimate small friction, that
this Billy Joe is in love with Brenda and Brenda is on the way to being in love
with him. And this is good, this is fine, this is what John Clark has wanted,
and he can go now and leave them together and not hesitate like he is doing
and wonder if he should somehow let Brenda know he is here and he will
stay if she needs him to, but he knows that is not right, that it is not her
thinking this way but him, and how strange it has always been for him to see
that when things end something else begins, and this is like that, very much
like what he has known. He knows, then, that all that's left here for him to do
is done. He can visit his pets back in the library, whisper a fond farewell in
their ears, and then be on his way. He could go and appear to them this last
time, stroke their fur, pat their heads, see his rooms with what was left of his
books and papers, and perhaps be glad that they are gone too, not here anymore, just like him. Maybe he will see all of this again, his family, his pets,
his books and papers and the strange wild nights of his life that have escaped
him for so long. He doesn't know. No one knows.

It comes to him that everyone is gathered together this day to scatter his
ashes. He knows they are going to do it in the backyard at sunset, in the
small garden by the garage where he liked to sit so often on so many nights.

This is good. He will leave them to it. His necessaries are embarked.

John Clark, since he seems to be in a farewell and adieu mode, thinks it
might now be fitting to go over to the Tasty Snacks warehouse and take a
look around there, maybe to make sure the place is still in business and
hasn't gone completely to seed these months since their ace delivery guy,
who was him hands down, had gone and got himself killed in the line of
duty. Maybe he can check and see if his truck was still in use or if as a tribute
to its slain driver it had been retired. He can close the books and know that
all his deliveries have been made, there is nothing else left for him to do.

All four trucks are parked outside the sliding doors, which would mean this
is a Saturday, as he thought it was but wasn't altogether certain, since days
and dates meant so little to him these days. His personal truck was down at
the end of the second door, and from the looks of the dust on its hood and
the sliding doors on the sides it appeared it hadn't been used too much since
he'd stopped coming in to work. Probably Jimmy and Donna hadn't hired
a replacement driver in his place yet and had simply divided John Clark's
routes up between the three other drivers, giving them the opportunity to
make extra commissions until the workload got behind and someone else
had to be hired. John Clark imagined that if the other three drivers couldn't
keep up the pace Donna would hop in a truck and go catch up the route on

her own. John Clark knew Jimmy for damn certain wouldn't do it, lazy slacker that he was, and for a moment wondered if he should have been by here before now to see if he could keep things going on this end from beyond the grave. Probably that wasn't a good idea. He thought about the places he'd visited the past few months, straightening up what mess had been left behind and completing any tasks that had been left undone. There had not been much to do, since he had never believed in letting things slide on his part, but the day to day wear required some hand keeping things from falling into disarray. Unless the machines were working and the product inside was fresh and well-stocked, people would stop using them and bring snacks of their own into work to placate themselves, even load up in their cars and go out to lunch. A route delivery salesman should never take his clients for granted. But there was only so much he could do. He couldn't keep delivering forever. There came a time when a fellow has no choice but to stop.

John Clark hesitated before entering the warehouse. He could slip through the cracks or go through the cinder walls if he wanted, or he could stay on the outside where he was and see in his mind what he wished to view. There was a part of him that said to remain in this area of his essence, but he already knew that was not going to be possible. The call was too great. He knew the warehouse was not deserted, Saturday or not. Donna was inside. He could sense her. He also was looking at her SUV parked ten feet away, so it wasn't like his supernatural senses were in full operational mode, because anybody else with vision could see it sitting there without Donna in it and deduce where she might be. It didn't take somebody who'd come back from the grave to put two and two together like a real live human being and come up with four. It wasn't like he was that advanced over everyone else.

Maybe he should simply leave. Maybe going inside was not the best idea.

But no, he couldn't leave yet. He also couldn't remain here fooling himself about why he was here, what mighty crusade he was on to see what he could do to save his handiwork before he left. The route would go on good or bad, he knew that. Sooner or later, a vacant Snickers slot wasn't going to change the spin of the planet one whit.

John Clark took a deep breath (or something like a breath, since he had finished breathing some time back but was still not accustomed to abandoning the practice) and allowed himself to appear at the far end of the warehouse. Here he was two rooms away from Donna's and Jimmy's office, an area which he thought was the best place to set down momentarily, just in case he came to his senses and decided to leave before seeing Donna this last time. One thing that had not left him despite gunshots and the stoppage of his bodily functions was that perpetual swirling longing that seemed not to want to go away. Perhaps it was to be expected, since he had always been a dreamer from way back, but he couldn't help wondering if it was always going to be with him, despite his departure from this life, wherever it was he landed. He had at first welcomed this part of his psyche when he was young. He had reveled in his desires, his foolishness about love and loss and a life that both giveth and taketh away, but he would have not believed that there would come a day when all this faded and died and drifted away from him, and he would be an old man devoid of dreams and desire and not really miss them that much. But this had never come to be. It was as strong in this afterlife stage as it had been when he turned thirteen. Maybe this is what they meant when they talked about eternal life.

Yes, Donna was here. She was sitting at her desk, looking at records, posting account receipts into her computer. It had been Donna who came up with a system to keep tabs on the financial stability of Tasty Snacks. John Clark doubted if Jimmy had figured out how to use her program yet, or if he even cared. He had always taken a step back and let Donna take care of everything. John Clark wondered if Jimmy knew what Donna kept in her heart as well.

He spiritually navigated toward the office where Donna was working. He knew he couldn't take off for the far yonder until he saw her again. The old Mamas and Papas song nagged and haggled him in his mind. I saw her again last night and you know that I shouldn't. He could see Mama Cass in her moo-moo dress, Papa John in that furry monstrosity that made him look like a Klondike trapper from a Jack London story, the entire group shimmering to and fro against the hallway wall that led past the three warehouse storage rooms to the corner office where Donna was. He wondered if he should this time, since this was the wind-up, the long goodbye that would never be long enough, this farewell my lovely I'll see you in my dreams moment, speak to her and tell her what was on his mind, what had resided there so long that he'd made certain never to speak about. It was getting late on this December afternoon, the sun setting already, and he knew there was only a few more minutes of light until the world was dark once more. He wondered what it was he could say to Donna to explain his life, his love for her, but maybe it was too late now. Maybe it was better for past dreams to remain unsaid, to not be brought out into what was left of the light of day to be heard and examined and perhaps catch a meaning that had never been there in the first place. He had refrained for the longest of times; it might be best to continue doing so this last time around.

Was this fear that was in his heart? Was he afraid that the section of his affections he had reserved for Donna all these passing years been merely something he had installed there to keep him feeling somewhat human, an artificial device within his dormant emotions to assure him that yes, he had love flowing through his veins too, just like all the other members of the world with their likes and attractions and spoken vows of love, words in a song, embraces on a movie screen, the imagery of a sonnet, he was as human as the next guy? Was he afraid that what transpired on one magical night with Donna was concocted in his head to keep him from feeling even more removed than he already was from his fellow travelers on earth? He hated to think that Donna was not in love with him after all, did not long for him like he wanted her to do, had never felt the desire for him that he liked to imagine was there. He wondered if Donna had been only another task he had chosen to maintain every day, some stop on his route he had to keep visiting regularly in his mind, making certain it was always stocked and in good working condition. He wondered if it was like that after all, and if he had to know what all this really had been here at the end?

He saw her sitting before her computer screen, exactly in the pose he had imagined she'd be, and he lingered a moment, wondering if he should disturb her, if he should make the effort to have her understand the road he'd traveled down without taking her with him, the endless nights he had slept alone without her at his side, and perhaps find out in return that she had not experienced the same solitary moments. He had seen her cry at his funeral, and he wondered now if it had been for love or because she had lost her one-time teacher and the best employee Tasty Snacks had ever had. He knew it was not so, those last few crass thoughts in his head, for he could look at her sitting before him and see that it had been for love, or at least something that closely resembled it.

Donna stopped entering figures from the worksheets lying on the desk. Her fingers rested for a moment on the keyboard and she stared at the monitor. For several seconds she did not move. She was wearing a sweatshirt that had a picture of the Saint Simons lighthouse on it, and John Clark remembered how he had taken each of his children to see that structure, one at a time so they could climb the steps together and he wouldn't have chaos going on with three of them in attendance simultaneously, possibly to have one of them while he wasn't looking climb the railing for a better look at the town and the beach and plunge to their death, no, it had been better to have been careful, one experience of bonding with a separate child at a time, with him keeping them from doing something crazy, a chore he'd been performing, it seemed, for everyone in his life for ages, an act of shepherding that also included himself. He was sorry Donna was not wearing something else, like the dress she'd had on at the party with her arms bare and the slight exposure of her breasts rising from the low neckline. He had never seen her undressed, and now he wondered if he was sorry about it or not. Would it have changed things? Would it have somehow made it less than what it had become in his heart and soul? He thought he knew the answer. He was starting to understand a few things after all. He was making progress here before it was too late.

He realized that all he had wished for had in actuality come to be. Perhaps he had believed for a time he had wanted to make love with Donna, but that was only because the conventional wisdom of the world told him it needed to be that way. The thing he'd soon discovered and probably had known all along was that he had never traveled along that highway where life got reduced to simple solutions to untranslatable questions. The truth, then, was what the world believed to be true and the way to fulfill its needs was to take the popular choice available and run with it. It had never been that way with him. He had to look the item in question up and down and over and out and discover for himself what all the consequences of his actions would be. Perhaps after a long study he would then act, but sometimes this research required a lifelong quest. That, he thought, was what had happened with Donna and the kiss. He had decided the road he was on should never end.

The lyrics of a song came into his head. Frank Sinatra sang as he stood watching Donna, trying to decide whether to come near her again or not. Someday, some way, Sinatra said, we both have a lifetime before us. Parting is not goodbye. We'll be together again. Was that so? John Clark smiled at the idea of it. One thing was certain. He was not to know for now.

It could be she was sitting here now, pausing during her work, waiting and listening for something that had pricked her soul here out of the blue. It just might be she knew he was close by and was waiting to hear his voice, perhaps even to see him once more.

Donna was four feet away from him, close enough for him to reach out his ghostly hand and touch, but for that moment he dared not move. He preferred rather to study this woman for a time that would never be long enough but would always be too short. He wished he had the power to know what she was thinking, but no one ever had that going for them either living or dead. He thought of Jeanne Dixon, of Kreskin, of Johnny Carson as Carnac the Magnificent, thinking of how everyone wanted to know the future, everyone wanted to know what others were thinking, everyone always wanted all the knowledge so they would know what to do next and not screw everything in their lives up. He, John Clark, was not that way. He had never been like that. He liked it better when he didn't know the truth all the way, inside out, just the facts. He liked better to not be in the fray of the action, to be somewhere out on a mountain looking down, up in the air, observing and seeing what happened next. He thought it best to keep it to himself, somewhere in his aura where others could not go. He liked the dreaming of it rather than the happening in the flesh and light of day. He liked staying in the dark, there with the moonlight and the stars, where it was easier to dream. He was this way now. He would be this way forever.

He saw it go by as he stood watching Donna. It had been slow to arrive but it was here now and he saw it clearly and knew it to be true. It was one of those things that had flickered by in his mind before, when he was reading or writing, when he was straight or high or sober or tipsy, when he was watching an old movie or with his children or Brenda when they had been in love and even later when they were not. It was in his mind when he had kissed Donna that one night where magic, like sugar plums, danced in his head, and mostly it was there with him as he drove his truck to the next stop on his route.

He saw it clearly this moment as Donna looked his way. He looked back, knowing immediately she couldn't see him no matter what he did. He was gone from her now as he was gone from everyone, as he was gone from all the world he had known. She had glimpsed him that once in the grocery store, and that was all. He realized that had been the way it had been all along. The world had sensed him leaving for an instant, then knew that he was gone. That was the way it worked.

He felt himself crossing over. He was moving on.

Donna looked at the keyboard and saved her work. That was enough for today. She was caught up enough on this Saturday. It was time to go home. Jimmy was there waiting for her. Maybe they could get a pizza and watch a movie together. It was something to look forward to, even if she had the feeling something was missing.

There was a goodbye playing in her head. She turned it over to dwell in a far corner of her mind for the tiniest of an instant, and then it was gone.

About the Author

Ralph Bland is the author of fourteen novels and three collections of stories. A graduate of Belmont University, he lives with his wife, three spoiled dogs, and an eccentric MG on the outskirts of Nashville, Tennessee.